EXION

Book One in the Maggie Johanson Chronicles

Written by Clinton Knox

Version 2 released 1-21-2

Prologue – From the Deceased

Dearest Samantha,

I write this to you so that maybe you can share my story with the world. These pages to follow are a retelling of my childhood being forced to grow up too fast in a world too dark. I always had a habit of writing down notes from the day in journals. Those will never be released as they contain things that only I should ever know. Rest assured I took care of them after writing this letter to you. They are gone forever. Even this text here was never meant to be released publicly. I wrote it only as a recounting of my life to fulfill my own desire to remember it for as long as possible. Writing always calmed me but I never had anything I wanted to share with others. So, I let my mind wander, my fingers dance across the keyboard and retell the stories of my life.

I realize that once I am gone from this universe and proceed on to the next what happens will no longer be within my control or frankly my concern. However, there is within me a desire to have the story properly told. The tales you have been told of me may or may not be true. There are many. Some believe in me as a Goddess, a power sent from the heavens to protect those less able to protect themselves. Others call me a curse, an outlaw. A traitor to my own. You can decide for yourself after reading through my story.

If you are reading this then I am dead. No longer an entity in the same universe you currently call home. Hopefully I am not non-existent as I believed back then as a child but only moved to another plane in another dimension of reality. Either way, I am entrusting to you above any others to protect my story and share it with anyone you can reach.

So that you know and understand as I retell my past, I never meant for any of this. I started as a frightened young girl both excited and terrified of moving on to her senior year in high school. Remember that when you read this, imagine having your entire world, your entire existence flipped on its head all in one day. Never again having a chance to regain your composure. Not having a place to stop and feel safe for a while. I pray your life is more than a constant battle but being who you are and what work still needs to be done, it will be. Above all others I know, you are my greatest pride. My largest hope for the future of our people. Of our morals.

Please go out and protect all that you can. Pick up where I left off and make it better. Do it with more empathy for the stricken. Maybe you can complete the mission in your lifetime. Even if you can't, as long as you do all that you can, then feel fulfilled. Be happy. Don't go out the way I have. Make sure to have love in your life. Be sure to value all around you. Don't push them away, keep them close. Know them, be with them. Those around you will make you stronger.

I Love you and wish you all the best this universe has to offer,

Your Grandmother,

Maggie Audrain Johanson

Chapter One

There was nothing remarkably different about that day the way I remember it now. At least to start with. It was the same as so many before it. Exploring the world around me, attempting to learn what I could. The only exception was how it all came to completion. In these final moments before my whole world changed, all seemed normal with the world. Looking back, I laugh at myself for being so dramatic as I knew nothing of what real drama was. Only the angst that accompanied me on a daily basis trying to find my way in a world that ignored me most times.

It was a wonderful day just as so many before it had been. Perfection. The birds were singing, deer were walking around the park at their leisure, the clear creek water was flowing calmly only a few feet away from the table I claimed as my own for the time. A warm summer spring morning with all the plant life blooming, a gentle breeze fluttering the newly developing leaves. I glanced down at the water and could see several small fish swimming against that gentle current on their way somewhere upstream. Possibly to their own origins to start a new generation of the creatures. At least that is what it was meant to seem like.

There was nothing here not to love, yet I had a hard time enjoying it. Everything unfavorable about this historical recreation was eliminated. No pesky bugs biting at your skin, no ants eating your picnic lunch. Children at play in the distance, other teenagers of my same age playing Frisbee off to the side.

I don't know why I can't just enjoy it. Instead, I always have this feeling of imprisonment here. Of being lied to. A reminder of what had been stolen from me before I was even born. My predecessors didn't care enough to save the real thing for me. Somewhere out there in the world this might be real, but not here. Not in the region of my birth. Nowhere at all according to our leaders. I was born into this world innocent but damned at the same time. Lost opportunities because those before me couldn't handle the freedoms they had.

In school, my teachers tell me to just enjoy it. "Not everyone gets to enjoy such natural beauty. You should never take it for granted. Some of us can't afford to put our eyes on such things but for a couple days per year. Most of your fellow students don't get to visit it weekly like you do. Try to appreciate what you have." Ugh, I hate hearing that. They were part of the problem. To be fair, some of my young teachers probably weren't around at the end of the previous world either but the older ones were. They did nothing to stop the end from coming.

What does it matter if I get to see this or not? Sure, it can be peaceful to come here and read a book or throw a Frisbee in the sun with a couple friends, but it isn't reality. Only an escape. Reality is my schoolwork. Being a Junior in high school required a lot of schoolwork. Preparation for starting my adult life that was coming so slowly. Then as my reward for years of hard work, my prize would be work. Whatever meaningless position I was instructed to take up. A course that would be decided for me based upon my attributes and perceived drive. Sure, I would have a vote in the end but only one vote of many. Instructors during my Senior year along with the placement committee would have the remaining ten votes.

Beyond schooling and the unknown future job that would consume the remainder of my productive life, reality is the apartment I share with my family. My Mother, my Father. Those two people who may be the only force in this world that really cares what happens to me down the road, yet they have little voice in that inevitability. They have guided me along my path giving tips and tricks along the way. Doing what they could to allow me the opportunities for growth and responsibility while still protecting my childhood. At least what childhood you could have in a regime that controlled all.

The final reality which is the most undeniable and unavoidable is the ongoing forward march into the oblivion that awaits us all upon our exit from this world.

Ha, that's another item I usually get scoffed at by others when I mention it. So many others believe in all these wonderful lands we can fall into after we die. An everlasting vacation with some kind of an overlord off in a fantasy world. Whether you call it Heaven, paradise, nirvana, the promised land, Neverland, etc. I know, I know, Neverland was a fictional land from a children's tale but really, are the others any more likely? Am I really to believe that such a place is real? That such an overwhelming power exists to create such a place? If that is so, then why is the world the way it is now? If an all-powerful, all planning, all controlling God is really out there then why would they allow their creation, this world, these people, to be so utterly devastated? A world so tormented by its own inhabitants. So rocked to its very core with centuries of unchecked rampaging through deposits of various materials to build even more devices of such destruction that we would now be relegated to small portions of the planet?

In the end though, what does it matter? What is done is done. I cannot take us back to the before. All I can do is continue my ever-moving march towards that oblivion. That point in time where I may cease to exist. Such an idea is difficult to comprehend with our animal minds. A world without our existence, no, a universe without our existence is so ridiculous that we search for answers to a question never even asked. We search for what will come after when there really is nothing. Absolute, nothing. It won't be cold, there won't be sadness, there won't be happiness. Just nothingness, complete and total.

Such things are so impossible for our minds to grasp that even a leap into a magical land of unlimited everything is easier to handle. We are an amazing species to be able to look past the obvious to the impossible and call that the only real answer. Do I like the finality of our deaths? Of course not. I wish I could believe in such fairy tales. I look at those that can see the oceans of beauty on the other side of this life and am truly filled with sadness that I cannot wrap myself in the same warmth and reassurance. I just can't.

Shivers down my spine shake me from my funk. Sometimes I am too dark even for me…

I went back to reading my book. No, trying to read my book I should say as I had been here for almost an hour and had barely covered two pages. The distractions in my own mind and out here in this so-called reality kept peeling my eyes away from the simple black and white. I wanted to hear the sounds, see the colors, smell the scents floating around the park. It was all so fantastic, but something was always missing each time I visited this park. Even with the overload of amazing, I always felt there was some void in this world. No matter how I focused on the beauty, it always crept back in around the edges. False, fake, a futile effort at re-imagining a lost land.

"You have to finish this book" I told myself out loud as if I was speaking to a group of equally sidetracked teens instead of just my own ever roaming mind. "It HAS to be done."

Mr. Coster assigned us all books to read and we had to write five-page essays on the words within to share with the rest of the class. That would be a fun day I thought to myself. What could be better than being forced to read a book you don't want to read and then being forced to listen to the same report on the same dull book multiple times by different classmates? Classmates that for the most part were pathetic attempts to continue the human race. There were exceptions. A few were at least capable of a continued thought that approached a mediocre level of intelligence. A half attempt at a mind that could function without the group leading it along. An exceptional few of that group might even be able to maintain a conversation about something other than the latest craze of backwards attire.

Yes, my generation of knuckle draggers had moved beyond the craze of yesteryear onto the current craze of wearing garments backwards. Why do you ask would someone do such a thing? Go ask them because I have no freaking clue whatsoever. That is really all I have to say on that topic. If forced to make a wild guess I would estimate the idiots wear their shirts backwards as some kind of thumb at authorities. What else can you do when you have a dress code that blends bland grays with more bland light blacks and dark whites?

When you have nothing to work with and must thumb your nose in some way then your options are limited. Of course, it could just be pure mindless acts of young rebellion that brings things like this on. The species I belong to is mostly a group of clothed monkeys with hardly a thought more than how to individualize our group mind. Think about that for a minute. We seek to become individuals and prove ourselves to be our own creature. Of our own guide. Steer our own canoe down the streams of existence yet in doing so we seek verification from those around us and start these crazes. Belong to these cliques. Once again, I must control my ever-rolling tongue and return to the point of my story.

At least Mr. Coster had only assigned four students to each book. There would be a bit of variety there. All the books were fairly dull though so no matter what, the next couple class periods were going to be a struggle to keep my sanity and stay awake. The book I had so fortunately been assigned really wasn't that terrible when I came to think of it.

If it wasn't an assigned project, I would most likely enjoy the book. The story was about spaceships zipping around the galaxy building new spaceships and hauling humans around from planet to planet expanding the human population. It seemed like every planet they went to was empty. Each would have gorgeous oceans and beaches with plentiful plant life. Perfect pristine water and clean clear air rich in oxygen and all the other required garbage. Never any other peoples or creatures though. Maybe some small animals like squirrels or rabbits but nothing large and never anything intelligent. The humans would disembark from their ships and build wonderful towns surrounded by nature. The air would be pure, trees large and abundant. Water steadily marching its way from mountain peaks, down streams and larger rivers all the way to the vast oceans of perfectly clear waters. The humans would build schools for their happy children, spread hydroelectric dams around and cover mountain sides in solar panels to produce all the power they needed. Civilizations prospered and all the people worked together for the common good.

"What a load of crock" I thought to myself. Humans will never be able to function in such a sustainable and controlled manner. Even today with the world the way it is when we should work together and maintain what little we have left we still as a species war with each other and further destroy the bits of habitable land we have remaining to us. Wars among the planets controlled by humans have been prevalent in years past. Even if we were able to reach beyond the limitations of current technology and possibly reach outside our own system, any planets we did find would most likely quickly be dug into for minerals and wildlife to harvest. Look at what we have done to the planets in our own system. They are all worse now than before we first reached them decades ago.

Sure, none have seen the swing our precious Earth has seen but we have had thousands of years to work over our Eden while only having less than a single lifetime to dig into the others we can reach at this point. Space travel for our species is still new in that we cannot reach other solar systems quite yet. I should add an asterisk to that and say we "can" reach other systems, we just can't return from them in a timely fashion. Ships have been sent out into the deep dark with slumbering hordes of our own aboard seeking out worlds to inhabit and claim for our own but most likely it will be tens or hundreds of generations yet before they land and generations after that before a signal or ship is able to return to tell of their exploits. That is if they are able to return or even find a world at all. We truly only have guesses to what is out there beyond the walls of empty space that surround our small collection of rocks.

Back to "reality", I could hear children playing off in the distance, some sort of kickball game. They were shouting and chasing each other this way and that. Each time one side would kick it, the other side would sprint to where they expected the ball to land and try to catch it. If they caught it, the kicker had to go sit in "jail" and one of their teammates got to leave jail. If they made contact but dropped the ball, the attempted catcher would have to go sit in jail. There were a few more rules apparently because children went in and out of jail for other reasons I couldn't quite understand from this distance. You know the game. There are versions everywhere that utilize various house rules during play. While I was watching, once again distracted from my assigned reading, one boy a bit larger than the rest kicked the ball so high all the others had to shade their eyes from the bright sun overhead to try and keep track of it. I watched it sail over their heads for a few seconds before it came plummeting back down to the ground right into one young girl's face. The ball overpowered her tiny neck and snapped her head back in such a ferocious movement I knew she would be broken. A neck can be fixed these days as long as you are cared for quickly enough, but it still can shut down your bodily functions for a time ample enough for brain damage to set in. With all the medical advances out there, the brain is one item that will possibly be forever outside the full grasp of medicine. Everyone froze for a second as the ball knocked her to the ground. Hard. The impact with the terrain was with such force it could break a bone easily on a girl as young as her. She couldn't have been more than four or five.

The girl didn't move.

She didn't move at all.

No one came to her immediate aid. She just lay there not moving. I couldn't even tell if she was breathing or not. She just laid there on the grass silent. The other children started to move towards her, but she suddenly arched her back and spun her body around till she was on her hands and knees. Then without hardly a strain in her face she jumped upright and snagged the ball from where it came to a stop nearby. She laughed her young laugh and hurled the ball back towards the young boy that had originally kicked it high into the air. It connected with his chest as he stood there dumbfounded and bounced away without him even getting the opportunity to flex a finger towards it.

He looked down at where the ball had hit him and then back at the girl. He gave a slight nod and a grin and proceeded to remove himself from the playing field moving past the other children to their improvised "Jail" area. The game went on after that with no issues, the young girl had no ill effects from the hard impact as none of them would. That wasn't possible in the park anymore. Children were never hurt while playing simple games these days. At least not in this world. You could say that was a good thing. Many said just that. I had an opinion on the subject that by now I am sure you could guess at. I understood the aim, I understood the why, no one could force me to agree with or like it though. When we have such a short existence to know before our reach into the oblivion, we should have the right to know all parts of that existence. The joy and the pain.

I laughed slightly at the girl's successful retaliatory attack on the boy and went back to my book. These humans had been on a new planet for a while at this point. Decades even. The main character who was but a child when the original group landed was now an adult with children of their own. They built cities. Large cities with industrial plants building more ships and components for space stations. It was a wondrous period of progress, and prosperity. There was plenty of work to be done and due to the somewhat small human populace, no one that wanted work went without.

Of course, everyone wanted work. Only the most driven humans came to this planet or any other planet for that matter. This original wave of settlers was all chosen precisely for their drive and abilities while on earth. The children that accompanied their qualified parents also went through screening processes to ensure they would be driven and productive in a new world just like their parents. There was no room for a couch potato or a leech. It would be nice to be able to have the time and support cushion to take time researching and weeding through people and find just the diamonds to send out. In the real world it usually ended up being shipments of desperation as areas became inhospitable and entire bases would be shipped at once or for the most blindly based missions into the deep, the worst among us would be chosen just to remove the problematic humans.

"I'm sure that will lead to the kind of prosperity depicted in books like the one I am reading." I think to myself laughing softly. "No way it will become total anarchy on the other end."

It was at this point I noticed a shadow creep into my field of vision slowly from the right. The shadow crept up onto the page of my book and stopped. Froze in place. Then it appeared to start curling towards me but only the uppermost portion of the shadow. It almost looked like a person holding some kind of .... thing. Some item about the size of a large beach ball but rectangular. A cooler? Why would someone be curling a cooler towards m--- I jumped up and swung to my left just in time to miss a wave of iced down water raining down on the spot I had been sitting. I wasn't quick enough to spare my entire self as a chill raced up my leg letting me know I was at least partially soaked now. As I spun back around to face where the shadow had been coming from, I saw Billy. He was standing there with a massive grin on his red face. He must have been exerting himself carrying that cooler so quietly. His face was bright red from holding his breath while carrying his weapon of choice in this prank attempt.

"Damn it Billy!! What the Hell are you doing?" I shouted at him. Instead of answering, he dropped the cooler and started rolling on the ground laughing. I ran around the bench to where he was and somewhat playfully kicked him in the side. "I told you there is no way you will get me with a silly prank like that. Why do you even keep trying? Your attempts never end up working like you want. Sometimes you can land a glancing blow," this part I said as I looked down at my leg which was tingling a bit due to the influx of blood trying to warm the chilled skin, "but your pranks never work out completely. Can't you find something a bit more age appropriate to be doing instead of these childish attempts at humor?"

"Oh, come on Maggie, try to have some fun for once. I almost had you that time." Billy was able to squeak out while trying to calm his laughing. "My ribs hurt so bad. Don't be too proud though, the pain is from all the laughing, not that puny thing you call a kick."

I retorted, "If I wanted to hurt you Billy, you wouldn't be laughing so hard right now, not with some ribs out of place. What are you doing anyways? Don't you have some reading to do?"

Still laughing, Billy retorted, "Reading, what in the world would I be reading for right now?"

"The book we are supposed to read and write a report on." I said.

Billy froze, stopped laughing immediately and climbed to his feet. "The report is due Monday?" he asked quietly, "This Monday? As in tomorrow?"

Realizing he probably hadn't thought a single time about the assignment since Mr. Coster had issued it to our class, I saw my revenge. "Yes, tomorrow Monday. We have to have the whole book read and a five-page paper written about it."

"Oh crap, I thought it was next Monday, I thought I had a whole other week to work on it."

"Billy, have you even started the book yet? You know Mr. Coster doesn't give an inch when it comes to due dates. Not for sick days, not for earthquakes, power outages, not for anything. You had better get to it and have that report ready first thing in the morning."

Billy stared at me for a long minute, his slightly plump face now red from embarrassment and increased stress as his new conundrum deepened in his mind. Billy had always been a friend. He was goofy and a bit nerdy, but he was always there for me. I almost felt bad about messing with his mind until I remembered that he was the one that always instigated these pranks back and forth. I only responded when necessary.

"Damn, I better get back to the house then and get started. I can't believe I forgot all about it. I really thought it was next week. We even have to read the report in front of the class, don't we?" Billy said in a defeated voice, all his joy and pride in a near perfect prank gone in an instant.

"We do, Mr. Coster told me he was going to be grading on the presentation most of all. A simple reading won't cut it this time around. He wants everyone to "feel" the book they read and portray it properly to the class."

"How far have you gotten so far?" Billy asked me.

"Oh, I am done with mine, I wrote the report last night also, just rereading the book now to make sure I didn't miss any subtle parts that Mr. Coster may find important and quiz me on during my presentation. You know how he likes to throw curve balls when he can. To test that you actually read and understood, didn't just use your tablet to scan the book and write a presentation for you."

"Ugh" Billy said resigned to his fate. "I gotta get back to the house and start on mine then. Guess I will see you tomorrow, if I survive the night pouring though the garbage they make us read. I would be more interested if we could have some good books, something with monsters, murderers or amazing wizards that can shoot flame from their hands."

With that last comment he waved bye to me and disappeared. Disappeared into nothing. That was so normal to me that I didn't even think about it. It wasn't until later in life that I started thinking about the simple things I took for granted during my time on earth. Before I found out we would be leaving it forever to go to a new planet that humans were settling. I didn't know about any of the plans yet, but many others did. Those I trusted the most knew all about it and didn't share. That would have an impact in my ability to trust later down the road. For some time now, my Father at least had known we would be leaving along with many others but no one else in my settlement could know for fear of causing hysteria on why they might not be joining us. So, I hadn't been told, just to keep one more source of a leak, me, closed up tight. I couldn't reveal what had been withheld from even me. That is a story for a later time though, back to the present.

After Billy had left, I turned back to my bench. I noticed the entire concrete seat was soaked now between the water and the now melting ice that had been so rudely dumped there. I picked my book up off the ground a few feet away. It had gone sailing when I jumped up and spun around. As I reached for the book, I peered closely at the grass. The turf appeared so luscious, soft and smelled just like it was recently mowed. Or at least that's what I assume. I had never really smelled fresh cut grass in real life, only what the simulation sent to my nostrils. I dropped my hand and grasped a handful of grass in it, rubbing the fine blades between my fingers. The grass rolled through my fingertips crisply and cleanly. It didn't tear, it didn't leave any green residue behind like the small squares of the stuff did in my science class. It just was. It was there but it wasn't. It was real but it wasn't. It smelt like grass, but it didn't. I was overthinking things again. Don't ask me how I knew it wasn't a perfect representation of what "nature" was at one point in the past, it just always seemed a bit off. My father told me it is even better than it was in the olden days because the simulations don't include nasty blood sucking bugs or any real dangers.

He always tells me, "Maggie, you can run around and play. Climb all over equipment, swing, slide down long twisty loops, hang from monkey bars, wrestle with other kids on the ground, all without having to worry about staining or tearing your clothes or even twisting an ankle." Like I would run around and climb anymore. I was too old for that, too near the end of my schooling, too near the end of my easy days of adolescence. Too near the crushing reality that soon I would be graduating and be old enough to join the work force. Required to contribute or be cast out of the settlement, out of civilization that was the only hope for humanity on earth. I heard stories of what lay outside the border gates but very few inside ever saw it with their own eyes. The few that had seen it were sworn to secrecy. Outside was that bad evidently.

The simulation does do a good job, even gets my real heart pumping. Sometimes though, I wish I could really smell the grass and maybe even get a nice stain on my dress. If I had a dress that is. A real one I mean. I loved the dresses I got to wear in this world. They flowed around me, I could tighten them up or loosen them out merely by scrolling through the menus that would pop up with a certain flick of my wrist. Still it wasn't the same as a real dress. I had a couple dresses back in a drawer at home, but they never came out. Clothes like that were so rare, you never wore them for fear of damage.

Why couldn't I just enjoy the grass and all the other wonders around me and forget the fact that it was all fake? It was my choice to see this as I wanted to, after all, if I didn't want this park, I could have gone to a beach or a snow slope. I could have gone to any old sports game saved in the digital files I wanted to or even a large circus. Even with the scene around me not being perfect, it was still a wonderful day and I should be happy I get to experience it. Not everyone does as I have been reminded so many times. This escape is not free by any means. My parents have a subscription which gives us so much time each month to get away into the simulation. Escape the harsh realities of the real world. The dying planet. My parents don't ever come into the Sim, they let me use all the time in our plan. They told me I needed the release and escape. They had been around at the very end of the world before this new reality. They had their own childhood memories, they wanted me to have the chance to experience it as best as we could at this point. I wanted to experience the real thing though and I blamed the older generations for their disregard for the planet when it was still green. When it still had a chance.

I looked back at the children that had been playing out in the open area. They were not playing anymore but instead taking a break and huddling around picnic tables covered in sweet treats and soda. In this simulation it wouldn't hurt them to have some junk foods. This was the only place you could get that kind of thing anymore anyways. With the depleted resources on the planet, all consumables not required to sustain life were no longer manufactured. Only things that kept the public at bay or moved humans off the planet quicker was produced now. I gazed around at the setting sun. It was just starting to drop down close to the horizon, signifying our time was nearly over.

Each session in these sims were one hour of real time but with the magic that was the sim, they always somehow felt like many hours. The sims did vary somewhat. Something to do with the group thought process. We were all linked in a way, so the system had to work with the group consciousness. This made our experience times vary from several hours to full days if you were lucky to match up with all the right minds at the right time. There were studies regularly on why some minds worked better with some others, but no real conclusions had been made yet. It seemed that even if you placed the same people in the same sim together their conceptual times would still vary. Maybe it had to do with moods, other thoughts going on, who knows. That was something for the science people to figure out. The human brain was so complex that even the rudimentary connection we all had in the sim impacted the whole thing.

The next group of people were probably waiting outside the simulation room getting their suits on, fitting helmets. I thought about leaving the simulation and with a certain eye motion the sensors in my helmet would recognize, I opened a menu. A simple flick of my wrist in the correct direction scrolled that menu and selected the exit prompt. Then I was out. Back in the real world again, just like that.

Outside of the simulation, I disconnected the chin strap holding my helmet on and lifted it up. A couple people in the room over on one end had a slightly different setup. They still removed a helmet, but their helmets were covered in electrodes. The helmet I had fed me real inputs. A screen wrapping around my eyes fed optical inputs. A tube pumped properly timed scents to my nostrils and tiny speakers sent sounds directly to my eardrums ready for my brain to interpret. These others at the edge of the room were more advanced versions. They had been developed with the eventual intent to eliminate the need for real inputs. They would send information directly into the brain tissue itself and bypass all our various physical senses. This seemed like black magic to me but that wasn't even the most advanced thing. I knew through the rumor mill that testing was going on with physical brain links. I don't know how close these were to being reality and released to the public, but they were being testing. Sim rooms that used to be open regularly had been cordoned off without more explanation than a simple "Out of Order" sign on the now locked doors. They had been Out of Order for months now. I doubt it was a basic breakdown that could be remedied within days. It had to be a test chamber for these new systems.

Physical brain links were talked about extensively in some of our texts and the state media covered it plenty. Some citizens held concerns that a person could theoretically plug another person in and implant information, memories, instructions into their minds but, in reality, the brain links were still too simple to handle that. There was no real input capability in the links yet.

They pulled information out so an individual could control simple equipment like having a fancy remote control. At least that is what I have heard. If the ruling class was doing testing in secret, then there must be a reason to keep it secret. Someone may have made a breakthrough and were well beyond what the media believed it knew. So, for now we still had to wear helmets fitted with all the proper gear or glasses with screens built in to see a sim and com links in our ears to hear the sim. This isn't wild Syfy after all, this is just reality. Boring reality.

Anyways, I came back to the land of the living and removed my helmet. I paused for a moment before continuing as one side effect of the sims was it took you so totally out of the real world and into another that it always took a few minutes for your mind to re center on what was going on. Once my senses smoothed out and recalibrated, I disconnected the support arm from the rear of my suit and hopped down from the perch I was on. When you were in the sim, you were suspended above the ground in a suit attached to an arm. The arm let you twist and run and jump in the sim. This controlled and limited motion allowing our bodies to still get exercise while we were in the sim. Even with the extensive sensory inputs from the helmets, humans needed real movement to buy into the sim. The suits would even relay pressures and temperatures to the skin so you could "feel" the sim. Just like the water that Billy had idiotically dumped on me. My leg never really felt the coldness or the moisture of iced water, but the suit chilled in the area and made my brain interpret it that way.

Looking around down from my perch, the room was painfully plain and maybe a bit on the large side at around forty by forty feet. White solid walls, dark industrial carpeted floors made up the flat surfaces with low LED lighting coming from recessed fixtures in the drop ceiling. The room didn't need to be much, nothing in the room but the suits and helmets provided any part of the simulation so not much was put into the room itself. The moment you step outside the simulation room, you remember that despite the beauty of the simulation itself, the blandness of the room wasn't all that special. The whole building is quite dull in fact.

The whole community was dull. Nearly all the buildings were the same. Off white and grey block or concrete walls with flat rooves on the outsides. A few of the original buildings were covered in a dark red brick but that was the only exception. Plain, regularly spaced square windows where appropriate. Few doors. Access points were always points of weakness in security so they were limited to usually two doors at the ground floor for each building. One regular entrance and a back entrance where workers for that specific structure would enter and exit bringing supplies in and wastes out. White and gray linoleum tiled floors in common areas, industrial carpets in rooms. Long, straight hallways. Plain and bare. No pictures hung from the walls, no decorations of any kind. The only thing lining the walls was the occasional emergency action posters on what to do if any number of emergencies occurred.

Where the nearest airtight bunker was. Where the nearest fire escape was and what to do in the event of a hurricane, tornado, earthquake or meteor strike. None of those emergencies scared anyone. There hadn't been a fire in years, not with all the synthetic materials and concrete used everywhere. Those didn't burn. The city was well protected from all kinds of "natural" disasters. Raids were the real dangers. The city had not lost a single structure or person in over a decade to anything natural. Besides the environmental issues encroaching closer every year to our hideaway, humans were the only danger worth evacuating for. People wanted in, or maybe just wanted us out. I didn't know and hoped to never find out. Humans in general were just poor company to keep it seemed. I had been around long enough to recognize that people were more a plague than anything good. We destroyed in general. There were good people among us, quite a few in all reality but overall, as a group we were locusts. Worse than locusts. At least all those historical insects ever did was fly around and eat everything. They never mined to the depths causing earthquakes and fractures to open up. At least they didn't build machines that burned away most resources. They didn't create weapons that could turn entire cities of the past into ash within seconds. They just ate. We do so much more.

I headed for our home after the simulation. It was getting later in the evening and I needed to get home before curfew set in. There was still plenty of time, but I was starving and wanted to get home before curfew (and my parents) so I could snag a bite to eat before chores and a late dinner. The community I lived in was under strict military rule and had multiple curfews in place for different segments of the population. Being in high school, I was in the second category. I had to be to my home building by 1800hrs each evening unless accompanied by a parent or other legal certified guardian. The only people that had to be inside ahead of me were younger children up to middle school. I despised the curfew but what was I going to do about that? Armed guards made rounds constantly but that didn't matter as much as the implant all citizens of Harrisburg were required to have placed when they were either born or were allowed into the city gates.

That implant was a whole separate deal to discuss at some later time. It fed vital signs and location to the central governing body so they could track all citizens and "ensure their health and happiness" if you believed the story line toted by the PR people within the government. We all knew it was just to keep tabs on us and make sure we were where we should be when required and not doing anything stupid on our limited off time. The implants also were our ID and our payment method for all commodities. You could just swipe your arm at any store and the goods you wanted would be charged to your government managed bank accounts.

We read this book once in school that mentioned something along the lines of our implants. It spoke of a mark that would be required by an authority. A mark that made you unable to accept God and go to heaven. Supposedly the mark was from the devil himself. Those fairy tales reared their heads regularly still. You would think that with all that was going on that such belief would wane, but it never seemed to. The worse things got; the more people turned that direction. Looking for the answer that would never come. I guess as long as it made them feel better then it didn't hurt anything. When the implants came about back when I was just a baby and had no voice to share, there were uprisings from the religious sect. Most of those voices quieted down once the authorities began sending people away through the gates when they refused the chip. Still today there are those few people that do speak about such things, but they still have their implants. Apparently, it is better to swallow that pill than be booted from the city gates to fend for themselves on the outside.

Chapter Two

Outside my home building I took a second to look up at the massive structure. It was a masterpiece of engineering. A monumental steel and glass work of art. Nothing like the rest of the barren community. It had endless windows to let in natural light, large ornamental decorations, huge front entrance that demanded respect. I was so proud to get to li-----.

Sorry, I can't go on with this ruse. I live on a sad, dark, damaged planet caused by thousands of years of devastating natural destruction, fighting between factions of my fellow humans, and more recently grand scheme speaking, a war that nearly wiped out humans as a whole. The end of the world as it was called. I don't know what caused it for sure since all I know is what my city leadership demands I am taught but I am sure it was stupid. Probably some idiot wanted something some other idiot had and shot at them. Then the second guy shot back at the first guy. The first guy's cousin was pissed so shot at the second guy. The second guy's brother's girlfriend's dad's stepsister was mad about that and shot at the third guy or maybe it was the first guy's cousin. Who knows right? All that really matters anyways is that pretty soon everyone was involved and so the nukes came out. End of story. The planet is ruined. Why else would we be locked in a gated city? Why else would I be spending part of my day in an expensive VR experience just to attempt a vain effort of experiencing a wondrous planet I will never have the chance to know? I was born into a world of devastation. A world on the brink of total collapse. The earth was dead and had been for a while. There was no nature, there was no need for an attempt at beauty here. The town was designed by military minds for military use until civilians started escaping here for refuge.

The building I really lived in was a dark, boring square. It was 10 stories tall, several hundred feet long and several hundred feet wide. Think large hotel. That is about what it was but more boring. I went in the plain front entry, large double doors for bringing furniture and supplies in and out easily, through the small lobby which had a desk and a guard watching a bank of monitors. The front doors had released as I walked up due to the sensors feeding an ok to the guard based off my implant. I didn't know the guard's name. Guards were rotated regularly, and it was frowned upon for anyone to familiarize themselves with them. Guards were there for security only, not for being friends or receiving that package you have been patiently waiting for.

Only approved people would be allowed in and anyone not in the building's database as a resident or approved visitor would be detained or shot on sight if any resistance was perceived. The guards were not mean people, not even unfriendly, but not your buddy either. They came from the military group. Trained professionals that knew how to handle a weapon and wouldn't need that weapon to take you down if that situation arose. I always made an effort to wave or nod with a smile to the guard on duty as I came and went but I couldn't tell you the name of any of them if my life depended on it beyond the last name they always wore on their uniforms.

I continued through the lobby and headed up the stairs. There was an elevator, but it was restricted to freight needs only. We lived on the fifth floor but the exertion from plodding up the stairs didn't faze me. Citizens were always expected to be fit and healthy. Not being able to jog up and down five flights of stairs would be considered a weakness the city could not afford to support. The bottom floors of each housing building were reserved for citizens that could not use the stairs. You had to have approval from the board which required some kind of debilitating issue that could not be fixed by modern technology. Even then you had to be worth enough to the government to have a debilitating issue overlooked.

There was no welfare or disability in this world. A lot of old illnesses and issues could be fixed that in times preceding ours would follow someone their entire lives. Lifespans had extended significantly if you could avoid the pitfalls of the modern world and personal health while alive was more assured due to advances in treatments. Cancers, blood conditions, muscle and bone deformities, injuries, all could be corrected now. Depending on how valuable someone was considered by the government, some brain and genetic conditions could be corrected now as well. At least corrected enough for the citizen to be considered useful in some position within the city.

Once I arrived at my unit's door, I swiped my arm across the sensor and waited for the audible click. The door opened easily and swung into my home. Families that lived here all got their own unit no matter the size. Each unit was a decently sized 2-bedroom apartment. Each was nearly identical with single small bathrooms, small eat in kitchens, small living rooms capable of housing a single couch and chair. Fortunately for me, my parents only had a single child, so I got a room all to myself. I knew some people at school that had three or even four siblings. That made for cramped quarters. Some had petitioned the city government long before for larger housing accommodations, but the governing body admonished those people for having too many children. They said if someone wanted more room in their dwellings then they could either have fewer children or leave the city and risk it out there.

People rarely left the city voluntarily and the government knew these families with children would never leave and put their families at risk. The governing body occupied the center of the base and owned all property. They did not expand the city's borders to build new structures. What was here was here and there would not be anything more. It was an effective means of population control without officially having any form of population control. Politicians still reigned supreme. There is a field that will never go out of date no matter how much it should.... When the city was too full, you could do one of three things. You could leave the city; you could deal with it or you could improve yourself and hope to push your way up the roster for off world colonization missions. It worked for the most part, but some families made do and grew their families even with the tightly cramped living areas.

No one was home when I got in, so I headed first for the kitchen just off the front entryway. I was starving from the day. Normally I would grab a snack of some kind from a street vendor on my way home but since the crackdown on consumables like food, street vendors prices skyrocketed, and my parents threw a fit when I got any. They told me if I wanted to spend my own money on a forty-credit hot dog, then I could go earn my own credits with after school service instead of going to the VR building so often. Of course, there was no after school service offering paid hours right now with the cutbacks so that was an empty offer by my parents. They would never allow me to join a service anyways as they were usually awful jobs filled by kids of low-level city residents that needed the extra credits to afford basic necessities. We were not wealthy upper class by any means, but my parents were proud people and made sure I had everything I needed without having to join these child labor groups.

After calming down my writhing stomach, I decided to shower and get ready for the evening with my parents. Usually on Sunday nights we would have a movie night in the unit just to ourselves. We would unplug from our tablets and spend time together. Just us. I went into my room and froze. The room was empty. It was still full of furniture, my bed, my desk, my chair, my stereo but it was empty. It felt empty. I slowly crept to my dresser and opened the top drawer. Normally it would be filled with underwear and socks but today it was empty, minus a couple scraps of old clothing and a couple hair ties. The next drawer down was the same thing. Only a couple old shirts remained. The rest of the dresser stayed true to the new normal. Empty, empty, empty but for a few scraps. "What the Hell?" I said out loud. "Were we robbed?" I stepped back and sat on my bed.

There was no way we were robbed I thought to myself. That is the whole reason we have guards and tight security everywhere. No one could even get in our unit without being approved and using their implant. Not to mention my room and the unit as a whole was clean, neat and tidy just as I had left it this morning. No thief is going to steal my clothes and leave everything else in place. I ran to my parents' room and found the same thing, their clothing was all gone besides a few random items that apparently didn't make whatever cut was going on.

I went out to the living room and the TV was still in place. Very few people had televisions anymore. They stopped production of televisions years ago due to the "Necessity to keep our citizens working towards a common goal. Televisions are unnecessary and keep our citizens from completing important daily tasks to keep the community running at its peak efficiency." TV programming had stopped at the same time so all we used ours for was re-watching old movies and shows on our regular weekly time together as a family.

If the TV was still here, then there was no way this was a common theft. That would be the first thing to be taken. What was going on? It didn't make any sense at all. Everything else was in its place except clothes? There had to be something else missing also. I slowly started noticing that our few personal items around the house were gone too. Everything that was specific to our family was gone. The couple portraits we had, my books, all gone. I walked around our unit some more and the utensils in the drawers were still there, but all our spare blankets were gone. I went back in my room and realized then my bed covers had been replaced by the standard issue gray coverings. It was almost like I had walked into a standard unit just the way they are when residents move in. Standard furniture and supplies plus the television of course. Hardly anything personal at all. The bathroom was exactly the same minus one thing. One pile that is. A single stack of clothing with a travel size container of body wash/shampoo/conditioner. It was my clothing, my cleaning product, my stuff. Left for me to change into after a shower it appeared.

Then it clicked, we must be moving to another unit. That's all. This happens rarely but it does happen. If a building needs work that is too extensive to live in during, the government will move all the families to another building. Once work is complete, new families will be moved in instead of moving the originals back. It was more efficient that way. Our building was old, and a few issues had crept up here and there. That must be it. My blood pressure and heart rate dropped back to their normal places and I took a long breath. We must be moving, and my parents wanted me to have a chance to shower before heading to the new unit. I didn't quite understand why I wouldn't just shower in the new unit once we moved in later that night but a lot of things my parents did didn't make sense to me. I took the hint and cranked the water on after first swiping my arm by the sensor so the shower would register who I was.

While showering I was daydreaming of where we may move. Maybe a top floor unit in downtown near the capital buildings. The buildings there were a bit nicer and it would be closer to school and the simulators.

As I was planning my future in a downtown location with roof top gardens and buildings with regular use elevators, I was rudely awakened by an icy cold only describable with profanities this world has never heard before The water had changed from the sweat lodge steam inducing temperature to an icy cold that would form ice on the shower door within minutes if allowed to continue. I decided to give up and get out to towel off. Another one of those wonderful efficiency items the local government believes is their duty to shove down the throats of the populace. The government is largely Women run so it never made sense to me that they would restrict us all to 5-minute showers once every other day but that is what they did. 5 minutes of course was only a suggestion. You could shower all day if you wanted to, but the city could only grant you 5 minutes of heated water at a time due to supply issues. Politicians again are magical beings able to create laws that control every aspect of our lives without ever creating a law at all.

As I toweled off, a murmur of speech wafted in from the living room. I quickly finished drying the best I could with the thin beige towel that had been left for me and slipped my clean dry clothes on. Fortunately, they were still infused with the wonderful heat from the previously steamy bathroom. I started to crank the door handle but stopped to listen to my parents for a second. They were speaking quietly but quickly and with a tinge on frustration or maybe fear on their voices.

"Jim, what do you mean the transport has been moved up?" my mother asked sharply. "I get home to find all our things gone and all you can tell me is the transport was moved up?"

"Honey, I --" My father tried to respond but my mother jumped right back in. "Don't honey me Jim, you told me we had another month at least before it was leaving. Maybe up to six months. We agreed to tell Maggie a day or two ahead so she could say goodbye to her friends first."

After a second of quiet, my father was able to respond in a quiet, calm and firm tone, "Barbara, I told you what I knew at the time, but that timeline has been moved up. There are intelligence reports that a group of Earthers are ramping up for a full-scale strike and they want as many Value 1 people out of the city as possible beforehand. Also, I never agreed to tell Maggie ahead. You know mission secrecy is top priority and if she so as mentioned it to anyone, it could destroy everything."

"I know we can't tell anyone Jim; I think Maggie could keep the secret fine."

"Then what would be the point of her knowing ahead of time?" My father quizzed, "You just said you wanted her to have a chance to say goodbye to her friends. The very act of doing that would share that we were leaving. We can't risk that knowledge getting out."

"So, she could have some kind of closure. More than just a random disappearance in the middle of the night. We all know we can't talk about leaving but she should at least get the chance to say goodbye."

"I'm sorry but she won't be getting that, none of us will. Guards will be here in a few minutes to escort us over to the launch platform. We are leaving tonight or possibly not leaving at all. There is nothing I can do or any of us can do at this point. You know we must get on this ship now or Maggie's chances of a life are near zero. There is nothing here --"

"You don't have to explain it all to me again Jim. I was in the meetings; I know the situation with the Earthers. I may know more about those situations than you do. You know I am constantly having to review, edit and translate messages between the Earthers and the government every day." My mother interrupted father again.

Tightly father retorted, "Barbara, no offense but you handle official communications between factions within the government. Communications that first go through other military translators and slated for either low, medium or maximum-security clearances. My office doesn't get to see the maximum-security messages either, but I can infer the tone of what is being said based on the shipping and receiving schedules between the space port and the launch platform along with the reports coming through my lab. The number of top brass coming in to look at my work has gone up dramatically. New guards have been placed, more secrecy, people are being followed home Barbara. It hasn't been this way in the past. This is all a huge ramp up to something that neither of us are being told about I am afraid.

"I'm sorry, I'm just scared"

"I know honey, I am too. We just have to do what we think gives Maggie the best chance for life. To do something other than die here in this city with no chance but work every day under a constant threat of attack."

At this point, I had had about enough listening to my parents talk about what was best for me. About us leaving the city and going where? Going to another city somewhere? No, dad spoke of the launch pad. That only sends ships into space. Why would we be moving to the space port? From what I had heard of families that moved back from up there after service rotations, it was even more dreary than on earth. Tight cramped quarters even smaller than on earth. Recycled air that supposedly smelled like wet socks all the time. A bland grey food that tasted like the feet that came out of those wet socks the air circulated through. I guess I should have expected this. My father works in government logistics. He deals with the space port and lunar farms every day. He managed a team that scheduled flights back and forth based on conditions on both ends. However, he did mention something about a lab. His lab. He is a logistics guy. Why would a logistics guy have or need a lab? I would have to think on that one a bit.

My mother worked in linguistics and communications earth side between the Earthers and various government factions around the world. It made sense that we may be rotated up to the space port for term of service. Both of them could work from either end, and anyone that held high positions like they both did were expected to be a part of the rotation. Normally if you had children school age, you were exempt from rotation but with any rules we lived by, they could change at the whim of the government and its leaders. I walked out into the living room to confront my parents.

Chapter Three

Riding in a transport truck from our old housing unit towards the launch pad I looked around angry, tired and a little scared. My confrontation with my parents did not go so well for me. Basically, I stormed into the room and they shut down. Eyes dropped to the floor and they didn't say a word. They let me rant and rave about how unfair it was for us to have to leave. For us to have to go to the space port. How much I hated their jobs and hated everything there ever was and would be in the future. I hated my life and I hated the entire existence of humans as a whole. Once I calmed down for a moment in a ball of sweat and tears I had worked up in my tirade, my father simply said he was sorry I felt that way and things would make more sense later.

Mother told me all they thought about was what was the best for me and if I could just trust them a little longer, it would all make sense. I wanted to protest, I wanted to scream some more but I didn't have it in me. My parents did do all they could for me. They made sure I was with the best teachers available to us and that my desire for the outdoor life was met with expensive subscriptions to the simulators. I had to trust them. What other choice did I have anyways?

So here I was riding in this bumpy, cramped, dirty transport truck. I had not been in one of these before. This was not public transport, but a government truck used to move troops from one area of the city to another. It was strange that this is the vehicle we were using to get to the launch pad. I figured it was just part of being sent to the space port. You got a special ride for your last few hours on earth. Possibly forever if things didn't go well up there. People were a lot more vulnerable on the space port than down here. Attacks on our base were rare and pretty useless to be honest. City defenses were strong and could shoot almost anything down long before it threatened anyone inside. The deadliest attacks were on space stations orbiting the earth. Any crude group of Earthers could cobble together a rocket to hit a station. Stations were slow and even though well-guarded, they were still easier to damage than bases on earth. Plus, these Earthers were more about keeping us on the earth to die together than just killing anyone already on the surface. They wanted to stop expeditions and technological growth unless it extended lives on the surface. Don't get me wrong, attacks were not a regular or highly threatening thing. It was just more likely to get you in space than on the surface.

I turned to my father who was staring out the windows of the old truck and saw his blank expression. Maybe a hint of sadness was there but nothing strong. He was deep in thought and I couldn't figure out what it was. His eyes came back to focus and he turned to face me. His lips curled up into a gentle smile as he wrapped his arm around me pulling me close. He didn't say anything and neither did I. We just rode there together in the darkness of the back seat bouncing down the street towards our exit from this place, the only place I have known, my home.

I started to doze a bit, wrapped in my father's warmth until the truck lurched sharply. I looked up at my Father and saw his eyes locked on something out in the distance. Turning to look the same direction I saw what had caused the sudden change in speed. A fireball closely resembling an atomic mushroom cloud was climbing up into the sky above the base far on the other end. The blast was huge. I was frozen staring at the display but the soldiers in control of our truck were trained too well to freeze in this situation. Instead of stopping to look or rubber necking, I felt the truck pull even harder under me as we accelerated and took a hard turn down another street facing us opposite of the blast source.

We tore down side streets in a roundabout way towards the launch pad. Another explosion rocked out in the general direction of the first one but a bit closer. I watched this cloud of angry gasses and burning debris grow large into the night sky. It reached far above the buildings nearest me. I was trying to think of where exactly the blasts were coming from. It had to be near our apartment building. We had been driving for only fifteen to twenty minutes when the first blast occurred. I couldn't tell exactly though with the darkness all around. I clenched harder to my father and hoped for the best since that is really all I could do. When the blast wave carrying sound arrived at our location, I could hear it above the roar of the engine and slapping of tire treads on the pavement. Such a deep rumbling sound. Suddenly the truck screeched to a halt. The abrupt end to our forward progress sent me reeling inside my head.

I knew we were not at the launch pad yet. I hadn't ever been there in any official capacity, but we had visited it a couple times during my school years, so I knew right where it was. My general interest in the area of space exploration probably helped me know more about the launch pad then someone of my age normally would have.

Why would we stop here in the middle of buildings when the launch pad would be more heavily fortified and protected? It was a critical part of the base so was protected nearly to a point of impenetrability. Nearly all our food was brought down to the space port which was part of the launch pad. If it was damaged, our supplies from Luna would have to be landed somewhere else and trucked in. I couldn't imagine how that would even work. Our trucks were all electric running off rails built into the pavement on the roadways. How would trucks even make it out somewhere not inside the base? I knew they had battery packs but had no idea how far those would carry a vehicle of such size.

My Father shifted me over to my Mother and stood. He patted a nearby soldier on the back and pointed outside the back of the covered bed. The soldier nodded while talking on radio with who I presumed was the soldiers in the cab of the truck. The commander most likely. My Father and the soldier walked to the rear of the truck and exited walking around towards the cab together. I turned to my Mother questioningly.

"What is Father doing? Why is he going with the soldier?"

"Maggie, he is trying to decide what needs to be done. Obviously, there has been some kind of attack on the base, and we want to make sure we don't drive into an ambush of some kind."

"But why is Father discussing it with the soldiers? Shouldn't that be up to the commander of this group?" I wasn't sure exactly how military hierarchy worked but I knew there was a hierarchy and civilians never had control in an active situation. The soldiers would be unhappy my Father was intervening.

"Honey, don't worry about that. Your Father know what he is doing. He has some experience in these situations and with his post comes authority to determine our best course and implement it. He will make sure we get to the launch pad safely."

About that time the truck lurched violently to the left. It knocked Mother and I out of our seats and onto the floor of the truck's cargo hold. I could see holes now in the tarp that wrapped this area. The holes were probably already there but against the night sky I hadn't been able to tell a difference. Now I could see those holes blazing with red in the background. Something had happened outside. The truck fired back up and started moving. Just as I was about to scream for my Father, he swung around the back of the truck with the soldier from before. They both jumped in and the truck sped off.

We rushed forward in the truck bouncing off curbs and sidewalks taking the corner out of our side street far too fast to be safe. I could hear the electric motor screaming as it went. When we cleared the side street, I could see through the open back a building near where we had been parked was on fire. One entire side was fully wrapped in flame and had most of the wall missing piled up in the street below where it shouldn't have been. Debris scattered into the road along with what I could swear were broken bodies scattered around. My eyes welled up with tears at the horror and met up with my Father's. He looked deep into me and motioned towards me to look away. I wanted to look away so badly but I couldn't. My Mother must have realized this fact and drug her hand over my face forcing my eyes to release the imagery in front of us. I wept into her arm.

The truck didn't stop again. It sped full force the remaining distance to the launch pad. When that explosion happened near where we had stopped to discuss options it must have cut said discussion quite short. The decision was made that we would be safer moving as quickly as possible to the safest area than to try and sneak around or wait for reinforcements. I only took a few minutes to regain composure. I knew of attacks on the base and people had been hurt. It was one thing though to hear about something happening while you are safety evacuated to a nearby bunker and kept in quiet comfort until the all clear was sounded than to be right on top of it when it happens. When you are vulnerable and in the open, even when surrounded by military, a bomb like what must have struck the building back there would make the security of this truck into a blender scattering our remaining bits among the debris of steel and rubber.

We arrived at the launch pad within a few more minutes screeching tires along the pavement until we passed the gates to the facility. The launch pad was amazing. I had never been in this entrance since citizens were not allowed on the physical facility for any reason. The field trips we had taken out here in the past used a different entrance and the visitor center overlooked the facility. We could see everything on the surface, but I had never been on the ground itself. Too many things we could mess up I had always assumed. The buildings were all stark white and the ground was nothing but black pavement and yellow paint. No grass, nothing else around but asphalt and concrete buildings. Along with all those tall poles and their near blinding lights.

Everything shined boldly in the glare of the overhead lights. Even though at this point it was the middle of the night, it was brighter than most days. Our atmosphere was clouded and the protective domes over parts of the community even as clear as they were designed never let all the light in like it should. Some was always refracted away. I had to shield my eyes as I tried to look up the sides of the ship, I assumed we would be riding into the space port. The ship looked like the end of a ball point pen. A near perfect rounded cone a bit more than double in height than it was wide with a small hole at the very tip. From my studies I knew that tip was an air induction system that fed the engines used in launch. This ship was designed to take off and land many times over its lifetime. I could tell it was a super launcher. Almost perfectly white with a bit of darkening like burns on the nose. The nose was pointed straight up into the sky, so it was hard to see well. That perceived darkening of the nose could have just been a shadow from something. More likely the bright lighting in the area just didn't show all the way to the tip as bright as here on the ground. I could make out the designation of the ship from here as the letters spilled down the side of the massive ship in large bold print. Expeditious.

The ship had large jets on the bottom for propulsion. There were no wings, no tails, just a smooth rounded cone shape that tried to touch the sky. It had to be 500 feet tall in total. 150 feet at the base. It was plain but immense and humbling. We would not be the only ones going up by far. They must be sending hundreds of people up at a time if they used a ship this large. The strange thing was that there were very few people around besides the soldiers we passed posted at the front gate, the soldiers with us and a few workers checking on the jets and other various items I knew little about. The small group I was with continued on and soon we were inside a building with the ship out of sight for now.

The next hour was a mad rush of technicians, passengers and stuff. All kinds of stuff. I saw baggage being hauled this way and that, crates of food being hauled by quickly. This was being hauled off the ship, not on. I quickly realized this wasn't supposed to be a passenger trip, the Super Launcher was actually set up to be a freighter that brought food down to the surface from the space port's moon farms. Then the ships would take raw materials and other small supplies manufactured on the ground not available in space back up with it. Mostly the ship was empty when it went up. That saved on fuel as it was easier to bring weight down controlled than haul things up. The factories in the space port made nearly everything they needed besides a few things that needed a more sensitive gravity-based manufacturing system. The only thing they didn't have was a few raw materials that were more plentiful and easier to get a hold of on the dying planet we were leaving. Most would be mined in space harvesting captured asteroids or even mining on other planets.

I wanted to ask a thousand questions but tried to stay quiet and follow the slew of instructions being thrown my way. Soon my parents and I were guided through the melee to a set of quiet, clean rooms. There were rows of simple padded chairs and a few dozen people already occupied most of them. We were apparently a bit late getting here as the moment we sat down a man came in ready to start some kind of speech. He wasn't an ugly man, but he would never be a leading man on any Bachelor season either. No, the Bachelor did not still exist in the modern world but as I said before, every Sunday night my parents and I would sit down to a move and classic tv night. My mother had found a full collection of 48 seasons of the show and we watched the first few episodes one night. It was one of those disasters you couldn't take your eyes away from. We hated the show but loved it at the same time. It was such a mess, but we were addicted immediately and had mixed episodes in as we felt necessary. When we had bad days and really needed to see people with much more messed up lives than our own. That kind of thing. Anyways, this man was neither ugly or attractive, a bit tall but lanky. Red hair and blue eyes made him seem a bit boyish even though he was clearly in his 40's. He still carried an air of authority and it was obvious he was in charge and we would be doing what he said whether we liked it or not.

"All, my name is Steven Barr and I am the Director of this launch pad. Now that all of you are finally here and accounted for", he eyeballed my father in such a manner you would expect a parent to eyeball their child that just dumped their entire bag of popcorn on the floor, "we can start preparations for launch. As you all know at this point, this is a very unusual launch for us, a first of its kind." I took advantage of the quick pause by Mr. Barr to spin my head towards my mother who was already looking at me with an expression of apology on her face. I looked over to my father and he just held a finger to his mouth in the universal "shhhh" sign and squeezed my shoulder with his other hand.

Mr. Barr continued, "Never before have we attempted a long range shot like this one with this type of ship. Normally we would have you rendezvous with a passenger carrier at the space port, but we can't do that any longer. The increased activity around this base has seemed to come to a peak tonight as some of you know. Not all our passengers made it tonight. You all are fortunate you did reach the base ahead of these latest attacks. I can assure you there will be no more before you all launch as the entire community has been put into a mandatory lock down. No movements around the area are allowed at this point without prior high-level authorization.

Due to this bump up in schedule we have been forced to send you all out to the Mars rendezvous point in the Expeditious. Problem is the undersized environmental systems on this Super Launcher. This ship class was designed to only support a crew of 10 for a trip to the space port or Luna. No further. We will be putting you all under for the launch except for our pilot team and a chosen few that will be expected to monitor life support systems on the way up. Once the ship is safely out of atmosphere it will continue to power towards the space port and past it towards Luna.

At that point you will slingshot around the Moon towards the new rendezvous point at Mars. After the slingshot maneuver and when the trip has steadied out into a cruise, the monitoring team will rotate into sleep chambers and a few others will be woke up for duty while you travel. Many of you will all take turns sleeping and taking monitoring duty as you make the thirty-day journey to Mars. Once arriving there, the ship will swing into orbit around the planet and dock up with our station out there. Once at that station, you will move from the Expeditious and into the ship that will take you along for the remainder of your trip. You will then accelerate out of our solar system towards the Exion system."

This must have been new information to most people in the room as there were coughs and choked cries from all around me. Where before most in the room were barely keeping their eyes open under the weight of their boredom and exhaustion, people started murmuring to their neighbors and then had to speak louder and louder as more people started trying to speak. Within a few seconds the room was growing loud and hysterical. My parents didn't move however, they sat stock still staring at Steven without expressions on their faces. They must have already known this apparently startling news ahead of time. What else were they not telling me?

"People, people, people." Our fearless leader at the front of the room nearly shouted to get our attention. "I know some of this was new information, most of the mission plan is the same as it always was but there has been a slight change in plans."

"Slight change in plans?" a woman near the rear spoke up. "I thought this ship was headed for Mars and that was as far as it was going? I have family there I was supposed to meet up with. Why are we going past Mars now? And what is this other ship?"

"Mrs. Ssss, um, Saaa," Steven looked at his notes quickly obviously forgetting the woman's name. "Sardona, Mrs. Sardona. Please let me assure you we understand your concerns. There was a change in plans this morning and we had not been able to update everyone. You will be meeting up with your family as will a number of you that were expecting to be stopping at the red planet. There was an incident on Mars last night that is leading to an evacuation of a few homestead bases on the planet. This is why your flights were originally pushed up suddenly.

Add in what is happening down here tonight and I expect a coordinated attack against our operations.

We needed to get people off the surface of the red planet immediately. The best place to go was the space station but it cannot support so many people for long as it was not designed to be a habitation. Just a shipyard and research base. The best way to guarantee their lives and make use of the available personnel is to launch this ship early, then have you all meet up with them and all of you together leave the system on the APEX.

When you get to Mars and start docking procedures, your extra passengers will already be there in emergency pods ready to transfer over to the new ship. That ship will then leave the Sol system for a new system. The ship outside here will load up with surviving usable equipment and goods to start transferring to other bases around Mars and elsewhere.

"But I never signed up to leave the system" a man from the far-right side of the room said, "I was supposed to stop at Mars for a year-long stay as a guard at one of the reactors there."

"True Mr. Weston," Barr responded curtly, "your assignment was to guard a reactor that will no longer be there in about seven days once the containment vessel completely erodes and leads to the destruction of that homestead base." He continued, "If you would like us to drop you off so you can go ahead and guard that melted reactor until your body is torn down to the bare atoms then we will drop a life boat as we pass by and let you do just that."

The man recoiled with that statement out and having landed hard. Barr continued, "Most of you were supposed to have assignments at the same base. That is not going to happen now. None of you will have family remaining on this planet either so the best thing for us to do was to reassign you to another region. We don't have a place for you here and we need to get those people still alive at that base off the planet. We don't have anywhere to put them either so the best thing for everyone is to send you all to another system that you can start fresh on. You will be needed, useful, productive. Better yet, you will be working to expand the human existence to another new planet. This planet is luscious, green, almost identical to earth in all the important ways. You are the lucky ones, If I could have been assigned to this mission, I would be in the front seat already strapped in and ready to take off. Count your blessings people."

Another man from the seat just right of my mother spoke up, "Sir, I am not arguing against the merits of such a mission or the sudden change in such mission but I know being an engineer working here at the launch pad that the ship we are slated to take cannot make it to Mars in 40 days as it sits out there on the pad." We won't make it half that far in that amount of time. A trip to Mars is usually a 100-day trip at best in this ship and that is by burning all fuel needing a refuel on the way. So that starts us off over double the timeline you have mentioned. Then you say we will transfer over to a new ship. Leaving out the difficulty of transferring this many people and that much gear from a ship with no gravity to another ship with no gravity, that new ship won't be any better for us.

I worked on the APEX back when she was new to the fleet. Just built in fact. I was on her for her first mission out to Mars. Was transferred off her after that trip but I was on her. She was a nice ship. Nearly top of the line but it is just a Super Freighter. Large and easily capable of travelling from one end of our system to another but not out into deep space. Into the true void. Exion is nearly 30 light years away from our sun. The system sounds all well and good with our limited information on it but there is no way we can travel that far in our lifetimes. The fastest we can get to sustained is maybe fourteen5,000 miles per hour with the APEX. It would take generations upon generations to get there if the ship held together. We would only have a dozen years of cruising through empty space before the reactors started failing due to lack of maintenance. If we can maintain enough of a fuel level to keep the reactors running that long. We don't truly know what number of stray atoms we can collect in route due to the fact that we have never heard back from any of our colony ships once they get out of range of regular communication.

Once we either run out of fuel or the reactors shut down from failures in the systems, we would only have weeks of backup power before life support failed. We could make it out of this system on that ship but have no way to get all the way to another system before we all die horrible deaths. This is an insane plan with no hopes of success. I would rather be dropped off at Mars to die quickly in a nuclear fission meltdown than slowly die out in space with no hope."

There was dead silence in the room after that. People slowly started to come back to and murmur to each other when Barr finally spoke back up.

"You are correct Andrew, as Director I am well aware of the fact that the Expeditious is a slow lumbering beast and the APEX cannot make it to another system on its own. The Expeditious will not make the journey on its own as it is known to be set up. Keyword known. This has all been planned out by our very own Mission Commander Jim Johanson. Jim, come on up here and explain to your crew how you will complete the quick jump to Mars and the groundbreaking long journey to Exion aboard your ship, the APEX."

My father stood up, releasing his grip he had on me. I held to him at first not even realizing I had such a strong hold on his arm until he started to pull away. He spun and looked at me with a soft expression on his face.

He leaned in quickly and whispered in my ear, "Hang on honey, this will make sense soon, just trust me." He walked up to the podium and turned to the gathered travelers. I was so confused; my father was just a logistics director. He wasn't a mission commander. He had never even left the planet before. Father began to speak but I was so confused and disoriented that I could hardly concentrate to make out the words. There was something about an experimental worm hole engine that was aboard the Expeditious that was meant for the APEX. If anyone had paid attention, they would realize the ship was much too large for such a small group of passengers. There was mention of using an experimental Photon laser against the Expeditious to increase our velocity to astounding numbers cutting our trip to Mars in less than half. Most of our fuel would be spent on the other end decelerating. After moving all our passengers and equipment to the APEX at Mars and picking up the remaining population of the Mars base, we would still be under 1000 total humans and our gear. The extra room in the new ship was being consumed by the experimental worm hole engine. It would perform some magic that sounded like sorcery to me to open a worm hole between our location at the time and where we plotted our destination. The math was immense, and they did not expect our initial results to be anywhere near accurate. Evidently even being within a couple light years of our destination was perfectly acceptable.

I completely zoned out at that point and just sat there listening and seeing nothing. I would be passenger on a theoretical ship doing something that until only recently was completely unfathomable but somehow my logistics director father and his team had discovered?? How is that even possible? It didn't matter, I was along for the ride and had no say in it whatsoever. My father must have finished his speech since people around me started raising their hands and asking questions. They would ask questions that meant nothing to me, then my father would answer them with words that didn't even ring as language in my head. I was breathing faster, and the room was spinning. Spinning. I tried to look over at my mother, but I couldn't tell which way she was, the room kept spinning so fast and the lights were so bright. It didn't make sense. I was a normal kid with normal parents. Normal, there was no way I was going on an experimental ship. Spinning, bright lights. I couldn't breathe anymore. The air was too thin here. There were too many people, they were taking all the air. Spinning, lights so bright. I think the speaking had stopped at this point and people were standing to leave the room. I tried to hold onto this world, the room was just spinning too fast. I couldn't get up; I could barely hold on to my chair. I felt someone shake me gently, pull on my shoulder, say something to me. I couldn't see, hear or understand them. I was disconnected from the world. The spinning world. I blacked out.

Chapter Four

Cold, why is it so cold? I tried to curl up, but my knees hit something solid. I was so cold. So tired. So very tired. I didn't want to move but I was too cold not to.

Minutes or maybe even hours after I had passed out in the meeting room at the launch pad, I finally came back to the world. It was slow at first, everything was still fuzzy but coming back to shape. I was in a chamber, lying flat on my back. At least the world wasn't spinning anymore. Everything was steady, still and solid. That was always a nice thing to see.

There was a clear dome over my head with the rest of my body bathed in darkness. All I could see from my obstructed sight were a few people walking around. One stopped and looked right at me. Into my eyes, they made a thumbs up sign towards me, but I didn't move. I frowned at the older woman but didn't respond to her. She started to walk closer, so I asked her where I was and what was going on, but she put a hand up to me and pointed to my left. Turning my head gingerly, a touch panel came into view near my shoulder. I reached my arm up to poke the panel but paused mid movement. Something else was off. My arm was so light. Weightless. Turning back to my arm now, I watched it hang there. Realization came to me that I was nearly weightless. My back was lightly pressed into the pod I was in but just barely. Straps wrapped up across my chest, hips, thighs and ankles. Then it hit me. We must be in space already.

I was out long enough to get loaded up into a pod, onto the ship and blasted off into space without me knowing.

Shit.

I wasn't on Earth anymore. Where the hell was I? Did they keep me out until we arrived at Mars, Exion? Am I now on board the APEX in another system after passing through wormholes and everything? I was starting to fume at the injustice of being ripped from my home system, from my planet, from my apartment with absolutely no discussion at all and kept asleep for the entire journey.

A light tap on the dome above me brought me back to the current situation. The nurse again pointed to my left. I nodded and reached over to turn on the com panel. It lit up with a few options; vital signs, ship locations, ship overview and coms. I picked coms and a directory came up with people listed last name first in alphabetical order. I heard a tap from the clear dome again and looked back up. The woman was pointing at a tag on her suit. Thompson. I turned back to the directory and scrolled to Thompson.

There were 2 entries, both had photos. One was Joseph Thompson who was a Larger older man probably in his 50's. He had a hard-lined face not unfriendly but one that obviously was not amused the day he had his official photo taken for the coms directory. The woman looking into my pod was definitely was not Joseph Thompson, so I scrolled to the next choice. Christina Thompson. This photo looked much more promising.

The woman in the photo and the one standing above me were both older, maybe her late 50's. It was hard for me to name an age, especially with women. It could vary so wildly depending on how much attention they paid to keeping themselves looking younger. They were both fit but not thin or hard lined. They both had the same warm easy smile. The only difference was the woman in the picture had perfectly maintained curly grey hair but the woman in front of me was more unkempt. She had wild grey strands shooting out around a headset holding a small screen in front of one eye. I assumed that was probably for viewing charts and other critical information about her charges. A click on her ID on the screen brought up a menu change and a generic ringing sound. Then Christina answered.

"How are you feeling Maggie? Any nausea, cramping, blurred vision, that sort of thing?" Christina's voice carried an accent I couldn't pinpoint but drew the words out. Maybe a Southern Accent from when the United States existed?

I tried to speak but could only get a small rough screech out.

"Take a drink, your mouth is probably dry as a sandy desert right now. There is a drinking tube to your right, bite down and suck on it gently. The system will activate and fill the tube with fresh cool water for you."

I took a long swig of the refreshing liquid and tried again. "I, I, where?" Several coughs racked my chest, clearing out gunk buildup from inactivity. I took another drink and after clearing my throat again, words formed more clearly for me. "Am I on the ship now?"

With a grin, Christina said, "Yes, you are Maggie. I knew you were out of it when we boarded but didn't realize how far out of it. You passed out back in the room when we were being told what changes had been made to our mission. Your father went to get you up after his speech, but you wouldn't move. You just slumped over. He picked you up and rushed you to medical."

"Ugh, so I messed everything up then didn't I? Been a problem even before we got a chance to get off the ground?"

"Not really Maggie, the doctors quickly scanned you and decided it was just from being overwhelmed with information you couldn't digest all at once. You were perfectly healthy, just needed some time to process. An anxiety attack I believe they called it. Since the plan was to put most of us under anyways for launch and the trip as a whole, you were probably the simplest. They just had to put you in a gown and plop you down in a chamber. You were already out so that was a pinch."

I looked down at my body for the first time since waking and realized I was in a gown and that was it. My clothes were gone.

"They undressed me?" I asked uneasily, "While I was unconscious someone undressed me and put me in a robe?"

"Yes, don't worry though honey, your mother took care of that part. No one but her was in the room when she changed you into the gown. You were already sedated at that point to help with your coping, so she took care of changing you into the gown and getting you prepped for a long nap."

"Long nap? I've only been asleep for a few hours though at the most. I know we are in space now but surely we haven't made it too far yet."

Christina nodded to me and continued, "Maggie you have only been out for a few hours. We launched with no problems and are in space now. Currently we are headed towards the Moon to start our slingshot maneuver. You were going to be out until we reached Mars, but your Mother and Father wanted a chance to speak with you before we went too far. I've already notified them both that you are awake. They should be arriving shortly to speak with you. For now, just relax. You can pop the top of the pod open and sit up when you are ready. The sedation you were given was short term but still strong. Be careful since your motor controls may still be a bit sluggish. One thing though honey, don't unstrap from the pod. From your chart here it looks like you have never had any zero G training and we don't want you to hurt yourself floating around in here."

I nodded back to her in agreement and mouthed thanks. It didn't take very long for me to find the pod hatch release option in the menu. As soon as I hit it, I could hear the electric motors whine and the clear capsule lid started to retract into the body of the pod. I tried to sit up but remembered the strap across my chest. Releasing that annoying bit of fabric, I could sit up straight. I heeded Christina's recommendation and left the strap on my hips in place. With the capsule open I could hear the soft clank, clank, clank of the few nurses walking around the bay checking various pods and their inhabitants. All around me were other pods. Dozens and dozens of them from wall to wall. Most of them were all full and closed with people's faces peering out eyes closed and peaceful.

The crew had already put most if not all the passengers to sleep before takeoff. They would probably stay out until we reached Mars. I wondered for a moment at the Nurses and how they moved freely but controlled around the bay until I got a good look at their footwear. Each one wore some kind of boot with red and green lights down the sides. Each time they would step down onto the deck the red lights would flash on, when they went to pull their heel up in a normal forward step the lights would flash to green and the boot would come up from the floor.

"They must be magnetic," I said to myself without thinking, "Each time they step it engages to hold them down and then releases when the little computer brains sense the user wants to take a step." I had read about these boots but never even seen one in real life yet. Their on-board computer processors tried to sense what the user wanted to do but it didn't always work perfectly. You had to walk a certain way to get the boots to activate when wanted and if you didn't do it quite right, they may not release when you wanted effectively tripping you. Then they would release thinking you wanted to move forward causing your already off-balance stance to shift further. The only good thing about the frustration of using them was if you did trip up it wasn't like you were going to pound into the pavement like on a planet.

While thinking to myself about the inner workings of zero-G boots my Mother appeared in my vision. I didn't notice at first and she quickly had a look of concern spread across her face.

"Maggie, are you there honey?"

I shook myself back to the present, "Sorry Mom, yea, I am here. Just fine. So, I guess we aren't on Earth anymore." I said this as I looked down and pointed at her footwear which happened to match the nurses strolling around in their clank, clank, clank patterns.

"No, we are not. You are on the Expeditious now and we are about halfway between the Moon and Earth. Are you feeling ok? I know that was quite a shocker back on Earth."

I wanted to respond with something like no shit but knew that wouldn't help anything in this situation. Keeping my calm, I responded with only a bit of peevishness poking through in my voice, "Yea Mom, I'm fine. Not quite sure what is going on yet though. Still processing that part but it sure seems like you and Dad kept me well in the dark about a lot of things going on lately. What's with all the secrecy?"

"After what happened on the way to the launch pad, I am a bit surprised you need to even ask that question." My Mother replied obviously referring to the multiple explosions we saw along the way including the one that nearly wiped us out along with the truck we were in and half a block of residential housing.

"Sorry, yea, I had kind of blocked that part, I guess. I understand something was happening and we had to get out but was someone after us or just attacking the base from outside?"

"Maggie, the domes."

That stumped me for a minute. What did the domes have to do with anything? I thought back to the madness of rushing through the streets, but I was in the truck under cover for nearly all of it. Then I did remember peering out after the first explosion and looking at the night sky. Through one of the domes. The solid intact dome. No holes, no cracks, no damage to the dome at all.

"Oh, that's right. The dome was intact. I didn't see any damage to it at all. The attack would have had to come from inside the dome. Inside the base. How is that even possible though? I thought security was extremely tight."

"Well honey, I have been speaking with your Father who has stayed in contact with his superiors on the ground and they think they have found out what happened there. It appears that earlier today a small group was able to overwhelm a security guard at a small weapons cache. The guard was on his own at the time and was taken out by small arms fire. We are not sure yet how the attackers acquired guns since they have been banned since before you were even walking but they were able to shoot the guard and steal what was in the cache."

"Oh, that poor security guard. Is he ok?"

Mother took a moment and looked at me. Maybe judging how to answer that question. She must have decided to just give it to me straight as then she continued, "No, he was killed instantly, possibly even before he knew he was in trouble. Anyways honey we don't have a lot of time before you have to close that pod back up so let me finish. Then you can ask whatever you want until we have to start the slingshot maneuvering."

I nodded at this last part as the realization that she must want to finally bring me up to speed on the entire mission came across me. That was my goal after all so if I could keep my mouth shut, all the information desired may come to me without digging. There was a lot to the story and there are probably portions I am not retelling correctly but basically what I remember at this point was she explained that they believed a group of Earthers was able to get weapons into the base somehow. That method was still unknown. They were able to kill a guard and steal a cache of weapons. This included some small shoulder fired rockets. The cache going missing and the guard being killed was the reason such a rush was put on the mission leaving asap.

Somehow the knowledge of our new rush got to the attackers and they improvised the best they could. They knew who my father was and attacked our building first. That was the first and second explosions we saw. Our building was first and the one next to it was after that. That building had been a secondary location for my family in the event of an emergency. The attackers had been smart though. They had placed another launcher nearer the launch pad just in case we had gotten out before the strike occurred. It was easy to know what path we would take to the launch pad since there was only one real route directly there. When the first 2 explosions had occurred, the soldiers turned off the main route thinking correctly in that would be the route to attack them on. When we stopped, the Earther gunning for my Father knew we had pulled over but couldn't get close enough to us for a clean shot. Instead they were impatient and fired at the building hoping to knock it over on us. The building held though and instead he probably just killed dozens of people while missing my Father. I wanted to ask so many questions, but my Mother kept talking so I hadn't been able to cut in yet.

What happened next was one of those moments you never forget. The ship lurched to one side sending me a bit off balance even with just sitting up in the pod strapped around the waist. I caught myself and so did my Mother. Her boots kept locked down tight, so she was able to stay stationary. I looked up at her just as alarms started sounding all over the ship. Immediately my Mother shoved me down into my pod and hit the close button on her side. I started to push back but she gave me a serious but pleading look letting me know she knew I didn't understand but this was the only chance I had. She then jumped up and took off out of the room.

I laid back and made sure my chest strap was tight again. Another wave of movement came across the ship and it spun around me. I couldn't hear much. Either the pods were very well insulated, and sound didn't travel into them very well or there was just too much happening too fast and my brain wasn't able to process the sound like it should. There were red flashing warning lights all over the place and sparks streaking across different parts of the ship around me. Something was happening and it wasn't good for our Expeditious. Then I could see stars from the corner of my eye. Not like when you are about to pass out but actual stars. Turning my head towards the new points of light, I could see the stars in the broad expanse of space. A nurse went flying by me sucked out into the newly opened hole in the ship's hull. All the air in the ship must have been ejected along with anything that air could pull along with it. I couldn't tell which nurse it was as the body sailed by so quickly. I was certain she died before leaving the ship. Her body was slammed against several pods in her forced exit leaving bloody splotches along the way.

Through the new gaping hole, I could see we were now spinning out of control. I saw stars fly by and then the moon entered view quickly leaving again by the opposite side. I felt a pressure in lines down my body. Only a few fractions of a second passed before I could determine the pressure was the straps on my body holding me to the pod. The ship had spun up enough now in its wild uncontrolled twirl towards an unknowable demise that the centrifugal forces were trying to pull my body up and away from the ship's floor. Once again, I thought to myself about the pointlessness of it all. I was going to die today, and nothing would come of it. Sure, if someone lived, they might miss me depending on who they were. I would be less than a foot note though. I would only be written about in context of me being my Father's daughter. He would be the story. The attack that took out the great mind of Jim Johanson. The creator apparently of the first working wormhole engine.

However maybe he wouldn't be remembered in such a way. After all, this was to be the test for that engine wasn't it? Meaning it hadn't actually been fired yet. So, I would be a footnote of a footnote in an obscure text somewhere holding absolutely no value. Maybe it was for the best. After all, a fear had been processing in the recesses of my mind in the few minutes since I found out what we were tasked with doing. After hearing our mission, my first thought wasn't about the glory of scientific discovery or the excitement of exploration but instead a question. Was it best if we were able to use that wormhole engine and spread across the galaxy? Maybe the Earthers had something right. Maybe we really were locusts like I had thought about before. Maybe we should all be stuck to this system so the disease of our existence could be limited and probably extinguished someday down the road.

If we were able to move on to other systems and spread, our desire for more and more may eventually sink the entire galaxy into a cycle of death and wasted planets. Consumed by the machine of our existence.

The hole I was watching opened further. At this point the hole was large enough that I could not see one edge from my position in my pod. It extended past the edge of my tiny protective bubble. I had no idea how far it went. I could tell we were slowing our rotation though. The pressure from the straps along my front had lessened significantly. This fading of pressure continued until the stars in my field of view had all but stabilized in front of me. Now I could see a small grey ball out in the distance.

It took me some time to realize what I was looking at. First glance you would think it was a man-made structure or a lump of sludge just hanging out in space but no that wasn't what it was. This image was rarely shown. We all knew it was out there, but the government authorities maintained that it be best if our books only shown the images from decades past.

What was once a luscious green and blue world was now a grey dot out in space. There was no green left on our Earth. There was but a grey haze over a muddy brown and tan planet. The land masses were brown and nearly stripped of all life. The oceans that once gleamed so bright blue from the heights of space were now a pale blue grey mix showing the debris and filth contained within. I instantly teared up again at this image. I wasn't sad about my near-death experience for the second time in a few hours. I was sad for the demonstrable effort we as humans had put in to killing each other along with our lifeboat in this abyss of darkness that was space. I wished the schools back down there would teach this view. Would blow up a huge rendition of what I see now and hang it on a wall in every classroom for all to see. Put it next to that pretty marble we are shown regularly. Show everyone what we have done as a species. As a disease released among the world.

At that moment I did not question if there was a God. An all-powerful being. I did not question why a being of that kind of greatness would allow such things to occur. I didn't question it because there was a simple answer. No God would create such beauty but then allow it to be destroyed without intervening before we took the truly innocent with us.

At this point in the midst of all this death and destruction, what did it matter? We would kill ourselves regardless. There was no turning back from this brink. The planet was done for. The only question was if we were going to make it out here in space or if we would tear ourselves apart and send the final component of a once great planet into a state of complete extinction just as we had done to everything else down there.

The thing I did question was what role I should play in our eventual inevitable demise. I was on the edge of becoming one of the first to prove a worm-hole engine. If this was successful, we would spread and do this to more worlds. If this was successful, the speed of which we could remove a planet from a livable gem to a state of disaster would be merely decades if that long. The way humans had destroyed its own birthplace with no way to move on to another world was so careless that if we now had the ability and the knowledge that we could move along once exhausting one place then our care for the natural state of things would be all but extinct on its own. We would feel free to remove what we wanted as we wanted with no regard for what was there before. As a species we could not have that ability. I decided there that no matter what my Father had created, it couldn't be allowed to be a success. It could not be allowed to continue. To carry our species away from this system. If need be, I would be the one to deny my species the future it was grasping at.

I lay there watching the open void beside me for some time wondering when I would be able to move again. What may be going on out there. If everyone on board was dead but me. I hadn't seen another living soul since that hole opened up. For all I knew the command deck of the ship was gone along with both my parents and any hope of rescue. The ship had to still have a functioning propulsion system since we stopped our wild spinning. I also knew the power was still on as sparks flew intermittently from the edges of the ship's gaping wound. If the Expeditious had active power still that meant it had to be mostly intact. Modern ships had the power units at an edge ready to jettison into space if a core overloaded or was damaged.

Instead of losing an entire ship to a meltdown or explosion, the power units could be released into space and the ship towed back to a service dock. If we still had power along with stabilizing propulsion, then we still had a command deck and the damage wouldn't be total. At least that is what I hoped for. I couldn't think about my parents being gone. Although that would make my promise to the universe of not allowing this mission to continue easier to follow through on. If my Father had perished due to some unforeseen accident, then it would free me of the implications of my promise. What I may have to do to keep that promise.

Still laying on my back with my head twisted sharply in order to see the missing wall, I noticed a shadow appear from one edge of the hull damage and creep across the opening steadily. I squinted hard and saw that the shadow was some kind of tarp for lack of a better word. It was being towed by a couple drones. They pulled the tarp across the great wound in the ship and then tight to her. From my position inside my pod I couldn't see how they attached the covering, but it secured to the hull in some manner I was sure. Once it was secured, the only light in this room was from the flashing red warning lights. I wanted to know what was going on but wasn't about to open my pod up for fear there was still no air or pressure on the outside. I continued to lay there for a while longer. At this point I knew I would be fine. The ship had survived. My adrenaline had subsided and was replaced with a crushing crash. A loss of all energy. I dozed out shortly thereafter with nothing else to keep my mind engaged.

A while later I woke with a start when a flashlight shown into my face. I squinted up at the sudden intruding light and glared at whatever was holding it in my face.

The light dropped away and behind the red spots now floating around in my vision was my Mother. The last person I saw before whatever it was that just happened was the first person that I saw after it ended. I felt a weight lift from my chest and began to cry openly. I was so happy to see her alive and without a scratch. She looked to be in perfect condition. Nothing wrong at all.

I immediately moved over to hit the release button on my pod. Just shy of hitting the release I paused. My mother had a face mask on and was waving at me to stop. I looked back at her questioningly and she pointed at the panel inside my pod and then at her ear. It took me just a moment to realize she wanted me to activate my pod's comms. I did as she motioned and heard her come over the speakers a bit altered from her normal voice. The receiver in her mask must not be the best. An old outdated version.

"Maggie, are you ok? The system shows your vitals are all great, but we never heard from you after the hull opened up."

I slapped myself in the forehead in an "I am a dumbass" motion to her and hit my transmit button, "Wow, I never thought to hit the comms. I just assumed you all would call me when you could. I didn't want to get in the middle of whatever was going on out there."

"Honey, these pods are not set up for us to call you. You have to open a channel to let us in. Normally nurses would be right here and can open a pod when needed. They just watch vitals, if someone needs assistance, chances are talking to them won't help."

"I didn't realize that. I am so sorry. What happened anyways? When can we get out of these pods?"

"You'll stay in yours for now," My Mother replied apologetically, "I know it is cramped and probably uncomfortable, but I don't see a reason to get you out. The ship is heavily damaged and at risk of breaking apart. The pods are the best place for you to be right now in case that happens. They can keep you alive for many hours even in open space on backup power. Plenty of time for the ships headed this way to catch up with us."

"Ok, I can see that but what are we going to do once the ships get here? Will they offload us all and transfer to another ship?"

"Unfortunately, no. There are no other ships that were within range and have that capability available right now. A couple tugs are coming instead and will tow us back to the space port. This ship won't be going anywhere for a while. It may just be scrapped. This was not the only section to have hull breaches."

"What happened to us anyways? Were we attacked by another ship?"

"We are not 100% positive yet, but your Father thinks we ran into a mine field. No other ships were detected in the area before or after we took damage. There are many spots where the hull is damaged and 5 where it was breached. We think some were from glancing blows and the 5 breaches were direct contact with some kind of mine. There is no way a mine would have survived takeoff from Earth so they must have been out here in our planned path waiting to detonate upon contact."

"A mine field? Why would a mine field be out here?" I asked this last one already feeling I knew the answer. We had already been attacked once on earth before we left. It made sense for an organized force to have a fall back plan in place ahead of first action in case things went poorly for their plan A.

"The command crew thinks it was Earthers. The attack on the ground was from a group of Earthers we know now. Since we launched, a group came out and claimed responsibility and condemned our flight. They made some information public about our mission that they should not of had any way of knowing. The whole system now knows we have an experimental drive on board. The military has ramped up protections and is stationing several warships around the space port in anticipation for our arrival."

As usual just as I was getting my head wrapped around my current situation, here comes another strong wind to totally blow me off balance. First, I was a normal High School student looking at what to do after their graduation. Little did I know my Father was a secret scientific genius working on a system to change all human existence. Then we were attacked while leaving earth's surface. Then we had been attacked again while attempting to transit away from Earth. Now we were returning to said planet orbit to swap ships or repair this one while being surrounded by large ships with large weapons that could destroy this ship and all its occupants easily. Part of me hoped they could protect us while another part let me know that if this ship was destroyed then my concerns of our disease escaping this system would be taken care of. My mind kept falling back to that point. Wouldn't it just be easier if we were stopped now never to leave high earth orbit again?

My Mother and I spoke a bit longer but then she had to go. The area I was in was under pressurized and frigid on the outside of my pod. The dome was icing some and my Mother had begun to shiver hard with cold. At first, she didn't want to leave my side until I reminded her that now that we had comms activated, she could be anywhere on board and talk to me. I would leave my line open so she could check in as she wanted. Still she refused to leave until I shut my coms off. Once she realized what I had done and would continue to do, she huffed and walked away. The moment she stood, I reactivated my coms and let her know I appreciated her, but she needed to go get warmed up.

What seemed like hours later but was probably only an hour at the most my Mother came over the coms and let me know the tugs were on site and would be connecting to us soon. I should hear some light clanks on the hull as they made connection and then a slight acceleration while they brought us to a stop in space and started pulling us back towards the space port. Fortunately, we hadn't been too far past the port when we were hit but due to the forces in space we had continued to fly in the same direction at the same speed until now. After the attack the main engines were disabled but our stabilizers had remained operational enough to arrest our spin. We could turn and adjust but couldn't change our overall course on our own.

I heard the clanks and felt the slight tug minutes later. The tug operators were efficient at what they did. I couldn't tell when we came to a stop and started heading back towards the station again. From inside my pod without any connection to the outside other than some slight rotational sense, all I could tell was my momentum was changing. A constant slight pull told me we were accelerating in a direction but whether that was a deceleration or acceleration in relation to the port I couldn't tell. Eventually my Mother came back over the coms and let me know we were headed to the port and should arrive in 10-12 hours. As my heart started to beat harder at the thought of another 12 hours in this pod my Mother continued and calmed those nerves immediately. She would be coming to get me out of my pod in minutes. Just had to find a good coat to bring me and another mask.

Chapter Five

Arrival at the Space Port was a bit dramatic. I was on the service deck with my Mother and most of the rest of the crew that was currently awake. A few crew members I only barely knew the names of at this point stayed back to monitor systems from the command deck. Father was standing at the airlock door speaking with someone on the other side through coms. I could only hear half the conversation of course but it was pretty easy to tell what was going on. The space port didn't want to grant us access because they said due to the rush of launching our ship from the surface, they couldn't guarantee all our occupants had been thoroughly checked out. My Father was quite angry but controlling his temper well. I knew him so I could tell he was pissed. He kept taking breaths before responding to whoever was on the other side. He would make calm and collected responses with tightly clenched fists and closed eyes. After several minutes of arguing, he concluded his exchange and turned to the rest of us.

"My apologies crew but it looks like we will be staying on this ship for the moment. Commander Markel aboard the I.S.E.P seems to feel we are a security risk. They understand our dilemma but also claim that we can stay safely on-board this ship for now until a process of checking out each occupant can be completed. They are providing power to the Expeditious to supplement our reduced power cores."

The I.S.E.P. or International Space Exploration Platform for those of you not around during its existence was a space station in high Earth orbit. It started out as the I.S.S. or International Space Station but after many decades and a couple wars that ended up pushing us to the stars whether we were ready or not, it was grown to the current behemoth. I doubt many that knew the I.S.S. would recognize her in this form. The basic design was the same but larger. There was no natural gravity in the station at all, all movement was either by swinging along hand holds or by wearing our well-loved magnetic boots like we had to do on the Expeditious.

Anyways, I was tired of just riding along without having a thing to say about anything, so I took the chance and spoke up, "Commander, what about our people in the medical chambers? All those people in pods sleeping away like they are on a vacation cruise unaware that the ship around them has been torn apart?"

My Father looked stunned for a moment, probably due to the way I had addressed him, but he gained back his resolve quickly and replied, "Ms. Johanson, while I can appreciate your concern for the others aboard this vessel, I can also assure you they are perfectly safe. They are safer there in their pods than we are standing here at this airlock. This area is currently pressurized but if something were to happen, we could immediately and without notice be sucked out into space and killed. Those in their pods are already in vacuum and only a direct hit on their specific pods would cause any harm."

"Ok, I can accept that Commander." I replied continuing the overly proper usage of titles. Everyone on board knew exactly who I was to my Father, so it wasn't fooling anyone. I was just in a mood and wanted to pick at anything I could. It helped me feel at least partially in control of what would happen. "What would you recommend we all do to make sure we don't get sucked out into space and die? I personally would like to continue breathing for a bit longer."

"Ms. Johanson, I recommend that you stay in your pod and let us handle this but for some reason I doubt you will do that. We will be allowed on-board the I.S.E.P as soon as we are all cleared to do so. It may take a few hours or a few days. If you insist on staying up and among us, I must ask that you stay clear of anyone working as we will have many tasks moving along as we wait." At this he turned to the group as a whole and started issuing orders. "Mr. Timmons, go back and take control of the command deck. Keep tabs on everything we have going on around the ship. Make sure that power keeps flowing to environmental systems and those pods. Let me know if anything happens in those areas immediately." I knew Michael Timmons well. He was one of Father's friends back on Earth. I knew they worked together but I thought they were both in logistics so seeing him in a command role almost threw me as much as seeing my own Father in a similar spot.

Father continued, "Mr. O'Malley, please see to the damage to this ship. If these bastards try and make us continue on with this ship, then I want to know how long it may take to repair the damages. Focus on structural issues. We can always swap new power cores in if need be, but it won't do us any good if the ship's shell can't take the force of the laser pushing us out towards Mars." Another man I didn't recognize nodded and turned to leave alongside Timmons. "Dr. Franco, please see to your nurses and keep an eye on those pods. If anything at all happens or you see the least bit of wavering of any life signs, let Mr. Timmons know immediately so we can get the damaged pods moved into a pressurized region of the ship and unloaded."

Another member of the group stepped forward. This woman was taller than my Mother and rail thin. Large glasses framed her face. "Commander Johanson, I am requesting to wake up 2 people from the pods immediately."

My Father already on to his next thought stopped and redirected towards the woman who I presumed was Dr. Franco, "Dr. why do you need to wake more up? I would like to wake everyone up, but you know as well as I that this ship cannot sustain too many people on its best day. This is not its best day by far."

"Sir, I lost two nurses in the attack. Mrs. Regalia and Mrs. Schroder both were pulled out of the hole in the hull before we were able to react and tie everyone in. I need to fill those positions if I am to keep an adequate eye on the rest of the personnel in pods."

Father took a moment and then responded with a tone sharing the apology of his words for the way he initially questioned her. "Sorry Doctor. I didn't think about that. I knew we had lost a few people in the attack but hadn't found out who yet. I am sorry for your loss. Yes, please wake 2 people up. I will leave the who to your discretion."

"Can I help do that please?" I asked before thinking. "I mean - I - umm, I just want to help do something and that seems like it's something I could help with. I promise I won't get in the way and will do exactly as you ask."

The woman looked back at me and shook her head, "I appreciate the offer Ms. Johanson, but I cannot accept. Waking someone from a pod isn't a learn on the job kind of task. If you want to observe I will allow that, but you cannot touch anything, do anything at this time." She changed directions and looked at my Mother, "Of course only if that is ok with your Mother."

"I am ok with it Evelen." My Mother replied, "I was actually going to offer a hand myself. If you need it."

"That's right, you do have experience and training in waking procedure don't you Barbara?" Dr. Franco questioned back a bit hopefully.

"Yes, I do. I haven't woken anyone but passed all those certifications when I trained for loading pods back on Earth. I may have to ask a few questions, but I should be able to do it without issue."

"Then yes, please come with me and we can get that process moving. I would like to have a couple people up and moving within an hour to help with rounds."

We started out the door together when my Father gave a slight cough. The Dr. and my Mother both stopped and turned to face him. He gave a wry smile and said jokingly, "So, I don't get a vote in what my Wife and Daughter are getting into? I could use a hand up here with communications and seems I could use a communications director for that."

"Bullshit Jim," My mother replied with an equal smile, "You just don't want us near that hole in the hull. If you wanted to keep us out of harm's way, then you may want to reconsider bringing us on an experimental voyage to another solar system. Seems a bit risky."

"I don't know Barbara, I think the dangers of staying here near or on Earth may be greater than us shooting out towards the stars. It would probably be safer even if all we had was an inflatable raft and a couple bottles of Oxygen strapped to us for thrust. Just be safe back there and keep your masks on. I don't like being hooked here with no backup plan."

My Mother turned back around and walked down the corridor towards the Medical area where all the pods were stored. Dr. Franco had already taken off in that direction. I looked at my Father one more time and gave him a bit of a wave. Then turned and followed My Mother. He waved back to me and then turned to the remaining couple people continuing his orders.

Three hours later we had two more people woken up and out of their pods. At first, we tried to wake them in the same room I had been in. It was still under pressurized and frigid cold. After about fifteen minutes of working with the controls on the pods we figured out it was just too darn cold to be working in there. I worked with my mother and Nurse Thompson worked with the

Doctor to unhook our chosen pods and guided them out of the room.

It took a bit of trial and error. I was still getting used to clanking around in my magnetic boots. Since we were at zero G here at the Space Port there was no way for us to generate any gravity with maneuvers or accelerations, so we got to work totally weightless. I had mostly mastered walking on my own but bending/twisting/stretching around or pushing was another thing. The boots kept trying to release when I wanted them to hold tight and hold tight when I wanted to release. I was stumbling around like I had been drinking all afternoon. My Mother wasn't a whole lot better. She had trained for zero G, but this was her first actual trip in space. All her training had been in simulators back on Earth. No matter how good they made those simulators, the real thing was always different to experience.

Both Dr. Franco and Mrs. Thompson had made several trips on other spacecraft so were well trained and used to the boots and their idiosyncrasies. With some cursing and a steep learning curve, I figured out how to manage my boots and we were able to push the pods through an airlock and into the hallway outside the medical area that was fully pressurized and most importantly warm.

The two we woke up were more of Dr. Franco's people which didn't surprise me. What did catch me was that they were both males. I knew there were plenty of male nurses but every nurse I had seen on board was female and my thought of a nurse had always been of females. Women are just usually more comforting than the big brutish men I knew. Of course, after I chastised myself a bit for the unintended sexism, I thought of other guys that could probably be good nurses. Billy came to mind. He was cute and gentle most of the time. He could get a bit temperamental if the right buttons were pushed, which of course I knew of each, but overall, he was a calm and caring person.

I caught myself daydreaming and had to chastise myself. Why was Billy even coming to mind? That didn't make any sense. Most likely I would never even see him again. Either we were going to go to another system and never come back or I was going to figure out a way to keep us from using that wormhole engine thing my Father developed and keep us here. If we did stay here though I would still never see Billy again. Once we got out far enough to even try the engine and realize it wasn't working anymore, we would be stuck out in the middle of nowhere and may not be able to figure out a way to return even from there. I wasn't sure yet how that would play out, but I still knew that I had to try and stop us from using the engine.

With the two replacement nurses up and moving around on their own checking on others in their pods, my Mother and I said our goodbyes for now and headed back towards the Command Deck. I figured if I was going to stop us from using that wormhole engine then I needed to first find out where it even was and what it was exactly. I didn't have the faintest idea. The thing could have been the size of a truck or a tablet. I really had no idea what kind of hardware you would need to tear a hole in space. I knew the basic theory behind a wormhole engine. You were supposed to be able to build a temporary bridge between two places spaced far apart somehow. Then you could cross that bridge and in turn cross that void in much less time. That was about as far as my knowledge went on the subject though.

"Mom, what is this engine thing that everyone keeps talking about? I know it is something Father developed or at least that is what I am assuming but what is it?"

My Mother slowed her step down the corridor and turned to me, "Honestly Maggie, I have never seen it. I didn't even know he was working on one until a few weeks ago. There was talk that his secret had been leaked and the Earther's were trying to infiltrate to destroy the wormhole engine. That is when he told me about the entire project."

"So, you didn't even know what he was doing? How could he keep a secret like that from you?"

"Honey, I am sure you have read in history books about many times leaders and governments have had to keep secrets from anyone they can. The larger the group, the higher the probability that information will be leaked. The smaller the group, the easier to keep things confidential."

"I understand that, but you're his wife. How could he keep that from you specifically? How could he keep it from me, his own daughter?"

"In your Father's defense, it really wasn't his choice. No, now wait a second and let me finish." She must have seen me clench my jaw as I was ready to take that apart. Of course, it was his choice. Whether he was told not to let us know or not, he chose to follow that rule and not tell us. He could have easily mentioned it to us and no one else would ever know.

My Mother continued, "Your Father could have told us sure. He was told not to, no he was ordered not to but sure, he could have told us. That would have been a terrible thing to do though. You don't think that our house was bugged? You don't think that everything we did wasn't recorded?"

"Recorded, bugged, what do you mean? Why were people listening to us? How would they even do that?"

"Think about it. We were the family of one of the highest-level Engineers and researchers in the entire base. Your father is possibly the highest value person alive right now. This secret was so huge that not only the Earther's wanted to destroy him if they had known who he was but other governments still in existence around the globe would have wanted those secrets too. They would have been perfectly willing to kill for those secretes. Of course, everything we did was recorded and tracked. They had to know if we would inadvertently or purposefully leak information. We couldn't be trusted. Your Father couldn't even be trusted. He probably had more trackers on and around him than anyone else to make sure he didn't mention a thing to anyone."

"If it was such a big deal then why wouldn't they just take us to the primary compound and keep us locked away in the capital buildings or whatever building his lab was in?" If all this was such a big secret and Father was so valuable, I didn't understand why we were living out with the general populace to begin with.

"I can only speculate there," My Mother started to answer but just as she did a voice came up from a corridor just down from where we were.

"Speculation is just bad guessing. I can tell you why and I can answer other questions you both may have now. Since we are off planet and have been attacked several times now, I don't see any danger in letting you in on the whole project." My Father pointed his arm down the corridor, "Let's find an area a bit more private than this open corridor though, it is still technically a state secret, so I don't need to go blathering it to the entire ship in case anyone else has woken and is moving around now."

We walked down the corridor to Father's private quarters. The door opened to a cramped little room. It looked to me like an opulent prison cell. About 12x12 in space but it contained everything a prisoner may need all in one convenient room. There were bunk beds on one wall with closing capsule tops and straps laid across them. That would be fun to sleep in. I could imagine myself there now trying to drift off while thinking about how I must be strapped in at any time and wrapped in a protective dome in case one of a thousand different things went wrong and killed everyone aboard....

The second wall has a tiny kitchen that consisted of a couple cabinets with labels that read MREs on the side. I could see the banquets now. The third wall was where the door we walked through was along with some bins that based off the labels held clean uniforms, dirty uniforms and some personal possessions. Maybe a few books of mine were in that bin. It looked to still be sealed from back on Earth. The final wall held the best part of the entire room. A zero-G toilet. There was a partition that stretched from floor to ceiling around the toilet. It was on tracks so you could pull it around you when using the facilities. I hadn't even thought about toilets yet but now that I had seen one, I cringed. This was going to be a long trip.

Father must have seen the expression roiling across my face as he gave me a bit of a wink and laughed. "You'll get used to it eventually," he started out, "maybe. I haven't yet but I'm sure I will someday. It really isn't all that bad. The privacy issue is a bit more pressing. I know you don't want to do that," He said this while pointing at the stainless-steel contraption, "with all of us standing around separated only by a thin sheet of polymer so let's make an agreement now that whenever we need that, anyone else in the room will go outside."

"Oh, geez Dad, that might be even worse. Then everyone will know what I am doing. I can't sit there and do my business while you two are standing outside the door of the room twiddling your thumbs."

"Well, I know I won't be in here much so it really would just be you and possibly your Mother when she isn't working on her own tasks. I think you'll be surprised at how busy living on a ship like this really is. There won't be much downtime for us. You'll basically have the place to yourself except for sleep shifts."

"Nope, that won't work either. Don't think for a second that you two are going to lock me in this room and go dance around the ship doing all your important adult stuff. I will be out there also. I am not some little kid. I have already survived two attacks and learned how to revive someone from a pod. You will have to give me a job to do or I will follow you around like a lost puppy dog until you do."

"Honey, this isn't a learn on –"

I interrupted him there, "the job kinda thing. Yea, I've already heard that today and I don't want to hear it again. If you didn't want me to learn on the job, then you shouldn't have kept me in the dark on the whole mission. I could have been training for months to be more useful, but you treated me like a little kid and now here we are. That is on you, not me."

"Fair," Father replied a bit softer almost like he knew he was in the wrong for a moment, "I did keep you in the dark and I wish I hadn't had to, but it was necessary. Not desirable but necessary."

"Even if it was, you still could have had me training on things that would be useful instead of letting me go hang out at the simulators doing nothing but reading a book near a stream. You could have had me doing sims that would actually teach me something."

"Ok, so you are telling me that if your Mother or I had told you which sims to do and those sims were only ones that had training regiments attached to them, you would have happily taken part in them and given them your all?"

I had to think about this one for a second. Of course, I wouldn't have done them. He had me there. If they would have directed my sim time, I just wouldn't have gone or would have gone in and just blew them off and did something else instead. I couldn't admit that though because then they would have the higher ground and be able to shut me down now. I had to keep them on their heels in order to get what I wanted now.

"We won't ever know, will we? I was never given the chance. I would have loved to learn something new. Now what are we going to do? I am asking for a job. I am asking for training. By your own description, if you tell me to sit right here in this room all day and do nothing then I will only go out and find something to get into. Wouldn't it be best if the something I was getting into would be a benefit instead of a problem for you?"

My Mother and Father eyed each other. Mother shrugged her arms and Father sighed closing his eyes and rubbing them with one of his fists like he hadn't slept in weeks. It was possible he hadn't slept. I know he was missing more and more from our apartment back on Earth there toward the end before we took off on this so far ill-fated trip. I figured he was busy at work and staying late which was true as it turned out. Just not the job I thought he was doing.

"Ok Maggie, I don't know what we can have you do quite yet, so you'll have to hold tight on that part. We will find you something though. It would be best if you could wait until we find out what is going to happen with this ship. Whether we get it repaired or move to another one."

Then the genius that is my own brain found my in. "Daddy, why don't I just stick with you? With your downtime until we see what the government will do with the ship, I am sure you'll be in your lab with your fancy contraption. Why don't I just tag along on that and you can show me around? You said you would answer our questions now that we are on the ship, it would be even easier to answer my questions right there by the thing now wouldn't it?"

He groaned and chewed that idea through his teeth while groaning some more. Him and my Mother looked to have an entire conversation back and forth using nothing but grunts, hisses and eyebrow waggling. I had seen it before. They had an entire language that was neither auditory nor motion. No hand signals to interpret, just grunts, hisses and eye wiggling. It was the oddest thing. Finally, my Father turned back to me and nodded. "We will start first thing start of the duty shift tomorrow. For now, I need to wrap up a few things on the Command Deck and I will be back down here for dinner. If you two can figure out what you want, I think we have quite the selection." We all looked at that bin that was labeled MREs and collectively groaned. Father left out the door and my Mother and I pulled the bin out to see what we had to choose from.

The night was sleepless. A mix of excitement and dread over what was to come. I knew it was the – no – I hoped it was the right thing to do to stop this trip out to the stars. Even if I was right, I had no idea how I would do the deed. Would this engine be a behemoth I would have to destroy to incapacitate or could it be as simple as unplugging a wire or two? Should I just disable it temporarily or go for the gold and really tear it apart? Of course, if I went too far and caused a catastrophic failure it could kill us all. I sure didn't want that either. If that happened, what would be the point in the entire process? What would I be saving? I would kill everyone on board possibly and for what? So that the species I belonged to couldn't go spread its disease across the galaxy? I would be gone though and none of my line would exist any longer at that point. My parents and I had no other living relatives at least that I knew of.

The last remaining family we had was my Uncle, my Father's brother. He died when I was little though. I barely even remember him, and no one ever brings him up. I don't even remember how he passed. I think it was some kind of accident at the launch pad, maybe an attack. I can't remember. I don't know that I ever really knew.

Like I said I was little back then so my parents probably tried to shield me from the horror of his death the best they could.

Really though, if my parents and I were to die, what am I saving the galaxy for? I wouldn't be protecting anyone I cared about. I would be protecting the other species. Yes, even if I came up with a way for us to survive the destruction of this engine, I wouldn't be saving MY family. Father would probably sink back into a lab somewhere to try and rebuild what was left after my handiwork. Mother and I would be left mostly alone. Humans would continue to work towards that goal. If my Father has built one of these then he could build another. The only way to keep this engine from firing up again later on down the road would be if my Father wasn't able to continue the work. The only way for that to happen is if he died. Again, I am back at catastrophic failure that would kill us all. Geez, there still is no point in that though. If my family is gone then why do I care what happens at that point. It's not like I would get any extra credit points for protecting other species from humans.

Wait, that is the point. Protection of innocent species that are yet undetected. Unexploited. Not yet tarnished by the overwhelming greed that my species saw as forward progress. That is who I would be protecting. That would be the value of my mission. Protecting those that don't even know they need protection. Those that have no idea the calamity that is about to befall them. Innocents that need this project to fail. I would make sure that they were protected. Even if it killed us all.

Chapter Six

I awoke from my weightless and fitful slumber suddenly. Not a gentle retreat from the depths of REM sleep but instead a sudden jerk back to a reality that had me dreading every moment of existence. My heart rate instantly jumped far past where it should go even during a full out sprint. Instantly I was freezing cold but sweating profusely. Why in the hell was I reacting like this? I wasn't having a nightmare, was I? I thought I had been in a pleasant dream but couldn't quite place it. Like so many dreams it was gone before I had the chance to try and recall it. I laid there for a minute or two pacing my breaths and working to calm myself.

Once stabilized to a point I felt safe sitting up I went ahead and unfastened the straps holding my upper body down on the bed. We were still weightless, so I guess that part was reality. Maybe that was my issue a minute ago during waking. My brain may have believed that the dream world was the real one and waking into this ship in this weightlessness was too much for my automatic responses to work out before a fight or flight response kicked in. A small part of me back in the back. The illogical portion filled with hopes and dreams was still hanging on to the possibility that this entire voyage so far was a dream of sorts and we would wake back on Earth at any moment. I needed to figure out how to kill that portion of my brain. Such a waste it was.

I hopped down or maybe it was better described as a gentle glide in a direction towards the floor of the room. It was a bit amazing how quickly a person could acclimate to weightlessness in their movements. Even though I had only been in space now for about a day I was already pretty used to moving in zero-g. It was important to always keep your hands out in front of you while moving just in case you got a bit overzealous and need to snag something to slow your progress. With my boots on it was easy as they took most of the effort out of maintaining control. With those off and truly floating through the ship you had to be more diligent of obstructions around you. A good knock to the head could spell disaster and wasn't in my plans for the day.

Looking around the room real quick was truly a work in efficiency. This tiny all-in-one room was easy to search in a moment. Nearly instantaneously I saw that neither of my parents were still in bed. Not surprising. I figured my Father would be up and out before I was. Even though I was supposed to work with him today, he wouldn't take the time to wake me and get me going. The clock read that there was still plenty of time before the start of the official duty shift but regardless of the time I was late evidently. Fine, as I felt my bowels notify me of my basic natural needs, I rejoiced a small fraction that I would at least have the privacy to take care of that dilemma. Into the "bathroom area" of the chamber I went pulling the curtain around me once inside. I won't go into details here but let me tell you gravity and regular plumbing couldn't come back to me fast enough. Wow.

I found my Father a bit later, on the Command Deck as I had figured. It was either that or his lab after all. The man had always been a bit of a control nut. Him being a Commander made some sense looking back at our history. He had always had a plan, a course of action we were supposed to follow. Things were lined out ahead of time and everyone had their role to play. I just thought of it as him being plain anal but turns out it was his profession to be anal. Mix being a Commander with a leading research scientist/engineer and good grief. It was amazing he was as laid back as he seemed. Maybe my Mother had something to do with that. She had always been the type to lay back and take the easy-going calm approach to things.

My Father saw me after I entered the Command Deck and nodded my way holding up his index finger to let me know it would be a minute or more probably. I nodded back to him and looked around the area. It looked a lot like any office complex really. Just a bit more open. There were stations all over the place, some in rows, some in square groupings. The room wasn't overly large but had enough room for maybe ten separate stations. Each station had a chair with the requisite lap strap to hold the operator down comfortably while working. The computer monitor in front of them was exceptionally thick I thought to myself. I was used to nearly paper-thin screens back home. These were bulky by any measure. A good 3 inches thick at least. I didn't know if that was a sign of how old the ship was or a design aspect. Some stations were manned, most were empty. I would imagine that with us sitting here tethered to the Space port dock and being fed power to supplement our own there wasn't a great deal to do in this room. These crew members would be here mostly for logistical purposes. Making sure the crews working in various areas of the ship could and were communicating effectively. After all, someone had to make sure the whole machine of skilled labor worked on the right parts and didn't get in the way of other ongoing work.

I browsed the various stations as I walked around the area listening to bits of the few various conversations going on. It sounded like the ship was in a bad way. Major structural damage had been stabilized on five of the twenty-four decks this ship had during my sleep shift. Stabilized only though. Major repairs were still needed. We were just at the point where the ship shouldn't break apart sitting at dock. Work now was going on to try and patch the holes in the hull well enough to start pressurizing damaged areas. My Father came up from behind and tapped me on the shoulder.

"Well, are you ready to get going now that you are up and around? Or are you still trying to eavesdrop on my crew and what they are working on?"

"I wasn't eavesdropping, and you could have let me know the duty shift was going to start before the duty shift. I believe I am still ahead of schedule based off what you told me last night."

"Ok, I will buy that you aren't slouching and are ahead of shift start but you can't claim you were not eavesdropping. Walking around the room stopping at each place someone is working is obviously eavesdropping. And may I add that eavesdropping on official communications is a punishable offense when you don't have proper clearance."

"I may have been listening in a bit but as far as being an offense, I don't see that."

"Oh really," My Father went on giving me a serious look that was obviously a poor cover up for the grin he held in reserve. "How do you not see it as an offense?"

"Because if it really was an offense to overhear anything said inside this room then management is at fault for me hearing it in the first place."

"How is it Management's fault you were listening in on things you shouldn't?"

"That would be a lack of mission security dear Commander. I, a mere minor with no official capacity aboard this ship was able to come up the lift and through the door over there into a controlled and sensitive area where apparently secret information is being shared freely with absolutely no questioning or having to prove in any way that I had a legitimate right to being here. No clearance was requested, no identification required. At that point I say it is an issue with the Command staff."

My Father laughed out loud at that and retorted, "Good point Ms. Johanson. I will take that under advisement and report it up to the very top of the chain here on this meager transport vessel. Are you ready to take a look around? I hear the guided tour is starting any minute now." He said that as he started walking towards the elevator with me following close.

The ship was laid out like a tall building with many floors. A central lift was the primary access up and down the ship. The lift was placed right near the center of the ship. The actual center was an air and mechanical shaft that fed air from the inlet at the top to the engines near the bottom. The lift ran right along that central air shaft. There were also open chutes that contained ladders near that central air shaft for backup access up and down the ship.

The upper floors of the ship were a lot smaller on the inside than it seemed looking at it from the launch pad back on earth. The top of the ship consisted of a fifty-foot-tall cone with the main air shaft running through the center. The remainder of the cone was either empty space or sensor arrays that looked forward while the ship was in motion. Below that was the command deck. Fifteen-foot-tall ceilings made the space feel a bit larger but most of that space was taken up by equipment. Due to being high up in the ship and within the narrower part of the nose it was only thirty feet across.

The next floor down was the upper service deck. We had already been here when we first docked with the station and had attempted to board it. The service deck was a bit larger around but filled nearly in its entirety with life support equipment making it a tight and confined deck. Below that was the science deck. Here is where the ceiling shrunk down a bit. It reminded me of a true medical ward back on Earth except for instead of patients, there was experimental equipment and computers. White all around and a sleek clean finish to everything. This was my Father's domain and I could tell it by how quickly he became distracted with different monitors and testing stations. To keep our tour moving along I had to nearly drag him from that area back onto the lift so we could continue down the backbone of our temporary home. I really didn't care all that much about what was going on in his lab at the moment. It was all equipment and computers. I wanted the worm-hole engine. That was my real intent in this tour after all. I wanted to see what I needed to destroy somehow.

Speaking of homes, the next deck down was the residential deck. We all but skipped this one since I was already familiar enough with it. Even if we were to look at them, all the units were the same basic design. Each room was a wedge shape as the outside wall that was closest to the outside hull of the ship was longer and the inner wall nearest the core was shorter. The rooms circled the outer skin of the ship. There were 11 doors to rooms around this deck leading to 10 private quarters and a utility room. The rest of the space was a small open area that housed a general mess hall area. It was large enough for a normal crew capacity but on the tight side with our crew. The area was meant for a maximum normal capacity of 10 as each room was designed for only a single space faring human.

Due to the abnormal mission we were on now, each room was retrofitted to house at least two crew and my own was set up to handle three. One more door in addition to the ten cabin doors lead to a utility room that allowed power conduits and other life support gear a pathway down through the ship separate from the main central shaft in case something happened there and cutoff power. It also housed the only functioning real shower on the ship. That was only unlocked and accessible while under acceleration. If you tried to shower in true weightlessness, you'd probably drown and spread liquids around the deck causing all kinds of havoc on electrical systems that were not hardened for such an attack of abundant moisture. Without even leaving the lift, we finished the tour of that floor and continued down the ship.

The next two decks were medical decks. Normally the two medical decks would really be a single cargo bay but medical didn't need large twenty-foot ceilings so a cargo deck was split into two with a temporary floor to make better use of the space. This was also the first point in the ship with major damage. The decks above had some scarring and issues, but this deck was the first with real extensive damage. The tarp that had been affixed to the outside of the hull had since been reinforced with some other materials so the floor could hold at least a partial pressure. Still not enough to maintain a constant livable atmosphere but you could go in there for short stents to check on things or make adjustments. Due to my personal term on those decks along with the fact that they were still under pressurized and beyond cold, we skipped those floors completely hitting the button for the second cargo bay.

The cargo bay was massive. Twenty-foot-tall ceilings and One-hundred feet across or close to that. I was a bit taken aback at first because if I hadn't known we were on a ship along with the ever-present feeling of weightlessness I would have thought we were in a nearly normal warehouse back on the surface. I had visited warehouses on many occasions. After all, my father was in logistics or at least that is what we had been made to believe. Or at least I had been made to believe that. I still wasn't perfectly clear on how much my Mother had known before the big reveal. He must have set up those kinds of visits just to keep the story alive and unquestioned. Racks lined the deck that reached the ceilings. Racks upon racks of materials. Pallets of gear. About the only thing I could see that pointed to us being on a ship compared to a normal warehouse back on the surface besides the whole gravity thing was the lack of robot pickers rolling this way and that grabbing items for shipment or storing items from delivery. Here it was utter silence.

Every now and then we would run across another crew member with a tablet in front of them checking off on some kind of list but other than that it was silent. Also setting it apart from an Earthen warehouse, everything was strapped, tarped or wrapped to keep it tightly confined to the pallet it rode upon. Each pallet was locked to the rack it sat on with straps or locking pins dependent on what kind of pallet and gear it held.

My father led me off the lift and down a row of racks. The pressure on this deck was perfect but the temperature was easy to sense as being well on the cold side of normal. The good pressure told me this deck must not have taken damage in the mine field attack, but the temperature was too cold to be normal. I immediately shoved my hands down in pockets and flicked on the warmer in my jacket. I wore this jacket nearly all the time now that we were on the ship. Regardless of the heaters keeping our vessel within an acceptable range for humans, I hadn't been able to shake the chill since I first exited the pod I rode up in. My coat kept me warm even in the colder parts of the ship I had been to so far. It contained warming circuits throughout that could be adjusted based on need. Small battery packs sat below the hand pockets in pouches on both sides. Each battery was good for about 8 hours of constant warming on a lower setting so the user could go a full 12-hour duty shift on a single load of battery packs with power to spare. I was cranking my heaters up higher than medium at this point which meant my batteries would drop to probably 3-4 hours each. That was fine though, I had charged the batteries overnight so I should have plenty of time to complete our tour.

I looked around the deck a bit more and noticed there was a huge section of the hull that almost looked like it was removable. It dawned on me that must be a door. At first, I was a bit taken aback by that idea but really this was a super launcher. It carried goods. This was basically a moveable warehouse. A sea faring freight carrier on astronomical scales. The crews on either end had to have a way to move goods in and out of the holds. I thought back hard to remember my trip to the launcher and started to pull memories from the haze of my mind.

I recalled standing in the visitor area overlooking a similar launcher, maybe even the same one being prepped for launch. My teacher at the time was standing next to another man that worked in the center. He was explaining that there were doors to the outside of the ship for easy loading and unloading. These doors were large and solidly built. Being the weakest point of the ship, they were heavily reinforced to the point where they needed support when opening on the surface of the planet. Whenever one of these super launchers were landed, they would be lifted by giant rams in the landing pad up high enough for a tracked machine to glide underneath. The ship would be lowered onto the cart and driven to the loading/unloading area.

That area held towers which were basically massive freight elevators. I could see what he was talking about out the window of the visitor center now in my memory. They had rolled the ship up to the tower and raised a platform to the appropriate deck level.

"A track system built into the tower catches an arm on the door and allows the door to apply a portion of its load to the tower as it swung open." The Visitor Center Employee kept going explaining the process. "That keeps the weight of the hinge mechanisms down, so they are not so intrusive. On a low gravity destination like the moon, the doors can swing open and closed on their own but on a full gravity planet they need extra support as to not tweak the ship itself."

Just knowing those large portions of the wall were doors to empty space made me a bit jittery. I shouldn't be as there was at least one airlock on each deck for emergencies on board. The only decks that didn't have any were the residential and command decks. Both were already packed in as they were and didn't have any room for additional equipment. I would be walking past those every day without a second thought, but these seemed different. For one thing, the air locks had multiple doors with safety interlocks that wouldn't allow both to be open at the same time. These were single doors. Single vulnerable points on the great ship. I had to get my mind off that. Nothing I could do, the doors were there and in all the history I knew, I had never heard of a cargo door failing unexpectedly and killing all on board. They may not be able to hold themselves up in gravity on their own but out in space they may be more rigid than the rest of the hull around them.

"Why is it so cold on this deck? Did we take any damage to the heating system?" I was a bit concerned, even with my warming coat on, if the ship wasn't producing heat for us anymore, we could be in serious trouble. Our coats would only warm us so much before being overwhelmed by the cold of space.

"Nothing to be worried about Maggie." My Father replied halting our forward progress and turning towards me. "The ship does have heaters on board in case we have to be on the backside of the plant or moon but out in normal space we really have more of a concern of overheating than getting cold."

"But what about the coldness of space? How could we overheat out here when there is no heat? Wouldn't it be siphoned off of us constantly?"

"If we were out in open space with nothing between us and the vacuum besides a single layer of metal then yes, we could have some problems. You have to remember though that this ship along with most in our fleet have very good multi-layer insulation. To the point that when we pass through an area facing the sun, we actually trap too much heat. The exterior coating reflects all it can but there is still radiation that warms the skin of the ship. That heat transfers inside warming the internals. When we pass through dark areas blocked by other structures, we lose that radiation but the insulation in the ship along with all the heat our equipment naturally makes keeps us warm."

"I guess that makes sense. I remember reading that ships had radiator systems that would use vinegar I think as coolant material. I thought that was for the engines though, not the ship itself."

"Ammonia not vinegar. Ammonia resists freezing down much colder than water and vinegar both. There are coolers on the engines also but usually the engines are fine. The radiated heat from the sun has little impact on them. The ship doesn't have to run the heat exchangers very much except for when we are in the sun's light for extended periods."

"If we don't need to worry about heat due to radiation from the sun, then why is this deck so cold?"

"Well, look around and tell me what you see."

Looking around I started to get a bit aggravated. I wasn't looking for a lecture or training session. I just asked a simple question and didn't understand why I couldn't be given a simple answer in return. Why did everything have to - My internal complaints stopped when I came across a label. Then it hit me, and my face started to turn a shade of red from the embarrassment that I even asked the question to begin with. The label read:

Kingdom - Plantae
Subkingdom - Tracheobionta
Superdivision - Spermatophyta
Division - Magnoliophyta
Class - Magnolipsida
Subclass - Rosidae
Order - Sapinales
Family - Aceraceae
Genus - Acer (North American Varieties, See pack inside)

Of course, I could say that I was so intelligent at this point in my young life that I knew exactly what that meant but then this story would lose some credibility. I was sixteen. I knew that Plantae meant the contents were some kind of seed for a plant. That is about all I knew when it came to specific scientific names for plant life. My Biology teacher would probably be a bit upset at that admission but I'm sorry I didn't learn all the specific names for all life that existed at one time on Earth. Most plants didn't even exist anymore in the natural world. There were trees within our borders of the city, but they were not plentiful. Also, they were protected to the point that you dare not touch one for fear of a hefty fine and punishment. My face turned red in embarrassment because of the handwritten labeling next to the nice clean official looking designation.

Maple Tree Seedlings

I looked to the next pallet and the carton on it had a similar long, drawn out label with scientific names. It started out with Plantae also but split off at the Subclass and ended up with Quercus Rubra. The hand-written note next to it had "Northern Red Oak Tree Saplings".

"Trees. This is a seed vault isn't it? That would make sense why it is kept so cold in here."

"Good job Maggie," My Father proudly boomed, "This is our very own seed vault. Each ship that goes out to the great beyond looking for a place to call home leaves the local area with a full or as full as they can get biological sampling for seeding a new world if we find it."

"I knew colony ships had vaults on board, but I thought it was only a small grouping of seeds. Enough to get some farmland going but that was about it. Everything else would need to be harvested from the new planet. This is huge. Surely, we don't send this much material out every time a colony ship leaves. Most of those ships are not expected to succeed so why waste what little we have left?"

"You are correct on that. Most ships that go out do NOT have nearly what we have here. This mission we are on has the highest chances of success of any previous mission. We not only have seeds for eighty-five percent of what was on the Earth, but we also have genetic material for a bit more than half of the animal life that was still in existence back in the early 2000's. It is not a complete set, but it is the largest grouping of any ship that has been launched since the beginning of these Colony missions."

I thought about that for a few seconds before responding again. Here I was focused on stopping this mission, but it almost sounded like humans had nearly all their chips bet on one mission. Everything was dependent upon us and our success. If this ship failed to make it and start a colony then we may be done as a species. If I stopped this mission, it could be that I am single handedly responsible for the extinction of my own species. I didn't necessarily want that to happen. I was of the belief that we should not leave our system and that if we were to survive it would be only by making do with what we still had left here but at the same time this was it.

"What happens if we don't make it? What happens if your wormhole engine fails or we are attacked again? What happens if everything we have with us is destroyed? Isn't it a bit much of a risk to put all our hopes into one mission?"

My Father looked a bit taken back by that line of questioning. He stared down at me from his still taller frame and seemed to debate his response. Finally, after what seemed to be minutes, he decided to speak. "Maggie, this mission will not fail. This mission cannot fail. This engine is my life's work. It is the thing I am most proud of besides you. I have poured everything I have into this project and will not let it die. Those bastard Earthers can throw whatever they want to at us. They probably already have. I am amazed they were able to get the mines out there like they did. They really don't have a lot of support behind them. Mostly radicals that don't really believe what they spew, they just want justification for their sick desire to murder and destroy. I know your Mother and I – no, that isn't right. Your Mother wasn't much more informed than you were sadly. This was a secret kept from all. I know I drug you and your Mother out here on this mission with me. Do you really think I would have done so if there was a shadow of a doubt in my mind that it wouldn't work? I know it will work. I have tested it again and again and it works."

"No offense intended but right there you made part of my point Dad. Besides your point that you have tested and tested the engine when I know there is no way you have tested the full-size version, you said you were surprised the Earthers were able to get mines out here like they did. If you were surprised and didn't think they had the capability, then how do you know they don't have more support than you realize also? How do you know we won't just be attacked again and again until they are successful?"

"The mines were one thing. I said I was surprised that they were able to get them out here like they did. I did not say it was an amazing accomplishment. Getting something out to the moon is basic operation. There are hundreds of individual private companies that have satellites in space. Dozens that have all kinds of sensors, cameras, telescopes all over the surface of the moon. Most are still there but dead now since the companies went under during the war. The ability to get something out to where the mines were is easy.

The surprising part was that they got them there without detection. That tells me there is someone in space on their side that has enough influence or control over networks to hide the rockets that would have been used to launch those mines from sensors. One thing you must understand about those mines is that they were tiny. Insignificant. If this had been any long-distance ship or warship, those mines would not have done more than dent the outer skin. The only reason they had any impact at all was because we are aboard a thin-skinned launcher. These ships are built to be light, so they are less expensive to launch from the ground. Any permanently space bound vessel is built heavier and would deflect those mines. Even with our weak ship the dozens of mines only did damage in a few of the direct contact explosions."

He seemed finished at this point but hadn't answered the other half on my questioning. I still wanted to know how he was so sure his test engine would actually work on full scale. I wasn't sure how hard to press the issue though. If I went too far and pushed too hard, he could pull back and decide he had work to do that was more important than feeding my curiosities. Then it may be weeks or months before I was able to get anyone to show me back down here and lower into the ship. I knew my ID wouldn't get me all the way down here. Father had started using his to get the lift to go further down.

I could always use the access shafts that move down through but there were doors at the entrances to each floor that I doubted would open for me. There was no real security on the control deck, but I had noticed that down here in the cargo areas security seemed to be of a higher priority. Evidently the governing bodies that controlled this type of ship were a bit more protective of the cargo being transferred. Ship control could be done from elsewhere so access to the control deck was one thing. Access to the precious goods being moved was another thing entirely.

I decided within a few seconds of silence between my Father and me that I would not press further. I could drop this now and resume it later after I had been able to put my eyes on the engine itself.

"I understand, I can't argue those points. Hopefully we won't have any more run-ins with the Earther groups. All we have to do is make it to Mars and by your words we should be home free. I did have one lagging question about the other ship though if you don't mind me asking."

"Always, Maggie, you can always ask me anything you want to. Don't hold back with me. I want you involved and invested in this mission all that I can."

"Well, I know you said this was a rushed deal in the final few days. The plan had been to bring the APEX to Earth and load it here. Then leave the system. Since that didn't happen, I know the worm-hole engine is on board this ship. Did it suffer any damage in the attack? Where is it?"

"You are correct to some extent. The plan was never to bring the Axion all the way to Earth to load. The APEX in its original format would have been fine to do so but the modifications that have been made to it have severely decreased its maneuverability. It is now a lumbering beast of a ship completely reconfigured for this mission. The original plan was to fly the Integrity out to Mars. Do you know what kind of ship the Integrity is?"

"Integrity, no, I can't think of it. Should I know that name?"

"No, its fine that you don't know it. That is the ship we used mainly to ferry parts and supplies to the APEX during the modification process. It is on its way back now since that was the plan but with our timeline pushed up, we had to leave early and took what we had."

"Ok, that makes sense, I guess. So, we took the Expeditious because we had it at the time we needed to move. I get that but still, with the damage we took on, did the engine get damaged?"

"Luckily no. The engine is not damaged. It is 3 decks below us now in one of the cargo holds. Do you want to go see it? I promise you won't be amazed." My Father said this last part with a bit of a grin.

Grinning back and giving him a playful wink, I spun on my heels and started back towards the lift without another word. He knew what I wanted to see. The fact that he asked had just proved that and the fact he was messing with me. I do think I threw him a bit with some of my questions but my end goal for this tour was known from the beginning. At least partially known. There was no way he could know my real intent on wanting to see his masterpiece. No way he could contemplate something like me wanting to disable it.

I climbed into the lift with my Father close behind me. He swiped his arm past the scanner and hit another button for a level 3 down from where we were currently. Each level had a button and a small screen next to it that read out what it was. The level we were on read out Organics. That made sense. The levels below read in order,

"Organics - Extension", "Construction Equipment" and "Farming Equipment". The level that read Construction Equipment though had a red flashing outline around the button similar to the yellow flashing border around the button for the medical levels. I hadn't noticed the flashing borders before. Looking further down the list I could see 3 other floors had Orange or Red flashing borders also.

"What are the colored borders for? Are those the decks that were damaged?"

"Yes, the Yellow one you know. That is more of a warning. No special permission to access more than normal is required. That only indicates a possible hazard you need to be aware of. The orange levels are ones that have a high risk associated with them. That particular one you are seeing is not a damaged deck, but it contains a lot of chemicals and fuels that provide a hazardous environment. You must have clearance to access that deck. The red decks that are flashing are damaged. The red indicates Severe risk hazard associated with them. The Construction equipment deck for example has a significant hole in it directly adjacent to the main door for that deck. The level is completely unpressurized and open to space. You would need a high clearance with maintenance authorization to get the door to open on that level. The two further down in the ship are similar situations."

"That is terrible. Why haven't the holes been fixed yet like the medical deck was?"

"One because there are much larger holes on those decks, so it is going to be much harder to patch or repair. Two because those decks have materials or equipment on them not impacted negatively by open space. They are a low priority to repair when compared to the medical decks that have living people on them. Those damaged decks are part of the reasons we are most likely moving to another ship before leaving the station. Along with some damage in the maintenance areas that have killed our engines, the damage to our structure on these red lined decks would cause our ship to disintegrate during the heavy forces applied to it during acceleration towards Mars."

"So, I take it there is no real risk to us right now?"

"Not really. They are weak points that allow easy access to the heart of the ship but with our safety procedures in place, only a very stupid and blatant effort would allow access that could cause injury. Those red levels require not only the proper access cards like I said before, but it also sends a signal to the command center above that access is being requested. The person manning the center has to approve the access which is only done when the access was previously scheduled. I couldn't even access the damaged decks right now if I tried. Same rules apply. I first have to schedule the work and get that approved by – well – myself but still it would have to be done ahead of time so access would be denied."

"Ha, so you have to approve your own visit but have to do it in advance so that you can approve it to be approved?"

"It may sound silly honey, but it is necessary. People make stupid mistakes all the time. As Commander I have to think of how someone could make a mistake and try to head that off." Same reason we have double doors on all our airlocks. That way if someone is stupid enough to get one open, the second door is always shut to at least protect the ship from catastrophic depressurization."

"I get it, makes sense. Let's not go on those decks. I don't think I'm dressed for it." I gave my Father a grin and he smiled back laughing lightly.

"Neither am I."

During our quick talk about safety procedures and damages to the ship, my Father had held the doors open much to the dismay of the little computer governing the machine. It was flashing and buzzing at him to remove his foot from the door's paths. Now that we were done, he let them close. As they slid towards each other I again peered out across the expanse of this collection of life aboard our current Ark. Could I still go all the way and destroy this ship or disable it to the point of not returning home with all this on board? I wanted to keep us all in the system and force us to use what we had but at the same time I still wanted us to live as a species. All this aboard was so much to lose. I don't know how hard fast my stance would be when destroying all this was in the cards.

I would need to be sure whatever I did couldn't kill the ship completely. I had to be positive my actions would only disable the engine. Even better, I should disable the engine before we left the system so that we could bail on the mission before it was too late and keep us from becoming stranded on the edge of accessible space. Once again though I thought to myself about the fact that my Father would never give up. He would fix the engine and we would head out again. Possibly with a smaller force, possibly with a larger one. It seemed the only option I had to keep us in this system as long as possible would be to destroy this ship, the engine and my Father all together. I shivered at the thought not knowing if I could really do such a thing.

The ride down to the lower cargo holds was short and basically weightless at the same time. It creeped me out a bit each time we went down in the lift. Being weightless it felt as though I was being stretched and pulled away from the lift floor each time. You know that feeling you get of dropping whenever you are on an elevator on any gravity well? Take that feeling multiplied by about ten. I already feel like I am floating all the time and only anchored by these magnetic boots but having the floor drop out below my feet taking my boots with them is a whole more intensive feeling. Almost like the roller coasters I was able to try out one time in the sim back on Earth.

There were these places called theme parks that had roller coasters. They were well gone by the time I was alive on Earth. For those of you who may not have roller coasters yet, they were giant tracks with cars carrying people. Not like trams going around town but the most open basic cart you could imagine riding on thin rails elevated high above the ground. The track would carry people up high and then drop very steeply back towards the ground. They would flip upside down or go in loops and twists. The feeling I had in the elevator now on this ship was similar to the feeling of a roller coaster dropping from its high peak down the steep track gaining speed. The only difference was in this lift, there was no wind and no image of a hard-packed ground coming up fast. Only the feeling, the motion, the having your body pulled down by what you were attached to. Each time the lift started down, it took a bit of my breath away.

We reached the desired floor only a few seconds later. With a ding and the doors rolling open, I caught my first glimpse of the engine. Or I think that is what it was. I wasn't entirely sure what I was seeing but it wasn't at all what I expected to see. When I think of an amazingly futuristic worm-hole generator, I think about brilliant lights, tubes of some kind, gigantic cables going from here to here. An absolutely massive central mass with control panels and steam rising from it. Now I know that the engine wasn't warmed up, so the image of steam is a bit excessive but really. Think about what you would expect when someone tells you they have built a working worm-hole generator that can rip holes in space large enough for entire spaceships to move through.

Have that image in your head yet? I can wait. Waiting, waiting. waiting.

Are you still thinking of that image?

Good now? Ok, then if you have that image set, here we go, almost there. Walking out the lift to get a better overall image of everything around me so I can explain it better.

3

2

1

Boxes. I saw boxes upon boxes. Crates, 6′x6′x6′ cubes really. The hold was full of these cubes on pallets. Crates. Dull metal crates. I turned to my Father and must have had a ridiculously confused look on my face because my Father looked back at me and started laughing.

"Ha-ha-ha, oh honey, you should see the look on your face. I am going to guess this isn't what you expected?", at this moment the smirk on his face was needing a good removal by slap but I withheld purely in the hopes that this was a stupid joke and the engine was one more floor down or something.

"Is this really it?" I asked cautiously.

"Yes ma'am, it sure is. This is the Star Drive system. It may not look impressive, but I can assure you it works. Or will work once put together."

"Put together, I thought you had already built it?"

"Well yes, we built it back on Earth, in a computer simulation, but I don't think it is quite what you are thinking. See, the star drive isn't just a magical box that sits inside the ship and makes things happen outside. The engine is hundreds of components all working together across the ship as a whole. Along with opening a wormhole in space, it also has to form a protective magnetic field around the ship to keep us in one piece. The effect I am creating with the drive system would also tear the ship down to base atoms without something holding it together. The magnetic bubble is almost more important than the wormhole itself."

"So, all these crates stack up like blocks to form the engine itself?"

"Not completely. There are many crates out there on this deck that are attached to the engine itself to make it work but most of what you see are control modules and very simplistically put specialized magnetic field emitters. The bubble that will be presented around us while transiting the wormhole is magnetic based."

"Magnets? What are magnets supposed to do to help us?"

"Not magnets really but magnetic emitters that will form a magnetic bubble around the ship. Similar to what is emitted and wraps the Earth to protect it from Solar winds. The Earth would never have become what it was without those magnetic fields. We were able to create a magnetic field for Mars decades ago. It wasn't perfect and still isn't, but it does shield Mars from much of the onslaught of solar wind. Some day we hope to be able to walk outside on Mars without full space suits. The same theory works for my plan. We create a magnetic field around the ship to deflect radiation and other debris within the wormhole and at the same time hold the ship together while it goes through an unknown number of and direction of opposing forces.

The wormhole won't be a nice place to be from all estimates. The big difference between the magnetic field on our ship vs the one at Mars is that ours will be substantially more powerful and densely formed. The other half of that is the basis for the wormhole itself is magnetic. We may need to keep an opposite magnetic charge on the ship to keep us in the center of the wormhole. If we touch one side or the other while transiting, I really have no idea what will happen. There are theories and I have my own but realistically no one yet knows for sure"

"Ok, so most of these crates have emitters. I can understand that, we have to mount them all over the ship. What about the engine itself? Where is it? Surely there is still some component that you can call an engine. Not all these crates alone"

My Father started walking away down one of the isles between stacks of crates. This deck didn't have nice racking built into it like the deck a few above with all the crates full of possible life. The equipment on this deck was more stackable and less prone to damage I would estimate. After all, from what I understood so far, this equipment would be mounted to the outside of the ship. It would have to be well built to stand up to being outside the ship. Space debris was a real risk to all ships and anything outside the protective skin had to be heavily reinforced in case of strikes with various debris.

Earlier humans on and around Earth were not careful about their worn-out gear. Instead of reclaiming it or at least flying it back to the atmosphere to burn up, most was just abandoned to fly in uncontrolled orbits around our planet and the surrounding areas. The first flights out to Mars were just as bad. Booster systems were ejected several times on each voyage until better systems were put in place.

There was junk in all kinds of odd orbits around the sun and nearly all the inner planets. By the time we made it to the outer planets we were much smarter about our debris and flight systems. Very little junk still hung out in that region of space unless it was something that happened to make it out there during those early flights. I wondered what would happen to all those colony ships as they died in route to various systems. They would all make it to their destinations most likely due to their momentum carrying them with very little resistance to slow them down.

My concern was when they reached their destinations as dead hulks. If the trajectories were correct, then they may get pulled into orbits around planets in those systems creating space junk for when later missions made it there with living cargo. Spreading our junk across the stars one way or another. We wouldn't necessarily have to concern ourselves with that junk, but regular space debris could be a major concern none the less.

I kept following my Father until he turned down another isle and the space opened up. This was much more what I was thinking of when I thought of what I anticipated a worm-hole engine would look like. Actually, a Star Drive engine. I should probably start calling it by the real name. My Father stopped and turned back to me while sweeping his arm across the more open area. The item in the center of the open area was large. Not quite as large as I would have expected but still large. Twenty-foot-long by nearly twenty tall just missing the ceiling by what looked like mere inches from my position. It was a cube really. Dark metal almost black with a bit of color to it in various fittings and screens mounted to the exterior. The screens were live with color. Graphs and other information scrolling along them. This thing was turned on.

"Why is it on? Are you running tests on it while we sit here attached to the station?"

"It isn't really on, the screens you see are more of a monitoring program we have running on the Star Drive all the time. It monitors the internal systems for irregularities, even when nothing is running."

"So, I guess this is the engine itself. The actual Star Drive?"

"In a way but not really. This is the brain of the system. Isn't it gorgeous?"

My Father looked over the monstrosity with utter love for lack of a better word. I don't think I had ever seen him look at even my Mother with the same desire on his face. This was truly what gave him a purpose. I couldn't blame him, it was amazing, but I was still lacking in the blow-me-away category.

"What is inside it?"

"Inside it? What do you mean?"

I walked up to it and took a closer look. It was ugly. There were pipes here and there. Screens, conduits. No artistic flair at all. Completely and utterly functional.

"I see a steel box with screens and a bunch of various pipes going from place to place. What is inside it? Does it have a power source, or is it powered by the ship? How do you communicate with it? I don't see any ports or anything. Surely you are not completely wireless with it. I know wireless is fast but with the kind of processing power you must be utilizing here, you have to be physically tied to it." I started peering around the edges of the device walking down the length of it to see if I could find a power conduit or a plug in attaching it to the ship.

"Yes and no on the power supply." was my Father's reply. "Yes, it does have a power source within it. A small fusion reactor is inside the body of the engine. That reactor is very small though and only powers the computer itself. Basically, it is there as a backup if power is cut to the unit somehow during transit. When powering up and creating the wormhole, the engine will pull power from the ship. This is not a small system to operate. It takes incredible power to make a wormhole. Far more than this ship can produce. That is why the Apex is a very special ship indeed."

"What kind of power are you talking about?"

"Well, the Apex has five 4000 MW fusion units on board and that isn't even close to producing enough power to fire up all the systems that are required. This box here," he said this as he walked up and put a hand firmly on what I believed to be the worm hole engine, "won't use all that power though. This box is the brain of the system. The most powerful quantum computer in the system currently. This computer alone can do the work of half the computing systems still on the planet. It is an absolute monster. That kind of power is required to run all the math needed to get a wormhole pointing in the direction we want. The wormhole itself is controlled by tiny fluctuations in the electromagnetic field my engine creates. This beast is the first to successfully break into the EFLOPS category of computing. That is one million trillion flops per second. It will only ramp up that high in emergency situations and at the very moment of jump. It isn't a level that can be continuously kept up."

"So how do you communicate with it?" I asked still walking around the behemoth.

"For small things we do have wireless setups for it but once aboard the APEX it will sit in a room specifically designed for it. The very cradle that holds it to the ship is also the data dock on that ship."

About then I rounded another corner of the box and noticed something that looked like a port. I went to it quickly and rubbed my fingers across the rectangular opening. Maybe an inch or so wide by maybe a quarter tall. "What is this for? It almost looks like a port of some kind."

Father wandered over to me and looked at what I was motioning toward. He turned a bit red at that point almost as though he was embarrassed. Like I had uncovered a deep held secret he didn't want to reveal. He grinned sheepishly and answered my questioning look before my mind wandered too far out of the scope of normal possibilities.

"Ha, well that is a USB port Maggie."

"A USB port?" I was confused at first thinking this must be some new thing but that didn't make sense to me. Modern ports were much smaller and of a completely different design. A connection point like this seemed like it would fit better on some old junk piece of hardware back in sch--. "Oh, a USB port. Like the ones on that old computer you had on Earth. The small PC you carried around sometimes. Wasn't that for connecting the old externals back in the day?"

"Yep, same thing. There are only two on this computer. Call me old fashioned but sometimes I like the feeling of the older tech. I am the only one that uses them though. Everyone else says the data transfer rates are too slow for them to deal with. Several iterations of this unit removed the ports all together but this final version I made sure still had a couple I could use when I felt nostalgic."

"Wow Dad, that is a bit sad." He was really that gung-ho on retaining some of his past to add in completely useless ports that no one else would ever use after him? Whatever, I guess that comes with being the inventor and Commander at the same time. You can force what you want through even if it makes absolutely no sense in any way. I made my way around the box putting the USB ports out of my mind and got back to the point of my visit.

"You said this computer won't use all the power from the ship. I imagine that the engine itself would be what uses all that power, so, this isn't the engine either?" I was starting to get a bit frustrated again. He knew I wanted to see the engine, but he kept pushing me off onto other items. Yes, the computer was impressive but once again it wasn't the engine.

"Not exactly, see the engine is hard to show you because it is not one item. I know you are expecting a physical engine to look at and touch but what you need to understand is that this is a large endeavor that I have worked on most of my adult life. It isn't just a shiny device with colors flickering around it shooting bolts of lightning out into space."

"I get that Dad but seriously, where is the engine? I have seen the magnetic field generators and now the computer that will run the whole thing, but I still haven't gotten to see the engine."

"Well, because I can't show you the engine honey. That is what I am trying to tell you. The engine isn't a box, it isn't a single item to point out on a shelf. The engine is much more than that."

"Then what is it?" I asked outwardly exasperated now over his bouncing around the real answer.

"The Apex Maggie. The engine is the Apex herself. We have been working on her for years. She is the engine. The engine is her. We are bringing her the final pieces of the puzzle. The brain to run it all is with us, the emitters are with us that need installed onto her, but she is the engine. She is the Star Drive."

Stunned would be a good word to use to describe my current mental stance. She was the Star Drive? The ship itself was the engine? What did that even mean? The ship was a ship. It was a large powerful super freighter but that is what it was. It wasn't a wormhole engine. It was built to move freight from planet to planet or station to station. It was built decades ago.... That is when I realized it. The whole damn thing was a massive secret. The Apex had never really been in service. It was built with the nameplate of a super freighter but the entire time it was destined to be the first true star ship. It wasn't going to be a super freighter at all. It may share enough of the architecture to keep watchful eyes from thinking otherwise but it was designed from the beginning as a wormhole engine. Father said he had been working on this his entire adult life. The ship was the Star Drive. Shit.

I was done after this tour. My Father offered to take me on down to see the engineering areas of our current boat, but I wasn't up for touring any more. I didn't want to learn any more today. I just wanted to curl up in a ball and cry. He gave me a concerned and confused look when I told him I wanted to go back up to the residential deck and take a break. I didn't care if he was concerned or confused. I ignored the look and walked back to the lift. After nearly a minute my Father also stepped onto the lift and swiped his arm over the reader.

I quickly stabbed at the button for the residential deck and we jerked upwards as the lift carried us up. The feeling now in the lift made me homesick. Gravity almost. As we moved up, we were pushed down into the floor simulating gravity just as the ship did when in transit. For a moment I felt like maybe we were back on a planet riding up a normal elevator. It was nice for a time until the lift stopped its acceleration bringing an end to the faux gravity. Then it stopped completely and that feeling of being stretched from my feet came to me again for just a moment. Now I felt the familiar sense of weightlessness. I stepped out of the elevator without looking back at my Father. As I swung our room's door open, I heard him mumble something about never understanding the moods of women. The elevator door shut just a moment before our shared room's door also swung to block out the world I had been forced into.

Back in my family's quarters I contemplated my options. I needed to stop the disease of humans from expanding across the universe. I wanted to protect all the other possible species either intelligent or not from being overwhelmed and removed from existence by my own. After my tour of the cargo bays and learning about my Father's invention I knew that stopping this ship would do practically nothing. The real engine, the ship itself was out there at Mars waiting for a crew to take her out. The only thing we really had on board with us was some emitters that could be reproduced easily and the brain for the entire operation. My Father's and the computer down in the holds. While being extremely valuable resources, neither would be the irreplaceable. He even mentioned there were several iterations of his computer, this was just the final version.

I should have thought of it sooner, of course there was no way the government we lived under on Earth would allow everything to go on one ship. They would play it smarter and spread the components out. Along with that, they would have duplicated my Father's research and his quantum computer. I would bet at least one of the earlier versions was already fully functional on Earth right now just in case something went completely sideways on this mission. I doubted they had another entire ship but these pieces of the puzzle aboard our improvised transit would be duplicated. Someone else could catch up to my Father's research and complete the mission.

Losing everything aboard would slow things down but only by maybe six months to a year. I knew my Father. There wouldn't be bins of papers to weed through to find his secrets. His collection of knowledge would be well documented and organized somewhere.

At this point the only option I saw was to wait to make any kind of move until we made it to the APEX. Anything I did here would make barely a blip on the historical radar. I could learn though. Learn the ins and outs of the engine, the process that builds a wormhole and allows us to transit into other regions of space. I could learn the way our ship functions and become a valuable element in this team. Then when the time was right an opportunity may place itself in front of me and show me the way to my goal. I had to maintain my secret desires for now and be very careful as to who I brought into my circle. No one could know. Not yet.

Chapter Seven

Time was dragging on here attached to the station. Yes, we were still here. To this point none of us had been permitted to enter the station or even leave the ship at all. Those that were asleep in their pods upon arrival were still in those same pods. We couldn't wake them because the ship even on its best day could not maintain life support systems with the pressure those people would have put on it. None of that was news though, we knew that before we even stepped foot on the ship back on Earth. Hence half the reason for the pods in the first place.

My Father had been in near constant contact with the Commander aboard the I.S.E.P. for the past few weeks along with government leadership on Earth. I of course was not allowed in those meetings and was not part of that conversation, but I could tell what was going on without being directly included. Between my Father's attitude and updates he gave my Mother at night after they believed me to be asleep in the bunk above them, I kept a decent grasp on what was going on.

Finally, each member of our awoken crew was cleared to board the space station in small groups as to not overwhelm the station with new crew aboard or leave the Expeditious without the crew it needed. Except for me. I was the youngest and only member of the team without an official rank, title, position or clearance. From several discussions I wasn't privy to but still was able to eavesdrop on, it was strongly recommended to my Father that I be put back into a pod for the duration of our trip. This greatly concerned me because well, I didn't want to sleep through the trip. I couldn't. I needed to be awake if I was to do anything in protecting lifeforms outside of our system. To my Father's credit, he never seemed to even consider that an option and blew it off whenever it was suggested.

Anyways, the day came that they allowed all of us but me to board the I.S.E.P. I wasn't all that upset about being left out since the station was far older and much more cramped than the ship we were stuck on. The good news was though that since we were now cleared to board, that also meant we were cleared to finally make some decisions and maybe get onto another ship for the remainder of our trip to Mars. It had been decided thankfully 1 week into our stay that the Expeditious would not be taking us the whole way due to extensive damage aboard. The structure had been repaired to an extent, but it needed much more work.

We still could not fully pressurize the cargo bays that we were using as medical areas for pods. The thin tarp was being replaced by another material. Thicker and insulating, it allowed the temperatures to be brought back to near normal, but the pressure was still limited by the seal we could maintain around the material. It was strong enough to withstand but there just wasn't any good way to retrofit a temporary seal between the material and the ship to ensure a full pressure wouldn't blow it out and once again drop us to full vacuum. Nurses could go into the ward now in relative comfort. But at a pressure similar to around 20,000 feet on Earth, they had to take it easy or wear an oxygen mask to keep their mind fluid. Our engines and 2 other cargo bays were also problems. The main space propulsion engines needed replaced completely. What was left could be rebuilt but only at a full shipyard. It would be much quicker to replace the engines and take the old ones to the shipyard for later rebuild.

I knew something was going to be announced tomorrow evening after the crew returned from the station. My Father was taking a group of 4 with him in the morning. Mr. Timmons, Mr. O'Malley, Dr. Hernandez and Dr. Franco were all going to accompany him first on the station. They were going to meet with command staff aboard to make decisions on a modified timeline for our mission. That meeting I did want to attend. There was no way that was going to happen, but I really wanted to. I had thought about trying to sneak onto the station but really there was no way to do that. The only way on board was through the airlock and that was monitored on both ends by their respective command crews. It wouldn't cycle without everyone knowing on both sides who was in there. That was a dead end.

I even thought about trying to bug the meeting but had no idea how to do that. I didn't have access to any tools, equipment, anything really. There were ways to bug of course but none that I had access to. Maybe if I had a drone, I could pull parts from or some kind of - then it hit me. I did have one option. One tool at my disposal. My communicator, each member had a small tablet device that was a communicator and a tablet that could access appropriate ship systems on the go. Access was determined by your position and what you needed control of.

I had a communicator, but it had no real access other than to see the most basic overlay of the ship with what was functioning and what was not. It also had a personnel tracker so I could see who was where but nothing beyond that. However, it did have a microphone and speaker since it was a communicator. Was there some way I could use that? Would it be worth it? I mean if I risk getting caught to hear the conversation, will I learn anything more than if I just waited until my Father relayed it to the remaining crew later? He had to tell us after all, it directly impacted us and when another ship docked nearby, and we started moving equipment over then the secret would kind of be out anyways. But what if they talked about other things also. Things that were not so obvious. Mission changes, risk factors. My Father could decide those items were more sensitive and not let anyone else know.

I didn't know if the risk would be worth the reward, but I really wanted to know and being the only member on board still without a position or job, I had plenty of time on my hands to think about ways to circumvent the chain of command. I pulled my tablet out and started punching buttons to see what it could do if I worked at it.

Dinner time came that evening and as was normal my Father was holding court with the other off duty crew members that decided to eat at the same time as our threesome. They were joking and laughing having a generally good time. My Father had always been a happy personality in public. He had no trouble getting along with most anyone. I had finished my meal of dry yet not crumbly wheat wafers with a topping of what was best described as a brown goop. It was a protein sludgy kind of stuff that tasted fine if a bit grainy. It was modeled after peanut butter. I had never had real peanut butter, so I have no idea if it was accurate or not, but it was edible. Most of our food was a bit on the bland side as it was more important to be nutritious and while in zero G clean to eat. Crumbs or loose liquid floating around the ship could cause problems after all.

Since I was done with my meal, I nudged my Mother and motioned to her that I was going to go ahead and fall back to our shared quarters. She gave me a slightly concerned look and mouthed "Are you ok?". I gave her a nod and motioned to Father moving my mouth in true blah, blah, blah fashion. She smiled and gave a light chuckle, nodded and sent me on my way with her approval. Quietly as to not garner any extra attention to myself, I removed the strap lightly holding me to my chair and rose moving towards our door.

Once inside I knew I had to move quickly. My Father always set his tablet down inside our quarters when he was off duty. One day when I noticed this and asked him about it, he told me it was important to put work down sometimes so you could really pay attention to those around you. Especially at mealtimes when people could connect on a deeper level. It was important to have your people on your side so that when things when badly, they would lose faith a lot more slowly when they had at least what they felt was a personal connection of some kind.

As a commander he told me he had to keep himself personally separated from his people but at the same time needed that connection so they would fight for him harder when the time came. Of course, he also chuckled when done with the short lecture and told me that when you were the commander on a ship in space you were never really off duty. There are intercoms on every deck so that even without his tablet, he was never disconnected. If anything were to happen, the command staff on duty would call him immediately. It was more of a for show thing.

This habit benefitted me on my desire to listen in on the meeting he had aboard the station the next day. I snagged his tablet from the table it was attached to with a small strip of Velcro causing the screen to instantly activate sensing movement. All the tablets were protected and secure so they would only open for those with proper authority. Any tablet would open for anyone but all the authorities they had or did not have would also apply on any tablet. You couldn't just grab the Commander's tablet and instantly have access to everything. You would still have access only to what you already had access to on your own tablet. This security system decreased the desire to steal another person's tablet since the benefit would not be there. I however had found a small crack in that security long ago back on Earth. We had our tablets back then also. During one of my specialized coding classes back in school we learned about cyber security and the system these tablets used. There was a kink in the armor the system provided.

I had a classmate whose mother worked for the government in the Cyber Security offices. She had warned her son off hand one day not to let anyone use his tablet. They had run into a problem where an official had misplaced their tablet. At least they had thought that. In reality, someone had stolen his tablet, loaded a program onto said tablet and returned it where the official would find it. When the official activated the now returned and altered tablet, it logged him in, and he went on his way not thinking anything of it. Unknown to him, when he activated it, a worm also activated and dug in. The worm's instructions were to alter the official's login credentials adjusting the way he looked in the system just enough to allow the thief from earlier to get in using a mask they had created to make themselves look like the official. Now that didn't do the entire trick, they still needed the access code the official used to validate his identity. They were not sure how the thief/hacker was able to acquire that part, but they did. It never came out, but I wouldn't be shocked if that official had used a junk passcode like 12345. He wasn't all that smart. Obviously.

My classmate told me that the thief/hacker was only in the network as the official for 5-10 minutes before they hole was noticed and closed off, but damage had been done. Hundreds of files were shared to the public network displaying several secret programs the official was working on along with some videos he had made with someone that was not his wife. It was a scandal and the official stepped down from his high position in disgrace. Don't worry about him though, he landed on his feet fine getting hired on by a "private" firm that did work for the government body. No one was fooled but that's how politics works after all isn't it.

What my classmates' mother had told him was that if he ever misplaced his tablet or thought someone might have gotten a hold of it, to not activate it and login until he brought it home and allowed her to look at it first. There were easy ways to tell if someone had altered it if you knew what to look for. After that scandal, the security systems were updated to require fingerprint along with facial recognition and now two passcodes. This was what I had to beat now.

The facial recognition I could do. I had been told since I was born that I was the spitting image of my Father. That drove me nuts sometimes since I am a girl and don't like the idea of looking like my Father but as I have gotten older, I can understand more what they mean. My facial features are like my Father's. I don't necessarily look like him but our eyes, our noses, our mouths, foreheads, all match very closely in shape and scale. He is larger than me and has more lines in his often furrowed forehead but I learned back on Earth that with a few alterations by holding my hair back, holding my smaller face close to the screen and coloring a few spots with a pen I acquired earlier today then the tablet would unlock for me. Sometimes. When I was patient and it was dark.

Fingerprint you ask?

That was even easier and is well known to not be a very good security layer. Security specialists will tell you that fingerprints are among the most useless methods of locking an account available, but it is a required layer by those in charge, so it is on every tablet. I pulled out the reusable drink pouch my Father had set down after finishing the lunch I brought him on the command deck earlier today. A quick dusting from a bit of ground up pepper from my dinner and a piece of tape from a laminated sign that had been hanging in the dining room and I had a near perfect replacement for his print I Folded the tape over on itself and placed it on the sensor backed up by my own finger to register the heat required. Once again according to Security specialists that made barely any difference as I was now proving but it was there so a bump to roll over.

Now on to the passcodes. Once again, such an easy thing to crack if you know what to look for. I had watched my Father unlock his tablet a few times to be sure I knew the codes, but I only had to watch once to know what they were. Like any good security conscious person out there, my father didn't use birthdays or anniversaries for his 5-digit codes. No, he was creative and used our initials. I won't tell you here what the codes were but if you think about it you might figure it out. After all, giving out secure information is a galactic crime these days. It wouldn't help you crack my Father's equipment since he is far removed from this universe at this point but still. There is the principal of it after all.

Inside my Father's tablet I went to work. There was a simple-ish way to do this. An app on my tablet when moved over to another tablet would let me hear through the receiver on the second tablet whenever I wanted to activate it. I didn't write it but got it from a very intelligent friend of mine back on Earth. A certain red headed boy.

A memory flashed in my mind bringing a bit of nostalgia to the forefront. My eyes teared up momentarily before I was able to push that away. Those feelings did me no good. When we had first gotten back to the station, I had wanted to contact my friends. I mean we were right up here above the planet anyways. There were many services that would allow me to call down. I had even brought the question up to my Mother without thinking about it first. She told me that we would not be allowed to make contact with anyone on the surface outside of our registered handlers. All information exchange was required to go through the government due to our highly vulnerable mission status. I should have known it wouldn't be allowed. Embarrassed to have even asked I dropped the subject and hadn't brought it up since.

I couldn't allow the memory to flood in any further. I knew I missed him but also knew there was no way for me to see him again. There was no reason to think about it so I wouldn't. I pushed the thought back out of my mind and continued. The app was written by my friend so that he and I could help each other out on tests in school. We had many of the same classes in different hours. Same teachers, same material, different times.

When big tests came up, we could use each other to figure out the answers through the app. Say I was the one in class taking an especially difficult test. Since tablets were an integral part of living in the modern world, they would always be within ear shot of the questions read verbally to the rest of us by the instructor. My friend, who shall not be named do to the ridiculous emotional reaction it inexplicably brings on, would look up the answers real quick using his tablet outside of class and would read it back to me utilizing the micro ear buds we both had. The ear buds were small enough that no one knew if you had any in or not.

Teachers knew this kind of thing was possible, but they had no real way to fight it. The whole reason tests were often given orally now was because when the invent of the first widely available smart contacts back before my time students quickly started using them to cheat on physical paper testing. Part of the contacts were that when they saw text, the processors read it and when it was a question, they answered after cruising the internet databases for the information. Schools tried to ban them, but the contacts were hard to spot, and it was quickly considered an invasion of privacy to check someone's eyes for the lenses.

There were even court battles where a slightly less naturally gifted person in the arena of sight sued for the right to wear the corrective smart lenses and was able to get it considered a right under various disability acts around the world. That was all before my time, but the subject had been covered in classes I had earlier in my school years. Ear buds were a similar case, since they were so small and inconspicuous, it was impossible to know if someone had them in without looking directly into the ear canal with a light source. That was an invasion of privacy, so teachers just had to live with it as we took advantage of it.

Really in the grand scheme of things, did it matter? The very fact that we have all this information at our fingertips at a moment's notice proved in my own mind that we don't need to be tested and forced into remembering it all. If on the rare occasion some of the information actually is useful, we can pull it up instantaneously. Only if the world completely collapsed and our technological advances and databases were lost would it finally impact us. At that point we would be more concerned about survival and the life supporting necessities we required than random trivia involving inconsequential historical events and certain mathematical formulas that explained various items from gravity to wildly powerful magnets used inside fusion reactors.

Anyways, with this app moved now over to my Father's tablet, I could activate it from my own at any time and would have audio from his microphone ported directly to my ear buds. As long as we didn't get too far apart that is. I was unsure if I could have that data go across the network as with him aboard the station during the meeting, the network he would be on would be the station's network which was military and very tight. That data would have to go through their servers and then to our own ship. I could probably get away with it on our own ship but if his tablet started streaming data from the station to our ship during the meeting, I doubted there was any way I would not get busted.

If that app was located, it would be immediately recognized what was going on. The app was not sophisticated. It was not hidden. It plainly had my IP in it as where to send the audio stream upon activation. The app was obvious and the only way for me to somewhat hide it was to bury it deep in some folders on his tablet. I would need to remove the app after the meeting to keep him from stumbling across it at some later point.

The only way for me to keep the connection semi secure was for me to be within direct communication range between the two devices. Each device had the ability to act as its' own signal tower. On Earth this was valuable to have so that the government didn't have to have network extenders all over the city. They could put a single repeater/booster on every few blocks and we would all be connected. Due to the signal range of the tablets, they could be connected directly from one device to another with a range of around 5000 feet give or take. Of course, we are on a station with a lot of interference so there would be no way they would reach that far. However, the station was only 7500 feet long at the longest point. We were all the way at one end of that length, but chances were the meeting room my Father would be in wasn't going to be on the opposite side. There wasn't much I could do about that part of the plan. If he ended up being outside of the direct com range, then I would miss out.

I doubted that would happen though. At least I hoped I was rightfully doubting that would happen. I could easily be wrong but what could I do? If it happened, so be it.

After locking my Father's tablet and velcroing it back where I had found it, on to bed I went.

Sleep would elude me for most of the night. My parents came in at one point not so long after I had laid my head down. As was normal, my Mother came and checked on me before doing anything else. She leaned in close and listened to my breathing which was controlled to make her believe I was fast asleep even though that was far from the truth. If they were going to talk to each other in private I wanted to know what was said.

They did end up speaking quietly for a while as they prepared for bed themselves, but it was of very little interest. Nothing important was said beyond my Mother recapping the plans for the next day. The meeting I would hopefully be eavesdropping in on and other details of no interest to me at the time. Fortunately, there was no speaking of a project or job for me. That meant I was free to do as I pleased which would be to stay right here in our room and listen in on what truly mattered. Eventually after I dozed in and out for a few hours, I was able to get my mind to shut down enough for a light and restless sleep.

Awakening in the morning was nothing special from previous days. I swung my head over the edge of my bunk and saw that both my parents were gone. Of course, they were. They always got up ahead of me. That worked for me though, today was going to be a big day. Whether I was able to listen in on the conversation or not, we should know what is going to happen from here on out in regard to this mission. If we will continue on in another ship immediately or do something else. I really couldn't see any other option. We already knew we were swapping ships. We just were not sure exactly which ship and what the timeline would be yet. I unstrapped from my bed and pushed myself off gently gliding to the floor near our kitchenette. I grabbed a breakfast bar and tore into the packaging. It was like most other snacks aboard a ship in weightlessness. Chewy and bland.

After breakfast, I took my time getting dressed and ready for the day. I pulled my washcloth out of a drawer and a bottle of all in one wash. Squirting a bit of the gel like fluid onto the cloth I proceeded to go to work scrubbing the areas most in need of cleaning. This was one of those rare moments when I looked back and wished I had the luxury of limited warm water showers on Earth in our apartment. I would love to have one of those now. Back then it seemed like such a regular activity that the pure limitation of time on it was a massive inconvenience but now even with that constraint it was much better than now. This method worked well enough to keep the funk off but was no comparison to a real shower. Hopefully once we finally got moving again, we could all take limited real showers again. There were showers set up on the residential floor in the utility room, but they were only usable while in flight as the G-forces of acceleration created a gravity substitute and water use as on earth worked again. Here in this weightlessness we couldn't do things like that. Activities you took for granted on a planet.

Completing my every other day ritual of a quick scrub down I dried off with another towel and placed both securely in a sealed laundry hamper. That was one thing that was nice about living on this ship. Each room had a laundry hamper that would be emptied, the items inside cleaned, folded and then returned to us later that day by an automated system aboard the ship. There were a few automated functions similar to what we had on Earth like cleaning bots for example but many other that we didn't have on Earth like automated laundry services. That was new and appreciated since I had done most of our laundry as one of my daily chores.

Since we couldn't really cook so to say while stationary, I didn't have to do dishes. All our meals were coming from precooked packages that were recyclable through the ship's regeneration facilities. I can explain that process later but basically anything "disposable" that was brought aboard was made of a specific plastic that upon being tossed out would be melted down and turned into pellets for production of new materials on board in flight.

I looked at my tablet and noticed the time. The big meeting was supposed to be sometime around mid-morning from what I had understood, and it was 8am standard time now so I needed to find out where my Father was. Fortunately, there was another app on my tablet that was used as a locator. Most people wouldn't have their commander's location set as trackable on their tablet. That capability of our systems were usually so the superior could keep tabs on their subordinates, by mission control to keep tabs on the crew as a whole and by doctors to keep tabs on their patients since the locators also showed a person's vitals at any given time. However, since the commander was also my Father, I had one special privilege that most others did not and yet no one batted an eye. I pulled that app up on the screen and set it to search for him. Not aboard the ship.

"Oh shit, I'm too late already," I spoke out loud staring at the screen as it moved back and forth showing what was being scanned in the vicinity.

"Too late for what Maggie?" My Mother's voice came up behind me. I had been so lost in my own thoughts I hadn't even noticed her unexpected visit to our humble room.

"Um, n-nothing. I a- was just hoping to catch a glimpse of Father going over to the station. You know, sneak a peek inside since I am not allowed over there."

Mother looked at me for a few seconds quizzically, "Maggie, you can see the inside of the station all you want. There are documented photos of it all over the net."

"Oh, I know that Mom but there is always something different about seeing an area with your own eyes, not through a camera lens and then a computer screen. Why is

Father over there already anyways? I thought you would be in the big meeting too."

"Not this one. I have too many other things to do over here on our ship getting ready for transfer to the new ship. I volunteered to help move pods when we are ready. I have been training all morning. Just stopped to see if you wanted to come join us. We could use another hand."

Crud. I needed to stay here to monitor the meeting audio, but I had been begging my parents for more inclusion with the crew aboard. I wanted a job. If I flaked now that opportunity may not come for much longer.

"If you are too busy though Maggie," I could see my Mother getting a bit perturbed by my lack of enthusiasm. I mean I knew I would find out the news later regardless, but I wanted to know now. I needed to find out when it was new. Before everyone else. I hated being just another person on board with no one thinking I had a right to know anything. What my Father would end up sharing with the crew may not even be the whole story. It would be edited, and I wanted to know the truth.

My Mother continued on as my mind raced for a way to do both. "Never mind Maggie. I can see you are not interested in grunt work. You know though if you want –"

"No Mom, I want to help." I spoke up suddenly breaking into the middle of her statement that was surely winding up to show her disappointment in me. "I would love to come learn moving pods around. Just give me a couple minutes. I was right in the middle of a lesson when I got distracted. Let me finish that and I will be ready to go."

"Well if you are working on lessons then maybe you should keep working on that. Sorry honey, I didn't even think about school. I knew you were keeping up with it since we left Earth, but it didn't even come to mind. I should have realized that. You keep on working and we will find another person to be our extra hand."

"No really Mom, I want to do it. I can finish my lesson later. That is the great thing about being on this ship. There is so little to do that even schoolwork is more interesting that sitting here twiddling my thumbs. I am already ahead if you consider the interruptions we have had so far on our voyage."

"Are you sure? You can get trained later. We will have to transfer again when we reach Mars anyways. You could help then."

"No, Mom, don't worry about it. Like I said, the lessons can wait. Really. Just give me 5 minutes and I can wrap this up."

"Ok. I guess that will work. Want me to look anything over for you? What are you working on anyways?" She stepped towards me and around to one side to get a look at my tablet with this. I spun away just a bit to hide my screen which still had my location search up for Father. It had found him I knew from the flashing green indicator I could see in my peripheral, but I hadn't dared to look down yet worried my Mother may recognize the reflection in my eye.

"Mom, really? I am working on some writing. I can't let you look at that. With your position in linguistics, my teachers already think that most of my answers are coming from you. I have to do this totally on my own to make it believable."

My Mother looked at me with a bit of a questioning expression, "Your teachers think I help you cheat on your writing assignments? I have never claimed to be a writer, linguistics is not writing. It is merely a conversion from one language to another. I do not create anything at all. How would I be helping you with a writing assignment?"

"Well, they um, the assignment is linguistics. It is writing but also linguistics." Eesh, that was a weak argument I knew immediately. Heading off another line of questioning I quickly added, "I have to um, write a supposed conversation between two officers and then translate that to an opposing language. It is supposed to show um, an ability to both create something creatively and then translate that message not just as words but as a cohesive thought." I paused there taking a breath. I wasn't sure where that load of crap had come from, but it sounded good once I got going.

"Interesting. I guess that is a good way to teach. It is very important in translating to not only convert the words but the feeling of the whole message. Many times, you do have to reconstruct the message in the new tongue to get a true translation. Some metaphors and examples we use in regular day to day life may mean something completely different to the other side if straight word for word converted over. Some languages wouldn't even make any sense if converted exactly. The two just don't match up in structure." She paused at this for a moment and then continued. "I can respect that. I appreciate your honesty also. You could easily get me talking on that subject and probably get me to do the work for you. Finish up what you are doing and meet me down at the upper medical level when you are ready. You should have the access to get there on your own."

"Yes, absolutely. Just give me 5 minutes. I will be right behind you."

I smiled at my Mother as she turned and left the room. As soon as the door closed behind her I released the tension that had built up inside me during our back and forth. Geez, I hated lying to her but what was I supposed to do? I couldn't show her I was tracking my Father. That would lead to questions I didn't want to answer right now. I was going to miss the meeting at this point that was easy to see now. I hadn't come up with a way to get out of the training session without hurting my future chances of being included in tasks around the ship. The only way I was going to get access to do anything of any measurable impact would be by gaining the accesses and knowledge I needed first.

Back to my tablet I set up a quick record function alongside the app. I would have to keep close watch on my tab as it would need to be active when the meeting started. The app I was using was really only meant for live communications since we used it for testing answers. Those only did us good live so there hadn't been a recording component added in. I could however use another app to record inbound signal data. Then I could replay that later to listen in to the whole meeting. There probably wouldn't be time to listen in before we were told what the meeting was about, but I could listen to the recording later and find out what was not mentioned publicly. It would have to do. After setting up the recording app, I went back to my tracker. It had found my Father aboard the station as I figured when he hadn't been on the ship. From what I could tell, I was correct on all accounts. The meeting room or at least a room was near the airlock we were attached to. Since I didn't have video, I could only assume it was a meeting room. That was really about all I could tell from the tracker alone, so I went over to my embedded app and started to listen in.

At first, I heard silence. The screen showed it was connected to Father's tablet so that wasn't an issue. His could have been stored away but that wouldn't make any sense. Most people used their tablets for note taking so it would only make sense if he had it on him and active. Turning up the volume I started to hear a light humming sound. That is when I realized that I had been hearing it the whole time. His tablet was active, but he must be waiting for the meeting to start. The humming was the same hum anyone on any spaceship hears all day every day. It is the presence that never ended all around us while floating around in our protective bubbles of metal and composite. The systems that keep us alive.

Continuing to listen carefully with the volume now turned up even greater, I could hear breathing. I imagine that must be my Father, but I could hear another as well. Offbeat, nearby but a separate sound. He must be sitting in a meeting room with another member of his team waiting for representatives from the station to come in. If that was the case, then the meeting must be starting soon. I decided to go ahead and start the recording function on my tablet but set it up to auto start when it heard an appreciable sound like doors opening and voices.

If I continued to listen now waiting, I would lose track of time and end up taking too long to catch up with my Mother on the medical decks. That would only raise further questioning and my already flimsy story could fall apart quickly. All my Mother would have to do is send a quick note to my program administrator to see what assignments I had out and how my progress was coming along. She would know immediately that my story was fabricated poorly. Leaving the room now, I locked my tablet and slipped it into a carry pouch on my waist like normal. Nothing irregular or suspicious here. Even going down a couple decks, my Father should still be in range of my tablet to continue the direct connection. There was a risk of dropping but nothing could be done about that.

Several hours passed during which I gained several new bruises and an ankle that would be sore for a couple days. By this point walking around with the magnetic boots had become second nature but all that changed quickly when you had to start pushing, pulling and twisting large heavy objects in confined areas. A correction here may need to be made, I guess the pods are not really heavy. Don't get me wrong, they are very heavy but out here with no gravity, they really aren't heavy. I can move them with one finger. They float in mid-air. A more correct description would be that they have a lot of mass. It takes a lot of effort to change their direction and momentum. Even though they may float in weightlessness, when you need to stop them before crashing into a wall, don't expect that to be an easy task.

After getting past basic maneuvering techniques which include nice slow controlled motions where each person guides one pod cautiously around the room, we moved on to the more hectic training environment. For this, we gently positioned 5 pods into the elevator with my Mother, myself and 3 other crew members. The lead on this expedition and training exercise was Dr. Franco. She taught us how to separate the pods from their docks and how to make sure the backup power supplies activated as they were supposed to. We moved the pods around some and now in the elevator we had to activate the magnetic clamps on the pod bottoms to keep them secured to the floor while the elevator took us lower into the bowels of the ship. That same effect that makes it feel like I am being stretched away from my feet when the elevator lowers would also haul the pods to the ceiling and crush anyone in their paths.

We lowered all the way down to an area lower yet than I had been with my Father previously when I was information shopping on the "Star drive" system. We kept going down to Deck 12. The little screen next to it read "Training". The doors opened and we climbed out one by one releasing each pod and taking them with us into the open space.

The next couple hours consisted of us working through various scenarios. While transiting, a pod may malfunction, causing you to have to take personal action to ensure the well-being of its occupant. Each pod was equipped with a backup system that would take over, but it had to be manually triggered. When docked, that could be done from the nurse's station that had monitoring systems of all the pods. When disconnected though that function had to be done manually at the pod. The pod could lose pressure, it could lose power, it could.... Well, that is about all that could go wrong. Either lose pressure or power. As long as those two things didn't happen there wasn't much else we could do ourselves while transiting. A whole host of other issues could happen but with my limited medical knowledge, that would come down to getting a nurse there quickly.

Our main training was over moving the pods during various scenarios aboard the ship. Sure, Dr. Franco threw in a pod failure from time to time but mostly it had to do with the ship losing power or the connection point between the ships failing. The magnetic holds on the pods failing. The one that got me though was when the good Doctor forced a failure in the automated release in my magnetic boots. I was walking along just fine down a corridor we had set up for this exercise and without warning, one of my boots held fast instead of releasing as usual when I moved forward. The correct procedure was to immediately lock the magnetics on the pod to stop it from continuing forward which would give a good jolt to the sleeping patient on board but not one they would ever know about. Instead, I twisted and wasted valuable time looking back at my boot and trying to get it to release. The pod continued on and ran right up my leg pushing me down to the floor and wrenching my ankle in the process. Dr. Franco gave a shove to the pod forcing the crushing momentum off of me and into the false wall of the corridor. Then she locked the magnetics and brought it to a halt.

"Well, can you tell me what went wrong there Ms. Johanson?"

"Yea, the damn pod tried to kill me is what happened. No wait, you tried to kill me. You're the one that caused that failure." I went to stand back up to give Franco a piece of my now infuriated mind but was brought back down to Earth (figuratively, obviously) by the pain that coursed up through my leg from my manhandled ankle.

"Ms. Johanson, I only brought about a simple equipment failure that can and does happen regularly. You need to know what to do in such an event. If this was a real-world incident, you could very well have a broken leg now from that pod continuing over you instead of being knocked to the side as I did. Do you know what you did wrong?"

I squelched my anger for a second as she was right. I did need to know what to do in this situation, we had talked about it already. Taking a breath, I replied calmly much to my own surprise, "Yes Ma'am. In the event of a boot malfunction we are to lock the magnetics of the pod to secure it until a repair can be made to the malfunctioning boot."

"Yes, and what else are you to do?"

"Then we are to call a supervisor, mainly you for assistance."

"Very good Ms. Johanson." She looked down at her tablet and after pushing a couple buttons my boot released like it should have already done relieving a good bit of pressure on the ankle I didn't even realize was still there. She then bent down on one knee and looked at me closely. "Now Maggie, how does it feel? Pain from 1-10?"

It took me a second but this woman that I knew but not well yet went from drill instructor tough to motherly concern in the time it took to stoop from standing to kneeling. "Um, I guess a 4 or 5. It hurts but I don't think anything is broken."

"Well, let's get you up on it just to see if you can put any pressure on it. Come on, hold my arm and use it to balance you. Keep that other boot held to the floor and push down on your ankle to check it out. Be careful though, don't put too much pressure on it too quick. Stop if it hurts above a 6."

I did what she asked and was able to stand and use my other magnetized boot to anchor me while I pressed down into the floor with the over flexed ankle. It still hurt but I wouldn't have put it at a 6. "I think it is ok. There is pain there but nothing substantial. A bit of ice this evening and it should be fine."

"Good Maggie, good." She then turned to my Mother who had been standing close but not interfering since I went down. She had been 2 people ahead of me in our progression, so it took several seconds to get her own pod stopped and return to my side. "Barbara, I would watch her tonight and check that ankle out. You know your daughter better than I do so you can see if she is putting on a strong façade or admitting to how much it really hurts. Children," she looked back at me when she said that, "can be hardheaded and think that just because they got hurt, they will be in trouble. They will dismiss it instead of taking care of it properly. I don't want her to cause more damage by putting on a strong face and bearing the pain."

"No problem Evelen. I will let you know if I suspect anything more than a simple strain."

"You know, I am still right here." I said back to them both. "You can talk to me. I mean I am the one that just got run over by a pod."

"Yes, you are right there but I can already tell that your pain when you put pressure on the ankle went above a 6. You just don't want to admit it to yourself for fear of being put back in your room to rest. I will leave it alone for now but you are still a child so we will make sure you really are ok to continue tomorrow."

"Tomorrow? What are we doing tomorrow?"

"Tomorrow's training will be on more pod movements. We need to perfect our standard movements and run through a few distress techniques."

"Distress Techniques? Didn't we cover pod malfunctions and ship problems today?" My Mother turned back to Dr. Franco in surprise. That made me feel a bit better that I wasn't the only one not kept in the loop as to our training.

"Yes and No. Today we only touched on mechanical malfunctions that could arise. Tomorrow we need to cover true distress scenarios as what to do if the ship came under attack while moving pods. It is not regular training, however, following our recent incidents aboard, I think it would be good practice to train for real evacuation procedures from one ship to another. Just in case anything further was to occur."

My Mother looked a bit horrified at the thought but nodded. The good Doctor continued to outline a few items for us that we needed to practice and read up on overnight and then released us back to our regular duties. My Mother and I both had appointments again in the morning to further our training on pod movements. We left the training room and took the elevator back up to the residential level. Neither of us spoke on the way up the lift but I could tell she was as nervous as I was. Training had kept our minds off the meetings that had been going on aboard the station but now that we were done for the day, both our minds had gone back to that. Mother was most likely thinking only of our safety and hoping we would get moved to a new ship quickly. I on the other hand kept running through scenarios and how I would need to adjust my plans in order to keep whatever ship we were on in this system.

Back in our shared room, my Mother and I found nothing. We didn't really expect to see my Father there as he was a workaholic and it would be extraordinary for him to have come back here after his meetings were over. Most likely he was up on the control deck or maybe down in his lab below us. I doubted that though. Whatever was discussed he would be getting plans put together whether it was to unload the ship or wait longer. About that time, both my Mother's and my own tablets went off with a high priority message. I pulled mine out and activated the screen. It scrolled a new message from ship control. A short and quick statement from the Commander only it wasn't Commander Johanson. This was Commander Thomas Carter. That wasn't right. That couldn't be right.

My Mother gasped but quickly cut it off and looked over at me. "I'm sure it's nothing honey. Just an error in the system. Nothing to be worried about."

"Yea right Mom. Come on. I'm not a dumb kid. I can see there is something going on. Why do we have a message coming from a new commander? Father was the commander."

"Your Father is still the commander Maggie." My Mother looked straight at me while pointing at her own screen turning the display towards me. "I am not sure why Mr. Carter is on the message but looking at the crew roster, it still shows your Father as overall Commander of this mission."

"Well maybe it hasn't been updated yet. Or maybe he is the commander of the now cancelled mission and we are being moved to another mission that this other guy has command of."

"No, the crew rosters are the first things to be updated when changes occur. A message would not have come out without updating the rosters first. All we have to do is search this Mr. Carter and see his position in the roster. I know the name, but he wasn't with us when we started out. Must be someone aboard the station."

I thought to myself again that I should have a recording of the entire meeting where something must have happened for us to be getting messages from a new Commander. I couldn't look at it though with my Mother in the room. No way she would let that go. I would be locked in our room without my tablet for the remainder of the mission if she knew what I had done. If I was allowed to stay on board at all. I needed to get away from her so I could listen to the recording and find out what happened. For now, though, we may as well read the message that was sent out by this Commander Carter.

"Mom, have you read the message yet?" I asked her as I finished the first sentence on the screen.

"No, I am trying to get a hold of your Father to find out what is going on. Why, what does it say?"

I started to read the message aloud to her while she continued trying to reach Father.

"Mission crew, you are required to attend a briefing at 1700 hrs. All awake crew will need to meet in the #12 cargo deck. No duty stations will be active during this time. The I.S.E.P. will maintain all monitoring functions aboard the Expeditious during this period. No exceptions to the attendance requirement will be granted. All crew must attend.

You will be informed of upcoming ship movements and new procedures we will be following immediately. Bring your tablets as you will be assigned new duties if needed of which will be sent to your screens for confirmation. All acceptable questions will be answered at that time."

I paused as I looked at the signature line of the message. It was simple and short but sent a shiver up my spine as I read it aloud to my Mother who by this point was looking over my shoulder reading along. I felt her tense up as well as my mouth formed the words.

"Commander Thomas Carter, Commander of Military Support Group, APEX mission, Brigadier General Earthen Navy"

This just got serious. From discussions I had overheard in the past few weeks I gathered that there was zero military force aboard the Expeditious. We were supposed to pick up some security forces personnel from Mars when we got to the APEX but that was the extent of our military strength. This was an experimental colony ship, not a warship. There was no need for extensive military power. When your species is the only ones to fly through the oblivion that is empty space, the need for large guns drops to near zero. Near Earth the need was high with unrest nearly everywhere. Up here though ships were so far and few between along with space so large that you just flew the other way. Maybe with the recent attacks this was going to change.

"Mom, why is there a Military Commander sending us orders?"

"I'm not sure honey but after you read the name, I pulled the roster back up and searched it. There is a new entry. Actually, twelve new entries. All military. All in a new crew group separate from the rest of us." She paused before continuing. "Well that's new. There are now four groups in our rosters when before there were only two. Before we had a group called active crew that held all the awake personnel on board. Then there was a second group called reserve crew that held anyone in a pod. Now there are four groups. Active Crew, Reserve Crew, Military Support and Colonist."

I thought about it for a second and then felt a bit of relief. "Did you say Military Support? It says support and not command or force?"

My Mother turned away from me and read the group names again as I did the same on my own tablet wanting to see what she had seen. "Yes, does that mean something to you?" She looked up at me with a questioning glance.

"I'm not sure. I think the fact that it specifically reads Support shows that they don't have control of the ship completely. They are here to support the crew. That sounds like a good thing. If the military was in control, then I wouldn't think it would list them as support."

"I can see that. It could just be to sound more political and less intrusive though." As soon as she said this, I could tell she wanted to take it back. I had come up with a positive twist on the situation all on my own and instead of allowing me to ride that out she instead shot a hole in my theory. "I mean, you are probably right. Military personnel wouldn't allow their position to be muddled by mere political wording. It would read more decisively."

"But you don't think so. If they were really just support staff, then why didn't Father send out the order instead of this other Commander? If he was still truly in charge wouldn't he have sent it out?"

"Maggie, I really don't know but I'm sure it will be fine. Still haven't reached your Father. I show he is on board now. His tracker is listing him on the Command Deck. I think I will run up there and speak to him. Will you be ok to wait here in the room until I get back? Shouldn't take too long."

"That's fine. I have a few things to do here anyways."

Mother turned back towards me curiously, "Things to do? Like what? What would you want to do that would overtake your natural curiosity? Here I was expecting you to demand to come with me."

I did want to come with her, but I also wanted to listen to my audio recordings from the day's meetings desperately. "I wanted to get started on our night's reading. Whether Father is still in overall command or not shouldn't stop our training tomorrow. At least I hope not. You go speak with him and I will get started on the reading. I can catch you up later when we go over it together. After all, if the military is taking over then I will need all the skills I can acquire to stay on the roster with crew and not be dropped back to Civilian. You know the first thing they will put into the procedures is that all Civilians stay in pods for the duration and will be the last to be awoken when we get to the other side. I want to be up and awake for the full trip."

"Ok Maggie. Deal. You start reading up on our materials and we can reconvene a while later." Looking at the clock on her tablet she continued, "One hour until the meeting in the cargo bay. If I am not back in time, make sure and head down there. We can meet up there."

With that she nodded to me and exited our room shutting the door behind her. I immediately walked over and locked that door to make sure I wasn't discovered with what I was now sitting down to watch. The app came open quickly after I sifted through a few folders to get to my hiding spot. Immediately I was shown a still image of my Father. It was his ID picture. It showed up since I was accessing his device at the time. There was an audio file there. 7 hours 58 minutes and 35 seconds of audio. Fortunately, when I had gone down to the training decks earlier in the day, my Father was already in the meeting room so the audio I wanted had to be near the beginning of this recording. I shouldn't have to search around for it for too long. I pushed the fast-forward button and jumped ahead 30 minutes and hit play.

A deep voice much deeper than my Fathers came up mid-sentence, "failure to keep the mission secure. He cannot be relied upon to." I hit the pause button quickly. That man couldn't be talking about my Father, could they? It wasn't his fault that we had been attacked. In fact, it was the military's fault to begin with. We were on a transport vessel. What was our Commander supposed to do to defend us better? The attacks back on Earth had been allowed to happen by the local government not catching them beforehand. Their guards allowed access to the armories the weapons were stolen from after all. The mines in space weren't my Father's fault either. That area should have been swept ahead of time by the military or at least they should have noticed the mines being placed there to begin with. Surely the speaker hadn't been referencing my Father. I hit the rewind button and went back twenty minutes and hit play again.

A much brighter tone came across the speaker mid-sentence. This one was lighter than the previous jerk but was still Male obviously. I thought it was the I.S.E.P. Commander but wasn't sure yet.

"for coming today. I know this meeting is very important to both the station crew and your ship's crew Commander Johanson. Nothing meant by this, but we want to see your ship off our docking port and gone just as badly as you also want to see that. If not more. We have more staff than normal working odd shifts to keep things in check with the added volatile mass of your ship clenched on. We are down docking ports even since we can't allow other ships to dock near your damaged vessel. I want to start out by saying that a way forward has been discussed and decided by leadership back on Earth. We already knew most of it since it had been decided that the Expeditious was far too damaged to make a quick trip out to Mars without extensive repairs.

Not to waste everyone's time I will get right to the heart of the decision. Commander Johanson, you will be taking the Walrus to get to Mars. This is not a surprise. I think everyone here figured that would be the ship. The Walrus is an old ship but will do fine for this trip. The ship should be docking in 2 days' time. You will NOT be moving supplies and personnel over while docked to the station though. The Walrus has some items we need here that will be offloaded. It will then be refueled from our auxiliary tanks. Your Expeditious will be released from our port and you will drift towards the moon into open space. Of course, this will be with the assistance of one of our tug ships as you were brought to the port to begin with.

Once you are safely positioned out between the station and the moon, the Walrus will be released and will transit to your location. The two ships will attach directly, and your crew and supplies will then be moved."

"Commander Markel, why are we only transferring out in empty space instead of while attached here at the station?" My Father asked a bit annoyed. "Why the extra steps of transiting a broken ship out a ways?"

"Well Mr. Johanson," I noticed the slap that was meant by purposefully leaving off my Father's rank when the station commander answered him. "Your ship is a hazard to anything around it. I wanted that ship removed from my station as quickly as possible. As soon as you are finished moving your necessities across to the Walrus, the Expeditious will be retired from service and disassembled where it sits at that point by a salvage crew. Being a super launcher, the engineering group does not feel confident it can be returned to full functionality. It will be better used for scrap material and spare parts for other ships of its class. The Expeditious is done."

"Understood, thank you for that clarification sir." My Father replied more courteous this time. He knew he needed friends out here not being a career space faring member of the military group.

"Continuing on, the Expeditious will be taken apart out in open space. The materials will be transferred by a local barge ship to one of the construction stations either on the moon or nearer Earth. That has not been decided yet. The Walrus will then continue your previous mission. The Walrus being a freighter is more along what you should have been on in the first place so your ride should be significantly more comfortable. I won't go into specifics about the ship as you are all aware of that class's capability and basic layout. You can check your tablets later for a detailed diagram of the ship. The main issue we have is the original push Earth had planned to give you once you sling-shot around the Moon will not be possible. The Walrus is much larger and does not have the components required. It is much faster than the Expeditious though so it should take only a couple weeks longer to make your rendezvous. That will put your mission 6 weeks behind schedule."

My Father jumped in again at this point. "What does that mean for the crew on the APEX right now along with our refugees off Mars?"

"They will be fine until then. Currently the evacuees are already aboard pods on the APEX waiting for you to arrive. There are enough reserves aboard the ship and support station to support the remaining on duty crew along with the work force you had out there finishing the ship."

"It would be much easier for me to maintain the construction schedule out there if I would again be granted access to the Mars communications system." My Father sounded a bit angry about this. I hadn't realized he was blocked from speaking with his own work force out by Mars. We had been locked down tighter than I had realized. The heavy deep voice I had heard before from later in the recording spoke for the first time now.

"Mr. Johanson, that was a security risk to allow you to continue communications. We did not know who was at fault for the attacks on the Expeditious."

My Father was now outwardly angry, "It is Commander Johanson to start with. I know that your military group was responsible for blocking my credentials from the network. What I do not understand is why you would think I was responsible in any way for attacking my own transport that I was aboard. Not only that but my family is aboard. My daughter was in a pod on one of the decks that was punctured. My wife had just left that deck shortly before and could have easily been killed if not by chance."

The deep voice returned, "Yes, Commander Johanson. I do know your family was aboard and it was a very fortunate circumstance that had both your daughter's pod and your wife close enough to be seen as in danger yet never really at risk." He said fortunate in such an exaggerated way he was obviously proposing that my Father had planned it that way. "While we are very happy that your crew for the most part escaped losses, it was protocol in this kind of terrorist attack to separate your crew from any other groups while we investigated the incident thoroughly. It could have been quicker if only we had some military intelligence on board during the initial trip out. Going into the investigation totally blind slowed us down some."

"We didn't have military on board because this was not a military mission. If the military had done its job in the first place, then those mines would have been blocked from placement or noticed before our transport ever made it out there." I could hear the anger still festering in Father's words, but he had been able to pull it back below a shout. His forced diplomacy rising again to the front pushing his rage down deep inside. "It was a terrible incident with the only ones being at fault were those inside the Earther group. Have the members of that group that were to blame for this attack been caught General Carter?"

General Carter? That was the Commander that had sent out the orders for everyone to meet here in another half hour or so. I hadn't been paying close attention to the time but knew I must have some left before having to take off and get down to the training deck before 1700 hours.

The deep voice I knew now to be General Carter continued. "Yes, we believe we did find the at fault parties that lead to that incident. There was a glitch in our systems two weeks ago that may have allowed devices to be sent out from the Earth to an orbit around the Moon. The operators on duty that night have been interviewed and the investigation's findings will be used appropriately."

"How about Earther's on the planet? There must have been a base to fire them from."

"Commander, I assure you that we are taking care of any known bases that may have launched the devices."

"What does that even mean? You are taking care of them. Can't you just destroy them and be done with it?"

"We could but it would do no good. Those locations will no longer be viable launch platforms due to our knowledge of the incident. They were abandoned already when we reached them. The launchers themselves were the only structures remaining. We have taken the launchers down and cleared the areas."

"So really, you have not caught anyone on the surface."

At this point the lighter, brighter voice of Commander Markel came back over the recording, "Gentleman, please let's not waste valuable time squabbling over things that have no further impact on our mission as it sits in front of us now. Commander Johanson, ground forces are doing all they can to ensure no more attacks can be launched from the planet. The station and space-based military forces are all on high alert and will continue to be for some time. At least until you and your crew are far beyond the reach of anything that could be launched. We will continue to work on catching those responsible and have plugged any holes we may have had on the space side of operations. Now, General Carter, please go over the future mission parameters that have been given to you."

"Yes sir, I have been tasked with a new mission. I am to join this crew along with my own security forces. Those forces are already aboard the Walrus now inspecting it and scanning it for any bugs or other equipment that should not be on board. We will be taking over all security operations for this mission."

"NO, that will not happen" My Father jumped back into the conversation with such anger in his voice it made me shrink back from the tablet and reach for the speaker down in my ear. "My primary demand for this mission when I first agreed to teaming up with the military was that this would not turn into a military mission. I refused to have military might on board the vessel and I still stick to that. This is exploratory only. Not military. I will not have my engine being annexed by the military."

I was surprised not to hear the General jump back in and argue his point again. Instead there was complete silence for fifteen long seconds before the I.S.E.P. Commander once more made himself known to the conversation. "Jim, you and I have known each other for years. Back when I was stationed on Earth, we knew each other pretty well. I had dinner at your house. You know I am in full support of your mission here. In the end we have the same bosses. There is no way you started working with the military and honestly thought they would not maintain some control over your creation. I know you are not that dense. You are not that blind. You knew this was coming so I ask you to drop the defiant attitude. You made it much further without a military presence than I could have imagined but after the attacks on your crew and equipment on the surface and now out in space you have to admit some security aid would be beneficial."

So, Father knew this Commander. The man who had kept us locked up nearly the entire time we had been attached to his station. If they knew each other so well then how come my Father had not been able to get us aboard the station sooner?

"Commander Markel, yes, we did know each other well back on Earth. When you were shipped up here though our relationship became official only. We had no personal contact. That was not my choice, that was yours. I believe you are in support of my mission, but I also have to protect it from being used purely as a conquest tool by military minds. I am maintaining control of it. Everyone involved knows that I alone am able to make this system work and I plan to keep it that way. You need me to run the machine whether the forces in power want it that way or not. If you want me out there running it then I will not be ruled over by a Military General."

Another long pause followed my Father's short tirade. So, he had the same concerns that I did. That made me feel better about the system as a whole. If it did work and we were able to transit through the stars, then at least I knew he was on my side not wanting to run around claiming worlds that had life already in abundance. That is what I gathered from his words. Also, it sounded like he had some kind of fail-safe that guaranteed that he would be the one running the engine. He alone could do it. There must have been a mechanism built in that required his presence or otherwise it would shut down on its own. He had not shared that secret with anyone. That makes sense on why there had been no true test flights and why he had been named Commander when he was a scientist alone. An extraordinarily intelligent scientist but still a scientist. Not a traditional Commander.

I could hear rustling and mumbles now but nothing intelligible. Almost as if someone was talking quietly on a com. Then Markel came back across, "General Carter, we have new orders across from command. Commander Johanson will maintain overall mission command. You will take over security forces as the military commander on ship. You will be reporting directly to Commander Johanson."

"With all due respect Commander Markel," The General started up with his low rumbling tone but with obvious disgust now overpowering his calm demeanor earlier. "Mr. Johanson has no military background and no official military rank. He is not fit to lead this mission and I cannot take official orders from a civilian while on mission."

"I have already told you I will not have Military Command on my ship. This is not a military vessel; it is not a military operation. If Command down on Earth feels it so important to protect us now, then they can send a military ship to escort us out to Mars and then for a ways after out until we reach our planned jump zone. That I will agree to. Otherwise we will not comply."

"You will do whatever you are ordered by government leadership Mr. Johanson." General Carter threw back at my father with ever increasing venom in his voice. "You have no right to refuse any order given from above. We could already be nearly to Mars if it wasn't for your failure to keep the mission secure. He cannot be relied upon to lead this mission any longer. This is too important a technology to be totally reliant on one man who believes himself to be above the leadership he begged to support his research in the first place. The mere fact that he was allowed to lock command and any other member of his own team out of the systems is ludicrous. Now he believes to have us all over a barrel unable to move without his approval." This last bit must have been aimed at Commander Markel and whatever further leadership was obviously listening in like I was.

To Markel's credit, he kept his calm demeanor throughout the entire exchange. Attempting to keep the discussion turned heated exchange into becoming a full blow out he interjected between my Father and the General. "Gentlemen, please sit down. Take a breath. We are all on the same team here. Before you start in again Jim, listen. We are all on the same team here. The Earth is dying. The very existence of the human race is diminishing. We as a species need this mission to succeed. Jim, you have to see that, and you have to see why you must accept military assistance at this point. I am not trying to point fingers but if you would have had a trained captain at the helm of your ship when you entered that mine field, they most likely would have been able to pick up on the devices and avoided most of them if not all of them entirely. Due to your persistence in making sure no military was aboard, you doomed your own ship to the damage it incurred.

If that ship would have been lost, nearly all hope in a human resurgence would have also been lost. You know what you have on board. You carry the very hope of a planet. You have in your protective grasp the biological key to a new planet, a new Earth that can be protected and preserved. We know humans can live in space at this point so we will not go extinct but our numbers will dwindle to such a small number that most of our history, most of our culture, most of our existence will be eliminated from the universe. Beyond our own species, the millions of species that we have purposefully expunged on Earth will be lost forever. No possible way to ever be recreated. You have your hands on the key to an entire planet Jim. You have to see that. Please I implore you, let General Carter join you. Let him come aboard and guide your decisions in a way that will help protect our investment in you. Our collective planet wide investment in you."

"Shelton, my old friend. I believe that you are trying to do the right thing. I understand that our planet is doomed, that is the reason I wanted to finish my predecessors work on this engine and make it work. I want to save the history of our planet in the living tissues. At the same time, it has been thrust upon me to protect other worlds as well. I cannot allow this engine to be used to conquer and that is what I am afraid will occur if a military force accompanies me."

I could here a long sigh from who I presumed was Markel. Then a bodily shift came through the speaker, squeak of a chair as if someone stood. Then the General came through again much calmer, more respectful, "Commander Johanson, Commander Markel, I do not know either of you personally nor do you know me. Let me tell you a bit about my history. I led a force back on Earth in my early days. At the tail end of the great war I was placed in a command position mostly due to the lack of personnel that were more capable than me. I learned though and I saw. We may have won that war, but we lost it at the same time.

This engine is what that war was about. We all know that. Word got out that an engine capable of spreading our species across the galaxy had been built. That was too much for many military minds to accept and the war broke out. Not because any of them thought the engine was a harmful thing, everyone only believed that they instead should be able to control it. There was fear of anyone that may control it becoming so overwhelmingly powerful that no force could stand against them. If someone was able to tame the beast of a machine, then they would reign supreme and whatever ideology that person or group belonged to would eliminate all others.

The same fear persists now. Word has gotten out that we have that machine again. Back during the war, the machine and its creator were destroyed. Commander Johanson, you have from what I understand recreated it and somehow have become the master that has tamed the beast. You are supremely powerful now due to your control of that machine, but you are also more vulnerable now than you have ever been. Even with most of the world's forces being too weak to do much, there are splinter groups like the Earthers who seek to simply destroy you. I don't think you quite grasp that. Otherwise you would accept the aid of the military without fighting it so hard."

"General, I understand the threat completely. I can concede to you that there is a threat I cannot defend against on my own. This new engine is more powerful than the old and it has been tamed. My concern now is exactly what so many were afraid of at the start of the great war. I know my desire to see this function is pure. I know that my goals are only to restore a planet worth of life on another world out there. My great concern is that someone will want to use my engine for conquer instead of rebuilding. We must not use this to take over other worlds that do not want us. We must only search for other worlds that have yet to develop and utilize them. There may be intelligence out there and we cannot pursue them and turn them into slaves or servants. We must ensure we only tame wild planets that have room for our kind."

"That is my goal as well. Jim, if I may call you Jim, our goals align. I only want what you want. The only difference is that I know what truly puts us at risk out here. I understand the threat. Allow me to lend you aid in your journey."

More silence followed this last statement by the General. His voice had almost taken on a soft tone even with its deep baritone vibrating the very substance that made up the room. I could feel that voice reverberate through me more than I could hear it with my ears. Even through the speaker on my tablet it rumbled through with such power. Almost calming it came across. Like a massager working through your cramped muscles and forcing you to relax into its embrace. Finally, through the quiet I heard my Father make his offer to the Station Commander and the General.

"General, Commander Markel, I believe we can work something out. If the good General sees fit to follow me and guide me as the Commander of our new security force, then I will allow a small contingent of no more than a dozen crew to join us. The General will have to report to me but will have autonomy within his security forces. I am overall Commander but all decisions that could impact security including navigation will be run through the Security team. Piloting and navigation positions will be filled with crew members approved by the General or by members of his crew."

"General, would this be acceptable to you?" Markel questioned the General in a hopeful tone.

"I can accept this. If the Commander accepts my input and puts it to good use along with allowing my people to pilot the ships. I do ask that I bring on fourteen crew including myself. If I am to pilot the ship full time, then I need a crew large enough to rotate a full team in and out of the command center. Also, I need another officer to accompany me to aid in the off shifts while I cannot be on the command deck myself."

"Understood and agreed. I will allow a total of fourteen. Twelve crew along with yourself and another officer to lead the crew while you are off. This is the limit though. There will be no others. I hope that you will vet this group very well as if anything else occurs on the ship, I will not be blamed so easily again. Now if we are done here for now, I need to get my people up to speed and working on preparing for the transition to the Walrus."

Markel added, "Commander, if you would allow, I think it would be a good idea to announce this to your crew all together at the same time this evening. Possibly bring everyone together on your ship to announce it in person. Then they could meet the General face to face as well and ease some of the tension these changes are bound to bring on."

"Commander Markel, I think that is a good idea. Commander Johanson, would this be ok with you?" General Carter asked of my Father.

"That works for me. It would be more appropriate to bring up this information in person. Please feel free to write up a directive for everyone to meet down on our Training Deck. It is Deck twelve. That deck is empty besides various training areas for differing tasks aboard the ship. I believe they were using it for pod movement training today prepping to move ships. Once I see your directive, I can follow up with everyone myself. It will be good to get your contact out there for them to have in their communicators. Also please get me a list of crew as soon as you can so we can add them all to the rosters."

With this I heard a chair scrape backwards as someone stood up.

"Now gentlemen, if we are done here, I will be getting back to my ship."

Both the other men gave verbal oks and quick goodbyes. I could hear them shake hands and then I heard a door swing open and click shut as magnetic footsteps slipped into the distance getting quieter until they were remnants repeated by my own mind. I sat there for a minute thinking about what all I had just heard. My father knew this Commander Markel from long ago but didn't seem to trust him completely anymore. Father had the same concerns and apprehensions that I did about this mission down to its very roots. He was driven though to preserve the innocent life he had in his control. That was in line almost perfectly with my own desires. Maybe with him in command it would be best to allow the ship to make a jump and keep us on the other side instead of returning. If those still on the planet thought our mission had failed, it may be decades or longer before they would try again.

On the other hand, my Father had just agreed to allow the military to join us. The General seemed genuinely on the same page as us as far as preserving Earth life along with whatever life we may stumble across along the way but how was I to know that was true? What if he was only saying what he needed to in order to get on the other side of the wormhole and then take over with force? Then conquer anything we may find out there for his own. He was military. He was used to fighting, to power, to conquering enemies. A lot of the time the only thing you needed in order to be classified as an enemy was a different heritage. Be from another state, another government. Out there in the great beyond, anything we crossed would naturally be on that list of others. They could be classified as enemies without ever doing anything against us.

As I thought about these things and turned my mind over and over again still fighting to keep my sanity in a world I seemed to be ever less able to influence I realized something. The footsteps had disappeared. That shouldn't have happened. They walked off into the distance and disappeared. I was listening to a recording from my Father's tablet. If he had it with him then why would his footsteps have trailed off? They should have stayed steady as the tablet was carried along. Even though it felt as though I had crossed another lightyear of distance in my mind, it had only been a few seconds since he left the meeting room. Then I heard voices of 2 men again. Familiar voices that would be nowhere near my Father at this point.

"Well Tom, that was a masterful display there. I thought we had lost him, but you turned him right around with that bull shit story of yours."

A deep chuckle across the recording penetrated deep into my core as the General allowed his cover to melt back. "Ha, ha yes. I felt it was a performance worthy an award. That pompous asshole scientist thinks he will keep the engine from us. He may have some control in there that will only allow his input but just give my crew time and they can beat it. I'm not worried about that one bit. I will bide my time and "guide" the prick along until he makes another critical error. Then we will push him to the side and gain full control over the device."

"Just so we are clear though, I don't want any harm to come to Jim." Markel added cautiously, "We only need to remove him from Command. He is still a brilliant man and we need him to pursue our goals. We need him on our side. Take it easy and don't push too hard. Allow him to make his own mistakes. Let him hang himself while keeping our hands clean."

"Precisely. I know we need him. Just because I can't stand the man doesn't mean I want him dead or detained. He is not fit to lead and won't for much longer. Don't worry Shelton, you brought in the right man. What I need from you now though is an official order from above that allows me full rights to take over that ship when we do run into trouble. It will be very hard to take it over without a fight unless I have official orders to fall back on. Either way we can take control once out there on the other side of the wormhole, but it will be less bloody and better for our future efforts if I can take it over without a fight."

"I will work on that for you. It may be a few weeks but by the time the Walrus makes it to Mars the order should be there waiting for you for when it is needed. Just keep him out of trouble on your way there. Make the transition to the APEX without incident and out to the jump point. Once on the other side you can take over. Keep it away from media camera drones on this side of the divide. Whatever you have to do on the other side won't be seen."

After that I heard another chair slide back and someone stand. A few mumbled words were shared that I couldn't make out and then the metal clank of magnetic boots rose across the recording. The clanks stopped and a hushed whisper was shared again outside of the reception of the microphone on Father's tablet. Then the whisper got louder only not louder. Clearer. The tablet must have been lifted closer to the men's mouths so I could hear them better. Markel's voice came across in a hushed tone, "This is his tablet but why would he have left it?"

Carter's voice came booming across without the slightest quietness to it, "Why are you whispering Shelton? You really think he is recording us? Check the tablet, there are no open apps. He probably just left it behind. Not used to open confrontations with leaders far more experienced than he. It got to him more than he let on. That is impressive but at the same time sad. We are technically on his side still and we spooked him enough for him to forget his tab."

"What if he did set it to record us though Tom? It could destroy our plans if he figures out what we are planning to do on the other side of the wormhole."

"Just give the damn thing to me then. I can run it by my guys on my way to the Expeditious. They will check it and wipe any audio recordings to be safe. I really doubt he was recording though. He would be smart enough to know that we would notice it sitting here and wipe anything we had said."

"True, true. Ok, take it by your guys then. While you are at it, go ahead and send out the order to attend the meeting this evening. If you do it now and Jim isn't able to add on to it for a while since he doesn't have his tab it may go ahead and create a bit of distrust in their Commander dropping off the radar during such an important time."

Then I heard the door open and could tell the tablet had been dropped into a pocket as all sounds suddenly became very muffled. Shit I thought to myself. If they check the tablet, then there is no way those experienced techs won't notice my app listening away.

Shit, shit, shit.

I am going to be busted for sure. Wait, if I just stop the transmission now from my end then they won't know. I set it up so I could set that app to self-delete with a command from my end. I went to type in the command when it dawned on me that I was being stupid. These recordings were from this morning. I was only 40 minutes into a recording that was nearly 8 hours old. If the General took the tab to his people to get looked at then they would have caught my stream hours ago. They must not have seen it since I'm you know, free and not in chains somewhere aboard the station. Still though why take a risk in case they hadn't gotten to it yet. I sent the command and instantly the connection was severed between the tablets.

I had a bit over eight hours of audio now that was probably mostly just empty time. I should delete the entire file now since I had already heard it, but something kept me from doing that. I wanted to check the rest to see if there was anything worthwhile. I couldn't do that now though as I looked at the clock. Nearly 1700 hours. I needed to get down to the training deck quickly so I wouldn't be late to the big gathering. My Mother had never returned so she must have gotten held up with my Father and would meet me down there. I pulled myself out of the fog of the conversation I just heard and left the shared room.

The trip down to the training room ended up taking a lot longer than I had expected. You know even in zero G where there really aren't weight limits in elevators there is still a limitation of how many people you can safely squeeze into a capsule. Beyond that, there is a limit on how many people I personally want to be pressed up against in said capsule. No one has ever told me that I was a big people person that loved physical contact or close quarters. The pods that had consumed a good deal of my time so far aboard were small but at least they were individual. There were no bumping elbows with other people or smelling their bodily odors from working long shifts upon long shifts while only being able to wipe down with a cloth every couple days.

When the lift had gotten to the residential deck of which apparently, I was the last person to leave, the doors slid open and revealed many more filled flight suits than I was comfortable squeezing in between. These must be all the crew from the command deck waiting until the last minute to leave their posts in the hands of the station controllers and head down. Only a half second elapsed from the opening of the doors to me swinging open a hatch into the vertical shaft that housed ladders. Since being aboard this ship, there had been a few times I had scurried from floor to floor around the lift, so this wasn't my first encounter with the shaft. It was still super creepy though to look at. It was well lit all the way down the ship so you could pretty well see clean to the other end or at least that is what I thought I saw. I did know it went at least all the way down to the lowest cargo bay. Into the Engineering decks I wasn't so sure. I hadn't gotten all the way to the bottom yet.

The meeting was supposed to be on cargo level twelve which was a full nine decks below me. One science deck and eight cargo decks one of which being the one converted into two medical decks. That was about 170 feet straight down into the belly of our ship. Climbing down 170 feet of ladder may not sound like an option to most people but out here in space on a stationary ship it was nearly as easy as taking the lift. I quickly flicked my boot's magnetic plates off and pulled myself more than jumped into the shaft. The simple part of using the chute in zero G is that once you get moving in any direction you really kept going the same general speed. Air resistance and various bumps against sides of the chute as you drop are the two things that slow you down. Once I got myself going in the right direction, progress was smooth and only needed a slight push off a wall or a kick off some ladder rungs to keep my momentum up. I could get to where I skipped twenty to thirty-foot sections of rungs between each push off.

Nearing cargo bay twelve, I stuck my arms and legs out and used basic friction against the walls of the chute to slow myself down to a speed that made it easy to grab the last few rungs before the appropriate hatch. Just like with the lift I had to swipe my arm across the scanner to get the hatch to allow access. Unlike a few of the decks my Father had needed to use his access authority to enter, the training deck had me registered along with every other member of the active crew. The system still required access to be granted to you before opening but pretty much anyone that was awake had that access granted already.

The hatch swung open and as I planted my feet back on an actual floor my boots sensed the action and turned the magnetics back on holding me fast and allowing me to regain my balance in this odd world of zero g navigation. The crowd was surprisingly large in the training room. Hundreds of people all surrounded a stage with diplomats and leaders all shaking hands and kissing babies. Ok, it wasn't all that grand really. I think we had maybe 20 people up and around at this point. That along with the 3 that came over from the station. It was standing room only but not due to crammed spaces but more because, well, you didn't really need a chair all that bad in zero G. We all kind of just floated there stuck to the floor with our boots. You had to keep a bit of tension in your legs to keep from just floating but there really wasn't any need to sit. Also, I may have been over stating the stage. I saw my Father along with the 3 new faces standing on the podium, but it was just a couple cargo crates folded down and strapped to the deck to form a slightly raised space for them to stand and be able to see us all. I'm betting that

that last lift full of crew was nearly half of who was down here.

Two of the three new faces were easy for me to guess on who they were. One was a grumpy looking older man in a fancy military uniform. He just looked angry. I would bet he held that look on his wrinkled-up face most of the time. The lines in his forehead supported that theory. That had to be General Thomas Carter. Or Commander Carter or whatever he was going to be called on this trip. The man next to the General was most likely Commander Markel. His body type fit the light voice I had heard on the recording. He was taller and skinny. He had a very proper stance to him. Up perfectly straight with his chin held elevated just enough for me to notice but not enough to make his disdain for anyone below him obvious to those not looking for it. Hearing him over the tablet had already set an opinion in my mind of him though so I could have been imagining the chin thing.

The third person I didn't have any idea. She was obviously military seeing the uniform, but I didn't know my insignias well enough to tell you what she was at that moment. I knew she wasn't another General or higher due to her position on the stage and that her insignia was different. She also wasn't an assistant or low-ranking officer as the way she held herself also relayed a sense of authority of her own. Beyond that I didn't know where she stood in the chain of command that was before our group. To the far left was my Father. He was at the edge of the thrown together stage leaned down speaking with my Mother in hushed tones. Whatever they were discussing it seemed to be the tail end. My Father gave her a squeeze on her shoulder and then stood straight turning back towards the other three.

Father started in as my Mother spotted me and walked around the small assembly towards me.

"Thank you all for coming. I believe it is time now and pretty certain I see everyone that needs to be here in attendance so we may as well get started right in. I would like to introduce to those of you that have not yet met our visitors here standing beside me." Pointing to the man I assumed was the station commander he continued, "This is Commander Shelton Markel of the I.S.E.P. He has commanded the station for many years now and was instrumental in getting ships to us in our time of distress. He led the charge to tow us back and get us docked and supplied. Without his leadership we would probably be sitting somewhere on the moon right now scattered across its surface alongside some of the hulks from early missions out towards Mars. Next to Commander Markel is a great example of our military might." The General gave a slight nod towards the small crowd as my Father moved on to him. "Brigadier General Thomas Carter has a long and decorated history with our military forces before, during and since the great wars that ravaged our world."

I was a bit surprised to hear my Father use the wars as a way to introduce the General. Usually the wars were never something that people referred to when you wanted them to think kindly upon you. The wars were devastating to everyone. Nearly all life on Earth and all hope of the planet recovering in our lifespans was wiped out during the wars. It was a conflict that once over, soldiers were not welcomed home with open arms. The few that did return were looked at with sideways glances. Most couldn't find work and were forced back into the service. My Father had told me about these times since he was still a young teen at the time and saw those returning firsthand. It was a terrible time for one to decide to leave the military. No one wanted to touch them. People knew that those soldiers were not at fault for the destruction and death that had plagued the world, but they did represent the loss. My Father continued his odd introduction.

"General Carter has offered to lend his lengthy experience to our mission into the unknown. He along with a small group of his most highly trusted and experienced security forces will join us aboard a new ship." Moving past the light murmurs that instantly started up with that last statement my Father continued to the third person in line. "Next on this prestigious stage is another great military mind that will be joining us. As the senior member of the team and second in command of the security forces, Major Robin Bonette will be an integral part of us making it safely to our destination. With the introductions of these fine members of our soon to be protective bubble completed, I will step back and allow Commander Markel to take center stage." With this my Father took a grand exaggerated step back and bowed slightly to the man next to him.

It took a moment for the Commander to get a grasp on what had just happened. From his delay I took it that this was not going at all how he had planned. My Father had evidently gone a bit rogue but not so much so that the Commander could take any direct action against it in front of the entire crew. A brilliant snub showing my Father wasn't on board with what was about to be said without directly saying as much and getting himself brought before a tribunal and possibly removed from his role. Although I doubt after all I heard in the meeting earlier that they could remove him. It sounded like he pretty well had them all in a noose for now. The only thing was how long that noose could stay there waiting before someone decided to cut it down or hang someone else with it.

"Thank you Commander Johanson for that welcoming introduction." That was the entirety of Markel being knocked off balance. Less than one sentence and he was back in obvious control of the situation before him. "I am happy to inform you all that you will be getting official backing of physical support from the military effective immediately. We will no longer allow the missteps that lead to the previous attack on your ship and the delay of your mission. As Commander Johanson already mentioned, General Carter next to me will be leading a small group of security forces blah, blah, blah, blah."

Sorry about that. I don't think he actually said blah blah blah but at this point he started rattling off about a bunch of information I had already heard from the recording earlier. Also, Mother had walked over to me by this point and was giving me a soft tug on my shirt letting me know she wanted me to follow her. As I started to turn, Markel locked eyes with me. I froze not knowing what I should do. It felt like his eyes stayed on me for minutes, but it was probably more like a fraction of a second or two at most. I could feel in that moment that he knew what I had done and knew what I had heard from my own tablet. My Mother's grip tightened ever so slightly as I held to my spot. Markel's gaze moved on past me still working his way through a prepared speech preaching now more than just speaking to the crew about how through our trials we would come out stronger by banding together with the new security forces that were joining us. He didn't skip a beat in his speech even while seeing right into me. I shuddered as I turned the rest of the way around and followed my Mother towards the lift. I could feel the eyes of a few other crew I had come to know well follow us as we made our way but only for a moment as they returned their focus to the show currently performing on stage.

In the lift now moving upwards towards the nose of our dead vessel my Mother broke her silence, "Why is all I want to know Maggie. Why in the hell would you risk it?" At first, I was puzzled both by her words and her tone. I can only think of a couple times I had heard my Mother curse and it had never been while speaking to me directly. As I made my way past the words alone and to the meaning behind them, I was certain what she must be referring to. I didn't want to admit it just yet though. If they were going to bust me for listening in, then I at least wanted to know how they figured it out. Although if they took away my tablet then learning a lesson may not benefit me at all. I could use how they caught me to improve my simple hacks. Without my tablet though, it wouldn't matter what I learned.

"Why did I risk what?"

"Don't you dare refuse to tell me now after what you have done! Don't act dumb, you know exactly what you did."

"I have done a lot of things Mother. I can't think of what I did that was so risky though. I went to the train-"

"Maggie Audrian Johanson! You stop this now! Your Father and I know about you trying to record the meeting on his tablet! He told me about it after I found him on the command deck earlier!"

My heart sunk. They did know what I had done. Although she wasn't exactly correct. I hadn't recorded anything to my Father's tablet, I had streamed it to my own and recorded it there. I felt that I still needed to fish some information out to see what exactly they thought I had done.

"Whoa, whoa. What do you all think I did? You think I somehow recorded the meeting from Father's tablet? How would I have done that? The meeting was going on while we were in training today. I was no-where near the tablet."

My Mother paused for a moment at that and thought. She quickly came up with an answer which was closer than I had hoped she would come to. "You must have activated it on a time delay or set it to start recording once it heard several individual voices like a meeting would have. How you did it isn't the point anyways. We know you did it. Father found the recording on his tablet.

Fortunately, the Military didn't figure that out on the station. If they had realized that your Father, even if inadvertently, was recording a high security clearance meeting, he could easily not only be thrown off this mission but arrested and tried for treason back on the planet. Is that what you want Maggie?"

So, they didn't know exactly what had happened. Beyond that my Father was lying to my Mother at least to some degree. Since I had already listened in on the recording, I knew that Father hadn't found anything on his tablet, he had left it behind in the meeting room. That was interesting. Why would he tell Mother a different story? I was sure there must be a reason. There was no way he would lie to Mother for no reason at all. I assumed I should play along with this story line and not reveal anything that wouldn't jive with the version of event my Mother thought she knew.

"Ok, Mom. I may have set up a recording on Father's tablet, but it wasn't fair that we were not included to what was being talked about. I mean it impacts us all on the mission. Why wouldn't we be allowed to know what was going on?"

"What the hell do you think the meeting downstairs just now was all about? Do you think they are all plotting behind our backs and will only tell us the bare minimum? The mission commander is your Father. HE won't keep things from us."

"NO!" I shouted back to her, "He won't keep things from you maybe. You both kept everything from me back on Earth. I didn't know anything about his true position or expertise. I didn't know anything about being shipped off planet or going into another solar system. I didn't know a damned thing!" Yelling at her wasn't going to do me any good but the rage I hadn't even thought about in quite some time rose inside me. How dare she proclaim that they would tell me the truth of what was going on? It had only been weeks since we launched and before that they had been lying to me for years. "On top of not telling me, he kept most of it from you too! How can you be so sure that he will suddenly tell you everything now!?!?"

As I finished my rant the lift stopped at lab deck and the door slid open for us to enter. I stepped out without even looking assuming we had been headed for the residential deck, not here. "What the hell are we doing here?" I asked my Mother who was following me off the lift into the large room of stark white dotted with various equipment, screens and chairs.

"Maggie, I know that what went on down on Earth was and is hard for you to swallow. Your Father and I did keep things from you down there and yes, he did keep things from me also. I knew some of the story but didn't have a complete picture. The difference now is that all that secrecy was there to keep us hidden and protected. Up here, everyone already knows what is going on. Everyone on the planet, on the station and on this ship know what we are doing. They know who we are, and they know what our mission is. There is no reason to keep things from you or me now."

"Bull shit." I threw that back at my Mother nearly spitting at her. "I can't believe that for a moment. If either of you thought that keeping something from me right now would possibly save me from some unknown hazard, then you would do it. You would lie to me all day long to protect me. At least you would do it if you thought it could protect me."

My Mother softened her gaze at me and walked closer lifting her arm and placing it on my shoulder gently. "Yes Maggie, I must admit that if I thought lying to you would protect you in some way, I probably would do that. On this ship though, you are part of the crew now. Anything that could cause harm to any of us would cause harm to us all. We have to work together and trust each other from here on out or we won't make it. Part of being a member of the team though also includes the requirement that you not risk others in the team. You can't go off on your own trying to snoop or keep secrets. That will only cause us problems. Do you understand?"

"Yea, I understand what you are saying." I wasn't about to agree to not keeping secrets though. I didn't want to lie to my Mother outright so just omitting some details sounded like a handy out for me. Plus, I knew my Father was keeping things and maybe out and out lying to my Mother right now so her whole speech was a bit moot. I still didn't like the idea of straight up lying to her about something important. "I promise not to purposefully put anyone on the crew in a position of danger for my own gain. If you promise to keep me informed of things that involve me or the ship."

"I can promise that honey. I won't keep anything important from you."

With that I turned to the room we were in sweeping my eyes across the area searching for why we were here. "So, what are we doing in Father's lab?"

"You are going to remove whatever programs you snuck onto your Father's tablet and are going to show me exactly how you broke into it in the first place. If you can hack in, you are either an expert hacker or found a way around security protocol which is a risk to the entire mission."

"Hmm, ok. I guess I can do that. It really wasn't all that impressive. I cheated a bit." At that point I saw my Father's tablet sitting on the table and went over to it. "I can't really do the facial part here though. It took me a bit of time and the room has to be dark."

"You make it sound like you have done this several times." My Mother said sounding a bit tired now. "I was hoping this was a one-off event."

"No, no. I haven't done it before. I just know how the systems work so I knew how to activate it. You have always told me I was my Father's daughter. I have his nose, his chin, his eyes." She started nodding slowly showing she understood where I was going with that. "I just need to be in a darker room and draw a few marks on my face with a pen to get close enough for the system to see him in me."

I proceeded to go through the steps explaining to my Mother how I broke through each level of security in rapid succession. When I got to the pass codes, she laughed out loud.

"Honestly I wish I had thought of that method. It wasn't secure enough to defeat your eye but still, not sure anyone else would have beaten those codes. That explains how you knew those at least. I was worried you had used a hacking virus to figure them out. That could have opened him up to an easy attack from outside. Basically, from what you are telling me, you beat security by pretending to be him in looks and thought."

"That is about the gist of it. Besides the fingerprint I really didn't need anything but me."

"Ok, now that you made it past his security, show me what you did from there."

I glanced down at the tablet again and realized for the first time that it was unlocked. Father must have unlocked it and set the security to open. That was a risky thing to do but being in his lab which he could control access to, he probably only allowed my Mother and me so we could do this while everyone was in the meeting down deeper in our ship. This part was going to be tricky. I didn't want to reveal to my Mother that I really had sent the audio to my own tablet. I had to think quickly about how to lead her along the lines my Father had already told her about and not reveal my secret.

"Ok, here on the main screen," I started to say scanning the home page and the various apps and folders there. I saw one and smiled slightly. He had thought of exactly this scenario and what I would need. "you can see this folder here labeled 'Maggie'. I opened that folder and copied over a version of an audio recorder app that is on all the tablets when programmed originally." In the folder just as I had hoped, along with several photos of me as a child growing up, there was an audio recording app with one recording on it. I had no idea what was on that recording but that didn't really matter to me as long as Mother didn't want to listen to it.

At this point I knew Father and I were on a team separate from my Mother. This folder had not been there before when I put my real hack on his tablet. All that had been there were work and communication apps along with a couple program file folders that most likely contained files related to various projects he was involved in. Now this 'Maggie' folder existed right there smack in the middle of the screen. Brilliant. I still didn't understand what had transpired between the time the Commander and the General had found his tablet and left the meeting room but somehow my hack had not been found and Father had regained the device. He must know about it though. Why else would he come up with this whole story? In fact, why did he come up with this story? He could have just kept it from my Mother completely and spoke to me privately later. Something else must be going on I hadn't yet figured out.

"Anyways, that is how I did it. Nothing fancy, I just wanted to know what was said in the meeting."

"Well how did you expect to listen to it?" My Mother asked quizzically. I don't know how long it took you to set all this up but surely you didn't think you'd have enough time to listen to the recording later on his tablet. No way you would get that much time alone with it in private."

"No of course not. I knew there would be no way to listen to it from his tablet. That part was the easiest. All I needed to do was wait until you two were asleep and I could move the file over to my own device. Then I could listen to it any time without anyone noticing. Plug into my earphones and listen to it whenever." That wasn't totally a lie I told myself. It was close to what I had planned, it was just going to send the recording to my tablet on its own instead of me having to manually do that.

"Ok, it is good to hear it was something that simple, I was concerned you had broken into more than just bypassing his login credentials. Thank you for telling me that. Now that this is cleared up, we can figure out where to go from here."

Well, here it came. I knew I was getting off easy compared to what I had really done and could have been caught with. Would I lose my tablet for a while or have extra controls put on it limiting what I could accomplish?

"For starters, you are grounded. In a way. You are going to be confined to our quarters and will have your tablet restricted. You will only be able to access the personnel locators and communicators of your Father and me. You will only be allowed out in the ship when accompanied by an approved escort which right now will be only your Father and me."

"That sucks but I can live with it. I understand."

"Also, you will be removed from the training group and will sit out the ship transfer activities besides moving yourself and our personal gear."

"Wait, what?" There was no way my Mother was pulling me from pod movements. "No way can you do that. We have been training for that ship movement. You can't keep me from that! We don't have the personnel to let me just sit around when I have been trained anyways!"

"Ahh, you don't know do you? Since you didn't get to listen to the entire meeting downstairs and hadn't gotten to the recording yet."

"Know what?" I was truly puzzled now. Unknown to her I had listened to the meeting already, but I couldn't say that. I still couldn't think of what she was talking about.

"The security team we are bringing on is already aboard the Walrus. They are checking that ship out now before we start the rendezvous maneuvers and start boarding." Now, I knew about that already, but it still didn't click. "The Security team is well trained in most things that have to do with ships in space. Pods are common out here, so they are trained on them just about as well as they are trained on using magnetic boots. We just gained 12 trained professionals that will be more than capable of helping with moving all the pods over."

Well shit, I hadn't thought of that. I knew they were well trained but hadn't thought of them doing tasks like moving pods and cargo over. I had assumed they would be mainly security making sure nothing would attack us and be prepared to fight back should something happen during the transition over to the Walrus.

"So, what am I supposed to do? Just sit in our room and wait until my babysitter of the day allows me to follow them aboard?"

"Exactly that Maggie. You can work on your studies and you can think about making better decisions that won't endanger your Father, the mission and yourself like the actions you took today."

With that she turned and walked towards the lift again. The door swung open and she stepped in turning back towards me.

"Unless you want to go up the chute to our deck, get on the elevator now."

I wanted to scream at her but once again I knew I was getting off much easier than I should be for what I really did. Instead of screaming I lowered my head and looked at the floor while stepping forward and onto the lift. I stood there next to my Mother as the lift rose ever so slightly gaining just enough elevation in comparison to the ship that we made it to the next floor above. The door opened and my Mother stepped out leading me to our room. Once inside, she tapped away on her tablet for a few moments, then motioned to my tablet. I passed it to her, and she proceeded to tap on that screen a few times also. Pleased with whatever she had done, she passed the tablet back to me.

"You are now officially restricted to communication with your Father and me only along with access to your school studies. Do not leave this room unless with one of us." Then an idea must have clicked in her head and she looked back down at her tablet punching away at buttons again. After maybe thirty more seconds of tapping she looked back up at me. "Now leaving this room isn't a choice. Since I don't know that I can trust you with even the most basic of options at this point, I have removed your authority to open any door on the ship. Effectively the ship believes you are confined to a pod. This room. There are food packs here in the room for when you get hungry."

With that my Mother turned and left closing the door behind her. When it clicked and I was finally alone I breathed a sigh of relief and tensed my hands in frustration at the same time. My Father knew the truth and was hiding something from me and my Mother in the least. Possibly hiding something from the whole crew. I couldn't be sure. What I did know was there was a recording on my tablet that I wanted to hear. Fortunately, my Mother had bought my story about the recording being on my Father's tablet, so she didn't look for anything on mine but at the same time I was locked out of that folder now that I was limited in my access. I hadn't thought to put that folder in with my schoolwork in case this had happened.

"AAAAAHHHHHH" I yelled out loud in frustration. "Shit, Shit, Shit".

Over the next several days, my parents held fast to my Mother's promise of not allowing me out of our quarters. I don't know what was said to anyone else aboard as they had to have noticed I was no longer moving about the ship during the course of the days. I never spoke to anyone much. There were hellos and nods as we passed here and there but as far as chatting about random things, that rarely happened. It was more interesting to find things to look at, things to read, things to learn. Now being confined to our shared room I was going a bit stir crazy. I had access to most any information I wanted on my tablet as I was able to quickly get my Mother to relent somewhat claiming that the web was vital to my studies as I needed to research things. Unless she wanted 20 calls a day asking for certain keywords to be unlocked then I needed access to the web.

What bugged me the most was that recording. I had expected my Father to come to me wanting to listen in on it since he had to know I had it. He never did and I dared not bring it up to him myself just in case he really didn't know. There was no way that would be the case though. Once again why would he have told my Mother what he did and then plant programs on his own tablet if he hadn't known what really happened. The thing that probably hurt me the most of all of this was that not only did he not bring up the recording with me, he didn't speak to me at all. The most I could get out of him was a simple look. He wouldn't say hello or goodbye. He wouldn't speak to me at all.

The third day of my incarceration was perhaps the worst of them all. We had detached from the station as planned and moved towards our rendezvous with the

Walrus. Connection had been made and the day of the move over I had been turned down when I offered to help with the pods. My Mother let me know simply that I had not finished my training and was not approved to touch a pod or anything else for that matter. So instead of helping, I sat in our room and listened to all the movement outside.

I could feel the rumblings from below decks when doors were opened, cargo decks went to vacuum and as the largest of the pallets were moved from ship to ship. As mass was transferred, I could feel shuddering run up the massive structure. I knew activity was frenzied outside my chamber, but I had no way to get in on the action without one of my parents releasing me. That was a far-fetched chance there. I doubt they even thought of me wrapped up in this room with nothing to do while they were out there guiding or taking part in the operation.

It took two days to move all the cargo and materials over from the crippled Expeditious to the much roomier Walrus. At the end of the first day, my Mother came and got me from our quarters. I had already packed all our personal gear into two bags that had been left for me that morning with a note attached to them. We each grabbed a weightless bag and moved out the doorway without a word. I knew we were moving to the Walrus now without her telling me. As we stepped onto the lift, I looked back and swept my eyes over the living area we had resided in for many weeks. This would be the last time I would see it. After all, here in a week or two the ship would start its dismantling, and no one would ever see it again.

Chapter Eight

"You can't keep me locked up forever Mother!"

I shouted at the woman who had been keeping me interned in my private room. It had been a week since we left the empty point in space where the contents of the doomed Expeditious were transferred to the Walrus we were on now. I could hear her footsteps clacking away quieter and quieter as she moved down the hallway away from my quarters.

"It's not fair! I cannot be kept alone in here! It is inhumane treatment! I demand a fair treatment instead of this disgusting display of overreaching one's authority! Just because I'm your kid doesn't mean I shouldn't receive at least equal treatment to a regular prisoner!"

There was no response from anyone. I know my statements were a bit overboard but that is what I was going for. All I had seen for the past week were these walls and the twice a day visit from my Mother when she brought me freeze dried portions of barely edible sustenance. I know I had stepped over a line, but solitary confinement was wildly over that same line. Beyond that even, was that I was now removed officially from my role on the ship. Not that there had been much of an official role before but at least I had been on the roster. That gave me the ability to move around the ship as I pleased. At least on decks that had been approved for me to be on in the first place.

My tablet was still locked down to where I could only see studies that had been assigned to me plus research resources pre-approved by my Mother and instructor. That was one of the most aggravating parts of this whole thing. I was expected to study up and take this opportunity to learn and grow as a person or at least that is what I had been told by the prison guard I had once known as my Mother. What company did I have to pass the days and help with my studies? A freaking teaching AI. We had these back on Earth too but only as a helping hand to aid human teachers. Now I was stuck alone with one full time.

Teaching AIs had been around for as long as I could remember, and they are helpful to an extent. They are smarter than a human teacher as all the information is locked in their artificial minds along with instantaneous access to all the information allowed by whatever governing body it was controlled by. What Teaching AI's were missing were two fundamental things.

The first was caring one damn bit about their charges. These systems were programmed to put forward a caring attitude in order to keep a child calm while going through difficult subjects. They had the end results of millennia worth of research built into them to aid in this portion. The problem was that no matter the amount of information an AI had built into it, it had no soul so to say. No thinking, creative mind. With all the improvements and advancements, it still wasn't even close to a true free conversation with a real person. It was only a machine with no real care in the world what occurred to it or anything else.

The second big thing was a physical form. The teaching AI's back on Earth as well as here on the ship with me now were built into our tablets as an avatar. The avatar was designed to have a human look and sound to it, but you knew deep in your mind that no matter how realistic, it wasn't real. It was a projection from a program some fat dude in his underwear coded while living in his parent's basement. At least that is what I envisioned. In reality, it was probably a well-educated group of professionals all working together in an office building collaborating and building truly marvelous programs. I know that but still doesn't make it any less creepy to me. This fake face trying to make me feel better.

So, for the past week I had been alone with this teaching AI aboard the ship. The thing drove me to learn and value the information I was presented with, but I couldn't care less. Sure, math and science I had no issues with. I had always taken to them with extreme ease that delighted my teachers. My parents were also happy, but I could tell that they expected it more than they were happy with it. I could see their point. Both of them were highly educated, successful people and beyond what I had known at the time, my Father was a planetary secret due to his intelligence and work. I mean hell, if my Father was the one to crack the secrets of and build a wormhole engine then I shouldn't have any issues with mathematical physics.

The true source of my aggravation with the planned course of study was history, economics and it hurt to even say it, psychology. Why should I care one damn bit about any of that?

History was a mess of assholes that just wanted their piece of the pie with little to no regard for human life or suffering. No regard for those that could not protect themselves. All the way from human to insect, no one seemed to care. Throughout history there were tyrants, kings, presidents, chancellors, prime ministers, Supreme Leaders, etc. I could find very few that ever showed any true care for anyone but themselves and their benefactors. Truly terrible people overall that did truly terrible things with their powers. Massacres on monumental scales. Destruction of the world through industry and war. People that would maintain power through threats, manipulation and money. I couldn't even believe much of the history I was given. Who knows what was correct and what was a fabrication or twisting of the truth by those that wrote the texts I now read? The victor writes the history after all. Those that died are not the ones who recorded history. Anything that was presented to me I had to automatically add several points of violence and disgrace to even think I may be close to the real truth.

Economics was a joke. Once again, a similar path alongside history appeared. Those with more money and more stuff were the same ones that ended up having the power and influence to impact history. The wealthy funded the power and they made sure to watch each other's backs. Additionally, what purpose would economics even have out here? We are flying around in a spaceship beyond the limits of where humans have travelled so far. IF we are able to jump through the great emptiness to another system with a habitable planet and are able to set up a new civilization, I can't see us having anything to do with money. It will all be what is best for the colony. What is best for the new human existence. We will be all together for one group under a leader. That is if we are able to jump at all. Who knows if that will work once we get out there to the edge of our system.

Now to my least favorite subject of them all. Psychology. This one I have to admit is probably useful at all times whether back on Earth or making sure people can deal with each other and the circumstance during a long voyage. My problem is that I just don't care. I hate having someone look at my mind. Leave my brain alone and let me be. There was a mandated yearly interview with a psychologist back on Earth.

That rule had been created decades before I was even born. Evidently back in the olden days, people ran around without ever having their minds checked on. They would go entire lives without ever having any doctor make sure their brain functioned normally. Even more people went to psychologists, but the findings were secret to all but the two involved. So many damaged people ran around popping medications that no one truly knew what they would do. Sometimes these people lead normal lives hiding their issues behind doors built upon pill bottles. Sometimes they would go insane. People who believed their minds were functioning perfectly could go insane. Some committed crimes thinking it was the right thing to do and some would commit suicide believing that end would be better for themselves and/or those around them.

Nowadays though, all people, at least all those that lived within our governed body, were required to visit a psychologist at least once per year for an interview. If the appointed professional would determine a mental health score and it would be reported up to the governing body called the Department of Health and Human Services. DHHS would then determine if that person was ok to continue their lives as currently lead or if they would be required to go through approved courses designed to correct whatever imbalance they saw. It was a feared appointment to many as if DHHS and their psychologists found something they did not like then you would be forced to go through whatever treatment they believed you needed regardless of your own personal desires. You could request a second opinion and be assigned to another psychologist but they were all trained by and approved by the same governing body so chances were the results would be the same. There was no refusal, you either followed the ruling or would be imprisoned and eventually expelled from the city if after a time you would not relent.

I heard many stories of families being taken apart because a certain member would be found abnormal in their mind. That would bring about a full review of the family unit to ensure the wrong thoughts did not infect other members of a household. You might ask how would the other civilians in your city allow such things to occur? Well, there were no protests against such things. That in itself would bring about a review of your own mind and family. Since the governing body ran the entire process from initial interview through reviews and "corrective plans" then it meant you would be openly accusing a group that had total control over your life of having total control over your life. Everyone knew what it was and also understood there really wasn't any way to fight it if you wanted to stay within the walls of our city.

I doubted my psychology program was anything more than a guideline of what would be expected from me as I went through life. The text showed what a normal mind should feel, should see, should expect from a full and productive existence in the civilization I was a part of. It told of problems in the mind that show up now and then and how those issues were corrected. Whether medicated or surgical. The whole process seemed frightening and angering at the same time to me. I dare not say it out loud but what right does any governing body have to direct my thoughts and feelings? Those are my own private things. Those are more private than anything else.

From the texts though there had been a massive decrease in the number of incidents stemming from believed instabilities of the mind whether that was true or not. Assuming they were accurate, you couldn't argue with the results. It may have been a major violation of one's privacy but in such times as we live in now, privacy and the rights of one person mattered little when put up against the welfare of an entire group. The days of personal rights and privacy had gone by the wayside along with most of the Earth's decadent green spaces that supported those lives. Once you reduce the regions capable of supporting life to the point where it no longer can do so, personal rights diminish to a point of being but a pin prick in the night sky.

I stepped back from the door that had been receiving a pounding from my bruised fist while also allowing my angry vocal cords to loosen and relax in my throat. There was no discussion of how long I was to be imprisoned here in this room and there had been no guidelines or a checklist that once completed would allow my release. I could live with a punishment, even a fairly harsh one such as this. The part that made my blood boil and my mind rush with thoughts of striking out violently was the pure unknown. It could be days, weeks, years until I was allowed to roam the ship again. This solitary life alone in my room here with little to do each day could not continue.

Maybe that is what they were waiting for. My Mother and Father. They wanted me to crash. They wanted me to breakdown and crack. They wanted to show me what would happen to me if I did something like I had done already and was caught by the authorities instead of by them alone. I had known what would happen to me though and I still did it because I wanted to know. I had needed to know what was truly going on behind closed doors. Back on Earth I may have been looking at a life with no real choices to make on my own but out here, leaving the grasp of the governing bodies behind, I was going to have control over my passage through time.

This imprisonment if anything has helped to strengthen my resolve to stop this mission. It is up to me alone at this point to pivot our current progress. Bring it to an abrupt end. I had believed that if my Father oversaw the mission then there was a chance that whatever we found out there would be safe. If we did find a world full of life and maybe even an intelligent civilization, we would not raze their world. We would monitor them sure, but we would protect them. I had no such trust in our species, but surely those that I had grown up with being my protectors would do the same for innocent life on another planet.

The past week however had shown me that at least my Mother would not care. If she was willing to lock her daughter away for causing no more than a simple nuisance then what would she be willing to look past on another world? My Father, the man who promised many years ago when I was but a little girl to protect me and support me always was allowing me to be locked away. He had the ultimate authority since this was a military backed and structured mission to release me without a hesitation, but he would not do it. The man I had trusted wholeheartedly was fine with keeping me imprisoned.

My resolve was hardened to the point now where I was ok with the death of either of them or both if it came to that. I may avoid it as much as possible if the opportunity arises but if unavoidable it would not cause a moment's hesitation from myself. What needed to be done would be done.

My own life however was still precious to me in that my path in time surely wasn't yet complete. Death was a black hole in my consciousness. A truly unknown end to a life that I didn't want to hand over yet. If it was a path to another world where I could continue on and grow while experiencing new trials and successes, then death would not concern me at all. If it was a place where I was to exist in perfect harmony with all that around me and be allowed all the possibilities of the universe then it seems I would quickly become bored with such an existence. That would still be preferable over my third option and still the most likely in my own mind. Nothingness. Nothingness as though I had never existed at all. I could not get past that bump in the road. If I was to die and drop into an abyss of which I could never climb out of or even know I was in. if I was to cease in my entirety then that destination was one I wanted to avoid for as long as possible.

I would work to end this mission still yet. I would find a way to stop it while doing what I could to protect my own fragile existence in this universe. At least until I could wrap my hand around something tangible on the other side.

Some days later I heard an unusual clacking on the floor outside my door. It sounded normal like they would any time someone walked up our hall. The sound wasn't the odd part. The timing. Mother wasn't due for my evening meal visit for hours yet. Then a knock came at my door. The knock reverberated around my room. The room that consisted of nothing more than a bed, the shower that was currently shut down due to a lack of gravity, a variable G toilet, my desk and that steel blockade to my escape. The door was solid. I had pounded on it for release not in the beginning and not in the past days but in the middle when I was angry to the point of disgrace. I had screamed and pounded like a wild animal attempting an escape of the live trap it had found itself in.

My tirades had become less pronounced and shorter lived since I had my epiphany. The cold decision to destroy the ship and my parents along with it if necessary. Since then I had calmed, realizing that my only escape from this trap was to fold into what they believed I should be. My act seemed to be working now. The knock that came now was softer than previous. The knock wasn't immediately followed by a simple passing through of more food packs as it had come to be the norm. From the other side of the still closed door came a softly spoken request.

"Maggie, are you doing ok in there?" It was my Father's voice coming through the closed door. He had not come to see me since we had moved to the Walrus that first day. Since this it had only been my Mother. "Maggie darling, are you up?"

Angrily I pushed back with my own much stronger voice before thinking, "Of course I am in here! Where else would a prisoner such as myself be!?" Then softer after catching myself and cooling my already once again hot temper, "Yes Father, I am in here. What brings you by? Been a while."

"Yes, yes it has been a while. Too long in fact. I am sorry I have not stopped in sooner, but things have been busy out here getting everything lined out."

"Of course, of course. I can understand how busy it must be out there in the world while I am locked away safely back here removed from it all." I spoke this last bit far more sarcastically than I had intended to. Really, how did he expect me to react to his sudden reappearance after so long though? Maybe eleven days doesn't seem like much but in near total isolation, it is a long time.

"Maggie, I am sorry you have been locked away but that is of your own doing. You know that. There was no way no punishment could befall you. Surely you didn't think that."

"No of course not Father. I expected punishment once I was caught. I did not however expect to be banished away from all others and left to bore my own mind out from the inside with my looping thoughts."

"Don't be so dramatic, you have not been completely alone, and you have had plenty to work on. Your schoolwork has been coming along nicely. I have been watching it daily."

"NOT ALONE!?!" I screamed this in complete disbelief. Then quieter, "Not Alone? Ha, that is quite a sad joke if it was meant to be one. How do you define alone if not by one's self with no other interactions?"

"Maggie, your Mother has been by and you have had your teacher to follow with."

"Mother? Mother has been by twice a day to deliver food to my door. She barely has said anything to me besides asking platonic questions such as how I am feeling. My Teacher? I have an AI. That is not interaction. That is a joke, a terrible attempt at duplicating humanity."

"Ok, I understand you are upset with me still. I can come back another time if you don't want to speak civilly to me now."

As desperate as I was to get rid of him and show the man how deep the hatred I had for him at the time was, I couldn't bear the thought of being alone again right now. If he went away, when would he return again? Would it be the next day or another week? Maybe another month? I couldn't know. There was no way to know. I had to keep him engaged.

"Every day you leave me here though is another day you go without the information you so crave. I know you want to know what happened after you left the room in your meeting."

A pause of silence drew long now. Did I overstep and go down the wrong rabbit hole? Did he already walk away? No, it couldn't be that as I hadn't heard his steps clanking away on the floor. The magnetic boots tapping along were a dead giveaway to someone coming and going. I waited a second more until he responded.

"What did you say?"

"You know what I said Father. I know you left your tablet on purpose. As angry as you act as though you are with me you knew what I had done before you even went into that meeting. You knew"

"That is nonsense Maggie, I am going to recommend an evaluation of your mind. You are obviously having nightmares that are bleeding over into your reality."

"Ha, you won't do that."

"Why wouldn't I Maggie?"

"You won't because you know that if you do, I will tell. All I have to do is open my mouth to Mother. Let her know what you did and what is still on my tablet. Yes, it is still there. She didn't erase anything and neither did I. The entire thing is still there."

His voice turned to acid, "Maggie, you have no right to threaten me. You are the one that hacked into my tablet and set it up to send you a recording of the meeting. You risked our entire mission, our family so that you could know what? What did you even learn? We shared all the information that was discussed in the meeting with the entire crew. There were no secrets."

"Of course, Father. There were no secrets while you were in there. It is what happened after you left that is of interest. At first, I questioned how you could have left your tablet in there but in the activity around the event I didn't have enough time to process it. Since I have been in this room though I have had time. All kinds of time. You knew I was listening in and you wanted to know what they would say once you left. That is why you left your tablet. So that I would have a recording for you to review later."

At that moment the door swung open and my Father stood there in the doorway with rage in his eyes. Rage but mixed with something else. Sorrow I thought. He is angry but immensely sad at the same time. This hurts him. Yes, he did use me to get what he wanted but only after I had injected myself into the situation to start with. Now I was attempting to blackmail him into my release. That made him angry with me. To do such a thing to one's Father was a horrid thing but to allow your daughter to be locked away while you carry some of the blame is an equally horrid thing.

Father took a deep breath after staring at me for a few moments and then asked calmly, "Do you still have the recording Maggie?"

"Of course, I do."

"What does it say? What happened after I left? I was able to get back in touch with the tablet before it was turned into the military intelligence guys. I knew that would be the General's first act. See what he could dig up on the tablet before giving it back."

"I don't know what it says dear old Dad. I hadn't had the chance to listen to it myself."

"What? If you haven't listened to it then how do you know what is on it if anything at all?"

"Well, I listened to it up until the point I had to run down to our meeting on the training deck of the Expeditious. At that point I had only gotten to when the General and the Station Commander got up to leave. I don't know if anything was said after that or not."

"I am surprised you have not listened to it since then." He looked at me puzzled while saying this. He must not know Mother had locked me out of my tablet. How would he not know that though?

"Well, it's a bit hard to listen to something while you are locked out of your own tablet. Mother blocked everything but school programs and limited pre-approved research topics."

"I know that Maggie, I had assumed you would just hack through that block. It isn't a very intricate wall. More of a roadblock, you just needed to jump the blockade and continue on."

I thought about that for a moment. Did I ever even attempt to get around her blockade? No, I didn't. At the time I had assumed it would alert my Mother and Father to any attempt to clear the block as soon as I started poking at it. After all, my Father would have been the one to create the block for my Mother to use right? Maybe not. Maybe she created it herself. If so, my Mother wasn't a very technologically advanced person so it wouldn't be complex. She knew her way around tech but was never a coder. I was suddenly angry at myself now. I never bothered to even look at it. Of course, even simpler, she probably just used some off the shelf parental control app to create the cordoned off area of my tablet.

A quick movement to my work desk and the tablet was in my hands with fingers clicking away. My Father looked on while I typed away on the screen. After no more than two minutes the block was still there but I had created a path around it effectively making it useless while leaving the block itself intact to keep my Mother from knowing it was defeated. I looked up and saw a fleeting grin on my Father's face. It quickly hardened back to an angry set, but I had caught it for a moment. He was proud of me defeating the firewall so easily.

"There it is." I announced as soon as I had the audio recording back up on the screen. Immediately my Father reached down and grabbed the tablet away. "Hey, what the hell?" I exclaimed surprised at his quick action.

Father put his hands up in front of him in a placating fashion. "Maggie, hold on. You are not going to listen in on this. I appreciate that you recorded it and the technological understanding that shows but you are still too young to get wrapped up so closely in things like these."

"Bullshit, you are not taking the very thing that I am in trouble for. I can still tell Mother what is really going on here." I crossed my arms at this and stood my ground. No way was he taking the recording I did all this to have and leaving me here in my cell to rot.

"I am taking it." Father continued through my outburst as he tapped away on the screen, "you will not listen to the recording and you will not be telling your Mother or anyone else for that matter anything." With this last part he looked up at me.

"Why wouldn't I tell her? Why should I keep any of this a secret?"

"You will not tell anyone for one because you have nothing to tell. She already knows you tried to listen in. She may not know that you had a recording still on your tablet, but she does already know you tried." Handing the tablet back to me he continued, "And because now you have no recording at all to show."

I looked down and sure enough where the file had been before was now blank. He had removed it. "What, why did you delete it? Now we won't ever know what was on the recording."

"I will know Maggie because now I have it. I didn't delete it. I only moved it from your tablet to my own. Not this one," he pointed to his own tablet protruding from a jacket pocket, "but my real tablet. The one I keep safe from any prying hands. Darling, you are going to learn over time to take precautions. You are going to play an important role in this group over time. You will lead it at some point in the future. Just not now. You are yet too young and too naïve for that to be now."

"I can still tell Mother. I can tell her you have another device somewhere on board too. She won't be happy about that."

"No, you won't. You will be too busy training to bring something as unimportant as that up."

I was truly puzzled now. "What are you talking about? I don't have any training scheduled other than the schoolwork I have assigned to me while interred here in this room."

"Once again you show your young mind Maggie. You need to think of an end and then determine the means to get you what you desire. I desire you to keep our little secret here," he tapped his faux tablet again, "between us. The means to get us to that end, that agreement is very simple the way I see it. You want out of this room and you want a place on this crew. I can make that happen."

I thought about it and this could be my ticket. It would require me to sell out to Father but with or without the recording, I could do no good trapped in this room through the end of our trip. If we made the jump while I was still locked away somewhere then I would lose. I needed to stop the ship before it jumped. What role could I have that would help me get to that end though?

"Ok, I do want out of the room and I do want a role aboard during the mission. I want you to put me back on the team that will be transferring pods once we reach the APEX out at Mars."

My Father looked almost disappointed in that request. He may think I was being too simple again, but I hadn't finished yet. "I can do that, consider yourself reinstated with that group. You will have to catch up some on training as the rest of the team is now experienced with an actual transfer."

"I will but first, I wasn't done yet with what I wanted out of our deal. I want to be on the pod team until we reach the APEX. Then I want to be trained as part of the flight team controlling the drones. I assume you will be using drones to place the magnetic field emitters."

"Why do you think we will need drones for that? It would be easier to just send people out on the ship before we take off?" Father was fishing, testing me I could tell. He knew exactly why he would be using drones but wanted to see how much I was picking up on. I can admit I was short sighted, and I will admit that was probably due more to my age and experience vs my brainpower. I could see this one though and he knew it.

"Well, we are far behind schedule already so you will want to get moving as soon as we reach the APEX. Also, the longer that ship sits there the longer it is a sitting duck for sabotage and/or attack. If you get it away from Mars and in open space on the way to the jump point, then attack is much less likely. The only thing you'll have to worry about after that is internal sabotage which is more and more unlikely the further out we are since the culprit would be condemning themselves to whatever fate comes to the ship. You can't send people out on the skin of the ship during transit as it poses too great a risk to them getting struck by stellar debris."

"Good Maggie, you are starting to pay attention. Yes, you are correct. We plan to use drones for equipment placement while in transit. This was going to be the process from the start though, not necessarily because of recent events. We accounted for the drone and equipment losses we are likely to incur going about it in this fashion. We have plenty of spares. While I cannot guarantee you a place on the drone team, I can promise you a shot at the drones. Your performance will then determine whether you make it on that team or not. You will not be put in place only because of who I am."

"I can accept that. I don't want your handout anyways, only a chance to prove my own ability."

Father looked at me one more time, pausing to take in the sight of his daughter I presumed. Either that or gauging if he believed I would keep his secret or spout off to Mother the moment he left the area. He eventually relented and turned to leave. "Maggie, consider yourself reinstated. I cannot stress this enough though. Pull something like you did before again and it will be the last shot you have in any official capacity. One more incident and you will be put back in a pod against your will if need be and put back to sleep for the duration of our trip. You will only be reawakened after we get to our destination and have a colony set up." With that he walked off down the hall clanking along.

I stood there expecting the door to swing shut when he walked away locking itself back like it had done each time my Mother had left. It didn't though. The door stood open. Moments later my tablet beeped and when I looked at it, all indications of a blocking program were gone. Cleared. I grabbed it and poked around on the screen seeing what I had access to. Everything, nothing I could find was blocked anymore. There were things I could not get into on the ship but that was the same as before my imprisonment. Almost immediately I received a notification from my Mother requesting me to meet her on the training deck for afternoon pod movements. Reading through the message I saw that she was going to be my instructor. Dr. Franco must be busy now on other things and since my Mother was fully trained now, she could teach me. I had no interest in going to see her yet but didn't really have a choice either. It was going to have to happen at some point. Might as well be now.

The Walrus was similar in design to the Expeditious. This made sense as both were cargo carriers. The biggest difference was the Walrus was much, much larger. Where the Expeditious was about 100 feet across and 500 feet long from tip to engines, the Walrus was nearly 500 feet across and 1000 feet long from tip to engines. The layout was similar with the foremost sections narrowing to a near point. Although there was no air in space to worry about pushing through, most ships were still designed in a conical shape due to debris contact. It was much easier to deflect speeding debris if you struck it at an angle. A large, flat nose on a ship would increase the likelihood of a direct strike that could cause serious damage. Hitting debris with an angled nose deflected most of the energy away from the ship bringing the thickness of protective armor plating needed down significantly.

Since the ships were so similar, I didn't have a hard time at all finding my way along the corridors. The residential deck was much larger to accommodate the normally much larger crew flying the ship on longer voyages between planetary bodies. I was back off a long corridor that put my room mostly by itself in comparison to the other rooms on this level. I went to what I believed was the center of the ship and found the usual main column through the core of the beast from front to rear or top to bottom however you wanted to look at it. Just like the Expeditious, the Walrus's decks were positioned so the cone of the ship could be considered the front or "above" you when you walked around with magnetics. This was so that during acceleration and deceleration the crew would experience the sense of gravity for a few hours. This would allow limited showers and pleasant walks without the bulky boots we had to wear otherwise to keep our feet planted to the floor.

As expected, there at the center core was an elevator. Only here, there were three elevators once again showing that the ship was designed for more active crew members at any given time. I grabbed the first one to open upon my summons and climbed in. Down into the belly of this new ship I dropped. Mother had messaged me that the training deck on this ship was also on level twelve. As the elevator dropped, I pulled my tablet out and looked at the overview schematics of the ship. It appeared when all the cargo and pods were moved over, they put everything back on the same level as it had been on the Expeditious. I would image that was just for ease of transfer. This ship had matching doors and matching levels so it would have been easiest to just line up the two ships and move all the cargo straight over.

The only difference in the layout of existing decks from the Expeditious was there only being one medical deck now instead of a sub deck also. Due to the large size of the ship, it appeared that medical now fit on one level eliminating the need to set up a half deck. That would make things easier as far as working with the pods. No more running those up and down the sub lift that went from the old main floor to the half deck above on the Walrus. Then of course many more decks that were unused at the moment. There were no labels on those decks, and I could not choose them to see the various camera feeds that were throughout the ship.

Soon enough, I felt my momentum change and some pressure was put on my feet as the lift slowed and stopped on Deck twelve. The door swung open before I had a chance to swipe my arm. This was a newer ship, so it was probably a bit smarter in the internal systems. The ship AI knew I was the only one on the lift and that I had approval to enter this area, so it didn't bother with formalities of swiping my arm. While I was standing there with my arm hovering in open air where a scanner would have normally been, I saw the stern, pinched face of my Mother. She really shouldn't hold that position for too long. It aged her many years with the wrinkles forming on her forehead and creases permeating outwards around her lips. I smiled a bit sheepishly and lowered my arm.

"You don't need to bother swiping your arm on this ship." My Mother started without a bit of a welcome or happy to see you coming from her. "The Walrus is more advanced than the Expeditious was. This ship always tracks all personnel on board. It will allow the lifts and doors to operate only for those that are allowed access at that point in time. No ID tag needed. The ship AI knows who you are and knows what you are allowed to do."

"Well, that's kind of creepy" I blurted without really thinking.

"You can head back up to your room if you don't like it." Mother said while shrugging back to me.

"I'd rather not. Been a prisoner up there for long enough. I'd bet the ship was watching me in there too. Now I just know about it."

"Maggie, you have not been a prisoner for the 50th time. You were grounded on a spaceship. What do you expect to happen on a mission like this? You had access to everything you needed. If you wanted freedom to move, then you shouldn't have broken the very most important rule there is."

"Ok, I hear you Mother. I screwed up. I get that. I shouldn't have eavesdropped on classified meetings. I should have just trusted you and Father. Can we move past this?"

"No, we cannot just move past this. The fact that you think this was a violation that we can just move past proves to me that you still do not understand exactly what you risked. What you violated in acting as you did. Eventually, hopefully we can put this behind us, but it will take time. Time to rebuild trust."

"What do you want me to do then?" I was getting angry again. I knew I screwed up but what good was going around and round about that going to do for us?

"Since your Father allowed you to leave the room and put you back on the roster, I guess what I want you to do is moot at this point."

"So, you didn't want me to get out? How long did you want me to stay in my room? How was I supposed to do anything to move past this if I was just locked in my room forever?"

"No, I wasn't ready for you to be out again. You needed to understand what you had done and what you had risked. I don't think that letting you galivant around the ship is going to allow that to happen. You will try to 'move past this' and forget it happened while not facing what you did. This allows to you make the same or similar mistake again later. The next time you may not be so lucky and get caught by someone other than your Father and I."

"Do I need to just go find something else to do?" I asked this truly wondering. If she couldn't let this go, then what was the point in me being down here. I could get off the pod crew and go do something else now instead of wasting my time.

"That is up to you Maggie. What I can tell you is that I don't trust you and I won't for some time. You are at the level of a recruit to me. No, lower than that since a recruit would start with an empty slate. You don't have an empty slate. Stay or leave I don't care. If you stay, you are a trainee and not my daughter. I won't take it easy on you just because of your last name."

This was a totally new person standing in front of me. My Mother had changed so much in the past couple weeks. She had always been a soft and caring person. Sure, there may be times that I was in trouble and received a stern talk but nothing like this. She didn't want me anywhere near her or the medical pods. It amazed me how she could knock me down and keep kicking with no regard to how much it hurt at all. I knew my parents were pissed at me but really all I did was eavesdrop a bit. If she acted this harsh on such a minor thing then maybe she wasn't the person I thought, she was. You know what though, I wasn't going to let this hurt me. I could block her out as a Mother and focus only as her being my trainer. After all, I needed this free access to the ship again. I squared my shoulders and replied with authority.

"Mrs. Johanson, I am electing to stay and train as I told my superior officer I would do. This is the assignment I have, and this is the assignment I will complete to the best of my abilities."

"So be it" My Mother, no, my instructor replied. She then turned and walked away. I assumed she intended for me to follow so I stepped forward and deeper into the training deck.

Two hours later I was exhausted, bruised and beat up. That was by far much worse than Dr. Franco ever pushed us before. I knew Mother was just trying to break me, but I wasn't going to allow it. After a quick review of what we had covered previous to my imprisonment she started throwing every disaster scenario at me she had at her disposal. The training deck on this ship was much better set up than what we had improvised on the Expeditious.

The Walrus had a full VR setup. We used real physical pods and temporary walls that could be moved around and snapped into place like before, but these walls were much more adjustable. Add in the VR helmet and body suit I wore and the scenarios I had to battle with were so much more realistic. It was incredible if you could push aside the pain.

The body suit added to the whole environment because Mother could use it to add in ship spins and violent shakes. The suit was connected to the ceiling with a giant arm that would suddenly spin me one way or another imitating what it would be like to have the ship rip out from under you one second and slam back into you again the next. Boots could only grip so well with their limited magnetics. They were designed to keep us latched down to the floor but were purposefully kept on the weak side so that you couldn't have your feet ripped from your body in a crisis situation. You could temporarily lock the boots down hard but that was something that took a second or two to activate, not immediate enough to activate before being thrown for a loop.

As soon as this training session was completed, Mother told me that I was to go for dinner and then return to my room. Even if Father had allowed me to rejoin the crew roster my crimes had not yet been paid for, so I was on lockdown unless at meals or in training. I wanted to push back but was too tired from training to really argue. To be honest all I wanted to do right then was eat and pass out in my bed. I nodded to her and agreed. I could tell she was somewhat surprised I hadn't battled back on her any for this ruling, but she quickly shook the look and turned walking away deeper towards a line of doors on one wall. I didn't know exactly where those doors led but I figured it was to some offices for this deck.

I spun on my aching feet and went for the lift. Back up above on the residential deck, I found my way to the mess hall. Since we were done accelerating and in zero G there was little on the menu beyond what I already had in my room. At least I learned my Mother hadn't been holding out the good stuff as part of my punishment. I found a bag of freeze-dried apple chips along with a sandwich and drink pouch and found an empty table to eat at. There were a dozen tables in here and most were empty. Even though we were on a bigger ship now that could handle many more active crew, it evidently had been determined not to wake anyone else until needed later on. All the faces I saw around me were people I recognized from the Expeditious. I didn't even see any of the extra military people around that I had expected to find.

Back in my room after eating, I remembered those first few days when we had first taken off and had enough acceleration to imitate some gravity. The showers had been active for nearly 2 days while we accelerated away from the old broken ship we had started out on. It had been wonderful being able to take a real cleansing shower. That was one of the only things that kept me from going a bit nutty earlier on in my imprisonment. Now I was back to my somewhat damp rag and dry soap. Ugh. I tended to the few cuts and scrapes I had managed to get while pushing pods around in my Mother's torture chamber and got in bed. Sleep came quickly before I realized it. The tablet I had been using when I dozed off into slumber drifted away from me as my fingers tightened slightly in response to a dream, I was already deep into.

The next few weeks were mostly training. Personally, I believe I was pushed far harder than need be during the training. Mother told me that when we started training before it was for pod movements only and only rushed like it was because of our timeline. Since we had more of that ever-desired commodity this time before we reached Mars and the APEX, we were going to take our time and train on all aspects of the pods.

This consisted of the first week being nearly all pod movements. More problems and glitches that I had to contend with while safely getting my charges from the Walrus on to the APEX. The plan was to dock with the station at Mars and use it as the path between the two ships. Our now beloved Walrus was able to attach direct to the old dead Expeditious because those two ships were so close in design and meant to dock together. The APEX was a super freighter in base design but I was told that it had been so highly modified through the years that even though it still held the core shape, extrusions from its skin made it impossible for a ship to pull alongside and connect.

Since they would not directly mesh, the two ships needed a go-between. Here fit the station at Mars. It was purpose built for the project Father had been spearheading for so many years. On the main arm that the APEX held onto, there were fifty cargo doors that all meshed up to doors along the side of the APEX. Those doors lined up for the most part, but the bulk of the Walrus couldn't snuggle up close enough to the APEX to reach them. The station was acting as an extension between the matching doors. The deck that was Medical on our Walrus and the deck that was to be medical on the APEX would connect via this extension off the station. We would have to leave the cargo door on the Walrus and turn. Then head down a short corridor and turn back towards the APEX again. The whole path was nearly seventy yards. So that is what we trained on. Back and forth, back and forth.

After the first week of constant pod movements and throbbing pains from the stresses of such training, we moved on to a classroom study for a week. I am sure during a normal process this section would have come along first since most of the material was utilized during our pod movements but Mother must have wanted to punish me as much as she could and try to force me into quitting so she pushed the physically demanding portions first. The book work covered controls on the pods, how to monitor life support, how to diagnose simple glitches and how to decant a resident from a pod if need be. No hands-on experience was gained during this week.

The third week was all hands on with the pods again but with very little pod movements. It entailed all the ins and outs of pod maintenance and repair. This was aimed more towards serious mechanical issues that could come up in the general day to day activities surrounding a pod. Interface boards fried; coolant systems deactivated. Power generation broke off requiring the backup power modules to kick in and save the day. Sometimes those failed and you had to diagnose the problem and get a secondary backup system connected and online within minutes or risk losing the occupant. I loved this week. I was always mechanically inclined and enjoyed the AI tinkering that went along with it.

There was even one training scenario where the AI was hit with a directed EMP from somewhere unknown. The backup module I snagged and tried had suffered a similar fate. The AI on the backup was still intact but had suffered a failure in the portion of its mind that controlled the oxygen balancing equipment aboard the pod. Everything else worked except the oxygen balancing portion. I was able to reprogram the AI to split another segment of its mind between Oxygen balancing and waste recycling. Neither function was incredibly demanding so it could operate both with one processor. The problem was that the processor I was partially hijacking operated through another port in the pod so I had to quickly build a jumper that would take signals across from the bad port to the newly redirected port.

In the end I was able to get the whole system to function correctly again and did it within five minutes. When I finished, I turned to my instructor and expected a nod and quick check mark on her tablet to record my satisfactory score. Instead I received a look of shock. Mother hadn't said anything for several seconds in which I was racking my brain trying to figure out what I had done wrong. From around a temporary wall came another woman who I knew quite well.

"Well done Maggie. Well done indeed. Barbara, where have you been hiding this exemplary trainee?" Dr. Franco kept looking right at me as she asked my Mother. "Maybe I am mistaken but wasn't that the special scenario we came up with to see how trainees dealt with defeat?"

My Mother still flabbergasted answered while looking at her tablet checking something I couldn't see. "Yes. Yes, it was. That was - unexpected."

"No, not really. Correct we did not expect anyone to complete it, but we also didn't expect your daughter to run any more scenarios after she was pulled from our training group back near Earth. I wish I understood why that was done by the way. From this performance alone I can see that she would have been a valuable member of our team at the time."

"I - I know you were taken aback by her sudden removal and containment, but it was for good reason. Direct from the Commander himself. If you ne-."

"No, Barbara no," the Doctor broke in mid-sentence stopping my Mother as she began to wind up a bit. "I was not questioning why you two did what you did. I mean I was, but I wasn't questioning your decision. I just wish I knew what had caused you two to pull such a promising trainee off the team just before we really needed her. I don't mean to interfere. I am sure you had your reasons. I am sure they were justified. It just puzzles me. Can we expect to keep her on this time around though?"

"Well Evelen, that will be up to her." My Mother said this pointing back towards me while looking me dead in the eyes. "She will be a member of this team for as long as she decides it is important enough to her. As long as that desire is strong enough to stay ahead of any other goals she may have in mind."

I wasn't sure what to say to that. Of course, I wanted to stay on the team, I was enjoying myself. I wasn't sure what the big deal was about the scenario that was just completed.

"I plan on staying on the team of course. At least through the exchange at Mars. After that there is talk that a spot may open up with the drone team."

Dr. Franco looked a bit saddened by that last statement and my Mother kept her eyes on me. Surely she had known about that plan. I hadn't told her, but I hadn't spoken to her much outside of just training information for the past few weeks. We had played the part of trainer and trainee. Nothing else.

"Father and I had spoken before that I would learn the pod work until we completed the transfer at Mars. Then you won't need as many people on that task, so I was going to move to drones. It's not like I won't help with pods again after that, but I wanted to keep expanding my knowledge and try different things."

"I understand that Maggie," Dr. Franco responded kindly. "I can't refuse being a bit saddened by your eventual exit from our team but you need to experience as many positions as you can early on so you can find which fits you the best before dedicating yourself to one thing or the other. I appreciate you being open to helping us further in the future if the need arises though."

"Thank you, Dr. Franco. Now what I don't understand is why are you both so shocked about this scenario? It seemed pretty obvious what the fix was to me."

Dr. Franco laughed out loud and a long missing grin grew across my Mothers face even while she tried to push it away. Franco was the first to speak. "Oh Maggie, that scenario was designed by both your Mother and me to stump our trainees. It is meant to be impossible. It was meant to push the trainees to the breaking point to see if they could handle having to walk away from a patient before endangering the mission overall. That didn't quite work out though since you beat it. You found a clever way around that actually worked."

The Doctor walked up to me and gave me a squeeze on my shoulders. "This shows that you are meant for great things young lady. If you keep your head on straight you will be a game changer like your Mother and Father both. Go explore different processes around the ship. Do your drone training. I don't think you will stay there either though."

"Where do you think I will end up?" I asked her really wanting an answer as I still had no idea.

"Oh, I don't have a clue. That isn't for me to decide anyways. We aren't on Earth anymore. We won't tell you what you must do out here. You need to figure that out. Wherever you do end up though, you will make an amazing impact. I am already a bit jealous of that team. Whichever one it is."

With that Dr. Franco walked away back where she had come from around the wall. I didn't follow her, but I did wonder what was back there. From behind me I heard another voice, "So that's how you were able to hack your Father's tablet. You know how to program an AI? When did you learn that?"

I was a bit stumped at first since that isn't what I did. I mean I guess I kind of did but not really. "I didn't reprogram the AI. I only asked it if it could work both systems through the same port. The AI let me know it could so I made the connections it would need. Really I was just the electrician that made the connections needed."

"But how did you think of that as a solution? We have trained two dozen others through this same scenario and every one of them has failed. Not you though."

"I don't know, it just seemed obvious to me like I said before."

"Well, I have to admit that was a good job. Go ahead and take the rest of the afternoon off. You deserve it. We are basically done with training. Take tomorrow off also, the day after we will start as a group. You have caught completely up to the rest of the team over the past three weeks. We are one week out from Mars and the APEX. We will push as a team for the final group trainings over the next week until we arrive. Then the big day will be upon us."

"Thanks. I could use a bit of rest to be honest with you. We have been pushing hard."

"We sure have. You have proven yourself though. I only hope you continue to prove yourself. We are close honey, very close but the bridge between us is still fragile. Please don't take it back down. I am almost there."

With that she turned and walked away. As she did most days, she walked across the open training deck to a door in the wall where I assumed her office was. The classroom we had used while I was doing book work was through one of the doors but never the one she used at the end of the day. The door we went through led to a stark white classroom similar to how the research deck had looked back on the Expeditious. I assumed the research deck looked the same on this ship but so far, the only decks I had seen were the residential and this training deck. I had not tried any others yet since I knew my footing was light still. Anyways, I doubted I had the clearance required so why bother pushing my luck. I still had plans but also knew I had to play as part of the team or there would never be an opportunity shown to me to complete my personal mission.

Our final week of training went without a hitch. I stayed the course and worked feverishly to make sure I finished out as high up in the standings I could in my class. There were thirteen of us total in the class but it was announced we would only need eight to move the pods in the same time frame as the cargo was expected to take. Dr. Franco had left my mother in charge of this project while she worked on other things so it would be up to her who was on the team and who would be held back as substitutes. The subs wouldn't get a vacation though, they would be helping move cargo instead. Pod movement was considered a higher-ranking position than cargo moving even though the actual work was nearly identical. The only real difference was that the regular cargo may get damaged if they screwed something up, but our cargo could die if we did something wrong. We were required to have so much extra training and pass exams because if something went wrong in the process of moving the pods it would be up to us to save the colonist inside.

Finally, two days out from the Mars station the ship started to fire boosters to slow our rate of approach. This was time for celebration across the ship as we regained a semblance of gravity again. Although it wasn't really gravity but just a change in inertia, we still called it gravity as that is what it felt like. Not full on gravity as on Earth but when you have been out in space for Months, it nearly felt like that. Even with our required daily exercises and medications to prevent muscle atrophy, it still happened. If we were to land back on Earth right now, it would take weeks to regain what we had lost and feel normal again.

Anyways, we were two days out from Mars and with the ship decelerating we had gravity again. That meant liquid systems aboard would be unlocked which included real normal toilets. Those were such a wondrous thing. The pleasure of just sitting down and doing your thing without suction systems and straps holding you down is amazing. Don't even mention the showers we were able to take. I don't care how well you wash with those damn damp towels and dry soaps; you don't get clean like you do with a shower.

These events are so popular with our mostly ground based crew that schedules had to be created and policed so the ship could even keep up with the sudden demand on systems not normally used. I was able to get two fifteen-minute showers. One each day during our deceleration. It was amazing. I did get the short end of the straw on both being the most junior active crew member as I was scheduled in the middle of the night, but I didn't care. The alarm that woke me was welcomed. The first night I hadn't even been able to sleep waiting for my slot to open up. I tell you though, I slept well afterwards.

The end of the final day of approach was when Mother announced who would be joining the select team. I knew I was going to be chosen and Mother had warned me to not be too outwardly excited and jubilant about it. Everyone in the training group knew I deserved to be on the team as I had put in the most hours and scored the highest scores but there was still a tinge of ill will towards me. After all, I was younger than was allowed by policy to even be active on a team and that was looked over because I was the Commander's daughter. It was obvious that I had every ability to do the job and do it better than anyone else but that didn't help people that believed there was favoritism going on. Fortunately, I had enough supporters that no one would openly say or do anything against me.

When the announcements came, I was on the team as expected along with seven of the best people in our group. My Mother sent the other five to another group that was preparing for the cargo transfers. Each deck would get a team of ten to twelve people to work the transfer. More had been awakened from pods to fill any empty spots we had. They were all trained ahead of time on cargo moving so they didn't have to get woken ahead of time a great deal. It was a good thing too because even being on this bigger ship, it still held many more people than it was designed to support. The oxygen systems had been working to build up a slight excess of oxygen over the past week and were cranked up to maximum now. Even with all that, we could only maintain this number of active people up and moving for four days. That would be plenty of time as we were only supposed to be at Mars for two days total, but it still made everyone a bit nervous.

My new team started prepping the medical deck for transfers to begin the next morning. We went through and assigned each team member an area of the deck to take care of. We checked over each pod completely. Every single pod was unplugged from its base and put on backup internal power to make sure it was working as planned. Out of all the pods we had to move, only two failed this test. Quick swaps with extra power cells fixed those issues. Each pod was also undocked from the floor clamps and then relocked to make sure those mechanisms hadn't seized up on our flight out here. No failures there, a couple needed a shot of heavy grease to the mechanism, but none failed to disconnect.

The final check was to make sure all pods were accounted for properly. We checked our lists and then the lists of two of our team-mates so that each group was checked over three times total. Each of us were also assigned a dozen empty pods to transfer over in addition to our occupied pods. These would be for any pod failures or if we needed to put more crew to sleep once we were all packed into the APEX. Once our checks were done, we all went back to the residential deck and joined in with every other active member aboard the ship. Everyone came, even the on-duty flight crew joined us. The ship was now in a safe orbit around Mars, so the ship AI was handling maintaining our position. If anything went wrong, it would notify the crew along with my Father and within thirty seconds they could be back on the command deck ready to deal with anything.

All personnel found seats either at the normal tables or the sporadically positioned chairs around the room. This would be the final time we were all on the ship in a group. After this we would all disperse and not see each other again as a group likely until we made it to our destination. As soon as everything was moved to the APEX and systems there were fired up, half our active crew would go to sleep again to save load on the life support systems aboard. My Father was the only one who was not sitting or even trying to find a spot. Mother and I hadn't even bothered saving him a spot as we knew he wouldn't sit. He wasn't the type to have a quiet dinner with us when everyone was here. He would float around here and there talking to each crew member one on one. He really was a great Commander and loved by the crew. Our crew at least.

The military contingent was less accepting I could tell. They were not mean or standoffish but there was a different demeanor there between Father and them and the General and them. They followed the General first. Although I had noticed in the last few weeks as I walked down the corridors or rode the lifts and ran across our military friends that they gravitated towards the woman officer that was with the group.

What was her name again?

I couldn't remember but I did remember she was a Major and served under the General. I figured that was just because the General was probably too highly ranked to get down in the trenches with the soldiers, but the Major made sure to be there with them. Appropriate full support and allegiance to the General was obvious but I had caught them in smaller groups from time to time and when they were with the Major, they all laughed and smiled more. With the General they were serious, professional but when with the Major, they were more comfortable, relaxed. From my nonmilitary standpoint it appeared they all like the Major more. I doubted it hurt that she was an absolutely gorgeous woman. Beautiful, intelligent and powerful all together in one package. There was no way the soldiers didn't have a thing for her. I even caught myself taking a second look once.

Sitting there reviewing my memories I realized that we were missing someone. She wasn't here, at least I couldn't find her in the crowd. We were up to about fifty people awake right now so it wasn't a crowd so thick you could get lost in it. I knew every face here. There was one that wasn't in view though. I searched around behind me, but I was backed up against a wall. The Major wasn't here yet.

"Everyone, if we could. I would like to mention a few things before we start to destroy this wonderful meal laid out before us." My Father had stood up where we now considered the front of the room. There wasn't really a real front or back but since he was speaking, and he was the Commander, that became the front now. "I think we are all here now." He looked around through the crowd while saying that, then continued. "Yes, I think I see everyone, wait. No, I do think we are missing one."

Everyone started looking around at their neighbors trying to figure out who was missing. Father leaned down and whispered in the General's ear who was sitting next to Father's improvised podium. The General looked around briefly and then to his tablet punching a few buttons. At that point the lift door opened and out stepped our missing military officer.

"Don't mind me everyone," The Major said upon seeing all eyes turned to her. "I just couldn't get myself out of the shower. I used every second of that fifteen minutes. After all, we won't have another chance for at least a few days until we are accelerating away in the APEX."

"No problem Major Bonnette." My Father said with a smile on his face. He had to say this through the cheers that raised up here and there around the room. Evidently people all over the ship felt the same way I did about the marvelous luxuries we had gotten to indulge in on for the last couple days. "I believe that was the last one as we will be dropping our final bit of momentum here if a few hours. At that time all liquid water systems aboard the Walrus will be shut down until further notice and we will return to true zero G. Speaking of which, let me make these announcements quickly so that we can all eat before that happens as tonight's dinner also won't be possible here in a few hours once we reach that line." As he said that last part, he motioned towards the buffet tables that had been set out but were still covered. When he motioned though, the lids pulled back revealing what I assumed was a full menu of items.

I wasn't looking at the buffet though. My eyes were still lingering on the Major. Something about her was off but I couldn't place it. It was more of a feeling than a definitive issue I took with her appearance. Yes, it could have been true that she had been taking a shower but that wouldn't have made her late. I had helped create the schedule itself a week or so ago before we started slowing. I didn't schedule the names, but Dr. Franco had requested that my Mother handle scheduling. Being the suck-up I was here lately trying to get back on her good side, I had volunteered myself to create the base schedule in the system so she would just have to fill in the names.

There was one thing though, the schedule had specifically followed a certain timing structure. I had set it up so that on the hour and at half past the hour, shower cycles would start. Each cycle was for fifteen minutes max. The system would cut water a quarter after the hour and a quarter till the next hour automatically if not shut off before-hand. That allowed the system to do a self-wash on the stall which took five minutes and then a regeneration filtering cycle on the water which took ten minutes. Problem was that the meeting we were starting now was booked to start at 1700 hrs. That means that last shower would have cut off automatically at 1645 hrs. Fifteen minutes was far more than any member of our crew needed to dry off, get dressed and get to the dinner.

Father continued talking but I wasn't listening in the least. I took my issue with her location further. I mean sure I guess she could have taken more time than normal to get prepped after her shower and get here late but the other issue I brought up in my mind now was where she came from. The shower stalls were on this level. On the residential deck. She had come from the lift. That didn't make any sense. If she had taken a shower, then she would have come from behind the center core that housed the lifts. Not from a lift itself. Maybe I was thinking too deeply into this. What else could she have been doing if not taking a shower. Why would she lie about what she was doing? Realizing I was still staring at her, I refocused and froze. She was staring right back at me now. Her golden eyes boring into mine. Thinking quickly, I shook my head as if I had only zoned out for a bit and shifted my gaze back to my Father who was still speaking.

From the corner of my eye I kept looking towards the Major trying to see if she bought my fake look away. I could see here face still turned towards my own in my peripheral, but I couldn't tell if she was still looking at me or just in my direction. I dared not look back towards her. I forced myself to listen back into what Father was saying. You never know, there might be something important in there.

"- team will start boarding the station at 0900hrs tomorrow. They will go though the arm we are connecting to and check all cargo door seals. Since we are completing our trip on the Walrus, our doors should seal up well. The doors on this station were designed to mesh with ours but when we were rushed off Earth on the Expeditious, they started modifying them to fit that ship instead. That ship's doors open differently than this ship so that the two could mesh together. That means that both doors are different and won't both mesh to the station. Since we are on the Walrus now though, the crew aboard the station has been hard at work undoing the modifications they had done in preparation. All work has been completed and checked but we need to recheck once more before letting loose on all the doors just in case anything was missed."

He kept going but good grief there was no way I could keep listening. My Father was a great Commander and scientist, but he had a bad habit of rambling on about things for hours. He was so intrigued by every little bit of information and could get derailed from a thought easily. Not that I am at all like him, but my mind began to wander again.

Where could the Major had been? Really that was silly to ask because she could have literally been anywhere aboard the ship. The lift she had gotten out of ran the full length of the ship. I assumed being military, she would have access to all decks too so that didn't cut down the possibilities. Most likely she had been on the command deck checking on things or maybe the deck we had reserved for the military segment. They needed ongoing training to keep their skills sharp but needing to run weapons training, they couldn't share our general training deck. I wasn't sure which level was theirs but somewhere down in the center of the mostly empty ship they had a deck or two just for them to train in. It wasn't like we were short on space, hell, they could have had a dozen decks down there for all I knew.

Back to my Father now I tried to refocus. "So, to recap before we all dig into this feast, I know I am torturing you all in keeping you from, docking with the station is planned for 0815hrs tomorrow. The station crew will check all locks and give us the go ahead for our advance team to disembark at 0900hrs. Once all seals are again checked and given the ok, we will open all cargo doors and start the transfer. I hope to have transfer started by 1000hrs but that may vary based on what the advance team finds. We will work on the transfer for twelve hours regardless of when we start. By the end of that shift we should be approximately half-way transferred. We will close up all cargo doors and reseal both ships for the overnight shift.

No movements will happen until 0800hrs again the next day. Similar process. Advance team will check all seals and once giving the go ahead we will open all cargo doors and run until the full contents of the Walrus are aboard the APEX and locked in. We will plan to disconnect from the station and disembark on the APEX by June 15th at 0800 hours. That gives us just shy of 48 hours to move all cargo over in two shifts. If you have any questions about the timelines, please get with your team leads. If team leads have any questions, please get with the member of command staff you have been assigned to. If for some reason you cannot get with them or still have an issue, please contact me directly.

Ok everyone, I am done here. Please go eat and eat well. The next two days are going to be beyond hectic."

With that Father stepped down from his podium and waved to everyone again for them to get up and go grab food. I held back though. The late arrival of our friendly neighborhood Major bothered me for some reason. Sure, she had several legitimate reasons for being a bit late but the one she gave didn't make sense and made me wonder why she would give that an the answer. Unless that was some kind of code to my Father and the General that was not meant for the rest of us.

Oh shit, of course. That was it. That had to be it. She was working on something, probably a security check with everyone being in here together. They didn't want to cause anyone to be worried about such a check and didn't want to tip anyone off if they were guilty of anything aboard, so they had worked out the code ahead of time. That must be it. I still had issue with why my Father would have called her out if it was to keep everyone in the dark but that may have been an honest mistake or part of the whole story. If she was going to be noticed arriving late, make sure it is noticed and addressed so any questions later would be easy to cover. Surely if timelines didn't mesh up then Father and the General would have noticed also. I wouldn't be the only one.

I glanced back towards the Major, but she wasn't there. I looked around the room and noticed her up in the growing food line. She was grinning while speaking to a technician that was ahead of her in line. Perfectly normal and part of the group. I needed to relax. My mind could get me in trouble sometimes.

"Maggie, honey, are you coming?" It was Mother, she was standing next to me now offering an extended hand to me as though I needed help getting up. I was a bit annoyed by that, no help was needed for me to get up, I had just been thinking but I let it pass. It would do me no good to show my annoyance to her now.

"Yea, sorry, just daydreaming. A bit nervous about tomorrow I guess so my mind is all over the place." I stood using her hand only enough to appease her offer of help. She looked at me a bit closer but appeared to accept my answer as she started to walk away toward the line.

"Well come on then. I don't want to be the last person in line. There might not be much left, do you want to get left out and stuck with another ration pack?"

I knew I didn't want that, I hurried to catch up to her and get in to line. In the end there was plenty of food for everyone. It was a good thing since there may have been a mutiny on my Father's hands if we had run out prematurely. Dinner went well and I was able to keep my head in the present and not off on wild good chases trying to track people's positions in this mission of ours. I didn't know what my Father and his military friends/adversaries had going on, so it was of no use for me to try and guess. I ate a full plate and then a second. By the end of that second plate, I was bursting and knew if I had any hope of being useful on our first day of transfers then it was time to call it a night. We were nearing zero hour for our deceleration anyways. Soon Father would have to start wrapping things up in here and pushing people to get things cleaned up and secured before our temporary inertial gravity dropped below a level heavy enough to keep our feet on the ground.

I didn't wait for the final round to be passed about though, it was late, and I was full. Happily, I went back to what had been my prison during the initial days of our current expedition only now it felt like a sanctuary. A space of my own I could escape to. A quiet place to relax in. Clothes were quickly changed, and my bed was sunk into. At least as far as one sunk with rapidly diminishing gravity. Laying there in my bed I could feel the change happening. There was still a pull there, but it was lessening measurably even with only my own senses as the instrument. Starting to doze I remembered with half a mind to attach the straps that would keep me held down once I again became weightless. By my internal clock and gyro, it may be happening now. I didn't think anything else that day as I drifted off into slumber. The pull on my body did cease shortly after while I slept, my body preparing for the next few days which were going to push me to my limits more than I knew at the time.

Chapter Nine

Finally, the day was here. I waited strapped into a chair on the medical deck surrounded by my charges waiting for the audible clunks of a connection being made. When they came, I didn't really hear them as much as felt them through my magnetic boots now locked to the floor. This morning I had forgotten in my barely woken mind about that change in status. I unstrapped from my bed and swung my legs over the side pushing off with my arms. Expecting to land softly on the floor it took a moment for me to realize my mistake and get hands up ahead of my vulnerable face before I plowed into the ceiling. The push off from my arms being meant to only give me the momentum to stand up had sent my body up to the higher limits of my room instead. Fortunately, I was able to catch myself while not incurring any embarrassing marks to explain away. After that near miss I had quickly slapped the boots on cursing the need for them. Zero G was cool for a few days, but it really did get old after a while. Having a bit of downward pull again for the last couple days had been a vacation. Now back to the daily grind.

The all clear sounded fifteen minutes after we had connected to the station. We were ok to unclamp from our seats and move about the deck at will, but it would likely be nearly another 2 hours before we would get to start our work of moving all these pods. I reviewed with my team once more what the plan was. Each member was to take two pods each at a time. The engineers aboard the APEX probably led by my Father, had designed little car like rigs that would clamp onto and carry two pods at a time. They were modified versions of what was used in the cargo bays. We would not ride on them but would guide them down corridors out the cargo door into the station. Then we would guide them through the station a short distance to the new ship. The bays were all marked I was told so there shouldn't be any misplacing of pods or cargo for that matter. Once inside the APEX, each pod had a designated spot to be connected and locked down.

I wasn't ecstatic about the carts as we hadn't trained with them. They were a new addition that we hadn't even seen in person yet. Since the APEX engineers had built them, they were still aboard that ship waiting for the all clear. Each of us would take our first round of pods by hand like we had trained to do and then bring a cart back with us. It shouldn't be an issue though as I had trained to drive book carts at the local library as part of my mandatory community service while in school. The carts at the library were smaller and simpler but I also operated them in smaller spaces inside the library.

The cargo decks and corridors on both ships and the station were large enough to easily maneuver without major concern. The carts themselves were smart also. We had been told this morning during our briefing that if I gave an order to the controls that the AI sensed would run the cart or myself into trouble, it would stop and require override before continuing such a course. Along with the 8 of us that would be operating carts and moving pods, we each got a nurse to help us. Christina happened to be placed with me so she would be helping me unload, position and connect the pods I would be moving one in the APEX. Each cycle was only supposed to take fifteen to twenty minutes so both of us would be moving fast to keep up with the schedule. I was excited to finally be doing something beneficial instead of only training all the time.

0915 hours we were given the go-ahead to open all cargo doors and start the transfer. The first round or two were a bit rough while we figured out what we were doing. With no ability to practice for real with these new carts, we had to learn on the job. I thought to myself while stumbling along on my first return to the APEX with a load of two pods that if these things had been designed and built in advance, you would think they could have been shown to us on screens ahead of time. We may have even been able to build a simulator for them instead of walking into it blind. I wasn't clear about why we hadn't known about the carts, but it didn't matter now. They were nice, efficient and took the strain off us movers having to alter the momentums of the large pods by hand. After the first couple rounds, we really sped up and began to make up for the slower start. The day went well. We were able to get an extra two rounds in by the end of our twelve hours which meant we would be ahead of the game for day two.

That evening after we were locked down again with all the cargo doors closed and secure, I stopped in the mess hall only long enough to grab a ration pack and say goodnight to my Father as he was doing the same. Difference was he wouldn't be heading to my parent's shared room for hours still. It wouldn't surprise me if he stayed up working the entire time we were docked. That was just how he was. Myself on the other hand wanted sleep so once I said good night to him, I headed on to my room and after a quick wipe down with a cold damp cleaning wipe went straight to bed and shortly after fell into a fitful sleep.

Dreams invaded my sleep and kept it fitful all night. You know how dreams work though so I won't pretend I have any idea what they were about. All I remember was that they were not kind dreams. Just shy of nightmares I think only because I never truly woke up during them. I only tossed and turned all night. Having that feeling of needing to move in your sleep could be much worse in space I learned because of the straps I had to maintain over me. They had sleeping bags we could use instead but I preferred my bed even though it meant I had to use straps to hold myself in position. The night drug on but eventually the alarm on my tablet went off bringing me out of my unfulfilling slumber.

After a quickly devoured breakfast smoothie from a pouch, I headed down to the medical deck again. The team minus half our nurse counterparts met up and went over the game plan for our second day. Half the nurses were already on the APEX. They had stayed aboard the previous night to monitor all the pods that had already been moved. The other half had stayed aboard the Walrus and watched over the pods left for today's move. The plan was the same for the most part. We had to wait until receiving the all clear, then the cargo doors would open, and we could start moving pods again. Since we had ended up ahead yesterday, it was expected we would end early today. As soon as we finished up, we would disperse to the cargo decks that still needed help and start working with them taking our carts with us. Since they were modified for pods, they wouldn't move as much cargo as the unmodified versions, but we could still help finish up where needed.

The all clear came right on time that second day and we took off. Ahead of schedule out of the gate things were going smooth. On my eighth or ninth round I noticed something was a bit off. Normally when I made the transition from Walrus to the station, the carts would beep as their AIs cleared the invisible network barriers between the systems and reconnected to the new system we had just gotten aboard. Then another beep once we crossed the threshold from Station to APEX. This time though when I crossed into the station, the cart beeped but an indicator light on it that was always green went yellow.

"Mrs. Johanson, I have a problem here with my cart, please advise." I called over the team chat radio. Mother and I had decided to go with me calling her by name as all the other team members would as to not cause any confusion. Across the radio my Mother replied.

"Maggie, I copy your report of a cart with a fault. Please advise your location and cart malfunction."

"My cart stopped when I crossed into the station and is flashing yellow."

Another voice came across the radio, "Mrs. Johanson. Abigale here, I have the same problem. I am in the APEX now, but my cart also went yellow and stopped."

"OK, all cart operators please relay your status immediately."

Responses came across the radio all reporting the same failure as mine and Abigale's. This couldn't be good I thought. What would cause all the carts to go out at the same time?

Lights flickered in and out and I went weightless suddenly. I was already weightless technically, but my boots disengaged. I came up off the floor along with my cart. The magnetic wheels it rolled upon must have let go too. It had a backup magnetic system that should have dropped feet to the floor but those didn't activate. Neither the cart or I went flying, but instead just lost our grip on the ship and started floating gently in whatever way our last motions pushed us. I was moving a lot quicker as I moved this way and that trying to grasp onto something. When I latched a hand onto the cart and pulled myself towards it, it pulled towards me at the same time. When we impacted gently together, the momentum of the cart reversed my direction and we both started floating towards a wall of the station we were nearest. When we got close, I grasped onto a handrail and pulled myself up and out from between the wall and the cart. The cart impacted the wall but hadn't gained any real velocity, so it was just a bump that left a blemish in the wall panel. That sent the cart off away from me and I lost my grip on it trying to secure myself. I watched it wander away across the corridor but couldn't do anything about it.

I heard screams come from down the corridor. As I looked down the long pathway, I could see other carts with cargo and one other cart with pods making similar bouncing movements in slow motion. It appeared we were not the only ones impacted. Then a cart carrying a large pallet far down the path at the edge of my vision appeared to run into a wall but not directly. With the lights flickering I couldn't be sure, but something was between it and the wall as they collided. The object in the middle stopped the collision but appeared to spread out in doing so. Then as just before the lights went out completely, I saw the red sprays radiating away from the impact point. Oh God, that was a person that had been there between the cart and the wall. I turned away but had already seen too much. The bile came up in my throat. Doing all I could to keep it down I fought to regain focus.

Holding to the wall tightly now that vision had been taken away from me with all lighting gone, I realized I hadn't heard anything back from my Mother since we had reported the failures. I called out across the channel, but no one answered. The team com must have gone down. I pulled the tablet from my pocket and called my Mother from it instead. It showed connected but I didn't hear anything. Just static. That meant that all our coms must be down. All I could hear besides the static filled frequency was the screams of fellow crew members trying to avoid their now errant carts and cargo. From the sounds of crashes increasing in frequency it seemed that cargo had come loose from many of the carts and was now taking separate routes from wall to ceiling to floor and around again. At least all the pieces should be slowing. Each time a cart or crate cracks into a wall it should lose momentum and eventually stop. Instead it sounded like the crashes were becoming harder but how would that be possible?

All I could do was hang on and hope that within a few more moments the radios would be back up. Hopefully command could reactive the boots too. As I thought about that I realized that if the boots did come back on suddenly then they would pull me to whatever surface was closest to them at the time. I was up high on a wall and needed to be on the floor. Starting to pull myself down the wall with whatever grips I could find, I looked back out down the hall and had to quickly pull hard to get out of the way of my cart as it swung through the air right at me. I ducked just in time as it crashed into the wall above me. It spun off the wall and appeared to pick up speed towards the ceiling. Following the yellow light that still shown and the glow from the pods that stayed on still it sure looked like the cart sped up moving away from me. I know that physics did not call for an increase in velocity but that is what it did.

There wasn't any time in the moment to work that through my mind though. All I could do was react and keep myself alive. Back to the Walrus I thought. There shouldn't be any loose cargo or pods in there. It was all tied down still. I started to pull myself along the wall in the direction I knew had to be the cargo door. That is when things got so much worse and I started to fear for my life. Since all station lights were out, I was having to operate by sound and the faint glow of pods and cart lights only. I heard before I saw but all down the corridor bulkhead doors started closing. The station was cordoning off each section of the corridor we were in. At the same time the wall under me rumbled and the door to the Walrus that I had been so close to reaching rammed home sealing me into what I figured was my tomb at that moment.

All the screaming was suddenly gone. There was a crash as my cart once again slammed into the wall just down from me careening back in my direction. As I shoved off the wall trying to evade the slow missile that approached, I bounced off a new wall that hadn't been there a few seconds ago. I must have been close to one of the bulkheads as what was a corridor was now a wall. My shoulder exploded in pain when it took the brunt of that impact. I cried out to no one and pushed off with my feet again but this time I pushed as hard as I could towards but under the path I estimated the cart would take next. I wanted to get away from that thing before it killed me. The cart cracked into the wall splitting one of the pods open. The blueish green glow emanating from the pod brightened now that it wasn't blocked by the think icy viewport and cover.

What I was forced to witness next will never leave my memory. The pod cracked open and a woman started floating out. She was still connected and asleep but in reaction to the sudden crisis, an automated response activated, and the pod injected her with a stimulant to bring her back to awareness. A glow from the open pod illuminated her face enough for me to see her awake with a jolt, her eyes bulged, and a look of sheer terror and confusion crossed her face. The cart with the pod still attached made hard contact with the new end of the corridor crushing her between it and the emergency door. Blood spewed out in every direction for just a second. The red fluid appearing green from being illuminated by the lone blue light available. Her torso was crushed but her head was above the carnage and staring at me. She had a look in her eyes that asked the universe why. I also asked why in my nightmares for months after the incident. Why did the damn pod have to wake her just in time to be crushed and killed in a bizarre way like this? I didn't have time to think about it right at that moment though.

As the woman's blood spurted out covering every surface within range of that dim glow, an explosion sounded behind me. I was still floating through open air not close enough to anything to grab hold of. I couldn't react. I spun my head to look towards the ear-splitting sound but saw nothing. I could feel the entire structure around me shudder even without touching the walls. The air itself rippled and roiled spinning me around. I was blinded by the very structure that was protecting me. There were no windows in this section or either of the bulkhead doors. I careened finally into a wall and was able to find purchase on a railing bringing my momentum to a halt. That was when it got bad. The entire room spun attempting to tear me free from my hold. I held tighter just hoping the cart and pod didn't find its way down here and crush me like it did that poor woman before.

A crackle came from one of my communicators tucked away deep in my ear. I couldn't understand it but there was something there. Then what I could only assume was an explosion occurred on the other side of the wall I was holding onto. The wall shuddered violently ripping the railing from my grasp and contorted inwards striking me hard. I felt fingers pop along with my wrist just as my left arm went completely numb. I could only imagine the force that was required to bend that wall inwards towards me. At the time though I was without active thought. All I knew was extreme pain. My arm was missing from the internal systems screaming at me for attention, but I knew it was in pain as well. I could feel things in my legs that I had never felt before. My head might as well be in a vice and my very insides felt as though they would explode through my skin at any moment. This tomb was tightening around me. Being dented in from things outside. The air was still holding but in a smaller and smaller container the pressures were quickly going to exceed my body's limits crushing me.

At that moment I knew I was dead. I didn't want to die though. Even this hell I now found myself in would be better than the emptiness of nonexistence that waited for me on the other side. Then I heard it again. The crackling in my ear. Only this time it was clearer. I could understand it. My father's commanding voice came through from the other end.

"Maggie, can you hear me? Do you copy me?

"Daddy, yes. I'm here. I think. I'm hurt though." I all but cried it through the radio. We had communications back. I might still be able to survive this.

"Maggie, where are you?"

"I'm in the corridor between the two ships, Daddy, what should I do?"

There was short silence that seemed like an eternity. I heard muted cursing and yelling, obviously my father had covered his microphone hoping to keep me from hearing his tirade.

"Maggie, I need you to listen very closely to me. I need you to do exactly what I tell you to do. Do you understand me Maggie?"

"What do I need to do? The corridor is crushing in on me!"

"Our system shows there are two pods in the corridor with you. Is that right? Are they intact?"

"Yes, there are two. One is smashed and the woman came out. It crushed her" I said this last part through clenched teeth trying to keep from crying out loud about the horrors I saw.

My father continued, "Maggie, the corridor you are in is about to be torn apart. You are on a direct path for the Walrus or what is left of her. I need you to get inside the pod that isn't damaged. I show it was empty. Climb in and activate it. It should protect you."

In the spinning turmoil I looked down the corridor at the mess at that end. In the dim blue light still emanating from the broken pod I could see the whole area was soaked in blood. What I was sure was warm fresh blood all from that poor woman. "Daddy, I can't, it's all covered in blood. I can't go down there."

My father didn't pause for a moment, he came back with an authoritative voice I had never heard before even when I was in major middle-name-using trouble. "Maggie, you get to the end of the corridor, you open that pod and you get in right now. If you do not, you will die. Get over yourself and get in that pod. THAT'S AN ORDER!"

I moved faster than I ever before. I was nearly an expert at this point in zero G maneuvers during all our training but not while in a spinning half crushed block of disintegrating alloys. I aimed the best I could and pushed off the wall towards the pods. One of my legs screamed out in anger as I did this. Whatever was wrong with that one was worse now. I felt it tear and break apart with the push. With one arm left functioning I reached the pod and grabbed hold of it. The hand hold I found was slick with thick liquid. I recoiled for just a moment but ignored it and wiped warm sticky blood from the control panel on the second pod. Before it was even fully open, I had swung my body in roughly and was jabbing at the controls to close it again. Blood followed me in and was soaking into my clothes, smearing on my face. I closed my eyes and tried not to breathe it in.

"I'm in and the pod door is shut" I yelled through clenched teeth.

"Good girl", my father responded in a much mellower voice than his previous order came through in. "We have you on our displays. Hang on honey, I can't do anything for you right this moment but as soon as your pod clears the debris field, we will be there to bring you aboard a Skater."

I cried out in pain as the last few moments of punishment tore back into my consciousness demanding attention. I couldn't identify which leg was the bad one as my whole body throbbed, but I only had one functioning one left. I just couldn't place which side it was on. As I was trying to do an inventory and announcing injuries into the comms hoping that would help the command crew prepare for whatever I may need everything slowed down to a crawl. I won't kid you here. I know that has been a story telling method in movies and books alike for millennia, but time truly seemed to come to a near standstill.

The corridor outside the window of my pod lit up like a small sun. It was just a small dot at first out too far for me to really see but then a wall of the corridor turned red hot and bent in towards me. It split open and the seam created wrapped around out of my view. Then a full-on burn came. Everything that was turned into a white-hot light. I had to shut my eyes and cover them with the one bloody hand I maintained control of. Still it was bright. Then I felt the shock wave. It was so violent that even inside my secure little life-giving pod I was slammed from one side to the other bashing my head hard enough to knock me out cold.

I came to in blackness. Total blackness. My head screamed at me in agony. Was I dead? Was this the emptiness that I had envisioned? No, what I had envisioned was nothingness. Not emptiness. I believed that everything would just end without knowledge of such a thing occurring or any memory of the life that had been ended. Pure unending nothingness that in itself did not exist. Could I have been wrong? Was there an afterlife? Some kind of existence beyond the physical presence in our universe? Surely this wouldn't be it though. If this was the afterlife, then I must be in some world between the two. A purgatory. A waiting room so to say. Possibly a processing center where it is decided whether you get to go to a land of plenty or a pit of despair. Which might I end up in? I was still a minor after all, but I had planned horrific things even if I had not followed through with them yet. I had denied the existence of any God or holy spirit. That could be blamed on my age though and being raised in a household without religion.

Wait, I smelled something. What was this thing that I smelled? It was all encompassing now. All I could smell. All I knew. I had no sight, no hearing, no touch but I did have smell. Blood. I smelled nothing but blood. Was that my blood or the blood of the woman I watched have the life ripped from her? I couldn't tell. I was sure at least some was mine with as bad as my head and one leg hurt but I couldn't be sure. Wait, my head and leg hurt. That was feeling. Could I touch? Reaching my arms out to the sides I felt. Yes, I feel a shell around me. My pod. I can feel my pod and sticky. So sticky. Dry and crackly in places but mostly sticky. That must be blood. My blood as that much didn't come in the pod with me. I was still mostly out of it. Dazed and in incredible pain, I twisted from side to side but could not see anything. No control panel lights, no light outside, just nothing. Was I blind? Please don't tell me I was blind. I had wanted to be a pilot of something. I hadn't decided what kind of pilot, but I knew I wanted to fly something.

No, not blind. I could see something now. My vision was coming in now slowly whether that was just eyes focusing on the new reality or my brain restarting and getting systems back online. I saw something.

A red dot. Small but there, reflecting enough light from our sun to reach my only slightly functioning eyes.

That must be Mars. Yes, it was a planet. It was so far away though. Too far. I couldn't be that far away from it. No way. Then I realized what happened in a flash as my mind truly woke with a start. The explosion that nearly blinded me must have shot my pod off like a bullet into space. I had been travelling at a high rate for who knows how long. I had been unconscious, and it appeared I had no power in the pod. The pods were meant to keep me alive for how long again? A few hours? Shit. I couldn't tell if the air was ok or not. All I could smell was that acrid blood floating around coating every surface.

What a way to die I thought. Survive an explosion and die in a tiny pod. I laughed when a thought crossed my mind. It was a bit like the caskets history books spoke of back when people buried their dead in boxes under the ground. Such a wasteful way to use precious land. Those were the days when they didn't live in tightly controlled communities/military bases/whatever those in charge wanted to call them at the time. All I had ever known was cremating people once they passed. We didn't use land to bury them, the state took the bodies and burned them in droves. Whatever was left of the mangled mass of used meats was disposed of outside our walls.

After a short burst of laughter of which I quickly realized I didn't hear, I returned to reality and my situation. I wasn't going to die. I survived too much already to go out like this. There had to be something I could do. My father said he was going to send a Skater. He would have at least one, maybe a dozen out here looking for me and other survivors. He wouldn't be able to locate me if the power was off and no beacon was on. I probably looked like every other piece of twisted wreckage out here. I had to get power back on at least enough to send a signal. Think, what could I do to get power back on?

These pods didn't have beacons built in as they were not meant to be used in open space, only on a ship. They did send signals to the control unit to monitor vitals, but no one was plugged into it so there was nothing to send. There should be a screen around here somewhere though.

I searched around and found it wiping it off with my good hand. Nothing. No response to touch at all. Shit. Shit, shit, shit, shit. Next idea, my comm link, Duh. I found it still in my ear, too deep. It was on the side I had cracked into the pod with. It was crammed down in my ear canal and it shot white bolts of pain through my brain when I tried to touch it. I called out a command and it buzzed in my ear sending waves of pain so severe I immediately vomited into the open space in front of me.

Great, I thought as the wave subsided to be replaced with a new scent mixed with the blood. Now I have vomit floating around in here. The com link wouldn't do me any good anyways I thought. They only work for about 60 yards at most. The only reason we can reach other people is that the ship relays everything.

No way my commlink would do any good out here without a real boost.

"Wait" I moved my lips and felt the vibrations emanate from my throat but heard nothing again reminding me how poor my condition was at the moment. I started to swim back into the rabbit hole that lead to nothing but despair and regret. NO, I couldn't allow myself to fall for that trap right now. Later I could feel sorry for myself but not now. I had to work on the problem in front of me and worry about the rest later.

Maybe I could boost it. If I could get my commlink tied into the pods wireless sending unit I might be able to send quick radio bursts strong enough to be picked up by any nearby ships. I needed that commlink. I took a deep breath and dug into my ear working through the pain and found purchase on it. The pain was incredible. It felt as though I was digging the very auditory nerve out of my ear. Pulling it along with the commlink. I felt the device slip free and then it was out in my hand. Fluids ran free from my ear expanding when they reached the outside, pooling wherever they felt the need whether that was in my hair or wrapping around my head invading the various cuts here and there. At this point I couldn't touch a spot on my own body that wasn't coated in some kind of bodily fluid.

I could feel consciousness fading in and out and knew I had to do whatever it was I was going to do quickly as I didn't know if I would stay awake much longer. Using my abused but still functional hand I punched out at the screen that wouldn't activate and felt it crack. I don't know that my hand fared much better, but I didn't have any tools with me. Again, I struck out and felt the screen give. A chunk stayed with my hand as I pulled away. That chunk was gripped by my teeth and pulled from my knuckles. I tore into the screen with my fingernails peeling two of them back from the beds, but progress was made into the deep internals behind that dead display. I felt around but couldn't find what I wanted by touch alone.

Remembering the flashlight all crew members were required to have on them I reached down and felt for the pocket I kept it in along my right leg. I found the pocket and reached in finding the flashlight. This felt wrong though, it was too smooth missing the rubber grip I should have felt and ragged at the end as though it had been broken off. A thought crossed my mind that the flashlight may have already been broken in the same explosive escape that seemed to have deadened that leg. Running fingers down the body of the flashlight I ran into the exposed meat of my leg. I couldn't feel the pressure from my leg directly but instead felt the warmth of it through my fingers. "Shit, Shit, Shit!" I screamed the curses into the pod. I couldn't hear the screams, but it still made me feel a bit better just to expel some of my anguish. The damn flashlight must have lodged into my leg. That was probably why I couldn't feel it. The leg had been impaled and to protect my ever-weakening consciousness, my body had removed the signal from my mind trying to keep me sane.

I still needed that power cell if it was intact though so I would have to bear it and pull the flashlight from my leg. There was no other way. I carefully wrapped my fingers around the slick cylinder hoping against hope that it would still be usable. I tugged lightly and everything exploded in white hot rage. I let go and pulled my hand back away from the spot. After another round of screamed curses tearing at my vocal cords but producing no sound I could sense, I breathed slower to regain control over my mind. It must be lodged in deeper than I expected.

I reached back down gingerly into my pocket reacquiring the flashlight's location. I felt it again but realized that it couldn't be my flashlight. Beyond that, I didn't know what it was. Now that I thought about it, if it had been the flashlight, it could only be imbedded in my leg by maybe a half an inch judging by the length protruding. I felt around the end of the shaft again and it clicked. My mind whirled spinning in pain again upon my realization that the item I had assumed was my flashlight was really my very leg. That was bone I had jerked on attempting to remove it. Again, I vomited into the air. Fortunately, this time though there was nothing remaining in my stomach, so the expulsion consisted mostly of saliva and blood. With what I was already soaked in, that was the least of my concern.

For what felt like the tenth time in mere minutes, I pulled myself together and reached deeper into the pocket. The bottom was gone, ripped out by something but I felt one of my torn back nails scrape across something metal. It was the clip of the flashlight. I knew it. Careful not to knock it loose, I was able to wrap a finger around the end and pull it through my pocket past the bone protruding terribly and out the top. Finally, with it in my hand I breathed a sigh of relief. There was still a chance. I turned the flashlight and clicked it on exposing the inside of my pod to a blazing white light that instantly forced my eyelids closed to shield the sensitive receptors underneath. Carefully I opened one eye alone allowing the other to stay trained to the darkness.

Aiming the light back into the now shattered dead screen, I found what I wanted. Two cables that ran from the onboard power supply to the electronics. One ran to the rear of the screen and another on through the shell surrounding me towards my feet where the transmitter would be. The cable was intact but that told me little. I needed to know if there was any power within that line going to the transmitter. I had no tester with me, but I knew if I shorted the cable that would tell me if there was power or not.

How to short the cable though? It was protected by the normal insulating coating. Thinking to myself, I came up with the idea to try and cut the insulation away. The metal clip on my flashlight was thin and durable. Possibly thin enough to serve as in improvised knife. Within a minute I was able to bend the clip away from the flashlight and began scraping lengthwise down the wire removing thin curls of insulation on each pass. I found the copper colored interior of the cable quickly and used the flashlight to try and short the wire to the metallic frame of the pod. Nothing. It was dead.

I had assumed it would be dead, so this was not a set-back in the direct sense. I had actually been hoping for this. If the screen and pod had been unresponsive with power still in the lines, then the chances of my next action working would have been near zero. The fact that the pod's power cell had run out causing my current outage was good news as it meant that most likely that was the only problem. If I could find an alternate power source, then I may still be able to transmit a signal. Fortunately, I held that very power source in my hand.

What would have normally taken me maybe a minute or two with two functioning hands ended up taking me around 5 according to my internal clock. I had no real idea whether that clock was accurate or not but I was still awake and functioning so it couldn't have taken me too long. I laid back completely flat and with a final prayer to a God whose existence I was still unsure of, I pinched the final wire to the back of my flashlight's exposed power cell. A dim light flared from a corner of the broken screen. The commlink now laying on the thin strip of skin between my nose and mouth buzzed shortly after the screen lit up.

I nearly cried right then. The commlink buzzing unprompted meant that it had indeed found something to link to which could only be the pod. I spoke as strongly as I could muster. Not able to hear myself I hoped it was understandable enough for the tiny computer within the pod and the link to process.

"Maggie Johanson for Commander Johanson. Critical need, bypass code 48972." This was the emergency bypass code my father had given me when we were first aboard the ship. It was supposed to bypass all walls and link me in directly with him. He had told me to only use it in the event of a life or death situation. Even during my time held within the confines of my room when we first got aboard the Walrus, I had never broken the word I had given him and used this code. Now though, it was the only way I could think of to get a direct link to what I needed. I waited but felt no vibrations return from my commlink. I had placed it there so it would be close to my voice and in an area sensitive enough to hopefully pick up on vibrations from the tiny speaker returning a message I would not hear.

Again, I spoke the phrase and waited. What felt like hours passed in mere seconds. "Well, that was it," I thought to myself still not feeling any return vibrations. This was it. There was nothing else I could do at this point. No other trick to try. I was going to bleed out I knew. There was too much of the sticky substance floating around in the pod or glued to every surface for me to survive any longer. I had no time left. Liquid blood was still seeping from many contusions across my body, I had bone sticking out of my leg, one arm was still completely nonfunctioning and my vision was narrowed down to possibly half its former glory. I guess now I would find out what was in the afterlife. Or not. I would either slip into nothingness and never know it as my essence dropped from the universe or I would awaken into a world of everlasting joy. I relaxed back and felt my being start slipping away. Parts of my mind shutting down. A slight rush of happiness tingled across my body. Something itched my upper lip though. I could feel my mind separating from my body, but my upper lip held firm. Keeping my soul from leaving just yet. A buzzing vibration was holding me firm. Keeping in my skin.

A sudden jolt of realization shot into my separated mind bringing me fully back into the body I had just given up on. I reacquainted myself with the pain and limited motor controls associated with this existence and spoke knowing that buzzing could only be a return signal from something. I had connected after all. With all the effort I still had within me, I drug the words up and spit them out through blood-soaked lips.

"I'm here, alive but injured. No power in the pod. I cannot hear anything from the comm link. I think it went through my eardrum. Daddy, if you can hear me, please help." I started to cry but stopped myself. Took a deep painful breath and continued, "I can see Mars. It is straight ahead of me but is small. About the size of a golf ball from here. That should give you an estimate of how far out I am if you can hear me. I don't know which way I flew but I think I can see a storm on the planet's surface. A whirling cloud formation is approximately at seven o'clock and nearly at the edge of the visible side to me. I can also see what looks like a crater, fresh at five o'clock about halfway between the center and the edge of my view. Daddy, please come find me." I took another deep breath, but this time was stopped by incredible pain coming from my chest. "Daddy, it hurts so bad I'm having trouble keeping my eyes open."

I sat there then repeating the same information hoping someone could hear me. After possibly the fourth rerun of similar information built more into an automatic reply than a conscious thought, the power cell in my flashlight gave out. The screen fragments still functioning dimmed out and then went back to black. My comm link buzzed again confirming I lost what connection there was. I didn't have any other options. This was it. Either someone heard me and would able to locate me with the information provided or they wouldn't.

I lay there looking through the burned and scarred glass of my pod. All the tiny lights out there surrounding the planet. All those other worlds. None of them knew what was coming their way. None of them knew to be scared. The mission would continue without me and I could only hope that with my father in charge, we would treat new worlds with respect. I doubted that would be the case, but it was beyond my grasp. The blackness was close again. I could feel it encroaching into my mind like before.

I would black out soon.

I may never wake.

The warmth of disconnection overtook me again. From my toes up through my body, I could feel the relaxing of strained muscles, the slowing of my heartbeat. The shallowness of my breath. I couldn't stay awake any longer. There was no desire to at this point. All efforts had been exhausted and I was too tired. Too tired. It was so comfortable here. Such a warm embrace. I blacked out.

Chapter Ten

"Billy, I told you I don't have any tens, go fish."

"I don't believe you Maggie, I think you are fibbing to me. I bet you have at least a couple tens. We have burned through nearly the whole deck, where else would they be?"

Billy smiled at me as he said this. I did have a ten, I just didn't want him to win again. For some reason he always beat me at this game. No matter what I did, he always won. I was better in nearly every subject in school and was smarter than him in every perceivable way but somehow, he always won at stupid Go Fish. I didn't understand.

"Seriously Billy, I don't have any tens, Go Fish."

Billy stared at me a moment longer, then let out a breath and drew a card out of the "pond" in the middle of the table. His mouth drooped a bit when he saw the card and put it in his hand. Must not have been what he had hoped for. Now for the fun part.

"Billy, do you have any," I paused here for just a second to build tension, "tens?" As soon as I said it, I burst out laughing. Billy stared at me in disbelief and then smiled. "Yea, I have a couple tens as a matter of fact, but you can't have them." His eyes twinkled just a little bit throwing me off a moment.

"What do you mean I can't have them? I asked for them and you have some so now you have to give them to me."

"Hmm, I don't think so. See I asked for them first and you denied having any, so you already decided that standard rules do not apply. However, I may be persuaded to give you my tens if you give me something else in trade."

"What might that be Billy? You want my twos or something?"

Billy had a stupid grin on his face and replied, "Well, now I know what to ask for next but no, I don't want any other cards, I want something else." When he said this last part, he reddened just a bit.

"What do you want then?"

"Well, see, I want." Billy cleared his throat just a bit. "I uh, I want a, see, I want a kiss."

It took me a few seconds to decide if he was joking or not. Don't get me wrong, I had thought of this before. Of course, I had. Billy and I had been friends since we were little bitty. We had always gotten along well. Always been friends. We just hadn't ever gone in that direction. Not that I hadn't thought about it from time to time. I mean Billy was cute. He wasn't a jock or anything but wasn't a scrawny little nerd either. About average I would say with an average mind for his age. I guess that was the reason I had never thought seriously about anything more. He was nice and a great friend, but he was just him. There wasn't anything wildly special and my young mind hadn't really put any importance on a real relationship yet. I realized I had been frozen for several seconds now thinking about this when Billy turned beat red and started backing away.

"Sorry Maggie, I shouldn't have said that. I was just joking. I, I need to get back home anyways, it's almost curfew now you know." He said this last part as he looked at his watch.

"Billy, no, don't go yet. I didn't refuse and we still have a game to finish." I leaned in as I finished telling him this and gave him a quick peck on the cheek. "I am not saying no but let's finish the game first."

"Ok, I can finish the game." Billy settled back down uncomfortably at the table and picked his cards back up. We kept playing a bit longer and just as we were about to wrap it up, I made a play, "Billy, I will make you a deal," He looked up at me as I continued, "If you win, you get a kiss." He grinned at this and spoke up, "Ok, but what if you win?". "If I win," I continued, "I get a kiss." I looked at him seriously for a minute and then, "have any eights?" Billy didn't pause for a moment, he laid his last two cards down saying, "I sure do, just happened to be my last ones. You win."

I put my cards down also and started to lean in towards him. I could feel my checks flush and my heart pound. I hadn't kissed anyone besides my parents, so this was something new. The world we lived in wasn't normally full of fanciful thirsting for others. It was a hard world that you had to find moments in. I hadn't found mine yet. This was my moment. Billy leaned in towards me, eyes already closed awkwardly aiming his lips towards my general direction. A slight grin showed through on my face. What a nerd I thought to myself. A nice nerd though. I could do a lot worse; I kept my eyes open as I leaned in further trying to meet his lips. Against my will my eyes did close at the last moment. It must be an automatic response the body plays on us. Just as you come to something important, something close and powerful, the body closes off other senses to improve the ones that matter most.

My eyes closed and then I realized I couldn't hear anything either. My ears must have shut down as well. Sending all my brainpower to my lips reaching out towards his, begging for contact, warmth of another person. I hadn't realized how much I wanted this until it was so close at hand. My heart was thundering in my chest, my blood rushing, my mind was racing. I waited for that needed contact. I kept moving forward but realized I wasn't moving at all. We should have come together by now. I tried to reopen my eyes, but I couldn't. It seemed like a cover had been pulled down over me. I reached out to him to feel his face that must be so close to mine, but I couldn't move. I didn't feel my arms. My heart wasn't pounding hard and fast anymore. In fact, I couldn't feel it at all. I had gone from such a vibrant, powerful scene of pure desire and need to this abyss. This land of nothingness. No feeling, no sight, no sound, no movement. What was this?

The world around me came back into focus slowly. The pain however came back in a flash. I hurt all over. Then I remembered what had happened. I was in an accident. I was stuck in a pod floating around out in space. I thought I was dead but if that had been true, I wouldn't be hurting. The pain must be a good thing. If I hurt, then I must be alive. If I am alive, I must have been rescued since there was no reason I would come back to in the pod. I was nearly out of air and totally out of time there. I reached out but couldn't. My arm didn't work like it should have. I worked my mouth to try and speak but couldn't move my tongue much. It was caught on something. I couldn't move my mouth much either. I realized then that I had a tube in my mouth. Another good sign in a sense. There were no breathing tubes in the pod so I must be on a ship in a medical ward.

This thought was comforting for a second until my heart really started racing. What if I was severely injured? Unable to move, unable to stand, unable to walk again? I didn't want to live on if that was the case. I started freaking out more but then got a hold of myself. Even if I was badly injured, we could fix it. This ship had a good enough medical ward and wonderfully trained medical people. We had the ability to regrow limbs to an extent, I would be up and moving before long. I just needed to remember that I was alive and that was what mattered.

As my heart started to calm down, I tried looking around again. I still couldn't see much but I could tell I could see. I wasn't blind, just blocked. I must have something over my eyes. I tried moving an arm again and felt it stir this time. Then I felt a warmth over that arm. It felt like a hand maybe. The warmth squeezed my arm lightly. It must be a person. Maybe my Mom. As soon as I felt that squeeze, I felt the covering over my eyes move. One eye was uncovered, and I could see! It wasn't focused and I had a hard time picking anything specific out, but I could see. That was the important part. My eyes kept trying to focus slowly bringing my surroundings into view. I indeed had a tube coming out of my mouth. It was taped around my cheeks holding in tight.

To my right was a woman, not just a woman but my mom. My Mom was right there as I came to, tears in her eyes. I saw her mouth move but couldn't make out any words. In fact, I couldn't hear anything at all. Then I realized, I couldn't hear anything. Nothing. It was totally quiet. That couldn't be right, if this was a medical ward, there should be constant beeping of machines, shuffling of equipment and feet along with quiet talking all around me. No way did we have an accident like we did at the station without having major commotion in the medical ward. There would be too many patients.

I started to feel my heart increase again. My mother looked away at something and then back to me. She said something but all I saw was her lips move. I had no idea what she was saying. Then a nurse nudged her shoulder and said something. I couldn't hear that either. They said a few words and then my mother returned her gaze to me. Sad eyes, she released my arm and took something from the nurse. She looked at it and worked with something out of my view for a moment. She looked back at me and lifted the item. A whiteboard. My Mom spun it around and showed it to me.

She had written,

Maggie darling, you are safe now. Just stay calm and rest. You will be fine. Just relax. Know we love you and are going to do everything we can to heal you.

Tears flooded my eyes as I finished reading. I closed my eyes and felt the warm salty liquid squeeze out and run down my face. I kept them closed for what felt like an eternity before opening them again. My eyes stung but I tried to keep them open. My mother had written a new message on the board and turned it towards me again.

You need to rest. We are going to let you sleep while we fix you. Just relax for us honey.

I didn't want to rest anymore, I wanted to get up and move but I couldn't. I was scared but there was nothing I could do about it. I was at the mercy of my mother and whoever else was around. I had no control. I shut my eyes and drifted off to troubled dreams where I rode in wheelchairs or never woke up at all. The thing I missed most was the near kiss. Was that a dream, a manufactured scene put in my head or a memory? It was so real I almost thought it was a memory, but it didn't quite fit. It had to be a dream. Had to have been.

Hours? Days? Weeks? I don't know. How long has it been since I was last awake? I knew I was still asleep, but it was an odd sleep. I could control my thoughts; nothing was completely ridiculous. I couldn't fly, couldn't conjure whatever I wanted to. I was in a structured state almost like the real world but not quite. The main reason I knew it wasn't real was my body felt off. It felt manufactured. I could walk around, run, jump, climb but it felt wrong. It felt like I was just controlling a robot. Not really my own body. I could converse with others but the thoughts they had were generic, nothing specific or new.

Information given was what I already had in my head. Everyone's focus was on me. They were not living out their own lives but were existing just to be here, just for existing. It was strange. It dawned on me after an unmeasurable amount of time in this existence that I must be in a Sim. This sim was different though since the sims I knew from home were more real. This one wasn't as powerful, not as realistic and the feedback on my body was much degraded and slow. I was currently walking through a park for probably the hundreth time today.

That was another thing, it was always daytime and sunny. It was never this sunny for so long in a real sim. Real sims had clouds pass by to keep the realism. This sim didn't have any. As was done for so long before, I kept walking. This time through the park was different though. A small squat brown concrete building that wasn't there before appeared. It hadn't slowly come up as I walked, it was just there suddenly. The building was a basic square, short, with a flat roof. I wanted to stop and think about this. There was no reason for a building to appear out of nothing. I looked closer and saw there was a door with a sign, so I kept moving towards it to see what the little plaque said. Once I was close enough, a word came into focus over the door. EXIT shown in bold red. I reached out for the doorknob and twisted it gently with hands that were not really my hands. The door clicked and swung inwards. There was nothing but darkness inside, but I went in anyways. No fear, no regret, just interest in seeing what was on the other side.

As soon as I cleared the door, it shut behind me latching audibly and that was all I knew. The world was gone and all that was left was this blackness. I felt comfortable though. Warm, clean, calm, loved. It was a nice feeling.

I awoke once again. Possibly this was just the second time since the accident but there could have been others. I wasn't sure. Immediately my body told me it had been a while since my last trip back. I opened my eyes and could see. Everything was blurry but nothing like before. My eyes quickly adjusted and brought the world back to me. Another change was I could move my mouth. That was a great sign. I must be breathing on my own since the tube was gone. I felt a hand on my arm and looked to see the hand, so fine and comforting. My eyes followed the hand to the thin but strong arm all the way up to the person it was connected to. It was my mother just like before only clearer this time.

I was glad to see her now in real form. I had seen her many times in my state of rest. It hadn't really been her, but a conjuring of details carried by my memories and recreated by the computer software controlling the sim. This however was real. I could tell immediately that this was really her. She looked better than last time also. Before she had been dirty, bags had been heavy under her eyes, she had scratches, blood, bruising. This time she was clean, strong, rested. That had to be a good sign also. I knew my mom wouldn't leave me alone so if she felt it was ok to clean up and rest then I knew I was ok.

I opened my mouth to say hello but as my lungs pushed air through and sound began to leave my mouth, I felt a wave of pain from my throat. It hurt. Screamed at me was probably a better representation. It felt like it was on fire. It must not have been that long ago that they removed the breathing tube. My throat would heal, I just needed to take it easy on the speech for a few days. Just as I had said hello to my mother, she put her finger to her mouth to quiet me. At the same time, she opened her mouth but then shut it again reddening just a bit. I looked at her stupidly but then realized that I still couldn't hear. It was perfectly quiet around me. Just like before but without the searing pain all over. I felt much better but still could not hear. My Mother picked up a now familiar white board and scribbled a quick note.

"Maggie darling, I am so happy to see you awake. Your ears took a pounding worse than the rest of you in the explosions. It should heal but will take more time. Can you move your arms?"

I read the message and then twisted my head to look down at my body. The mere movement of my neck brought about more pain, but this pain was more of a soreness probably from not being used for too long. Overcoming it, I peered down at an arm. I could see it, that was a good sign. The fact that I could move my head this time was a great sign. Before I had been strapped down, so movement was restricted. I looked for my arms and found them. I concentrated and yes, my right arm moved. Just a shiver at first, then a wobble, then it lifted off the bed. My arm didn't move fast or with any power, but it lifted. I took a few seconds twisting my arm around at the elbow and the wrist, moving the whole assembly around at the shoulder. Everything seemed to work besides being weak. I looked back at my mom and she smiled back to me holding a thumbs up sign in my direction. I thought to myself well, progress is progress no matter how small.... Mother had a new message for me then on the board.

Your body is in good condition, most of your injuries have healed. Test your other arm. I will get you a board so you can try to write.

I looked to my other arm and it moved also. It felt great. Slow, weak but great. I could tell I wouldn't be boxing anytime soon but I could move. That was all that mattered. I peered down further and saw my legs lying motionless under the sheet. I sent a signal to lift my left leg and it shifted. Not a lot, it didn't even come all the way off the bed, but it shifted. Moving to my right leg I noticed there was something different about it. I shot the same signal down to it but had no response. My right leg was significantly bigger around than my left. Looking back up I saw my Mother returning as promised with another smaller white board ready for me. She didn't move closer though, instead she looked at me studying my responses. She had a clinical look on her face. Her face shifted back into a concerned motherly look as she moved to my side. She handed the board to me along with a black marker. I tried to write but it was just squiggles. I looked back to her as she was writing down another message. When she spun it back around it read;

"Take your time, it may take some practice to get your coordination and strength back. How do you feel, does anything hurt?"

I wiggled my hand twisting it slightly showing a so-so sign. Looking back down at my right leg I motioned to it and tried to speak again with no real success. Mother was writing on her board again while I continued to look at my nonfunctional limb. A touch to my shoulder brought my attention back to the board now with new words written across them;

"Your leg will be ok in time. It was shattered in twelve places, three of which broke through the skin."

I wasn't really all that shocked at her statement. As she smiled at me with that concerned smile a Mother gives when trying to reassure her child while unsure herself, I thought back to my time in the pod. That leg had been useless. Completely dead to me. Being shattered sounded about right. The good thing was that it was still there. If it had been hopeless, a prosthetic would have been a near automatic decision to make. The fact that doctors had left my naturally born leg in place meant that it was going to heal. Maybe not perfectly but it would heal and become useful again. Better than dead. I grinned to myself showing my Mother my teeth unintentionally with the thought.

She smiled back and I could see the tension release from her. The concern over how I would take my current status must have been weighing heavy upon her. I pointed at myself and gave another thumbs up to indicate I didn't feel any significant pain. There were some tingles and uncomfortable cramping in muscles apparently too long not used but overall, I wasn't in any real pain.

We worked on my writing for a while, but I tired quickly. I was able to jot down a couple quick notes that wouldn't be winning me any literary awards but were legible enough to understand.

"I feel good, just weak

Where are we now?"

My mother answered back and asked other questions about different things. Apparently, we were on the APEX now and were headed out away from the gravity wells of the planets. I had been out for a couple weeks so far. If all went well, we should be arriving at our planned point in space where we were supposed to "jump away" in several more weeks. About this time, it dawned on me that I was having to use my musculature to keep my head up, to keep my arms up while writing. I was fighting gravity. Quickly I scribbled another masterpiece to Mother asking what was up with the gravity?

In response to my question Mother laughed lightly. I could see the laughter on her face and in the movement of her shoulders but heard nothing. She went to her whiteboard and spent a bit more time this time spelling something out for me. When she spun it back around it wasn't a long description but only 5 words and a small crudely drawn diagram of a ship with a circular ring around its belly. The message read;

"APEX has a gravity ring."

That threw me for a loop. Some ships did have gravity rings, but it was very rare and mostly only for vacation cruise ships for the ultra-elite leadership. No one spent money on gravity rings for freighters or colony ships. I didn't know why we would have one on this ship, but I quickly accepted it pleased. That meant that we would have running water and showers during our time on this ship. That in itself was enough for me to say a quick thanks and move along to other things without asking too many questions.

Mother also let me know that my hearing should come back over time. My ears were totally destroyed internally by the comms I had in at the time of the accident along with the pressure waves from the explosion itself. I was thrown around so violently that the comm link drove deep into my inner ear. Surgeons with our advanced equipment had removed all the damaged parts from my inner ear and replaced both with manufactured parts. I was pretty much a cyborg in that regard now. Tiny electronics picked up sounds and transmitted the signals directly to my brain. The nerves needed time to heal and calm before they would activate the devices though. Oh well, at least I was alive right? I smiled again to myself and nodded off to a restful sleep where I had real dreams again.

Chapter Eleven

Two weeks after the Mars fiasco and one week after being awoken from my fitful slumber in a fake sim I was up out of the medical bed and on my feet. The sim had been designed to keep me calm but cerebrally active during my retrofit into a functioning cyborg - ok, maybe cyborg is a bit strong but I really kind of liked it. It was a cool thing to think about and made me feel like a bad ass. Anyways, a couple weeks after Mars and a week after waking up I was back to work training and getting into whatever trouble I could find on board our APEX ship.

It took a full week of physical training and constantly scribbling on whiteboards before I was deemed fit to leave the sick bay. I was still hobbling around with a crutch since my right leg was still more pulp than rigid bone. That would take several more weeks I was told before it would be back to normal again. Until then I would progress from crutches to a cane until I could finally walk on my own again. The last day there in the medical ward, my powerful cyborg hearing powers were turned on for the first time. Wow, that was a shocker and painful.

Apparently, the connections they were able to make were a bit stronger than anticipated because when the devices were cranked on, I thought my head would explode. I could hear everything. And loudly. A normal voice was like someone screaming with a megaphone directly into my shredded ear canal. A quick shriek from me and a barely slower adjustment by a tech and I was back into normal ranges of hearing. The tech started to apologize for the incredible headache that was now forming between my ears, but I stopped them thanking them for everything the whole team had done for me. In the grand scheme a little headache for a bit was nothing compared to what I had endured. However, I would have to remember that I could hear much more strongly later. That could come in quite handy in the right circumstances.

During that week after my miraculous recovery from what I would be told for the rest of my life was an amazing work of engineering and luck along with the outstanding efforts of my Father's crew in finding and tracking my weakened signals was me working my butt off in physical training trying to get all my strength back. Apparently muscles atrophy pretty quickly when you are totally lifeless in a pod. During this time, I also learned how amazing I was with my quick thinking and tactic of using a flashlight power cell to send a signal out through the pod. I was reminded of how lucky I was to have such a dedicated father in control of the mission that would not leave me behind. I was even reminded of how everyone thought I was quite incredible by staying alive and sending out a distress signal with just a flashlight batt – oh wait, I already said that didn't I?

Yea, well, people kept telling me and reminding me and telling me and reminding me. Everyone I spoke to wanted to congratulate me and remind me and tell me. At first it was neat. I had never had people so interested in what I had done but that faded quickly. I realized I didn't like being the absolute center of attention. Recognition was great but it wasn't like I saved a ship of innocent passengers or that poor woman that was crushed while I was transporting her from the Walrus to the APEX. All I did was save myself. I took it all in the best I could and kept moving forward the only way I knew how.

Week four I was finally cleared back to limited duty. I couldn't take on a real full duty assignment since I was still a minor not to mention hobbled on my one good leg and a crutch. Since I had only really been trained on moving pods, which hopefully we wouldn't need to do again, it was easier for my Father to move me to drones. Following the diagrams on my tablet which had been updated to include schematics of the new APEX, I eventually found a flight deck that was being used for drone practice. Unfortunately, and honestly expected, the flight deck of the big ship was not on the gravity ring. The only thing that was on the gravity ring was living quarters, a medical area and some garden sections. Being a long flight and a colony ship at that, we started producing some of our own food along the way.

The ship overall was still a super freighter. A heavily modified one at that but still a super freighter. The main body had living quarters which were empty as of now, a medical bay which was being used on severe trauma cases only where zero G was best for recovery, and of course cargo bays. As with the Walrus, we were using two of the cargo bays for pods. The only difference is that unlike the empty decks of the Walrus, all the decks on the APEX were loaded down. After all, this was the ship that was supposed to carry us out into the great unknown beyond our own system. As a true colony ship it came with a full compliment of equipment for starting a colony. Prefab panels to build hundreds of structures from homes to hospitals to barns and more. Equipment like tractors with all their implements, dirt working equipment like excavators, dump trucks, etc. The ship was truly loaded with everything we should need to start a colony. It even had dormant fusion reactors that could be flown down to the surface of a planet to provide power for that burgeoning colony.

This was my first time moving from the gravity ring back into real zero G. It was nerve racking. I knew how to move in zero G and had my magnetic boots back on but being many weeks out of practice with my strength not quite back to 100% it had me on edge. The way the ship had been designed was more function than finesse when it came to the transition from ring to the main ship. The ring was connected to the ship via structural arms that led from the outer ring to the center of the ship ending in a smaller ring that rotated around the specially modified round cargo hold. The cargo hold had been modified to handle the massive rotating structure. The normal squarish body of the ship was trimmed down to a circular shape at this deck. This enormous wagon wheel rotated around the circular deck without touching it using a magnetic field like the old maglev trains on Earth. There was no real metal to metal contact as the ring rode around on and on. That lowered resistance and eliminated wear points but served for an odd transition for the crew.

The biggest issue was you could only move from ring to ship via a full space suit. With the ring rotating and the ship not, there was a small gap in the skin where the two came together on the magnetic track. Due to this, the entire cargo bay was kept at full vacuum instead of trying to fully seal that rotating joint. There was an elevator that ran down each of the structural arms all convening on that center cargo bay. According to the training video I watched before attempting the transition, the elevators would stop just past the end of the legs putting you inside the ship by a few feet. At that point you had to activate your magnetic boots and step from what had been the floor of the elevator to one of the walls which was marked to let you know which one. Then what was the bottom of the elevator a minute ago opened up like a door allowing the crew members to walk out the end onto a raised platform in the correct orientation for the rest of the ship.

After going through the video again in my mind and still aboard the ring, I put on my full suit and climbed into the elevator. Looking out the elevator door I was sad to see the ring environment go. Yes, there were metallic walls here just like aboard the ship but out here on the ring there were plants. Here you could walk around without clunky boots on. There was always a definite up and down. On Earth I really took basic gravity for granted and even with only being up and around on the ring for a few weeks I realized I had already started to take it for granted again. Investigating my new environment as the doors closed, I saw familiar grey metallic walls. I could still feel gravity holding me down and I hadn't activated my magnetic boots yet. My mind pleaded for me to soak up this feeling as long as I could. Again, I reminded myself this was only a day trip for a few hours. Come the end of my day aboard the ship, I would travel back up the elevator and be able to bask in the sense of gravity again.

On board the elevator now, I was reminded of not having any buttons to push like an elevator on Earth as it was controlled by a team that operated the elevators. The doors slid shut and almost immediately I felt my stomach drop deep into my abdomen as I was thrusted upwards in my steel box. I felt my breathing ratchet up along with my heart rate. Why was I rising? The ship was below us on the inside of the ring, not outside out towards the stars. I should be dropping down to the ship. This was all wrong.

"Maggie, everything ok?" The deep, strong, but caring voice came across my commlink. The commlink that was now permanently in my ear after having my natural eardrums blown out and replaced by artificial devices. Having the implants now had the benefit of never having to remember my commlinks. On the other hand, I could never use forgetting them as an excuse to not answer either…

"Maggie. Please respond." That deep soothing voice came across again but with a tighter note this time around. Showing some concern? Why would they be worried? I was just flying out into space all by myself. That was it. I was again heading out into the black on my own in a pod not meant to support me out here. I wouldn't make it back this time. I could feel tinges of dark flowing around the outer reaches of my vision. Were those stars? Could I see through the walls of this box now?

"Maggie. Come back to me baby. You need to take a breath. Your heart rate is too high." That voice again. What was that voice? I knew that voice from somewhere. Forcing myself to take a breath I thought about it and then it came back all at once. That was Joe. Christina's husband. He was our mechanic on the Expeditious and Walrus but had lost his place when we came on the APEX. It was a bit out of his scope of experience, so he had been reassigned to man the transports from the outer ring to the ship.

"Joe? Is that you?" I was able to bring myself to finally croak. My throat was restricted down to a string.

"There you go Maggie. Take another few breaths. Are you ok?" Joe's voice was back to his loving deep tone. A tinge of concern still lingered there but he hid it well. Catching my breath again and bringing my mind back in focus I was able to put together what was going on.

"S-Sorry Mr. Thompson, it just felt like the elevator rose. I wasn't expecting to feel it rise and it put me back in my pod on the station there for a moment." I responded in a shaky voice.

"Maggie, for the hundredth time, just call me Joe. Remember, gravity on the ring pulls us out away from the core of the ship. So even though the ship is below us, it is really above us looking from our point of view when we are standing."

"Oh yea, sorry Joe. First time on the elevator is getting me a bit jumpy I guess. I knew that." I could feel my heart slowing some, my breathing coming back near a normal level.

"No problem Maggie, it gets most of us the first time. Very disorienting. Do I need to bring you back down here? Let you get a breather in?"

"No Joe, no. Thanks, but I've got this. Just threw me for a minute, I think I'm fine now."

"Ok honey, I can see your heart rate dropping back into normal range now. Don't worry, you'll get used to it before long. Just a heads up on what to expect here on out. In the next minute or so you should feel a drop in gravity and go into a zero G state. At that point you will be around three quarters the way to the ship. You'll want to spin yourself around and place your feet on the red end of the elevator. Don't lock your boots in though. Just use the handles in the elevator to orient yourself and hold there."

"Yea, I remember that from the training vid. Once the elevator car stops, I have to swing around and stand on the blue wall, right?"

"That is correct Maggie. That's when you can lock your boots in again. Then I will open the red end which will be a wall to you at that point. You should be in the correct orientation at that point to just walk out onto the raised platform in the ship. To me you'll be standing on the wall of the elevator but to the ship you'll be standing on the floor."

"I remember, thanks. I will let you know if anything feels wrong."

"Be safe Maggie. Just remember to take a big step across the threshold between elevator and ship platform. The elevator will seem to be moving slowly and it can still be disorienting the first few times."

"Thanks again Joe. See you when I come back aboard later."

As Joe had warned, it almost felt like the elevator started slowing even though it maintained speed. As we came closer to the ship, the spin rate dropped off lowering the centrifugal gravity effect. Pretty soon it felt as though the elevator reversed course and plummeted away from me. I was back in zero G. Close enough to the ship that my centrifugal speed was too low to give me any sense of gravity. I spun around and put my feet on the now glowing red end of the elevator. This was the roof before but as the elevator began to slow down, I floated to that end and it became the floor.

A clank sounded through the steel box as I felt it settle into its clamps on the ship side. I was still technically aboard the ring but now just inside the skin of the APEX. The elevator never actually touched the ship but rode on rails into the ship as it sat still beneath me.

"Ok Maggie, you are docked now and secure, go ahead and move over to the blue wall."

Without responding I used the grab handles mounted to the opposing walls and swung my feet to stand on the blue wall. Then I locked my boots in and gave a thumbs up knowing Joe could see me from the various cameras installed in the elevator. No sooner had I given the thumbs up the red floor, now a wall, spread apart and opened to the ship. I peered out and saw exactly what I had seen in the video. The expansive interior of the ship spread out before me. I held tight on the grab handles still and peered out as far as I could reach my neck. There was indeed a metal platform that circled the entire room about ten feet from the outer wall. There were giant rails built into those walls and a gap between the rails. That is where I rode. Seven other elevator doors stood spread around the massive area. I could just make out the doors near the one opposite from myself. The one directly across was hidden behind the massive core shaft of the great ship.

Looking down now at the joint between my elevator and the curved walkway I could see there was a gap, but a portion of metal extended out from my elevator and rode just an inch above the platform. Thinking back, I could remember stepping off an old rusty merry go round as a child. This was similar to that. From my point of view the ground I was about to step off onto was moving even though it was what was standing still. I took my big step out, far exaggerating what was needed to clear the junction and landed clumsily on the walkway. Immediately I felt my whole world spin to my left. In my mind I knew that it wasn't the ship that was spinning but it was me that suddenly stopped. That didn't keep the feeling from hitting me. I reached out and grabbed the walkway railing and steadied myself for a few seconds. The ship stopped spinning under my feet, and I felt better. Standing fully upright again I turned and watched my elevator slide away in an arc following the outer skin of the circular room. It didn't move fast but was still a very odd site. The red doors then slid shut and the whole box reversed up out of the ship.

I kept watching as my elevator slid further and further away both while circling me and by sliding away up the shaft leading back out to my sanctuary on the ring. I longed to return to that safe place but that was just the childish portion of me. My analytical mind knew I had a task to complete and my emotional side would only be rewarded once that task was finished. Fortunately, the child within receded back into the depths of my mind and left me alone to continue on. With that weakness quieted for now I could focus on the job. My goal. First thing to do was to find the flight deck and my drone crew. Training was supposed to start within the hour. I gathered myself and walked ahead.

Every fifty feet or so around the raised platform was a set of stairs that led down to the real floor of this level. Just as with the Walrus and Expeditious before it, this ship also utilized a central shaft to house various forms of transport up and down the spine of the ship. Even though there wasn't an air shaft in this ship, it still had the same basic layout. Seemed once people had gotten used to this layout, they used it over and over again, even in the largest of ships that would never see an atmosphere and never need to suck air down to the engines. Instead massive pipes ran from end to end carrying breathable air along with liquids and wastes from various operations going on.

I walked across the expansive deck to the center core. The core here on this deck was larger than any other aboard as it doubled as an air lock since this cargo bay was kept at full vacuum.

Upon my walking up, the ship sensed me and automatically cycled a door open. I stepped inside and it closed behind me clicking shut. Air began to stream in even though it made no sound in my ears. These suits were very well insulated from cold and sound it turned out. Once the airlock had filled to a level deemed safe, a light on each wall lit up green. I checked the screen on my forearm and it showed a green glow along with several readings of gas levels. Everything looked to be where it should have been, so I hid the acknowledge button and the door ahead of me swung open. I walked through and allowed the door to swing back shut and latch behind me before beginning to pull myself from the suit.

It took several minutes to remove myself from the suit completely. These suits were pretty user friendly but still took some effort to take on and off. The biggest thing was having to remove the top half. Even with being weightless, it was still awkward to remove. The bottoms were simple as they just dropped down around my legs and slid off as I stepped from them. The magnetic boots were part of the suit but fortunately a locker had been assigned to me and a separate pair of magnetic boots were left in the bottom for me to use while on the ship.

Once I was all put back together, my suit stuffed in the locker and standing again magnetically held to the floor it was time to move on. Using my tablet as a guide I climbed into a waiting elevator, selected the appropriate deck and continued my trek. When the elevator stopped and the door slid open, it revealed another cargo bay that had been retrofitted as a flight deck. This deck was meant only for the drones though. It housed all the drones, the flight controls for each and a training area where we could practice flying the old-fashioned way in air. I went into the bay and hooked up with one of the team members. He pointed me towards the captain's office where I was to meet up with Mr. Tremmon. My father had set this whole thing up for me as part of our previous deal, so Mr. Tremmon was expecting me.

We already knew each other reasonably well. I remembered back on Earth Mr. Tremmon would come by our home from time to time to speak with my Father. I don't think they were friends or even coworkers, but they knew each other and must have known they were part of the same mission. After speaking with Mr. Tremmon for a while about what I wanted to accomplish as part of his team, I was officially assigned.

My training started immediately that day. I joined up with another member of the team and followed them around learning the ins and outs of the drones we had at our fingertips. There were several types of drones, but they were all based on the same platform. Some were better for handling parts. Some were better for wielding tools. Each drone pilot was assigned to a group of five drones to manage. They could fly around via ground controls or by using their own AI systems on board. The AI was basic, it couldn't complete complicated procedures on its own but if you gave it instructions on what you wanted, it could usually handle the small details of not running into obstacles and get to the destinations you listed. That is why the pilots were assigned to multiple units. As a pilot I could send a drone to fetch a part over here while having another drone with a cutting rig remove a damaged component. When the part carrying drone came back, a third set up with various tools could then attach the new part. It was truly a team effort with the pilot playing the part of head coach.

Each drone had small power cells to keep the weight down or could be fitted with larger cells for longer missions. There were specialized drones that carried mini fusion reactors aboard, but those were reserved for major issues and only the most seasoned pilots were approved to operate them. They were big enough they could do major damage if ran improperly.

The drones I would get to use were originally designed for atmosphere and had 6 small propellers each powered by its own tiny motor. The tech really wasn't all that advanced besides the motors being highly efficient and them carrying small solar cells on their backs to partially recharge while flying when in bright enough conditions. I had always been interested in drone flying back on earth but had never really gotten the opportunity to fly them in much detail. Drones were hard to come by back on earth, especially for the untrained. They were normally reserved for the military but sometimes used to deliver materials around the city. These drones were modified a bit for vacuum. Each propeller was replaced by a tiny reactionless engine to push it around out in space near our ship. They didn't have a great deal of thrust but were able to manage the task at hand.

Each training session was three hours, so I still had plenty of time each day for studying. Yes, my parents enrolled me in a school that my mother helped put together for the minors on board. There was a dozen of us total now, grades from fifth to twelfth. I thought I might get out of schooling now that I had been assigned to a new team and the fact that we were aboard a ship hundreds of thousands of miles from the closest outpost but no, apparently my Earth mandated education was still very important even if the plan was to never return if the mission went ahead ok.

Once training was done for the day, I headed back to the cargo bay that contained my bridge to the ring. I wanted to check out more of the ship but between you and me, I was exhausted. This first outing into the "real world" since my accident had taken a lot out of me. Today was the start of a pattern lasting a full week. I got up in the mornings, ate breakfast and attended my schooling aboard the ring. Mid-day I ate lunch aboard the ring and then transferred down to the ship for drone training. Then back to the ring after for dinner and continued recuperation in the form of time in the gym to build my strength back to its pre accident levels.

Five weeks into our seven-week trip out to an empty void far enough from any gravity wells that my Father's team could get a wormhole to open I was where I finally needed to be. The previous several weeks had been a back and forth emotional roller coaster for me. Each day I felt us get closer and closer to that point where we would jump and my aspirations of keeping us confined to one system would be eliminated. I knew I was quickly running out of time but my request to join the drone team had been a strategic one.

I woke with a start hearing the alarm blaring on my tablet. "Today is the day" I told myself out loud laying in the dark. "Lights on" I spoke out loud. The words were followed by a slow increase in what was visible to my human eyes. As the lights came up, I swung out of bed and dropped my already booted feet to the floor. After a long argument with myself the previous day which continued late into the night, it had been decided that today was the start of my personal mission. Training had gone well for a week and I had passed qualifiers without any difficulty. The drones were easy to fly and being the daughter of the commander never hurt when I wanted something. I tried not to wave that flag too often as I knew it also brought a small bit of resentment from my fellow crew members. If it hadn't been for my connection to the top, someone of my age would never be given the accesses that I had gathered. I knew that but I also knew that I worked for each one. I only used my connections to open doors, never to pass qualification barriers. If I couldn't do something, I didn't want to force it. One mistake could collapse the entire mountain I had climbed and staked my flag upon.

I stood stretching out sore muscles. My leg was back to 100% along with the arm that had been damaged. Everything worked as it should and was probably stronger now than before anything happened due to my persistence in the gym. The difference now though was I could feel the joints. I could feel my bones. They still fought me, told me to slow down but I couldn't. I was strong and I was solid. I would not allow simple bones to keep me from my mission. The thing lacking from my plan now was knowledge. The goal was still the same as before only modified. The magnetic field emitters needed to be switched off or adjusted to cause a cascading failure during start up. A simple bug in the system could cause the emitters to do things that might lead the crew to believe they were fine when the opposite was true. The only way to figure out how to make an impact that would stop our transit but not kill the crew was to go to the source of the ship system design. My Father was that source. He held the answers I wanted. Getting them without tipping him off to what I was doing was the trick.

Within five minutes of waking, I had brushed out the tangles in my hair, freshened up my breath with a quick rinse, straightened out my uniform (enough to keep it from appearing I had slept in it which of course I had) and was walking out the door of my quarters. My walk to the nearest elevator took only another five minutes. The control room for this elevator wasn't occupied by Joe's presence right now. I was so used to seeing his welcoming face that when I opened the door to enter and saw another man, I stopped frozen in place for a moment before realizing of course he wasn't here. I had only been transiting down to the ship in the afternoons during Joe's shifts. This was early first thing in the morning before even breakfast had begun being served in the galley.

I nodded to the man whose name I didn't know off hand. He returned my nod and peered at his computer screen. I knew as soon as I had opened the door the ship would have brought my information up on his monitor offering up details of my clearances and schedules for the day. Fortunately, everything had been approved previously. Late in the evening while arguing with myself I had the forethought to message my Father and request a meeting with him this morning.

Using the all too true reason of wanting to get to know his work better but leaving out the reason for wanting that information, I had convinced him to allow me to shadow him for a half a day instead of attending my normal schooling. I imagine it caused a slight rift between my Mother and him, but she would have eventually agreed to it anyways as the importance of understanding the ship and our mission was more crucial than the few items we would be taught today in our classes. This would not fly for more than a day here or there but all I hoped to need was today.

Once the man behind the operator's desk standing before me confirmed that I was indeed allowed to transit down, he pushed a button opening the access door to my right. Now done being the blockade to my destination he nodded to me. I proceeded through the door thanking him heading straight to my locker. By this point the act of donning my suit was second nature and subsequently I was ready to jump on the elevator now a mere 15 minutes after first waking. The ride down to the ship was uneventful now being as basic and trivial an act as simply hoping on the subway or a bus back on Earth. Once aboard the ship proper walking and gazing again at the wonder of the engineering that brought this beast to life, I reached the air lock and transited through, removing my suit before the interior door had even opened all the way. I quickly packed my suit away in the same locker as always and went out to the open section around the central spine of the APEX.

A quick ride on one of the elevators took me to the deck my Father had designed for himself. It contained both the quantum computer core and his labs. Likely being the highest security level aboard the ship, it was his special hideout. As we flew through the emptiness of space out to our proposed jump point, my Father had left basic operations and flight of the ship to his command crew while he relegated himself to his labs. I knew this section of the ship meant more to him than any other single part. It was buried deep in the center of the great vessel protected as best as it could be from anything coming at us.

Once on board the APEX, the massive computer core my Father had shown me what seemed like years ago was placed in the core of the ship. It was in a tightly guarded area along with my Father's labs. This ship was his pride and joy. A monstrosity of a ship that had been hidden from most on Earth for safety reasons. It had in fact originally been a super freighter but that was only in the beginning. From that point it had been flown out to Mars and parked at the station we picked it up at. The one that was blown to pieces.

At the correct level I waited for the elevator doors to open. They held fast. I had clearance to be down here as the elevator wouldn't have even allowed the floor selection if I wasn't allowed. Puzzling for a moment, I wasn't sure what to do. Should I call my Father? No, I knew I had clearance to be here. I always had clearance and didn't need an appointment to reach this deck. Getting down from the ring to the ship itself was something I needed to be on the schedule for but being on the ship already and showing up at this level I shouldn't need anything for.

Another privilege of being the Commander's daughter. Father spent more time here than anywhere else, so I had been allowed unlimited access here in order to reach him anytime it was needed.

The doors parted finally and tension building in my chest quickly released finding its way out of my core by escaping with a sigh from parted lips. Looking out the doors, I tried to spot my Father. Instead I saw no one. No technicians, not my Father. The deck was empty. White walls and floors extended as far as I could see circling around me. Walking out into the area, I started heading around the center core housing the elevators I just got off. Maybe he was around the corner out of direct eyesight. Nothing as I walked around the core scanning each area. The room was set up as one large open area besides one section walled off with its own security point. That was where the computer core was located. Even if you were allowed on this level, it didn't automatically mean you were cleared to enter that room. I wasn't even able to talk my way into that room. It was secured against everyone besides the very top command crew and a couple specific technicians that had worked closely with my Father on Earth.

The rest of the area was open. There were separate sections where different devices and equipment were set up. I kept looking but didn't see my Father anywhere. Then the doors on the computer room slid open revealing the man I was looking for.

"Sorry dear, I lost track of time in there." Father threw his thumb over his shoulder pointing back into the tightly protected room while walking out towards me. "The system alerted me you had come on board, but I was right in the middle of a code tweak. I had to finish that up real quick before coming out to greet you."

"No problem Daddy. Thanks for agreeing to have me shadow you for a while. I really want to get to know what you have created here a bit better." I was a little frustrated that he had 'lost track of time' but what could I expect. This was his passion and holding it against him would gain me nothing but stress.

"Of course, Maggie, anytime. I was excited to hear you were interested in the jump system again. I feared after our talk on the Expeditious that you were unimpressed."

"No, I was very impressed. If you remember though a lot happened after that and it just hasn't lined up for me to revisit your lab. Now that we are getting close to our jump point and I am helping place all the Magnetic field emitters, I wanted to get a better handle on how the whole thing would work. See if there is anything I can look for out there while we are working."

"Have you seen something you feel isn't right?" Father said this part with a concerned look.

"No, no. That isn't it at all. Everything seems to be going just fine. I just want to make sure I knew what to look for."

"Well Mr. Tremmon should be going over all that with you as you train. It is quite simple. The emitters themselves are not complex units. As long as they are attached in the correct positions on the ship then all will be fine."

"Yes of course Mr. Tremmon has shown us all and taught me well. I guess what I am getting at is with all the problems this mission has had to this point, how do we know there is not still a sabotage plan when we get to our jump point?"

Father's eyes lightened up and a smile came across his face. "Ok, I understand now. You are worried that someone might try to mess with an emitter and disrupt our jump?"

"Basically yes, that is the thought. What would happen if they did?"

"For one, we would know almost immediately. As I am sure you already understand, as soon as you place an emitter it is logged, and my team runs diagnostics on the device to make sure it is working correctly. Then once it is cleared by the system, it is put into a cycled monitoring system controlled by the core quantum computer. The core cycles through all active emitters every 30 seconds. That means the longest any emitter goes unwatched is 30 seconds."

"A lot can happen in 30 seconds though" I said raising concern in my voice. This was great information to have. If I needed to do something, I had 30 seconds to do it within.

"Yes, you are right, but the thing is that the core does that only while we are on standby. Once we reach our jump point and start the final preparations, the core will start inspecting each individual emitter every second. Every single emitter will be inspected each second. Then when we are within 10 minutes of the jump and through until the jump is complete, the status of each emitter will be checked one thousand times per second and adjustments will be made if needed at the same pace."

"Wow, that is amazing but if someone altered the emitters before the final few minutes, they would still have time to change code in between inspections."

"Ok, in theory, yes you are correct. If they could get through the firewalls, then they could inject some damaging code within the delays between inspections but it wouldn't matter. Part of each unit's inspection is not only a status inspection but a debugging inspection. The code is checked to make sure no new data is there. No worms or viruses. If anything like that is injected, then the system will flag it and halt all other processes."

My heart dropped a bit then. My idea had been to inject a virus into the system that caused the emitters to burn out when they were brought to full power. That would have caused the field to drop off before the wormhole was opened and would give the crew plenty of time to cancel the jump before we entered the wormhole and tore ourselves apart. If the emitters had a full debugging each second and then even faster right before firing up, then there was no way that would not be caught.

"Maggie, is that not what you were hoping for?" My Father looked at me puzzled. Obviously, I had not hidden my disappointment well enough and was sharing it with him now. Quickly I shut that sharing off and tried to lead him away.

"No, that is great. Sorry. Just thinking hard. It sounds like the emitters can't be messed with. What about the core itself? There was a bomb on the Walrus we didn't know about. What if someone was able to sneak one on this ship too and brought it down here?"

"Well, IF someone was able to get another bomb on the APEX, I don't think they would have waited this long to activate it. If the goal was just to blow the ship up with a crude device like that then they should have done it while we were in disarray after the explosion at Mars. I highly doubt anyone has one on board at this point. It just wouldn't make sense."

"Yea, I can see that I guess. Is there any way someone could get to the core then? What if a virus was injected into it?"

"Maggie, that would be impossible, and I don't even mean impossible like unlikely. It is literally impossible. For one, only 5 people on board even have access into that room. Those are only the most trusted people aboard. Impossible."

"But what if someone stole one of their ID badges?"

Father re-examined me for a moment before responding. "Maggie, are you really asking that question? Did you swipe an ID badge when you came in here?"

"Well, no but," He cut me off holding a hand up in a stop motion and spoke again, "Maggie, the ship is far beyond ID badges. Every movement you make is tracked and recorded with bio metrics. The ship knows who you are and what you are allowed to do on board without any tags or badges needed. I don't care if someone stole MY ID badge. They would get no further with it than without it. The badges at this point are really just a holdover from the past with no real use other than allowing you to know someone's name and title even if you don't know them."

"That makes sense. Ok, so I guess no real reason for me to be worried about that then?"

"You have nothing to worry about darling. This is my ship. We had issues on the others because they were rushed or improvised transports that were not planned out. This is my ship. This is my creation. This is my safe house. Nothing will get us here. I promise you are safe." Standing back up straight and looking around the room, "Now hopefully you didn't come here just to talk catastrophe. Want a tour?"

"Of course I do!" I said excitedly. Deep inside I was cursing in frustration. I was no closer to figuring out how to stop the ship without destroying it than I had been before our talk. I couldn't let that show through again. My Father was a smart man and intuitive. He would see through me if I slipped up too many times. We moved on to a few areas of the lab talking about different projects he was working on at the time. Most centered around the wormhole but he seemed very content with where they were at on that. He told me there wasn't a lot more they could do on that front until all the emitters were in place and wired in. Then they could start doing system checks and prepare for the jump.

During our tour around the lab looking at all the different experiments and projects in the works I was able to get him on the topic of what happened at Mars. Mother had kept me partially up to date during my stent in rehab, but I wanted to see what I could get out of my Father also. The overview of what he told me explained that the explosion which was officially still under investigation at this point was still very much a mystery. There was little known on who was responsible for the attack. The team my Father placed in charge of the investigation knew the explosion originated in the Walrus itself. One of the cargo pallets detonated, wiping out a team on that deck along with half of the Walrus itself and the entire station we were attached to.

The pallet had originally been near the front of the move list as it was noted as medical supplies but something with the scanners had malfunctioned causing the pallet to be categorized wrong in the system. When the first team had reached it and got the erroneous reading off its tag, they moved it aside and kept moving other pallets. The problem pallet was noted in the system but put on a low priority, so no one made it to checking the pallet out in time.

For an unknown reason it detonated aboard the Walrus taking a team with it. The explosion spun the Walrus into the main section of the station. The resulting wad of twisted wreckage spun away from the vulnerable APEX. Fortunately saving the ship from major damage or destruction. Just as the crew aboard the APEX was able to get her engines fired up and the ship moved away from the immediate scene, the Walrus/Station combination exploded in a white-hot ball of fast escaping gasses and debris. Before that final explosion, I had been in the section of station still attached to the fleeing APEX. The waves of plasma and debris escaping from the ensuing explosion ripped my section of station away from the APEX and in an impact with some other random debris it had shredded spewing broken pods and bodies out into the void.

The crew had known I along with a few others were in pods floating away at high speed and tracked them with active sensors. The pods travelled so fast and were so small that most were lost before the big APEX could accelerate after them all. Fortunately for me by the time I regained consciousness and was able to get my pod to transmit the APEX crew happened to be listening for signals from my area and caught mine. They dispatched skaters and retrieved my pod. Only one other had also been recovered alive. A woman from Earth who never knew anything was wrong at all. In fact, she still didn't as she was in stasis when the explosion occurred, but her pod was spared from any damage. Sensing the vacuum, the pod did not wake her up and instead broadcasted an emergency beacon like mine should have done. A skater recovered her pod before mine and once on board the APEX, along with a thorough inspection, it was determined she was fine, and she was placed in storage with the other colonists still asleep.

Back on the doomed Walrus, we lost two of our military contingents in the explosion. Three were still aboard the APEX. Major Bonette had taken up the control deck on the Walrus during our transition while the rest of the crew moved to the APEX to get her ready for transit. Two soldiers were on the deck above the explosion when it went off. They were helping move cargo and were in the wrong place at the wrong time. Their bodies were lost to time and space most likely consumed entirely in the instant after the explosion. The Major was able to eject in an escape capsule before the Walrus went critical and ended its existence in our universe as a tightly bound grouping of organized atoms. With the good Major being in an escape capsule, she was able to use its propulsion system to get to the APEX as it accelerated away towards the hurled pods.

In total we lost 34 crew including the two soldiers. While I was out of commission, the remaining crew woke replacements and mourned the loss of those gone forever. It was luck the pallet had remained on board the Walrus as long as it did. The way Father explained it, there was a failure in his operations since the moment the pallet had scanned bad, a tech should have been on the pallet and fixed the issue putting it back on the schedule to be moved but because of the mad rush to move everything over, that pallet had slipped through the net and been left. No one caught hell for that failure though as it had probably saved the lives of thousands and the hopes of millions.

As we continued our tour around the lab, I reflected on the attack. Part of me wished the attack would have been successful as it would have solved my internal crisis. The explosion would have destroyed all parts of the worm hole engine and system. It would have killed all those that knew the system inside and out. It would have wiped out the ship that was designed just for this purpose and it would have killed me. Not only would I not have had to worry about the escape from our solar system by my invasive, destructive species, but it would have also ended my existence and with it my concern about everything. I could have known true peace. Or not known anything at all depending on how you looked at it.

In the end I was glad I was alive. That told me that I wanted my life and I wanted it to mean something. I still did not know what may lay on the other side of that great divide, but I did know I wanted to stay on this side for as long as possible. I also knew I could not bring about my Mother or Father's demise. I simply couldn't be responsible for that. Even if in the end it had no impact on my afterlife or lack of, I simply would not be able to bring myself to manufacturing their ending prematurely. That made my internal struggle a bit harder as I still wanted badly to keep us within our home system but now had to ensure that whatever I did would not bring about the deaths of any of my own people.

I stayed with him until just after lunch opting to stay aboard the ship instead of returning to the ring only to have to transit back down again to get to my drone training session an hour later. That seemed to make him happy, but I could also tell he was itching to get back to work. I took up his entire morning, during which time he wasn't able to do any real work. Acting more as a tour guide than a scientist didn't suit him. He would never admit it, but I know there was relief in his face when I announced it was time for me to move on and get to my training session. It bothered me some, but I knew he loved me in his way.

During training that day I thought about what I was going to do. My theory was to train with the drone team, who over the past few weeks and over the next few weeks had been and would be placing the magnetic field emitters all over the skin of the ship. We had brought the emitters with us from Earth on the Expeditious and then the Walrus. Enough made it aboard the APEX to satisfy my Father that we would be able to create the magnetic bubble around the ship required to protect it while transiting the wormhole. If I could cause failures at enough of those emitters, then we would have to delay the mission in order to get new ones. This could delay us years depending on how long it took to build them and ship them out to us. That could buy me enough time to work up another plan to more permanently keep us in system.

After speaking with my Father though, the challenge would be designing a failure that would go undetected until the emitters were fired up to full strength. It couldn't be a software failure but a hardware failure in the device. Maybe something within the power supply. I needed to get an emitter to myself for a while so I could dissect it and figure out what all was inside them. Find a weak point.

Six weeks into our flight I was handed the controls of an unregulated drone team. This wasn't the first time I was allowed to fly the drones on the outside of the ship, but it was the first time I wasn't linked directly to a trainer's console to be watched. My practice time was complete and now as a full-fledged drone pilot I could work on the project at hand. My first magnetic field emitter (MFE) placement went without a hitch. I took a 3-drone team out and was able to fly the MFE to the correct latching point and lock it into position. One drone carried the unit, guiding it through open space. While that drone was bringing the unit out, a lead drone arrived first and prepped the location by removing a cover and pulling cables from the ship.

When the MFE arrived, I had the prep drone attach the cables to the emitter by plugging in the specially designed connector. The connectors were nearly robotic themselves. Created to ease the installation process, the two halves would sense each other, and tiny actuators would spin clamps to bring the ends together making a tight connection that couldn't vibrate loose. With the wires connected, the prep drone took the panel it had removed and brought it back to the drone bay to be stored away for future use when/if it was needed. The third drone on my team paired up with my carrier drone and between the two of them I guided the emitter to its connection point and twisted it in until the unit latched to the ship. More smart connectors activated locking pins securing the emitter tightly to the ship.

With my first mission being a complete success, I brought the drones back into the bay and parked them. After parking and confirming with the team lead, I removed my VR helmet and stepped away from the operator's controls. I noticed one of my fellow pilots speaking animatedly with an engineer and one of the other team leads down at the end of the row of control modules.

I walked down towards them and overheard an argument over what to do with an emitter that was unresponsive. The pilot, John I think his name was, wanted to bring the emitter back on board the ship for repair since it was unresponsive from the moment of installation while the engineer thought they could repair it in place.

As I walked up, the engineer noticed me and quieted down. His sudden change must have tipped off the other two as they also turned to see me approaching. I raised my hand as though waving and trying to seem welcoming I said, "Hey guys, what's going on over here? Is there a problem with an emitter? Maybe I can help."

The engineer, a tall large man topped with a wad of rough red hair that reminded me of Billy back home, huffed but quickly regained his composure and spoke up next in a voice a bit higher than I would have expected coming from a man of his size, "Sorry, I don't think you can help with this repair. It is quite a complicated unit to work on. I don't think you have the expertise required."

"I can understand that," I said understanding where he was coming from but hating the tone he used basically letting me know he thought I was too stupid to understand, "However I do have some experience working on the emitters. After all, you know who my Father is. You don't think I grew up in the same house and never saw any of the equipment do you?" Of course I never had, in fact I didn't even know who my Father really was until we first launched from Earth but I didn't know any of these guys so it was likely we picked them up on Mars and that would mean they wouldn't know that I was stretching the truth pretty far.

"Listen little one, I know who your Father is, and I respect him, but this issue does not concern you. Why don't you run on back to your station and drive your drones around some more?" With that the engineer waved his arm showing what direction he wanted me to scamper off in. This pissed me off. I don't mind someone underestimating me but if you try to blow me off to my face with that kind of attitude it really digs under my skin.

"Listen," I paused and looked for his badge. Finding it sticking out of a pants pocket but not readable I reached out and snagged it to read the name. "Arnold Becker, I know you probably think I am a spoiled little brat that couldn't ever be nearly as smart as a brilliant engineer such as yourself but I will tell you right now I bet I could fix that emitter quicker than you."

This got a chuckle out of the team lead and John while it turned Arnold's face a bright shade of red that I think was made more up of anger than embarrassment over being called out by a minor. I turned to John like he was my accomplice and said "Can you fly that emitter back in here for us? I want to show this snobby engineer where he ranks in the mental hierarchy." I knew this was a gamble but pretty sure these guys would love to see me go up against the man I already pinned as a grade A narcissist.

"Sure thing Ms. Johanson. I think I could bring it back in for you." John replied to me smiling. "It ought to be fun to see you two go at it." At that, he turned back to his station and slipped his helmet on going to work to remove and bring the broken emitter back to the drone bay.

"Ok, Mr. Becker. Why don't we circle around to the parts airlock so we can retrieve the emitter when it comes back on board?"

"Ms. Johanson, now I know you think I am an idiot and you are so much more brilliant than I but how do you expect us to see who is smarter here? There is only one emitter that needs looked at."

I thought about that one for a moment. He was right and I hadn't really thought about it that far out. Really, I only wanted to get in front of an emitter with some tools to pull the covers off. I had yet to see inside one of the things and only had an idea of how they worked. My entire goal was to see the innards to see if there was a way to break them without anyone noticing until it was too late. Then I had an idea.

"Simple really, kind of surprised you hadn't already surmised what my idea was seeing how smart you are. What I propose is that we bring the emitter in. Set it inside the staging area and pull the covers off. We can even have one of the other engineers do it so neither of us gets a sneak peek. Then we both get five minutes to poke around at it together. After time is up, we both write down our solutions and then we see which one is right."

Arnold thought about that for a minute still stewing on my assertion that he was slower than me to the punch.

"Fine Ms. Johanson. That will work for me. I may need a tester though to check certain components."

"Ok, any testing that is done on the unit will have results shared to both parties."

"Not a chance. I am not going to give you my results."

I figured I ought to try and drive the knife in a bit further and twist. Really get him going. The angrier I could get him ahead of time the more likely he would overlook a simple issue and give me the score.

"Well, then we will only waste valuable diagnostic time since you will just copycat any tests I perform anyways. I'm not really interested in your tests, I just figured it would save us both time for me to give you mine so we can move on."

By this time, we had made our way to the prep area behind the airlock and apparently our conversation was being overheard by more people now garnering more attention than before. I heard a few chuckles when I finished my last antagonistic statement. Arnold started to respond in a rash counterattack but seeing the same people grouping up around us got him to take a breath. No matter the outcome of our challenge, he could tell it would do him no good to be in a knife throwing contest with a little girl half his age. A mere child against a big ole trained engineer.

"Ms. Johanson, we will share any testing results with each other. Our inferences from that data will be of our own until we reveal our diagnosis and plan for repair. Deal?"

I acted as though I was thinking about that for a moment just to keep the tension high but after a moment reached my hand out to shake. He reached his out and we shook. As we shook, a drone piggybacking an emitter flew into the bay. It glided up and placed the emitter on a cart which locked onto the emitter as soon as it touched down. The drone reversed course and backed away while the cart started rolling towards us still on the vacuum side of the barrier separating us from outside. After the air lock cycled through, the cart rolled up to an assigned parking spot. One of the other engineers started pulling panels off of it while Arnold and I kept our backs turned. Maybe ten minutes later all the panels were removed, and we were told it was ready to go. I turned slowly not allowing myself to be outwardly excited. I had to play this off as old news if I was to keep my story supported.

Before me was the emitter as I was used to it but with the internals uncovered. Arnold was already digging in, but I stayed back looking over his shoulder to take in the whole device. A disc of stainless steel about three feet in diameter. Maybe ten inches tall in the center. It was the shape of a large hockey puck. Nearly flat across the top and bottom besides the connection port on the underside. The top had a cross design supporting the four now removed panels. Each panel would normally be attached with hex headed screws all the way around. Those threaded holes were now displayed empty with the panels gone.

Inside the emitter I could see the largest portion of the device was a circular chunk of metal that was hollowed out in the center with a coil wrapping it all the way around. A rod physically separate from the coil-wrapped donut protruded out from the center and ended just inside the cross structure supporting where the panels would sit. That portion would be the actual emitter. I didn't see anything there that could help me. If I touched that coil, the entire unit would be completely dead. That could be the problem today, but I wasn't really worried about that. I wanted to know what I could do to break one when planned.

Tracing my eyes around the donut I found the heavy cables that fed it. Those had to be the power cables. They led back to a solid relay block which was connected via smaller wires to another block. A panel had been removed from that smaller block revealing circuit boards inside. That is where Arnold was focusing his attention at the moment. He had a testing device in his hands checking terminals all over those boards. With that section covered, I figured my time would be better spent looking at the relay and power cables. After all, Father had told me that the ship checked the units constantly so anything I did to the circuit boards would probably be noticed quickly. The relay block looked like a solid piece. Probably not much I could do there. It was held in with 4 bolts.

I turned to the engineer that had removed the panels previously and asked him if he could remove those bolts to allow inspection under the relay. Arnold looked up smiled snidely and said in a demeaning tone, "Ahh, can you not operate any tools on your own? Need someone to help you with the wrenches? That wasn't part of the deal. You are hunting the wrong game anyways. Those relays are solid, they never fail. I've got this easy. It is obviously going to be in the control board."

I ignored him and motioned to the other engineer. He nodded and grabbed some tools. Arnold scoffed again but went back to his control boards running the tester back and forth on terminals. While the other engineer went about removing the bolts, I turned back to the team leader.

"How did you all determine this unit was bad anyways?"

"Well, when they turned it on there was no signal. Nothing. Completely dead. No reaction."

"So, it never gave any feedback at all? No failure signal, no momentary blip?"

"No ma'am. DOA."

I thought about that for a minute. Running through my mind how that could come about. If there was a problem with the control boards that Arnold was solely focused on, then it should have at least sent a failure code back to the ship. The only way there would be nothing at all would be if either the boards were completely shot which would show visibly with burn marks or no power ever made it to the emitter at all. I watched as the engineer removed the bolts and lifted the main relay out turning it over.

He looked at the relay and then to me with big eyes. He knew right then just as I did what had happened. I grinned and put a finger to my lips to keep him from announcing my discovery for Arnold to hear. Shifting over, I peered around Arnold's frame to get a closer look at the control boards. As I did so, the larger man adjusted to block my view.

"Not so sure about your power relays over there, now are you? Want to reverse course and look over my shoulders? No way, you picked your area, now live with it." He said in such a way I could nearly feel his disdain for this stupid young lady trying to push his buttons.

The guy was so full of himself I thought to myself. I went into this little competition fully expecting to lose. I had hoped to pull out an upset as that would help me even more but all I needed was to get the chance to see the internals of the emitters. Now I really did want to win just to shove it in his face. Deciding to really try and dig into him and keep him from thinking too clearly, I responded starting with a solid snorting laugh, "Ha-ha, really I already figured out what the cause of the issue was. I just wanted to make sure you were still well behind on your diagnosis. Good luck to you. You'll need it."

"You think you diagnosed the issue already?" Arnold kept at working his circuit boards, but I saw a tense in his body flow. I had thrown him a bit there. "I doubt that. There is no way you already figured it out. You haven't even actually touched the emitter."

"Oh Arnold, that's fine. Some of us don't think with our hands. Some of us can use our minds to come to conclusions. I guess the real determination will be when we both reveal our diagnosis here in about two more minutes."

I stepped back with that and watched Arnold. He paused and looked over at me with an expression of confusion on his face. He reddened and went back to his testing. Watching as he worked feverishly, I waited for the clock to wind down on our little competition which I had already won I was sure of. Even better, I had figured out what to do to create my failure point. I thought at least. There was no real way to know for sure yet, but I was fairly confident.

Besides Arnold's various curses and threats to the machine under his breath, everyone stayed quiet. There were a few murmurs in the crowd but nothing loud enough to discern. It could have been crew members betting back and forth or sharing disbelief in the little girl who so assuredly just stood there watching as her competitor kept working away. Soon enough though the Team Lead spoke up announcing the end of our time.

"Arnold, please step back. Times up man"

Arnold stepped back at that with his arms raised. I watched his face, but it was pointed away from me keeping any decoding of his expression from me. The Team Lead spoke up again,

"Ok, that is the end of your diagnostic time. How are you wanting to reveal what you determined?"

"Arnold can go first," I spoke up trying to maintain control over the situation. Arnold spun around towards me with a look of near rage on his face and spit out,

"You would love me to go first. I don't think so. You don't have a clue what is wrong with the emitter and just want to ride in on my work to make it look like you did."

Well I thought to myself, that worked out nicely. I didn't want him to go first but I had a feeling he had no clue himself and wanted me to go first. Instead I went another way.

"You are probably right big guy. I would hate for you to go first and then I say the same thing. Would make for a hard decision on who was really correct. I think I will just write down what I believe to be the issue on my tablet here. You can do the same and then we can reveal to our friendly neighborhood Team Leader for him to decide."

"Why don't you just reveal now out loud?" Arnold asked before he could stop himself. I saw him realize his mistake the moment the words left his mouth.

"Oh, so you are saying you need my ideas out there first before you can reveal your own? You aren't having issues coming up with your own diagnosis, are you?"

"No-no, no. I know what my diagnosis is. Just don't see the need for a confusing turn of explaining it on our tablets when you could just announce yours. If you want to be difficult about it though then fine. Have it your way."

I nodded to him in agreement and we both pulled our tablets out. Quickly I typed out my discovery and what I felt needed done. It took maybe fifteen seconds to write out and submit to the Team Leader. I let my tablet drop to my side and looked over to Arnold who was bent over his screen typing away with both hands. He kept going. And going. After probably a good minute and a half he finally looked up and over at me. A panicked look was there on his face. I knew he didn't have it. What he had been typing out though I couldn't think of. So much typing for such a simple problem.

The Team Leader spoke up then, "Alright everyone," I peered around quickly and at that moment noticed the number of people who had shown up. There had to be two dozen or more crew now all on this deck in this area watching to see what the results of an experienced senior engineer going up against an untrained minor would be. The Lead continued, "I have reviewed both of your explanations of the issue at hand and your recommendations for repair. At this point it is obvious to me that one is correct. Neither answer matches the other in any way so only one of you was correct. Ms. Johanson, thank you for your input. I am determining that at this time you are correct in your diagnosis. Arnold, I am sorry, but you are incorrect in your assertion."

"WHAT?!?" Arnold exclaimed loudly. "How can you even know that? Neither diagnosis has been tested yet. You cannot possibly know which of us is correct." Pointing at me he continued, "She didn't even touch the damn thing. There is no way she found something I did not. The only thing she even looked at was the main power relay and I know that isn't the problem. I put that relay together and installed it in this unit myself!!"

Looking back, it was not the best time to lose control of my outbursts, but I couldn't help it. Of course, I had no idea Arnold himself had worked on this unit, but it should have been apparent to me since he was the engineer looking into the problem with it. Obvious to me after the fact he would have been the one to prep the unit and do all the final checks before releasing it for placement out on the hull. I snickered when he said he had put it together himself. Well, a snicker may be a bit of an understatement. What I really did was a combination snicker/cough/sneeze/laugh that was not covered up by my hand quickly enough allowing a wad of snot to sail away from me and right onto the side of Arnold's uniform sleeve. He spun towards me with a furious look on his face.

"What the hell do you find so funny?" He snarled at me. I could only respond with a choked apology from what I knew was coming next.

"Mr. Becker, please control your temper. You are only damaging your own position here losing control like that. Ms. Johanson, same goes to you. If you cannot act professional here, we don't need either of you on the deck." The Team lead looked both of us over and not getting any further responses from either, he continued.

"As I said, Ms. Johanson's diagnosis is my pick for the correct one. Yes Arnold, we cannot know for sure until we test it but once you hear her reasoning, I believe you will also side with my decision whether you like it or not." With that he moved over next to the emitter and reached in grabbing the main relay with one hand and rotating it up so that we could all see the side we needed to. A few gasps rose up from those crowded around us and then some chuckles. The chuckles quickly died out as the Team Lead shot the offenders with deadly looks. I looked over and Arnold stared at the relay in disbelief. Then shame overtook his face and he turned as though to walk away. I reached out to him suddenly feeling bad for making a mockery of him in such a public fashion.

"Sorry Arnold. I didn't know you were the one to put it together. It should be an easy fix at least. No damage done."

The big man spun back to me, his mess of red hair following him quickly behind as it floated behind him. That hair wasn't ridiculously long but being as bright as it was against the regular dreary grays and silvers of the ship all while floating in the zero G of space, it stood out making it appear to be longer and more flowing than it otherwise would. On a planet it probably didn't even bring much attention but up here it floated around his head almost making it appear as though he was surrounded in flame all the time. His eyes locked on mine, icy anger flaring inside. He started to respond to me with vile words tickling the end of his tongue but as I watched he was able to reel himself in. Calming somewhat.

"Ms. Johanson. I admit to my own defeats. I was the one that put that unit together and obviously I made a mistake on this one. You may have made a mockery of me today, but I still believe that you are reaching well beyond your own understanding into a world you know little about. You were lucky here today. Be careful with how proud you are of this small victory as it could came back to haunt you later on."

With those words Arnold walked away, magnetic boots clanking away. I turned back to the Team lead who was now joined by another engineer pointing out the repair that needed done. I approached the duo and whether it was right or not I injected myself back into the discussion.

"Sirs, if you wouldn't mind, I would like to fix this emitter." They both broke their conversation and turned to face me. I continued, "It was my diagnosis anyways, right?" The engineer turned and waited for guidance from his Team lead who had been presiding over the entire process. The Lead motioned for the engineer to leave and waved me over. He reached his hand out for a shake.

"Ms. Johanson. You were correct in your diagnosis, but something tells me it was more luck than knowledge on your part. In 95% of cases, an emitter failure would be in the boards Arnold was looking at. Why did you think it would be in the relay on this unit?"

"Well" I looked for his name really quick so I could remember him later on. "Well, Mr. Wilson, it really wasn't all that intuitive. I am not an engineer, but I have taken some courses and did my research on these emitters. I know that you all test the emitter on board the ship before sending them out to be mounted. Because of that I felt that if the emitter never responded at all then it was unlikely it had a total board failure at the very moment it was connected. The only other option was the power feeds never worked. Once again since the feeds from the ship are tested and monitored, it had to be within the emitter itself. The only part that it could be was the relay. The main power never goes to the boards, the boards just activate a relay which sends power to the emitter coils."

"Very good Ms. Johanson. That was a correct assumption but also a very simple one. Could you have diagnosed anything wrong with the boards?"

"Maybe, maybe not. Mr. Wilson, I wasn't looking to make Arnold look bad or embarrass him. When I heard you all arguing over it, there was an opportunity to get my hands dirty in an aspect of the ship I was interested in but hadn't gotten to see up close yet, so I took it. Not to place blame on others but if Arnold wouldn't have spoken in such a derogatory way to me to start with, I probably wouldn't have challenged him at all. It struck me wrong and I reacted poorly. I do apologize for that and would like to speak with Arnold again at some point to clear the air."

"That would be a good idea to do and I am happy to hear you admit that you may have let your own feelings get away from you. I think you could be a hell of an engineer at some point, but it is important to not burn bridges. You never know when you may need help from someone. You don't want that person to hold a grudge when your day of need arrives."

"Understood Sir. Once again, I do apologize to you for getting a bit carried away. Could I help with the repair to this unit so it can be flown back out and put into service?"

"I don't see why not young lady. I will leave it to you. Check in with me once you think you have it ready to go. I will look it over and sign off on it. Then you can fly it back out and connect it yourself." With that, Wilson walked away leaving me alone with the emitter and a small collection of tools to work on it with.

I quickly dove into the emitter. The problem I had seen that made my victory so easy and upset Arnold was one cable that led from the plug to the relay was pulled out at the plug end. That plug was what connected to the ship once in place. When the emitters are tested aboard ship, the testing cables are connected to special ports on the relay to feed power. The cable from relay to power port is one of those smart self-connecting plugs that are not meant to be plugged and unplugged repeatedly so it is bypassed during testing. I had to assume that was going to change now. I took just a moment to bet myself that within a week the new testing apparatus would connect directly to the power port just as the ship would be doing on the hull.

Connecting the power cable to the relay was a bit harder than I expected. The amount of power running through those cables was quite tremendous in order to create the kind of magnetic field that was needed. Each cable was a solid piece, no braided flexible cables here. It didn't want to bend at all for me. This was perfect though because as I was working with it, I tested my theory of how to fix these emitters so they would fail only at the final moment causing us to have to stay in system longer. My idea, which I tried out here in this emitter first, was a simple slice from the same power cable I was connecting. These cables were designed to carry the full load of transit through a worm hole.

They were designed to do just that; no extra material would have been added beyond what was required as material was expensive. Each cable could handle it's expected load but no more. So, a simple cut out of a single power cable would decrease the load it could handle before it failed. I also knew though that due to the extreme power required, full load testing would not be done on the emitters before the actual transit. Partial load testing would be done but no full load testing. Removing a tab of material from a single cable that equaled about half its diameter would create a point that should survive all the partial load tests that would be run but would not show any failures to the computers. Then upon transit, the cables would melt down at the point of full load causing failures on enough emitters to force a cancellation of our transit. It would take time to fix all the damaged emitters. Time in which I could think of a better, more long-term plan to halt our transit.

I notched the cable and slid the protective insulation back over my modification. Then I connected the cable to the relay and bolted the relay back in its place. Where the notch was in the cable, it was now hidden by the body of the relay. Once I was happy with my work, I called Mr. Wilson back over to inspect it. He approved and authorized the cart to return to the vacuum of the drone deck. I went back to my station and fitted my helmet and drive gear. An hour later I had the customized emitter back out on the hull of the ship and reconnected. It wouldn't be tested today as it was nearly the end of the shift at this point, but it would be tested the next day and hopefully would pass all initial tests with flying colors. No problems should arise with it until the final day.

My mission for the day was complete and I felt great for it. In the back of my mind, there was still a reminder letting me know this was not an end game solution, but only a stop gap measure. This would give me time to find another way to keep us in this system. For now, I didn't have time to think of that long-term solution, I still needed to modify enough emitters to keep us here in the short term. I figured if I could cause a cascading failure of around five percent of emitters, that would force my Father to abandon. Five percent all in one area would be enough to weaken the magnetic field to a point where he would not be able to guarantee us safe passage through a wormhole. This was all theoretical and I wasn't working off any real numbers but it sounded good to me so that was what I had to go with.

Over the remainder of that fifth week and the entirety of the sixth, I went to my duty station each day to run drones and affix emitters. The first day after my victory against Arnold, I went up to him and apologized for my actions. He wouldn't accept it saying he was the one who let my trash talk get to him. He was supposed to be an adult and take a higher road. We worked out a truce and he agreed to let me hang around while he worked on different projects. I had an ulterior motive here also, since I really didn't want to be pals with the guy. He was still a narcissistic jerk and at every opportunity he would remind me of how much smarter he was than myself. I took in all the knowledge he handed off regardless of how he presented it. I did learn a lot and had plenty of opportunities to bring my plan into reality.

Arnold and I worked into a routine. Each afternoon after I flew my emitter mounting missions for the day, I would move over to the engineering area and help Arnold get emitters ready for testing and to be placed the next day. He would assemble the emitters and work on all the technical details while he allowed me to put the relays in and run the power cables. On one hand it was what I wanted to work on as it gave me all the time I needed to notch power cables. On the other hand, it bugged me as I knew he was having me work on this section only because it was very basic and he still didn't think I could handle anything more technical than cable A goes in slot A, etc....

July 28th rolled around, and I was done. Deciding I had sabotaged enough emitters to complete the mission I had laid out for myself, I called it good. Enough of a failure rate should occur as to shut down our transit and give me more time to come up with a longer-term solution. I didn't have much time before the day of our transit attempt as it was scheduled for August second, a mere six days away. The ship had already started deceleration. We were slowing at a rate small enough as to not impact our regular activities. If you were out in the gravity ring and watched a bowl of water carefully you could see it gather more on one side than the other as if the bowl was out of level. If you stood quiet and still enough you could feel the almost imperceptible tug towards the rear of the ship as the engines fired slowing us. Father had wanted to leave the gravity ring turning as long as possible to keep morale up. Even with being a space faring species now, we were still naturally happier in gravity than in Zero G.

The ring would be shut down before our transit attempt but only just before. The Saturday morning before our wormhole jump, I flew my final missions to place the emitters that had been completed the day before. Normally they would have waited for Monday shifts to start but Father had requested that we get them all in so his team could have extra time to go through tests and make sure all was ready to go. I didn't really want his group to have more testing time as that would only leave more opportunity for them to uncover my actions, but I couldn't just not do my job as that would put the spotlight on myself. I had to trust in the plan that was already in motion and hope that all modifications that had been made were well done enough to survive testing without issue.

Finally, the big day came. We had travelled far enough out of the system for my father and his team to feel safe trying to jump. I hadn't seen my father much in preceding weeks. After our last talk down in his labs, I was working non-stop between the drone team, helping Arnold put together the emitters and my school requirements. I know Father had been busy during that time also but even if he hadn't, we still wouldn't have seen each other much. There was part of me that didn't want to see him. I knew I was working directly to destroy the creation he had spent his professional life building. That guilt rode with me but I didn't see any other way.

I did know that Father was working feverishly on our trip out. The APEX had only taken minor damage in the explosion that removed the Walrus and the station above Mars from existence, but the damage was extensive enough to take what was left of his attention after focusing the majority on his main project. The engine that should take us from one part of the galaxy to another.

His team had been working on that engine and the controlling supercomputer non-stop since Mars. Rounds and rounds of numbers, self-checks, adjustments and more checks. Everything had been run over thousands of times. Plans for every conceivable event had been hammered out and put into place within the massive computer. At the point of wormhole creation, the ship should take care of all the fine details on its own with no human hands intervening. The sheer scale of calculations and adjustments were so immense that there was no way for even the smartest human in existence to keep up with the process. It was simply beyond the limitations of our organic minds.

Now Father's team believed the system to be ready for a test fire of the engine. Most of the crew that weren't in stasis pods were taken to conference rooms around the ship that had been fitted with seat restraints. The gravity ring had also been stopped; all liquid water stored away to keep it from floating around in the zero G where it shouldn't be. Everyone out on that ring had been moved down to the ship in case something happened to it while transiting the wormhole. No one really knew what would happen in transit so we wanted to make sure that if we did get bounced around or if worse case, the wormhole wasn't as large as we planned for then we would at least not have people flying all over slamming into things or in a ring that was torn from the ship.

As for myself, after much moaning, groaning and claiming that I just wanted to spend time with good 'ole Daddy, I got to be in the Command Center with my mother and father. I wanted to see exactly what my hard work over the past couple weeks accomplished. I wanted to know if I had succeeded or killed us all or made no difference whatsoever. Here in the control room I should be able to see what went on. Anywhere else on the ship I may not get to see real information. I would be stuck only with what was officially released by my Father's staff.

Mother and I were strapped into jump seats lining the outer perimeter of the central shaft while my Father and his executive crew were all strapped in at their respective stations.

"Okay people, lets run the power up and start charging capacitors" Father started, "Power generation, how do you report?"

"Power generation reports all generators in the green sir" responded a crew member with O'Malley on his shirt.

"Where are the capacitor banks at?" My father replied back to O'Malley.

"Capacitor banks at 67% and rising steadily sir."

"Good, let me know when they hit 90%. General Carter, all your gear locked in tight?"

"My military personnel and equipment are locked in and tight Mission Commander." General Carter replied with a tense tone in his voice. I had not gotten to know the General very well on this trip so far, but I also didn't go out of my way to run into him. The guy gave me the creeps. The few times our paths had crossed, he did not seem like a pleasant person to know and he obviously didn't like playing second fiddle to basically a civilian leader on board.

My father kept going down his checklist seemingly either not noticing the Generals tone or not really giving a damn one way or the other.

"Dr. Franco, are all personnel strapped in tight?"

"Yes sir, all personnel are accounted for and in their designated locations" Dr. Franco responded.

"Are all our plants, foods, livestock accounted for and contained properly?" my father continued.

"Yes sir, all plants and livestock are contained."

I hadn't realized we had real live livestock on board. I know we didn't when we left Earth so we must have picked them up at Mars. With everything going on since then, I hadn't toured the entire ship like I did on the Walrus and Expeditious. There was no way they were awake and roaming around inside the ship. They must have put any livestock in pods like our human cargo.

"Good, how about all our food and other inventory?"

Timmons spoke up again, "Sir, all our inventories are tied down and secured in the cargo bays. If anything comes loose it will be contained from causing harm elsewhere aboard. Also, all our equipment is tied down in the cargo bays as well. All cargo bays are closed and locked down"

"Understood Timmons. Tremmon, are our Skaters, pods, drones all locked down and secured?"

Tremmon responded quickly, "Yes sir, all onboard ships, pods, drones and other gear associated with them are locked in and secure. I have staffed each Skater with a pilot and copilot in case we need immediate help on the outside after our jump. The engines are warmed but shut down per your orders. They can be quickly restarted and flown if needed."

"Excellent, I believe that about covers it all. Where are we on the charge Timmons?"

"85% sir and climbing. Still steady. All systems are green, no problems so far."

"Good, I am going to make a quick announcement to the general population, let me know if anything changes."

My father then turned on the intercom system broadcasting to all the speakers in the ship, "Crew on board the APEX. We are within minutes of starting our Star Drive and doing something humans have never done and to our knowledge no other intelligent species have ever done. We are preparing to move slowly but at such a pace that we will travel many times the speed of light. No matter how this ends, you are all noted in the history books as brave boundary pushers. The very first to travel fully beyond the limits of our own solar system. Here is to what will come, and we will see you on the other side." My father then turned off the intercom just in time to see his control panel light up angry red.

"Status?" My father shouted to his team.

Timmons was first to respond, "Sir, capacitor bank five just overloaded. It was showing ahead of the others but still within safe range. I don't understand what happened yet. It must have shorted out internally. I am dumping that power now; we should have plenty of power still from the other banks."

"NO, don't dump that power yet, we need it to make the jump," my father ordered, "if we don't have that power all our calculations are junk. Do what you can to hold it together. Bank five is back at the rear of the ship away from everything else. If it goes, it won't damage too much of the ship."

"Yes sir, I understand but – " my father cut Timmons off, "Timmons, I don't care about any buts. Do as ordered. Where are we at on the charging?"

"90% just now sir"

"O'Malley, initiate the jump engine on my count. 5, 4," An amazing sound wound up in my head. It wasn't really an audible sound but a feeling almost. I could hear it, but it was almost like a powerful deep bass from a speaker. You couldn't decide if you felt it or heard it more. "3, 2" The whole ship shuddered as the sound intensified. I could see in the status feeds on control panels ahead of me lighting up with red. One after another changed from green or blue to red. I wasn't well experienced in our flight systems but red was never good. I had expected yellow but saw none of that.

"1, initiate." The moment Father finished speaking initiate the ship stopped shuddering and the sounds that had built up began to fade as though a massive electric motor was winding down in freewheel from an extraordinarily high RPM. Had I been successful? I couldn't be sure. There was no shouting back and forth at the control panels. No operators yelling for assistance. A calm fell over the entire group as though they all realized something long before I was able to grasp it. Father drooped his head a bit but then brought it back up rigid grinding his teeth some.

"Report, Timmons, what happened with our ship?"

"Sir, it appears the moment of initiation the computers shut the process down. I'm not sure why yet but we have major failure in the magnetic field. Give me a minute to put the data together."

"Is it safe to send skaters out?" Father asked this directing it I assumed towards Timmons, but O'Malley spoke instead, "Yes Sir, I have brought the engine and emitters back offline for now. There is no danger to ships leaving from their holds."

"Mr. Tremmon get your skaters out there to look around at our ship. See if they can see anything obvious out there."

"Yes sir, they are already on the move. Should have eyes on the ship within thirty seconds."

"Direct their video feeds straight to the monitors in here. I want to see for myself."

The command deck was silent for what felt like minutes but was more likely only a handful of seconds. Then video feeds began springing up on various monitors around the command deck. Immediately I could tell we were looking at the APEX. The giant ship extended off into the far distance and the ring hung there suspended in space where it should have been. There were no sparks of discharge coming from torn off sections of the ship. It appeared all was perfectly fine out there.

"Can anyone tell me what happened?" Father asked the group.

After conferring with a few of his underlings along with O'Malley, Timmons turned to Father and began his brief report, "Sir, it will take some time to decipher exactly why we had the problem we did but initial reports from the control computer show significant failure in our emitters. The magnetic field collapsed just as we ramped it up to full power. There were not enough emitters remaining for the computer to compensate with, so it overrode our commands and discharged our stored power out into space. A wormhole never even began to form."

"The emitters failed?" Father asked. "How could so many emitters fail? We tested the emitters extensively."

"As of now I cannot tell you why they failed but it does appear they were mainly in one area of the ship. A group of them failed together just as we built up power supply to them. They showed no problems until we got up over 85% power. Then they all dropped out of service together."

"Get if figured out and report back to me. Mr. Tremmon gather your people and start pulling those defective emitters off the hull. Get them inside and let me know the moment the first pair land. I want to look at them myself."

With that Father left the command center presumably for his labs where the quantum computer sat. I hung around for only a moment longer before hearing my name called by Mr. Tremmon. Frozen for a moment, I wondered why he would be calling me. Did they already figure out who had worked on all those emitters? Wait, did they record who worked on the emitters? If they did then that would trace straight back to me immediately. I would be called out within hours and would lose every chance to ever take part in any exercise on board the ship. I may be put back into a pod until we reached our destination if they decided to pull me back out at that late point in time. It could be decades.

"Ms. Johanson!" I heard Mr. Tremmon again but couldn't move. I was frozen in place terrified of the disappointment and anger my parents and the other crew would have towards me. I only wanted what was best for the universe. The universe. I really was thinking of the entire universe? Assuming that I knew what the universe needed? Was that really my decision to make in the end?

A softer voice now broke through the wall of thoughts racing around my mind, "Maggie. Maggie honey, are you ok?" I came back to reality with a start. It was my Mother, concern in her eyes as mine turned and brought her into focus. "Sorry, yea. Just kind of shocked about the whole thing. I'm good." I replied to her weakly. Then turning to my drone team commander, "Mr. Tremmon, yes sir."

"Maggie, are you back with us? Can I count on you to keep your head in the game? We need to figure this out now, if you can't focus then I need to put someone else with your drones."

"Sir, I am more than capable and back in control." I said more strongly. More confident on the outside while still reeling on the inside.

"Then get off your ass and let's go!" Tremmon ordered sharply and stepped into the lift next to my seat against the wall. I quickly removed the harness that had been holding me and relied on my boots to keep me grounded to the ship. I slipped into the lift along with Tremmon and we started dropping into the belly of the APEX.

Chapter Twelve

It took two days, but we were able to pull the impacted emitters off the hull in their entirety and bring them back on board the ship. It was a rough two days of working nearly nonstop. After an initial twelve-hour shift, Tremmon finally forced most of us to take a six-hour break from flight missions. I was exhausted and didn't want to pull the emitters off but didn't have a choice as any refusal would obviously implicate me in some way. I could have feigned illness or mental breakdown, but that would have only removed me from service during a critical point. Whether this implicated me or not would not change if I retreated to my quarters balling my eyes out. If I stayed on the team though and an opportunity rose, I may be able to help myself out.

As Father had instructed, the moment the first two emitters came aboard he and some of his team were there within minutes to inspect them. This was where I was able to make use of me being on the drone team again. I knew that I had not placed all the impacted drones as that was an obvious way to bring the blame back around towards me. While working with Arnold, I made sure to put the emitters in the que so that I would get some unmodified emitters to place along with some modified ones. There were failures in some emitters that were not part of the ones I modified as was expected. Father always knew some emitters would burn out. It was supposed to be a negligible number of them though. From the list I was given, the first one I retrieved was an emitter that had failed but was not a modified unit.

My unmodified but burned out emitter was the second one to get back to the door. I tried to hurry as fast as I could but one of the other drone pilots was able to beat me bringing in another drone that was one that I had modified. There wasn't much I could do about that other than make sure that my unmodified emitter was right there. Once I landed my emitter back on the ship, I could only hope Father would look at mine first and be thrown by another issue that would take time to clear out.

When Father and his team arrived to inspect, I was already focused on pulling in more emitters. Beyond that first one to try and throw the investigation some I didn't have much of an option. There was one more emitter on my list that was an unmodified one but beyond that all of them were ones I had tampered with. There was no way for me to hide that that I could think of at the moment. With the helmet on that gave me full visual senses from my drone's standpoints, I couldn't keep an eye on Father and couldn't hear a thing from them as I had to focus on traffic control's directions. In such a rush project such as this, there was heavy traffic around the drone bay coming and going and traffic control had to orchestrate the entire affair.

At the end of my first shift bringing in my assigned emitters I was a bit over halfway done. I was completely spent but wanted to see what I could find out about Father's findings so far. I walked over to his team's work area and saw dozens of emitters already torn down to the frames. Components in bags floating all over the place. In their rush, the investigation crew hadn't taken the time to carefully stow away all the extra parts but instead had bags full of parts floating here and there tied off to the tables where the remaining frames of the emitter they went to sat strapped down. It was the very definition of an organized chaos.

Frames of Drones were on numerous tables cleaned of all the sensitive electronics. It appeared that a vast majority still held their coils also. A few were missing but most were intact and in place. Closer inspection relayed to me that the power supplies and main relays were missing out of every single unit. My heart sunk understanding that they must have already figured it out. No way they could have found the issue almost immediately and not tie it back to me. There was nothing I could do at this point. It may take a day or so to get back to me, but I was well screwed at this point. Sure, I wasn't the tech on the final assembly records for these drones since Arnold was the engineer responsible for them but the moment they realized Arnold's name showed up over and over and confronted him about the issue, he would throw it all on me.

There was no reason for him to lie after all. Letting it all fall on him would put him in that spot of being a proven traitor to the mission and would have him removed from his position, put back into a pod and most likely imprisoned once he was woken at some point in the future.

A hand came up and fell upon my shoulder as I was running through scenarios of me being held in a pod until my parents had both fallen into old age and passed away. Awoken only to find out that everyone I ever loved was dead and gone. If I was ever awoken at all. The hand gripped me tightly and went to turn me around. Being torn from my thoughts I started to fight back against the hand, but it was powerful. Small I thought as the pressure was applied across a relatively diminutive portion of my shoulder but strong none the less. I allowed myself to spin around slowly, my boots disengaging long enough to give motion to my feet keeping the connected lower body in line with my rotating upper torso.

My eyes started up high expecting a large male to be there with stern eyes demanding that I come with him. To be walked away in shame, fellow pilots and team members watching me go wondering what the daughter of our esteemed Commander could have done. I was met with eyes but not the ones I anticipated. These eyes were gorgeous. A fire raging inside them made of golden flame. The eyes glaring back at me were framed in a soft, friendly face but those eyes. They burned into me. They let me know this person knew what was going on but didn't want to make a scene of it here. Maybe somewhere else but not here.

"Ms. Johanson. You need to come with me right now." The strong voice of our Military Major came to me. I immediately nodded my head in agreement and dropped my gaze to the floor. I was caught dead to rights. At least she wasn't going to make a scene of it here in front of those crew I had grown to consider friends over the past weeks.

We walked off the drone deck together with her leading, me following trying not to look at anyone else as we went. I couldn't help it though and snuck several peeks before openly gazing around at a nearly empty deck. There was almost no one here anymore. None of my fellow pilots were within eye shot. Tremmon was no where to be seen. All I could catch in my vision was a sole representative from my Father's team watching over the gathering of parts and pieces. The graveyard of emitters that had formed around the airlock doors.

I wasn't being walked out in shame. I was being led away without fanfare. Where this march of the damned was going though I had no idea.

"You Stupid little girl!" The Major nearly yelled at me as the door swung shut behind us. We were back in my room. She had let me up to the residential deck and to my own room. I had no idea as we marched up here together why we would head here but we did. "Please explain to me what in the Hell you were thinking! What the hell your plan was!"

"What?" I was puzzled as to what she meant. Expecting to be put in front of an immediate court proceeding with my Father as acting Judge and sentence this threw me.

"Don't act innocent Maggie. I know exactly what you did and while I can applaud you for your ingenuity, I can only question your sanity by leaving it so obvious."

"Major, I really don't know what you are talking about." Really, I did as I was catching on now but what was still unknown was how much did she really know? I didn't want to give anything away I didn't have to. After all, this could just be a ploy to get me to admit what I had done while the room was bugged relaying my words and visuals straight to a jury of my peers.

"You did this. I am not completely sure on how you did it, but I know you did it. You did all this. This failure we find ourselves in now. You brought it on. Why? How?"

"What are you talking about? This failure? You mean the aborted jump? I didn't have anything to do with that. How would I? All I did was place some emitters."

"Oh, come on Maggie. I am not that stupid. You may not think much of us military brass on the ship, but I have eyes and ears. The moment the jump failed I knew what had happened. No way that many emitters failed without there being a reason. In fact, I had expected a failure in the jump but not the failure that had occurred."

"You expected a failure in our jump?" I asked before thinking. It was an automatic reaction. Why would she expect a failure in our jump? What kind of failure was she expecting?

"Yes, I knew something would go wrong but most of us did. This untested behemoth your Father has been promising to our government for years isn't going to work. It never should have existed in the first place. The investment to make this thing come together has been extraordinary. Untested though, no proof the concept will work at all. I expected a failure, but I expected it to be catastrophic. Not a minor delay. The moment I realized we hadn't jumped but were still alive and in one piece I knew sabotage was the only option. Imagine my surprise when 95% of the failed emitters were registered to one engineer."

I still didn't want to give anything up voluntarily but so far, she was on a roll. I could see where this was going. She continued, "So my first stop was with this engineer. Arnold. You seem to know Arnold pretty well, don't you?"

"Well, I guess I know him somewhat. I mean, I know who he is."

"Yes, yes you do know who he is. You two had a run in on a broken emitter a couple weeks ago and have been best friends ever since."

"I wouldn't say best friends. I don't even think he likes me, he just tolerated me because of who I am. He shows me a few pointers here and there on the emitters."

"Bull shit Maggie, you are much closer than that. You know, I went to talk with Arnold, and he let me know that you have been helping him with emitters for the past couple weeks. I couldn't believe that at first since let's be honest, Arnold is a bit of a prick. An asshole. He isn't the type to let some random little girl hang around him all the time. You must have been doing something for him and you know my first thought wasn't technical expertise. My first thought was he might have been taking advantage of a young woman to fulfill some of his desires."

I thought about that last sentence for a moment. His desires? What was she getting at? Then it clicked, did she seriously think I was sleeping with Arnold? Is that why he let me hang around? Did she think we had some kind of sick relationship going on? The sudden look of disgust that went across my face must have been what she was looking for as she eased up some and gave a soft laugh moving over to my 'bathroom' stall which had the curtain pulled around closed. She pulled the curtain back revealing Arnold. He didn't look very happy though as I noticed his right eye was swollen with a fresh bruise forming around it. Then I saw his feet were tied together and his hands were behind his back presumably tied there also.

"Thank you for that reassurance Maggie. If there is one thing I won't tolerate, it is a child predator. I may have taken matters into my hands a bit prematurely, but you must understand, that kind of shit won't happen under my watch no matter what. Before I untie this big wad of meat, please let me know what you two were up to if it wasn't getting him off."

"He was just showing me some of the technical stuff surrounding the emitters. You know who my Father is so I'm sure you can understand the kind of pressure I am under to become something like him. Some technical issues have never come easily to me so I try and get real world tutoring whenever I can. Arnold was just showing me some details about the drones and in return I helped him put a few together."

"Pressure to be like your Daddy? Really, that's the reasoning you are giving me?" With this she turned and punched Arnold hard in the gut causing him to wrench over while still tied and off balance.

"You Bitch" Arnold croaked while crumpling in on himself. He didn't move from that spot though. Didn't try to step away or rush her. I had to imagine the Major had locked his boots in place along with tying him up. "Tell me the truth now or I will keep hurting him."

"Why do you think there is more going on? Really that is all it was. I helped him out on the labor side, and he showed me a few things with the emitters." I took a step backwards trying to get back within reach of my door in case I needed to make a quick escape.

"Don't bother trying the door Maggie. I've sealed it. Benefit of my authority aboard our ship here. Even with your inexcusable access, you can't override my lock codes." She turned again and gave Arnold another brutal shot to the abdomen. He had just uncovered the area starting to recover from the previous blow. Arnold doubled over again. Coughing this time, he tried to protest, "Robin, stop please. I told you we didn't do anything."

"Arnold, don't make me tie your mouth shut. Not another word." Turning back to me she continued, "Here, let's make a deal. You be honest with me and I will be honest with you. How about that? Can we agree to that much at least?"

"Honest with you and you'll be honest with me?" I didn't quite understand here. Did she mean she had something to share with me also? The Major nodded back to me so I thought for a moment. Could she be on the same side as me? I was busted regardless. She obviously knew it was me that sabotaged the emitters. I couldn't come up with any other explanation for what was going on here. She may have thought Arnold was taking advantage of me at first but they had obviously already had rounds so he would have revealed to her what was going on. I came up with a question for her and continued, "I will answer your questions 1 for 1. However, I get to go first. Why are you on this mission?"

Without missing a beat, she responded openly, "I volunteered for this assignment because I want to make sure this ship does not leave the system."

I stood there stunned for a minute. She didn't want it to leave the system? Just like me? "You don't want us to succeed? Why not?"

"No, no. Deal was 1 for 1 so now I get my turn. Did you sabotage the emitters to keep us in system?"

Well, here goes nothing I thought to myself. Either I found an ally that can help me, or I am dooming myself to imprisonment. I started to stammer but got myself under control as I revealed everything. "Yes, yes I am the one who sabotaged the emitters. Arnold had nothing to do with it. It was just me. Alone."

Major Bonette stood there for a moment like she was contemplating but then became annoyed with the apparent delay. "Your turn to ask a question or are you already out of them?"

"Sorry, no, um, why don't you want us to leave the system?"

"Simple, we as a race are destructive to everything we encounter. If we see a new species on Earth, instead of allowing it to live uninterrupted we have to seize it and test it. Study it to learn all there is to know about the new creature's design. What it needs to survive, what it provides to the ecology. Then what do we do after finding out about this new amazing creature? We destroy the habitat around it for our own purposes and imprison the newly found and now newly endangered creature to "protect it"."

Holy shit! I thought to myself. Is she really on my side? Does she want to stop the ship for the same reasons of protecting live out in the galaxy? This could be my ticket to winning my battle. With her access and abilities, we might be able to turn this ship back.

"You want to protect any alien species we come across? That is why I am doing this too. I just don't want us to harm anyone out there. You know as well as I do or even better with your position that if we find another habitable world out there and there are creatures already calling it home whether intelligent or not, we will just wipe them out and claim the planet for our own to rape and destroy over time."

"That is exactly what I want Maggie. I want to keep us here in system. I want us to return to Earth and forget leaving our star. Can you help me do that?"

At this point Arnold was standing back up nearly straight. He was still a bit hunched over showing his abused abdomen was bothering him but not enough to keep him doubled over on himself. He spoke next interrupting our back and forth, "See I told you Robin. She is on our side. You really think she was able to do all that without me noticing?"

"Shut up you disgrace for an agent. You didn't do anything to help her and if you knew what was going on, you didn't report it to me which was a requirement of your mission."

"Wait, Arnold is an agent? An agent of what?"

"No, no, no. See you are out of turn now. You have to answer my question first. Can you help me keep us in this system?"

I had so many questions but could tell I wasn't going to get them all answered right now. All I could look at now was the information I had at hand. She seemed to be on my side. It could still be a trap to ensnare me, but she already had a confession so if that was the case, I was done for. She wouldn't need anything else. Also, by the way she was treating Arnold I had to imagine this was outside the boundaries of her official role. There was no way beating a suspect was permissible under the rules of engagement she would be tied down with on this mission.

"I can help you but only with conditions."

"Oh Maggie, I don't think you are in a position to be making any kind of demands other than keeping this from your Father. See, it was easy for me to track down who worked on those emitters. Easy for me to figure out they almost entirely came from Arnold since those things are tracked. That took me minutes to figure out. Your Father is so set on figuring out why they failed, he didn't first look at who may of caused them to fail. I already took the liberty of adjusting some records to show the failures were dispersed across all the engineers and amazingly all the failed parts came from one shipment from Earth. That way it looks like a manufacturing defect instead of treason."

She had me there. It did look bad. I hadn't thought about them tracing it back to me through Arnold, but it did make sense. He would have had to sign off on each emitter as we completed it. Even though my name wasn't there, the moment they traced it to Arnold, he could have rolled over and threw me under the bus. It would only take a quick check of security records to find out I was indeed in the drone bay well past my scheduled shifts for the past two weeks. I couldn't let the Major spook me though. She seemed a bit on the edge. Someone that could jump over and stoop to killing people on purpose just to meet her goals.

"Major, you need me. If you didn't, then we wouldn't even be here talking right now. The only reason you are revealing yourself to me is because you need me. I don't even have difficult demands either. All I want from you is two things. Number one, we do not do anything that will harm people aboard this ship. Number two, we do not do anything to pin my Father as a traitor. Whatever we do has to be a fundamental flaw in the system that may label him as a failure but cannot frame him with any kind of conspiracy."

Major Bonette stood there for a few seconds contemplating my demands or at least made it look like she was contemplating them. A grin flowed across her face, almost a creepy grin then she spoke quietly and steadily, "Maggie my dear, I think we will be able to make this work between you and me. While I cannot promise you absolutely no harm to the crew aboard as you could not even guarantee that for your personal attempt. There was no way to know what would happen when that many emitters failed. You took a chance and we will have to do the same. What I will promise you is that we will not purposefully hurt anyone on the ship. As far as what those back home on Earth think when we return, there is no way I can guarantee they won't find a way to pin it on your Father. He is the commander after all.

You have to decide right here and now if it is more important to save all the possible species out there or protect your Father's good name as a scientist and leader. Which will it be Maggie?"

I had to think about that. Was there any way we could realistically do this without damaging his name? Any failure would naturally come back on him just as the Major said. That was a risk we would have to take.

"Ok, I will agree to that. As long as we promise not to do something that appears to be a direct product of his input. A failure in the system only."

"Understood and agreed to. Now we need to decide how to continue. This delay will only take a week or so to remedy. I already saw what you did and with Arnold here we worked out a timeline to replace the components and go for attempt number two."

I didn't realize there were enough components still on the ship in order to repair that many emitters but that did make sense. This was a colony ship along with an experimental one, so it probably had some very wide-ranging manufacturing capabilities. Raw materials were most likely packed in some of the cargo bays below us waiting for a purpose to be used for.

"So, if you two are working towards the same goal as me," I started back in questioning if they had been really working on anything at all, "what have you done so far? Why didn't you come up with the idea I ended up going with? It would have been a lot simpler for Arnold here to do it than me sneaking around putting myself in the position to do it without being noticed."

"We did think of it. The idea of setting the emitters up for failure was already an option I had on the table previously. Arnold told me it couldn't be done in such a way for the ship to not notice before attempting a transit, so we threw the idea away." Looking over at Arnold with a glare she continued, "He told me the only thing we could do would be to create a failure point in the control boards but those are checked hundreds of times before the actual transit attempt and are checked hundreds of times per second during the attempt." Looking back at me now she perked back up to an almost joyous tone, "But you my dear figured out a way to do it that He didn't even think of. You modified the power cabling coming out of the relays. You made it hold up until the final seconds when full power was sent to the emitters. That was a brilliant move and almost worked."

"Well it did work." I corrected her before she continued with what almost seemed like a prepared speech. "My goal was to give myself more time to come up with a better plan. I knew this wasn't a permanent solution, but I did think it would stall us out longer than a few days or a week. I was hoping fresh cables would have to be shipped out here from Mars. Something that would give me months."

"That was never going to happen." Robin jumped right back in before I could continue, "This ship can manufacture most of what it needs as long as we have the raw material. Unfortunately for you we have plenty in stock right now. We need a plan that will disable the very heart of your Father's system. If we can kill the computer in the center of the whole process, then we will have to return to Earth. This ship may be able to manufacture a lot, but it can't build a new quantum computer from scratch. Not out here. Some of the methods of creating that big machine require gravity in order to pull off. Our gravity ring doesn't spin up enough for full Earth pull and we can't keep up a high enough acceleration long enough to do it either. It has to be done on a planet."

"Ok, we have to kill the computer. I get that but how do you propose it? I know it is protected every second of every day by its own security systems. Systems that record everything, analyze it for risk and react all on its own. It is even self-contained. You can't just shut the power off or overload it. Neither would do anything besides burn out a couple safety relays that could be easily replaced."

"That is where Arnold here comes to be slightly less useless than normal." She pointed over at Arnold and motioned for him to step up and speak.

Still tied up and bent over slightly from either the pain in his gut or due to his arms being strained behind him he looked towards me keeping his eyes away from the Major, "Um, yes. I have a work around to kill the main drive computer systems. I wrote a virus back on Earth that when injected will adjust the parameters that the computer uses for its computations. If injected at the correct time, it will throw calculations off enough on power control that in fact it will overload itself frying those sensitive internal components we can't replace out here."

I couldn't see that working. Father had told me that it checked itself for irregular code millions of times over per minute leading up to the time of transit. During which time the secure room it was in was locked down and didn't allow anyone at all in for any reason. Before that lock down period only a handful of personnel were able to access it. I could see that both the Major and Arnold were waiting for a response from me. They were scoring me based off my next response I realized. If I just go along then they will probably kill me not thinking there is a use for me. If I balk, then the same ending would probably come to me. It would be easy enough for them to kill me in such a way that would look self-inflicted, then pin the whole emitter thing on me to solidify the case.

"That could work but there are problems that will need to be worked out." I started with still not completely sure what way to go with this. "Problem I see is that the computer locks itself completely down from outside influence well before transit occurs. Then checks itself over for any new code and clears it. It would notice the virus and wipe it out before we were able to do anything at all."

Major Bonette waited a few seconds and then made a hurry up motion with her hand prompting me to continue on with my thought.

"In order to make this happen we would need to get the virus inside before the lock down but not be injected into the computer until the very moments before transit when the system is loaded down to a point it shuts down its own internal checks. I have no idea when that is though or even if it does that. I am just assuming it wouldn't be able to continue the internal checks and a transit at the same time."

Now grinning again but this time a smile of real happiness instead of the creepy hungry smile she had before she answered my final concern. "We are in luck there my new friend. While completing my security investigation upon boarding this ship I was told by one of your Father's techs that the computer does shut its own internal audit system down before transit. We have 3 minutes to inject our virus."

"If you already have that figured out then why didn't you do this the first time?" I asked truly wondering why.

"The problem we ran into was that the computer locks down access in the room it resides 15 minutes before transit. We cannot get inside to manually inject the virus and there is no way we have found to get the virus to it without being inside that room."

"So, you need someone to be in the room ahead of the lockdown and stay in there for the duration until 3 minutes to go. Then they can inject the virus and will have to ride it out in the room if I am understanding." A thought came to me making me realize the problem with such a simple idea. "But of course, you can't do that because of the system cooling. As part of the security features not only does the room lock down but it also floods with coolant instead of running pipes through the machine."

"Very good, I was wondering if you knew that much about your Father's system. It does indeed flood the room with liquid ammonia coolant. The computer puts off a lot of heat when it ramps up, so it is first flooded with coolant that has been sitting in pipes exposed to the vacuum, so they are extraordinarily cold. No way we can get a suit in here that would protect a person from that for long enough not even counting the force of the coolant rushing around the computer would keep someone from being able to function inside."

I drummed my fingers on my chin deep in thought. There must be a way to do this I was telling myself. We need a way to inject the virus into the computer without being able to access it directly and without being able to remote a virus into it from outside. Could we remotely activate the virus so it laid dormant until a signal told it to start up? No, the security system of the computer didn't only look for active threats but any change in its own code from the millisecond before. Any additional code would be noticed even if it was tiny and dormant. Then I had it. Snapping my fingers, I started back in with my solution.

"Here is what we do," I started. "I need that virus loaded onto a memory stick. An old fashioned one. Do either of you have an old USB stick anywhere? My father uses one sometimes to connect some of his older equipment to the computer. No one else uses those ports but there are still 2 I remember seeing when he showed me around earlier on our flight."

"A USB stick?" Major Bonette replied questioningly. "Why would anyone have one of those? They went out of mainstream use decades ago. The speed/storage space and security of them was so poor they had to be abandoned."

At that point Arnold spoke up deciding to break his self-imposed vow of silence that had held fast through much of the Major and I's back and forth conversation. He didn't say much but it did pull both of our attentions straight over to him. "I have one." I looked at the Major, but she held firm on Arnold.

"You have a USB memory card? Why the hell do you have one of those? Aren't you supposed to be a highly evolved engineer using the best and latest tech?"

"Well yea but I can understand why her Father would have a couple still in use on his computer even with how low tech it is. Sometimes you just need the ease of use and basic utility of the old-style devices. They are easier to work with when modifying. I have a couple I keep music on for safe keeping."

"Do either of them allow wireless interfacing?" I asked getting more excited. If they did then my plan would work perfectly.

"No, no none of them do but that wouldn't be hard to integrate. I would just need to wire in a transmitter. I would have to wire in a small power cell also. If the USB is a power drain on the system even in the slightest bit, then it will be noticed and burned out before we can use it."

"Fine, that would work. How far will that transmitter work? How long would it take you to put together and load your virus onto?"

"Whoa, whoa. Before we get too far ahead," Major Bonette jumped back in splitting Arnold and I in our conversation. "What makes you think this plan would work at all? Using old tech in an old port? How is that supposed to fix anything?"

"Untie me and release my boots and I will explain it to you." Arnold said a bit peevishly. He obviously wasn't a fan of being tied up, but I could tell it took a bit out of him to stand up to the Major like that. He was terrified of her I thought to myself. Should I be a bit afraid of her also? The major turned to Arnold and pulled a blade from her pocket. With one fluid motion she knelt, cut the ties that held his legs together and rose along his body just missing his exposed portions but slicing as close as possible to him maintaining the overwhelming authority of violence over him. She ended with tracing that blade up his arms and through the ties there at his wrists releasing him from his bindings. Then she took a step back and waiting for him to continue with the explanation.

"If we load the virus on a USB stick with its own power supply and tiny transmitter, all we have to do is get that USB plugged in as close to the final cutoff as possible to avoid detection by someone walking around the computer. The USB will stick out like a sore thumb from the side of the machine. Anyone that walks near it will see it clearly but the machine itself won't notice. Then when the machine locks down and floods the room, we just wait until the final 3-minute mark. Send a simple activation code to the USB bringing it to life. Until that point the USB would be completely dormant not sending or taking any power or data to or from the computer. Once activated it will inject the virus which will immediately replace some of the coding inside causing the mathematical failures that will bring too much power through the external power couplings and fry the entire computer."

Bonette turned and looked at me looking like she expected a counter argument. I nodded in agreement and added one final detail, "The only thing I can add to this part is make certain that when you set the USB up that you put a control in there so it won't return anything in the basic act of plugging it in. If the computer's host controller sees something plugged in even if it isn't active, the controller will burn the unknown device out in the name of security."

With a note of annoyance, Arnold responded to me without looking my way. "Of course, yes. I can modify the port on my USB so that it doesn't even contact the data port until activated. That way the computer will never sense something is plugged in until we activate. At that point it will be too late with the internal security shut down for transit calculations."

Moving on ignoring Arnold's peeved tone I presented the next problem on my list. "How do we get access to the computer room?" I knew that I did not have clearance to get in on my own without my Father present. There was no way I would be able to set the USB with him in there with me.

Bonette answered that question quickly, "That would be my job in this. I have the appropriate security clearance already. I am head of security on this ship reporting to the General. Every system aboard is accessible by me."

"Ok then, so what are we missing here?" I responded.

"The final piece of the puzzle," Bonette continued, "is where we will all be. From this conversation, Arnold has the drive and the virus. He can prep that and get it to me by end of today. I will carry it with me until a few minutes before the lockdown procedures start. I need a reason to be there though. To be in the lab where the computer room is positioned. Normally for this event I would be at the security control board in the command center."

I thought for a moment and came up with an idea to bypass that issue also. "Simple, we need to stage a physical attack on the computer system ahead of time. A failure of course but enough to demand security presence at the time of our transit."

"Ok, I like that. I will take care of staging the mock attack." Bonette seemed happy to stage an attack so I wasn't about to argue there. She could have that. To remind her of our agreement though I did interject on the rules for her mock attack.

"Just as long as the attack doesn't harm anyone. I don't want to hurt anyone. We all need to make it through this together. All the crew aboard."

"Once again I will remind you my young counterpart, there is no way to guarantee anyone's safety in this endeavor, but I will not purposely harm anyone."

"Ok fine, but when will you do it? When will you stage the attack?"

"It will need to be right before the transit attempt. If too far in advance, then I will be expected to secure the area and then still be at my station on the command deck."

"That makes sense. What are you going to do?"

"Don't worry about that," Pointing at Arnold, Bonette continued, "Arnold and I will take care of the mock attack. Once he gets me the drive, he won't have any other tasks to perform so he can help me on that part."

"Ok, but what are you going to do?"

"Let's keep that between Arnold and I." Bonette turned away from me at that point and towards the door. "You need to be surprised after all. Your Father will be watching you."

I watched her open my door and start to walk through, Arnold following close behind. I had one more question though as she started down the hallway. "What else do I need to do?"

"Nothing Maggie. Just be yourself. You have helped us enough for now. Leave it to the professionals and soon we will be headed back to Earth. Keep an eye on your Father though. Stay close to him. Make sure he doesn't expect anything."

With that she and her red headed puppet were gone around the corner and out of sight. I turned and looked around my room. The now cut ties were still laying on the floor from holding Arnold hostage. "Well" I said out loud but only to myself, "I guess that's it. We burn out the computer and we go home." I sure hoped that was all. The Major bothered me some. She seemed disconnected in a way. Fearless and determined but disconnected from reality. Maybe it was me that was disconnected. I kept wanting to keep us in this system but didn't want to hurt anyone. Could I live with myself if my plan ended with people dying? Would I be able to sleep afterwards? The real question was would I be able to live with myself if I did nothing and then had to watch another world be invaded and torn apart by the very people whose lives I worried about now.

I knew I wasn't going to sleep much that night, but I had to try after all.

Chapter Thirteen

It ended up taking eight days to construct enough new cable assemblies, install them into the impacted emitters and reinstall them all out on the ship. I did as I was asked and hung as close to my Father as I could. He ended up ordering us to remove more emitters. A random sampling from all over the ship just to check and make sure no others had a similar issue with the power cables. No others were found but a few singed control boards were replaced. The failures that everyone had expected from day one.

Just as the Major had promised, when the investigation was complete, it was judged that the failure was due to a basic failure in the parts built on Earth and sent out with us. All were determined to be from the same batch and were replaced by the manufacturing systems on the APEX.

I hadn't spoken to Arnold or the Major since our conversation in my room. I didn't even see the Major at all. Arnold, I saw each day back in the corner of the drone deck working on various emitters. He never would glance up at me though. No eye contact, even when I tried to catch his attention from afar. I just wanted to ask how the USB was going but it was too risky to be seen together or to message him on our tablet messenger system. All that was tracked after all.

Now I was again in the Command Center alongside my Mother. This time it didn't take any complaining from me to get there. No one stood in my way and my parents never told me I couldn't be there. I don't think either of them wanted the fight. They knew I would end up there one way or another so might as well just allow it. I had been having some second thoughts on the whole destroying the quantum computer plan but kept shoving that down deep in my throat. All around me there were people walking back and forth or sitting in their console chairs monitoring varying systems. Sometimes a red light would flash here or there, and radio calls would be made to teams around the ship.

I sat quietly next to my Mother. She was grasping my hand and whispering comforting words in my ear like a Mother does. While the effort was appreciated, it did very little for my nerves. Maybe in normal circumstances it would be different but here in this moment, those comforting words has little impact while my mind raced. At that time, the Major walked in with a small entourage of security personnel. She went to her normal station and sat down without even a glance in my direction.

The General sat behind her strapped to another jump seat similar to mine. He had the look of a very disinterested man, not caring what was going on around him. If only he knew what was afoot on this ship. Maybe he did know. After all the Major was the supposed ringleader but how sure of that was I? She could merely be another pawn being moved around the board by the General. He always struck me as the very death of the party anywhere he went. Always so serious and not once had I seen the man smile. Not even a fake make-everyone-feel-better kind of smile. It didn't matter at this point. Even if I was having second thoughts it was too late for me to change it. I was powerless here in my seat and had to hope the Major knew what she was doing and would hold to her word with me.

While I was contemplating my life choices a ding came to my ear. A new message had come to my tablet and it was notifying me via my hearing implants. Who would be messaging me at this time? Looking up at the countdown clock, we were just shy of thirty minutes out from ship transit. Everyone should be locked down at this point. Random chatting would be between crew jabbing at each other with nothing better to do than sit there and wait. I had made a point not to form that kind of relationship with anyone though. Only a small handful of people ever messaged me, and I knew none of them would be doing that now as most were up in the Command Center with me. My only ongoing friendships not up here were with Christina and Joe. They were both down in the medical ward waiting with the few crew there that needed some special attention from various ailments and injuries suffered aboard.

I pulled the tablet up from my jacket pocket and activated the screen making sure to angle it just so no one around me could read the messages. There was a new one there but from an unknown contact. That was odd, everyone on board was automatically in the system so it was impossible to have an unknown contact. Curiosity raging now in my mind, I clicked on the message needing to know what this was all about.

- Maggie, she is going to blow the ship up. Its too late for me but you can still stop her. I won't be a pawn in her games any longer. Don't hesitate or you all die.

"What the hell?" I thought to myself without speaking. I tensed enough though to prompt some attention from my Mother who leaned around to look at the screen.

"What's wrong honey?" She asked concerned. "Everything ok?"

"Um, yea, no. Nothing, sorry. Just a crude joke from one of the other drone pilots. I will have to punch him later for that." I let out a small nervous laugh trying to hide my apprehension. Quickly I deleted the message.

"Ugh, do I need to talk to someone? I really don't like you hanging out with some of those guys. Its not a good place for a young woman."

"No, really Mom, its fine. I don't mind."

What was I supposed to do with that message? I couldn't just share it with my parents or anyone else on the ship. Who could that have been? Not going to be her pawn anymore. Who's pawn? I looked up and scanned the room trying to find a set of eyes peering back at me that might answer my question of who but came back with nothing. I searched again and paused on Major Bonette. Could she be the her in the message? Maybe it was from Arnold? She or Major Bonette was going to blow the ship up? Arnold couldn't be her pawn anymore?

That did fit. From that first day in my room when I saw them together, I could tell he was just a pawn to her. A piece to play with to her advantage and disregard when he wasn't useful anymore. Watching the Major I could see she glanced up at the countdown clock, crinkled up her forehead and looked down at her screen checking for something. What was she checking for? I looked up at the countdown clock also and saw it was at 29:37, 29:36, 29:35. Looking back across to the Major, we locked eyes. I shrugged my shoulders ever so slightly and looked back up at the clock. 29:30, 29:29, 29:28. Was something supposed to have happened at 30 minutes until transit? Maybe that was when Arnold had agreed to launch his fake attack on the control computer system. The attack that would prompt the Major to station herself down there.

I kept going back and forth between the Major and the countdown clock. When the clock hit 29:00 I looked over and saw the Major now standing. Something aggravated her. Her motions were stiff, forced. She didn't want to leave her console without a reason but apparently that reason wasn't coming as planned. She bent over and said something to the General I couldn't pick up on. He snarled back and made a comment I could only assume was derogatory or inflammatory. The Major bristled, spun towards where I was sitting and started walking my way anger clearly shown across her face. She looked me dead in the eyes again and I could see that fire. Fire like she had that day in my room. A flame wrapped up in the orbs of her eyes waiting to erupt and engulf everything around her. Just short of my seat she turned and stepped into the lift. Doors rolled shut behind her as she entered, and I could feel the lift start descending immediately.

"I wonder what that was all about." Mother commented from beside me evidently watching the same scene I had been. "Major Bonette looked awful angry about something."

"Yea," I responded to her quietly, my eyes on the General who was moving from his jump seat to the console that had just been vacated, "The General doesn't look any happier."

I kept watching the General while trying to not be too obvious about it. A quick glance at the countdown clock showed 27:45, 27:44, 27:43. Time was slowly eroding, and my mind was racing. I needed to figure out what Arnold had meant by that message. He was done being her pawn. What could that mean? I get that he didn't want to work for her anymore and must have refused to follow plans and stage an attack but what would he be doing instead? I pulled my tablet back up and searched the roster for his name. Normally someone of my status would not be able to look up information such as someone's location but I had hacked into more than I was supposed to over the past weeks travel time so much more was accessible to me than should have been.

Arnold's information came up and I clicked on the locate option. A diagram of the ship came up and after a moment or two, started zooming in on one portion of the ship. Right there he was. In the lab. Right where he was supposed to be. If he was there, then why hadn't he activated the attack like he was planned to do. If he didn't want to partake then why was he there at all? Wouldn't it make more sense to just stay in his room or down on the drone bay? Why make the trip to the lab if he wasn't going to do anything. Right next to the dot on the screen showing his location was a vital sign. Not anything specific but a simple indicator. The indicator showed green which meant all was well with the man.

I looked back up at the clock. 26:58, 26:57, 26:56. I needed to see where the Major was. Quickly splitting my screen so I could keep tabs on Arnold, I pulled up another query and searched Major Bonette. The same wide view diagram popped up and zoomed in on a dot showing her location. She was in the lab too. Near the lift about 20 feet from the green dot that was Arnold. I watched for a few moments wondering what was going on. Then Arnold's dot turned red and flashed on my screen. I froze. The Major's dot then moved closer to Arnold's now red indicator until they were bumped up against each other. Then the two dots both moved together around ten feet until they separated again, Major Bonette's green indicator moving over towards the computer's containment room door. It stayed there for a few moments and then went into the room.

It came to me then that something was terribly wrong with this situation. Arnold was supposed to set off some kind of alarm to provoke the Major to come down and post herself down there. Instead he sent me a warning and refused to stage the mock attack. Then when the Major went down on her own, he died. She must have killed him. Shot him maybe but firearms were not allowed on the ship. We had some but they were locked away per Father's requirement when he allowed military to join us after the attacks we endured on the Expeditious. She was the second in command of the security forces on board though so if anyone had access to the armory it would be her. I didn't have another explanation for what I was watching unfold on my tablet. Arnold's indicator turning red all of a sudden and then maybe being dragged away to be deposited behind a desk out of shot of a camera.

Wait, a camera. That's right, there were cameras all over the station and I could pull the feeds up on my tablet. I jumped out of the screen I was in and moved over to the camera feeds finding the right one. Many times, I had pulled this feed up over many weeks as it was one of the only ways I could check up on my Father. He had allowed me this one for that very reason. Immediately I saw the Major inside the glass walled room with the computer core. Just outside the door on the floor was a smear of red on the floor, curving around and out of site behind a desk. Not even enough to notice normally unless you were looking for something. It didn't take much though in a stark white room to stand out.

I rewound the camera feed several minutes and hit play. Instead of using the tablet speaker, I routed the audio straight into my implant so no one around me could hear the same thing. There was Arnold pacing back and forth in front of that glass room with his tablet out in front of him.

"Dammit Maggie, do something. Tell your Father, raise the alarm you stupid damn girl. I knew we shouldn't have started this."

I could hear the doors to the lift slide open at that point and the back of Bonette's head came into view. Arnold turned and froze when he saw the new entry in the room.

"But I thought you couldn't leave the command center without a reason?"

"You don't think I can move around the ship whenever I please?" The Major was obviously angry by her tone and the way Arnold started to recoil by her voice alone. He knew immediately what was coming. I saw that much in his posture.

"Why Arnold? Why are you abandoning the plan now? Are you too stupid to follow through with a simple plan? Was it so much for your diminutive brain you simply couldn't handle anymore?

"I can't do it Robin. I can't go through with it. I don't want to be responsible for killing everyone on board."

Even from looking at the back of her head I could tell in that moment that Bonette's entire demeanor changed from rage to a concerned motherly stance and tone, "What? Is that it? You just have cold feet? Ok, don't worry about it. You don't have to be responsible for killing anyone. I understand."

She then raised her arm and a flash leaped from the end. There was no sound that I heard through the feed, but the flash was there for only an instant and then gone. Arnold didn't speak again. Instead, red started spreading around his head emanating from a black hole right in the middle of his forehead. What took me a few seconds to recognize as blood didn't pour out into the air around him but instead rolled out of the new orifice and spread across his skin. A few droplets escaped and floated out away from him, but most just hung there wrapping him in a new liquid skin. His body went limp but hung in space gently folding over backwards as the final moments of inertia transmitted into his body pushed him over.

Bonette walked over to what I truly understood to be Arnold's corpse and grabbed both arms. She started to pull but his legs were held fast with the magnetic boots still engaged. She growled and bent down pushing the override on his boots. They released with a click. Instead of circling back to his arms, she pulled his body by the legs around a lab table out of view of the cameras. As she made it around the table, his torso and head had floated all the way around and made contact with the floor leaving a small trail of blood behind. She noticed that and looked up at the camera. Glancing around she found a rag in a drawer and quickly wiped up what she could, shoving the rag somewhere behind the table where it wouldn't be seen by general glances at the video feed.

I felt like I needed to vomit. If Arnold had decided against helping her because she was going to blow the ship up and kill all on board then with him out of the way, there was no reason not to follow through. I looked up at the countdown clock at froze. It counted down 16:49, 16:48, 16:47. Back on my tablet I went to the live feed and saw the Major plugging the drive into a socket on the far side of the computer. I had to stop her but couldn't tell anyone in this room.

That meant I would have to reveal everything I knew including my part in this plan to destroy my Father's life work. I couldn't do that. Maybe there was a way for me to stop this on my own. If I could remove the drive before the fifteen-minute mark, then nothing would happen, and we would transit. Sure, I would fail on my mission to stop us from transiting but at least I wouldn't be responsible for getting all these people killed. All the life aboard this ship whether in crew, colonists, livestock, plant and animal DNA samples, all the hopes of my species. I never wanted to destroy it all, just keep it here.

I turned to my Mother and nearly vomited in her lap. I had to swallow it back down and control my panic enough to speak. "Mom, I, I think I'm going to be sick." I swallowed another wad of bile back down which prompted more to seek an escape. She turned towards me and I could see the concern come over her face.

"Honey, oh my. Are you ok?"

"No, my stomach is rolling. I need to get out of here and find a bag. I don't want to make a mess in here."

"Oh of course, here I will help –"

"No, no, stay here, I can find something myself." I held one hand out to her putting it on her buckle to keep her strapped in while removing mine with my other hand.

"Honey, I can come help you though. Oh baby, you look terrible."

"No really Mo-," Another wave of bile made its way up and the taste flooded my mouth. Immediately a wave of saliva met it and I was able to force the whole wad back down as I stood up. "I'll be fine. I just need to fi-," This time a bit escaped my mouth, but I kept it contained with one hand. I swung into the lift and hit the button to go down to the residential deck. As the doors closed, I looked around, but it didn't appear anyone else noticed my quick escape. I lost my hold over the pool of vomit residing in my throat and spewed it into the lift. Funny thing about vomiting in space is the vomit is truly projectile. It keeps going until running into a surface to break the momentum. It found and stuck to the door on the lift, spreading across its surface while some bounced back across the space still moving away from me. There was an emergency suit strapped to the wall that made for a quick vomit bag. Once I cleared my system out the best I could and used the suit to wipe up the majority of what was clinging to the walls and doors, I forced myself to take a deep calming breath.

I had little time to recover from my vomit fest though as the doors start to slide open leading to my Father's lab. They moved open maybe two feet and halted partially open. That was incredibly strange as there was no reason for them to do that. Then they started to slide back closed and I realized the Major was attempting to lock me out so I couldn't interfere. The only two aboard that could override her would be my Father and the General. By the time I convinced either to come down here our time would already be up. I'm sure that by this point she had come up with another fail safe plan in case her improvisation was found out. I jumped through the doors just as they pinched down on me and cleared them making a grand uncontrolled entrance into the room.

Having deactivated my boots in order to sail through the doors I lost all control in the empty air with nothing to grab and stop myself. I reached out for anything trying to find some kind of traction even if it was just air resistance from flapping my arms wildly. Just as I came close to snagging a cable leading down to a workstation, everything went black. I didn't know that though. There was nothing in that void my mind resided in for several minutes. To me I was flying through the air about to snag an anchor line and then the next moment I was in a fog, my mind was so blurred that I couldn't even recognize that I was only seeing from one blurred eye.

Then the pain came. Absolutely dreadful pain. Pain that was beyond the normal 1-10 scale the nurses used to judge our ailments. This was easily a 15-18 on that scale. My brain felt as though it was being forced through a rupture in the very bony home it resided. The pain was persistent and total. All other senses were voided, not strong enough to overwhelm the singularity that was my existence at that moment. With all things though, the pain failed to maintain a totalitarian hold over my mind. As my other senses began to come back to me, I understood I was screaming. Not a shout of terror or a scream of frustration but an outright bellowing of absolute anger mixed with the desire to end it all right then and there. Not to end myself but to end all those who crossed me in any way throughout the history of my life. I roared up off whatever surface I was on and swung to see my attacker but there was nothing there. I'm not saying I was in an empty room but the area my vision did relay to me was a mess of red and black. Foggy shades of grey mixed in. All of it shifted in waves as I looked around. I reached one hand up to touch what was ahead of me and came up empty.

Seeing now in my mind what the problem was, I connected the splitting pain in my head with the nonfunctioning of one eye and rubbed away the gore that had seeped into it. Blood was seeping from somewhere pooling up in the cavity that was my eye socket. Clearing the badly needed bodily fluids I blinked again and pulled into view a woman laughing.

"What a Bitch." I said this to myself and out loud to the woman at the same time. I couldn't place who she was but the lone fact that she was laughing at me while I wiped blood from my eye was enough to convince me of her being exactly what I said.

"That was quite a yell there Maggie." The woman said. "You have to tell me how that all feels. I didn't expect to get such a direct shot, but you came through that door with no direction at all except right into my swing. It was perfect. Honestly, I thought you were done. The way your blood flowed freely, and your skull split open I didn't expect a recovery but WOW! There you are."

"Who are you?" I honestly wanted to know. This woman who I had no recollection of was telling me she nearly killed me and enjoyed it. There had to be a good reason for that. I was pretty foggy, but I still understood basic principals of community and being a normal human. Usually you weren't supposed to enjoy bringing such injury to others of your kind.

"Who am I? Isn't that great. I knocked the memory right out of your useless head. You must have realized what I was going to do and thought you had a chance in Hell of stopping me. Well good job."

"Lady, no offense but I have no idea who you are. Why would I care what you were doing?"

"Wow, you really are out of it. Well, you asked, and I guess it doesn't matter since we have," the woman looked down at a tablet in her hand, "one-minute left before activation of the virus."

"Virus?"

The woman seemed to become bored with me, sighing as she answered my question, "Yes Maggie, the virus you helped me create and inject into the ship to keep us here to protect your precious unknown species out there somewhere in the void."

"What are you talking about?" I looked around at our surroundings and felt much worse as I moved my head around. Waves of Nausea slammed into me bringing more bile up into my throat. Wait, more bile? I thought hard and remembered coming down a lift on a ship in a panic trying to get somewhere. "No way I was helping you with a virus." I told the woman trying to force a memory to form in my head.

"Well Maggie, it was all your idea. I just improved upon it. See, this is the end here. I have been trying to end this entire experiment for months ever since you lifted off from Earth. This mission to the stars. The whole damn thing, I wanted to wipe it all out. I led up the mine effort that took out your first ship. That was less impactful than I had hoped but what can you do with homegrown explosives launched in secret? You get what you get. Then again at Mars. That was my way to survive and come back to Earth so I could continue on working to bring all of the human race back to Earth and limit us there. That one didn't quite work out either but that was your Father's fault, not mine. The explosive did exactly what it was supposed to, your people just failed to get it on the right ship in time. Now we are here. This is my final stand and my final victory. I will have my victory. There is no way around it now."

The woman I still couldn't place but felt a building hatred for looked back at her tablet again.

"Look at that, times up. I wish I could wait a bit longer until you regained some of your memories so I could really enjoy the horror on your face but oh well. I guess this is it. We don't have forever after all."

The woman smiled a broad grin at me but those eyes. They were a blaze with fury. Hatred, beautiful evil. She looked away from me and down at her tablet, her arm moved towards it in slow motion from my vantage point. I didn't know why it was in slow motion and I didn't understand what she was doing yet but I did grasp that it was bad. Very bad. I searched for something to throw at her but there was nothing near me and just the motion of my eye looking made everything swim around me. Something was terribly wrong with my mind. It wouldn't focus. I started to drift away but was brought back with a strike to my face.

My head swung to the side and struck something hard. Another wave of unbending pain raged through me. I cried out but didn't hear anything. I don't know that sound even escaped my mouth. My vision blurred out white and then came back to a red fog. A hand roughly wiped away what I remembered to be blood and then tugged on my chin. Sound came through again and I recognized that woman again. Yelling in my face. Spittle flowing freely impacting me.

"YOU WILL LOOK AT ME WHILE I TRIUMPH. I WILL NOT BE DENIED THIS FINAL AUDIENCE! This was going to be for Arnold to watch but I had to kill him early. Now you will be my audience. Watch as I destroy the only hope any of us to exist. We are doomed back on Earth and we will all be removed from our existence. Our destruction will be repaired over time and life will again be allowed to live on."

As this strange creature in front of me screamed in my face so loud I could feel the sound waves bouncing around inside of my head, I couldn't focus on what was being said. It was only words with no meaning. I heard a snap somewhere nearby and the woman fell silent. She slowly moved away from me. Good I thought to myself. Now I could sleep and have some peace. Maybe she can have some peace also. I hope she could because being so angry all the time would be so sad.

My head was again pulled not by my own hand but by another. I noted this one was gentler, larger and rough but not so demanding as the other one.

"Dr. Franco, I need someone down here in the lab immediately" The voice was deep, strong. Nothing like the shrill angry voice before.

"General, is that you? I can't move anyone just this moment, we are transiting or getting ready to."

"Franco, I am telling you we need someone down at the lab now. I have three down."

"Oh my, ok. I'm headed that way"

What was all that going on? People talking but not everyone was here. I was having a hard time grasping what was going on around me but then heard something loud coming from around us. Not a person but a voice still yet.

"Transit in 10, 9"

The deep voice interrupted the other voice, "Maggie, hold on. This might be rough."

"8, 7, 6"

I could feel something in my chest. Not coming from my chest but maybe the floor I was laid on. A rumbling that felt like deep bass. It felt nice, focusing on that deep feeling inside me took away from the white noise trying to get attention in my mind.

"5,4,3"

The rumbling was so fantastic now. A rough jerk to one side came then.

"2,1"

The floor beneath my skull leapt up and sent another shock wave of violence into my brain. I gasped at the pain while feeling the comforting hands of this man that knelt above me. I couldn't see him and didn't know what General meant but I did feel good knowing he was there. That was the last thing I remembered. Understanding that it was ok for me to sleep. Ok if I didn't fight the warm embrace of the void.

Chapter Fourteen – From My Father's Eyes

This was the moment the human species would finally jump through the stars and become a true space faring force. To this point we had mastered our own solar system. We had stations, colonies, ships but every attempt to leave the borders of emptiness that kept us in had failed. Probes had been sent out to the far reaches of our system and sailed off into the nothingness never sending anything back past a certain point. Our manned missions have had similar fates. Dropping off the map and never returning signals.

My mission will fix this. My creation, my life work will turn our collective future around. We will finally reach another planet able to sustain life. I am so close to this final completion. No matter what happens after, I will have succeeded. I will have become the leader of a new civilization. Under my guidance a new branch of our history will evolve and grow. I will be the shepherd we need at this time.

"Commander, we are up to 50% in all power banks."

"Good Timmons. Keep me appraised. How is number five doing this time around?"

"So far just fine Sir. I think our fix is holding. Should I hold it back some just to be safe?"

"No, no. We need all that power. You do have the bulkheads closed between all sections though right?"

"Yes sir, absolutely. Also, each ejection module is prepped and ready in case we have a major failure."

"Let's hope it doesn't come to that. We cannot guarantee what will happen if an ejection is required while in transit."

I hoped nothing would happen in transit. Outwardly, very little questioning was shown from my words. I worked to stay solid, an immovable presence of control and authority. Inside I was much less confident. The math had been done. Testing as far as we could test had been done. Everything worked on paper and in our simulations but all those things, the equations, the basis upon what the simulator was built upon was all theoretical. She told me the theory would hold. All of her power, her knowledge shown to me proved it, yet still not enough. She was built upon my own understanding and as this was not even my own theory, but one created by a beloved predecessor to myself, I was uncertain of her ability to understand completely. After all, he was unable to bring the experiment full circle and into reality. Too many failures in testing. I was the one that brought it to reality. That was my victory. I had pushed and twisted arms and put myself in a position that was able to make this happen.

My mind was on a cliff's edge at this point. Whether I failed or succeeded, I knew I could not return to the system behind us. Now or ever. Too many bridges burned, too many secrets withheld. Too many calls from Earth refused. No one here would know. I kept the calls secret, no record stood in the databases. I peered up at the countdown clock in my Command Center. 38 minutes and counting. Soon Jim, soon you would see it. You will see the inside of a wormhole. We will finally know for sure what it is, how it feels, how it tastes. The work will not be complete though. No, the work will only continue. I will be required then more than ever. There are forces at work on this ship outside of my vision. I know this but have not been able to pin them down yet.

Three groups exist at a minimum working against the other two at every turn. It would be up to me to guide this crew, guide this ship, guide my species, guide her to an ending that unites all those vested. That or see the detractors eliminated. Normally I would balk at such ideas, but it has come to be in my understanding that simply keeping people working together is not enough to bridge all gaps. She has shown me that solidarity in words alone is not enough. Solidarity in thought will be required soon. At some point, we must all agree on the basics or war is all there is. We cannot afford another great war. Most did not survive the last with our planet being one of the greatest losses. If we are to live out here beyond the limits, then we must stay the course and work towards one central vision. Mine. Hers. Ours.

I glance around the room in between frequent questions from the crew and checked those sitting around the perimeter. There, near the lift is my wife, my daughter. The very people I do all this for. It is for them. My daughter is to inherit the species. She is not to only thrive in a land of new opportunities, but is to take the reigns when my time comes to a close and lead these people. She will be required to step up. To make hard choices, to lead. I will show her the proper way. I will show her what must be done to continue our kind. We will build our own legends. We will become the very legends that we create. Those that follow us will forever remember our names. The names of myself and my daughter.

Back to the checking and rechecking of system status screens. All is still in the green. I notice a few yellow dots around the shape of our ship. Selecting one I see an MFE has failed. I cringe ever so slightly. This is expected as the vast amounts of power surging through these devices are bound to burn a few out. I thought this same thought at our first attempted transit. More had failed than expected. A flaw was found in the materials used to build the devices. At least that is what I had been told. Of my own accord, I inspected some of the units and saw the flaw. It was not only a flaw but instead a purposeful failure point created only to cause a cascading crash of the magnetic field. Fortunately for us all she caught it in time and stopped the wormhole before it opened. A great amount of power was dispersed into the universe the end points of which I had no idea.

This time we would not have another failure of such magnitude. Each emitter was tested in turn over the past week to ensure none had similar errors in their construction. The boards were still weak points that would be remedied eventually but for now all I needed was for one transit. One time through the chasm and we would be able to take our time improving the entire structure of our creation. Those around me of similar rank as myself all believed the purpose was to return here after dropping cargo and supplies at the destination point. I knew other needs would quickly subsume that concept after we arrived. By design these things would occur. Whether manufactured or by simple circumstance.

She beckons me speaking into my mind. I don't hear her but feel her desires, her demands walk into my head and make their presence known. I need to look at the time again. Something is wrong but she does not understand. I turn my eyes and looked. Thirty-two minutes before transit. Nothing wrong there. I look towards the man I have known for decades. Of all people he is possibly the most trusted. More so than my own wife or daughter as the both of them do not understand. Not yet. He does.

"Timmons, status?"

"Yes Commander, power banks at 68% and climbing steadily. Bank five is still in the green. Holding steady with the others."

I look in on myself wondering what she could be concerned with as I see nothing of note here in front of me. I feel the need to look at cameras, but I do not understand. Why do I care about cameras at this point in our history? With everything else there is to see, everything else there is to monitor, why do you desire my attention on the cameras? I bend to her demands and pull a camera feed up on the tablet I hold in my hands keeping it covered enough so that my eyes only can see it. I see a man near her mind. I recognize him. I relax. Its Arnold. He is another trusted friend that has stood by me during much of our struggles with building her. He knows her nearly as well as I myself do. He would have been up here on this floor with me if not for his desire to stay in his position as an engineer. For reasons I was never able to grasp, he wanted to work on the drones and subsystems of the ship. I allowed his requests but in return he watched over my emitters.

A thought came to me then, could he have brought about the failure in the MFEs? He did have the access and was the controlling influence on all manufacturing of components. The opportunity was there but why after devoting such time to the work would he then attempt to destroy it? Plus, he knew her so much better. He knew how fragile she was. He knew her code. If he had wanted to hurt us, another way would have been his preferred course. No, I could not start distrusting those that did not deserve it at this point. There were many I feared worked against me but not him.

I responded back to her not within my thoughts as no matter how hard I worked towards that end goal, it still eluded me. True unspoken conversation was a difficult ending blocked by an unseen barrier. She could speak into my mind, but I could not into hers without a keyboard or speech. For that reason, I now typed onto my tablet, gesturing short cuts. My message back to her was one of calm. Not to worry. It was only her uncle. One she could trust. She argued back that he seemed different than the usual but calmed. We agreed for her to watch and report any changes.

A commotion from my left brought my always demanded attention from the tablet in my hands up to see Major Bonette in what appeared to be a disagreement with the General. I disliked them both. So did she. On this we agreed very easily. We did not like weapons. Weapons were the tools of war and had no place in our new world. They would need to be handled but a time to do such things had not presented itself yet. When those that carry the weapons were forced upon us, we were vulnerable. We had little leverage. Tensions were already strong and a breakdown inevitable. Only time separating us. I was forced to accept their addition to us.

Now the Major walked away towards the lift. She was supposed to be at the security station during transit monitoring the trace information I allowed her to see. Her access was unlimited but only in the networks I allowed her. It almost seemed like Maggie and the Major locked eyes for a moment as she stepped on the lift. They had nothing to do with each other though. He had seen to it that they never intermingled. When I knew the Major would be somewhere, I made sure my daughter had other things to do. It may not have been me directly but a quick order to a superior or a request to her Mother would make quick work of a scheduling conflict.

I stepped around to the General and motioned to him. Once his attention was up on me, I asked him, "General, where was the Major off to? Is there a problem I need to be aware of?"

"No Commander," he responded, that constantly angry expression he carried wearing on my patience with his team as a whole, "she needed to step out for a minute. Some kind of intestinal…"

I stopped him right there putting my hand up and nodding.

"Enough said General, enough said."

I stepped back away from the General and proceeded to check over displays aimed at various officers around the deck. Each showed green, some had yellow markers here and there but still all within expected numbers. The countdown clock now read twenty-four minutes remaining. I again looked towards my world. My meaning for existence and my future. Maggie was bent over in her seat looking at her tablet. I groaned inwardly forcing myself not to reprimand her right then. All that was going on around her and she was focusing on her tablet. Most likely playing a game, honing her skills as a drone pilot. I had hoped she would grow bored with such things, but she had instead flourished and loved it. Such a menial task being a pilot. It was beneath her, but I could not refuse her the enjoyment. What little time she still had for things like that.

"Sir, Bank five is pulsing on us. Need you to look at this!"

"Timmons, send your screen over here to me. I'm going to go ahead and strap in. If we need to jump early, we may have to."

I dropped into an open spot and the screen instantly brought up a feed of the power banks. There was five. That pain in the ass. It had given us grief all the way out here from Mars. All the other banks were up to 74% now but five was bouncing between 72 and 76%. I quickly forgot about what my daughter was doing and got to work in the system working on a solution. A patch that would modulate the bounce. I watched the indicators climb and started to get bank five leveled off. It was now gaining slower than the others but had steadied. 88% now and looking up at the clock we had fifteen minutes left to go. That's when she reached out to me again, speaking directly into my mind.

What is it now? I need to stay in the moment with these power banks. Something was wrong though. She wanted me to check cameras again, but I didn't have the time. I sent her a message requesting more details, but she didn't respond. Video came up on my screen being pushed there without my request. She wanted me to see something.

"Sir, bank five is dropping charge now!"

I pushed the video feed away and brought the meters up again. It was dropping. This was not good. If that bank failed on us, we may not be able to complete the transit as scheduled. Temperatures were climbing fast on it. I hollered back at my friend who I badly needed to regain control over the power network.

"Timmons, dammit man, get that bank under control."

"Commander Sir, I can't. I have completely shut the power feed down into it and it is still acting as though it is shorting out."

"Nail down what section of the bank is shorting and cut it off from the rest then!" I shouted back to him. He needed to get this under control. I watched the temperatures and they continued to rise. Even cutting the power supply to those bad cells within the bank wouldn't stop a cascading failure now. It was too hot. I bypassed Timmons and went to his second in command.

"O'Malley, dump the air in five and open it to vacuum!"

"Sir, that kind of pressure change might rupture more of it."

"That's an order O'Malley, do it now or the whole thing is going to go anyways!"

"Done sir, vented to vacuum."

Timmons jumped back into the back and forth as yellow and red indicators flashed across my screen.

"Commander, we have bulkhead failures between bank one and five. Not total yet but one is purging air into the vacuum through five."

"That's fine Timmons, it won't hurt four to lose any air. That's why we evacuated the area and closed the bulkheads. They may perform better open to the cold of space."

"Yes sir. We will keep monitoring."

O'Malley spoke up then, "Sirs, it appears temperatures in bank five are dropping off. I have been able to identify and separate the shorted cells within it. They are still burning themselves up, but it isn't leaching over into surrounding cells."

"Good man O'Malley. Keep it up. Do what you can to hold onto one and five. Start feeding power back into the remainder of five. We still need all we can get in it before that clock hits zero." I pointed up at the countdown and looked realizing we were within five minutes.

Glancing around the room looking for any other flashing lights or warning indicators I noticed the security station was vacant now. Good I thought to myself. I don't need that group looking over my shoulder all the time anyways. As soon as we transit, I won't need them anymore at all. They will be a liability at that point. Things started to calm but I have a nagging feeling in my head. My heart rate slowing I was able to concentrate more and realized she was trying to tell me something. She needed me. Someone was hurting her. Not her but her. I pulled the messenger back up and sent a short note.

"Who is hurting you?" I asked in text.

The thought came back through my mind nearing a spoken word. "Not me, someone is hurting her. Yours."

I didn't understand what she was telling me or attempting to.

"Who is being hurt?"

In my mind again came, "She is. Maggie is being hurt."

I froze at that, looking over I saw Maggie's seat empty. Her Mother looked at me and seeing the sudden horror come over my face, she paled looking over at the empty seat next to her. It was too late though, the thoughts coming across into my mind warning me of what was happening went silent. I tried to undo the harness holding me tight to my seat, but it would not release. I typed out a message demanding she release my restraints, but no response came. She was not speaking to me now. Looking over my dear wife was pounding at her buckle also, tears running down her face. Looking up I realized why the sudden quiet had come. Less than 3 minutes remained on the clock. She had shut down. Pulled back into herself and reached out to every edge of the ship. Sending and receiving amounts of data that far exceeded anything before her.

"Timmons, where are the banks?" I asked, the only thing I could do was to hope my daughter survived whatever transit was coming our way.

"97% sir. Bank five is still lagging behind but it is holding steady, no more failures."

"It should be enough, just keep everything working. O'Malley, initiate the final sequence, hand off control to the APEX."

"Handed off sir. It's all hers."

That was it, there was nothing else to do. She had the ship now and was not telling me anything. That was designed in, not an indication of failure or problem. Even with her massive abilities, she still had to focus just as a human would when dealing with a complex problem. I could only hope she was still there. I could only hope my daughter was still there. If she was not, if something happened to her there would be no reason to continue. My concern was not only the future of myself or my species but her future. Everything I did was for her.

My dread built up within me as the seconds ticked down and the minutes fell to zero. When thirty seconds came left on the clock I started to feel the vibrations. The APEX was starting. Building the field that would carry us through to the other side. They were slight at first, I had to work to feel her movements, but it was there. More yellow came up here and there around the room but no red. ten seconds, eight, seven. Now the floor, walls, ceiling, consoles around me vibrated outwardly. I could feel it within myself. Such a power was all around us. The full output of four massive fusion power plants and eight power banks. All working in concert to eject enough power out into space to energize a city on Earth for a year.

Through the screen in front of me I saw outside the ship. Out in front of our ship opened a hole in space. There was no bright light ringing the hole. Just a blacker void within a black backdrop unseen besides the realization that stars blinked out in a circular pattern. A true hole in space that distorted the universe around this great ship. Around my life. four seconds, three, two, one. The timer ran out and everything went silent.

I breathed. I felt the pain in my right wrist from the arthritis that had started to plague me over the past few months. I knew I was alive but didn't know where I existed. Were we inside the wormhole? Maybe this was transit. I breathed in and licked my lips.

"Did it work?" I asked out loud hoping someone else would be awake as I was.

"We don't know yet sir, we need to calibrate the systems. All systems shut down; we are on backup power now." Answered O'Malley.

Screens all around us flashed back to life, updating information for us all at once. Red flooded the monitor in front of me and others nearby illuminated the space around us all in red.

Timmons spoke first, "Sir, I am discharging the final remnants of power from bank five. It held together but I believe it is toast now. From here it appears it melted down three sections of the bank. The other banks look to be in good shape. Bank one is in the yellow but stable, I am discharging it as well to be safe. Banks two, three, four, six and seven are all stable and in the green. They are down to twelve percent and should take a charge once the generators come back up"

"Understood Timmons, do what you can to discharge one and five. You only mentioned through seven. How is bank eight?"

"Bank eight is not responding. It was in the green before the jump but is not responding now. I don't know what it is doing. We need to send a tech down there to check it out manually."

"O'Malley, send someone down there now to check it out. How are systems coming? We need to know where we are."

"Systems are coming online now. Another couple minutes and we should be up and running again. I will dispatch a team to bank eight now."

"I suggest you hold off on that team" A male voice spoke up I didn't immediately recognize, "I am getting pressure fluctuations near bank eight's location. One of our cargo bays containing livestock is back there. I am showing fluctuations and I have lost all life signs in that section."

Not thinking too much into the voice for the moment I reacted, "Ok, I need an update from that area, O'Malley, tell your team to continue that way but take all precautions. Don't open bulkhead doors without confirming what is on the other side first. Mr. Tremmon, I need your team to get a Skater on the outside now to confirm status of eight and the structure in that area."

"Yes sir, dispatching a skater now" Tremmon responded. He spun back to his station and radioed to his crew ordering two skaters outside immediately to put eyes on that section.

I turned to the voice wanting to know who it was but before I asked, a thought came into my mind. Immediately I recognized it. She was back. She had survived the transit and was speaking to me again. I listened to her but nearly collapsed at what she had to tell me. Then Dr. Franco was in my ear.

"Jim, get me power to the medical bay. Its still dark down here and you need me to have everything I can get to work."

I couldn't think. I felt her presence in my mind again, telling me to unstrap and take command. She would get power flowing again but she needed complete control of the ship. That could only be done from the main command console. In my hurry to help regulate bank five before transit I had strapped into a regular station that happened to be empty at the time. She pushed me to move. I released my straps and stood making sure to engage my boots to release and reattach as I stepped.

The ship shook violently to one side. Then the other. I reeled against the movements trying to maintain my balance and to keep myself from slamming against either a wall or consoles. People yelled around me wanting help. Needing answers but I had none. She kept urging me forward, demanding I move. In order to save those I loved, she needed control. I complied and kept moving. Reaching my primary console, I activated it with a finger and retina scan. I punched in my override code and allowed her access to it all. Immediately she left my mind. Stopped urging me. Over my earpiece I heard the Dr. again.

"Thanks Jim, we have light down here. Calm the ship down, that jerking around isn't helping me. Send Barbara down if you can. Maggie needs her mother."

I turned towards my Wife, but she was already gone as well. General Carter stood there instead. His uniform was smeared in blood. A tear hung to the grizzled old military man's eye lashes. That alone more even than Evelen's concern over the radio crushed me. He nodded to me and instantly regaining his controlling demeanor, spoke to the crew.

"What the hell was that jarring all about? How is the ship?"

"Sir, I jettisoned bank five. It wasn't draining fast enough and internal temperatures were spiking well beyond safety levels. Sorry sir" Timmons answered looking at me now. I couldn't focus and just hung there drifting about my magnetically locked feet.

"Both jerks were bank five?" The General asked, "Did we take any damage?"

"Yes sir, both were bank five. The first was me jettisoning it, the second was the debris from it peppering the exterior skin. Internal temperatures spiked causing catastrophic loss of the bank. It did not cause significant damage to the ship. The debris field was easily deflected by our outer shell. If it had exploded while still inside, it could have done significant damage."

A voice came through my mind again bringing me a sense of joy and wonderment. I could not fathom the feeling, but it was there. She was trying to raise me to my feet. She was telling me everything would be ok. I pulled my tablet out and cycled it bringing Evelyn's name up and calling her. She ignored my call. I pulled my wife up and again an ignore came through. I spoke aloud so she could hear me.

"Why are you telling me to be happy and joyful when my daughter is in such pain?"

"But she is not in any pain. She feels nothing." Came the response within my mind.

"She is injured terribly though. Please, what is her condition, will she survive?" No one turned towards me through the commotion still going on around the Command Deck.

"She will survive Jim. Evelyn and Barbara are working very hard on her. I can see into her brain. It is damaged but will recover. I will help them if needed but for now they do not. They do need you though. The General does not know me like you do. I cannot access many systems. My drive units are out. You need to take command to keep me functioning. Let Evelyn do her job, you do yours."

I understood then. If the ship fell apart then Maggie would die. I had to push aside my fears of her death in order to do my part in keeping her alive. I fought against the dread, the sorrow, the uncertainty and brought myself back to the present. It was chaos around me. Red lights flickered all over. Crew members yelled back and forth. The General was bright red and yelling at Timmons about something. Reaching down, I typed in a code on my panel and the room when bright white only for a moment and an alarm blared. Everyone cut their conversations short and turned to me.

I looked first at the General who had spittle extending out from his mouth starting to rebound along itself back to his face. "My ship General. Thank you."

He nodded, wiped his chin removing the offending string of saliva and replied, "Your ship Commander."

Turning to Timmons next, "Timmons, I need a status on the ship."

Timmons started to speak but Tremmon beside him went white pulling my eyes over to him instead. He croaked out, "Sir, bank eight is gone."

"What do you mean gone?" I replied already feeling my blood cool again.

"Gone sir, it isn't there anymore. The Skater crews are reporting that from the cargo bay bank seven is in, the ship curves in through where eight used to be and continues to curve around through where one of the main drives was. It's all just gone. Sheared clean off. No tearing, no damage, they are telling me it looks like we just cut the ship off clean on a curve. Other than a few sparks from power systems shorting out, you can't tell anything is wrong"

Thinking for a second, I told my crew, "I think we know now what happens if you are not through the wormhole fast enough. Although we were through instantly so I don't think we can call it a wormhole anymore either. It was more like a window. We passed through it like there was no real distance to it. Just a window to another area. When that window shut, it sheared off everything not through as it closed around us. We must not have been centered perfectly so it only carved off one side of us."

Wow, that is an amazing bit of knowledge to have learned already and we just made it to this side. Already I could think of ways to improve a future transit if I ever deemed one to be necessary. I kicked myself for getting off the here and now and turned to O'Malley realizing a problem. "O'Malley let your crew know where to stop. Check all bays in the vicinity to confirm condition but do not go outside. Fortunately, we planned for this and each bulkhead is designed to take the effects of being outside. They were already closed before we transited for this kind of event. The ship should be fine once we cut the power feeds to those broken lines. We need to block the bulkhead doors though to make sure no one accidentally opens one not realizing they are now at the exit door."

O'Malley didn't even respond; he was already speaking to his teams around the ship. Crew members were getting orders and moving from their restraints to start work on damaged areas. The ship shuddered again. Not a huge shock wave but enough that everyone noticed and grabbed onto anything nearby to stabilize themselves.

Timmons spoke up, "That was bank one. It started to overload also so I ejected it to be safe. It may not explode but I didn't want to risk it. If it cools down and stays together, we can always go back and grab it. I didn't launch it hard. We would be able to easily catch up with it."

I nodded to him and replied, "So we are down to six banks now?"

"Technically sir we are down to five functional banks. We lost eight in transit, five exploded, one was just jettisoned and seven malfunctioned and is now offline and fully discharged. I will not know condition of that bank until we get an opportunity to look it over in person."

"Well then, I guess we best figure out where we are because our engine was not designed to work with fewer than six fully functional banks and even then, it will be a strain on all systems. Seven is what we needed really. The eight was a backup…. Let's get crews assessing all areas of the ship. I want a preliminary report on all sections down to each room within the next two hours. Do we know where we are yet?" My father continued, "I need to know where we are and what is nearby. We have equipment on board to build new power banks, but we need somewhere to gather materials. We have some but not enough to rebuild three power banks. Tremmon, go ahead and put together a plan to retrieve bank one if it holds together. We may be able to rebuild it or at least harvest some materials."

No one argued with me and went back to what they were working on. Some left the command deck to go on specific missions handed down to them from their superiors while others stayed in the center locked into consoles working there. I stepped to the station Dr. Franco would normally be at and found the voice I had heard earlier but hadn't thought about who it came from.

"Sir, I have something you may want to look at." Dorian Franco, Dr. Franco's son said. I knew this boy well enough but had never spent any time directly conversing with him. He was one of those faces that grew up in front of me but just out of my reach. Always on the fringe as the Dr. and I worked together on many things but not as closely as I worked with my engineers. She focused on the biotic while I focused on the mechanical.

"What do you have for me? Any idea where we are?" I wanted to ask him if he had heard anything from his mother, but I knew he would not have. The moment she could step away from Maggie, she would let me know where they stood. For now, I had to keep my mind on the business at hand. While I waited for reports to come back on the ship's status, I needed to find out where we were and if there were any dangers out there.

"Commander, it worked." He clicked a few more buttons and a shot appeared on the large screen in the command center that to this point had been empty. "Do you see that blue ball just off to the right and below center? I think that's the second planet. Just ahead of us towards the sun.", Dorian waved his arm and the screen changed to a shot from one of the Skaters still outside checking the skin of the ship, "I think that is Exionous. It fits what we expected the profile of the sun to be. I am working on the profile now, but it matches. I don't see the first planet yet but it may be on the other side of the sun right now. I believe we are detecting the third planet out to our right", he swung to another view from a telescope on the APEX. "Its way out there and I can only see a dot right now, but I think we did it. I think you did it. We need to confirm but we are in the Exion system."

A quiet cheer came up from the remaining crew in the command center. I quickly quieted them down and reminded them, "That is good news and not what I expected but we have grim issues to deal with before we can celebrate. We need to stabilize the ship immediately and check for any wounded. Timmons, I am putting you in charge of stabilization efforts for all critical systems on board the ship besides the power banks and wormhole engine. Dr. Hernandez, work with Timmons on those systems. O'Malley, you oversee the power banks. Stabilize them is all I need, do not try to start building them back up to any minimum standard. If we lose any more banks, it won't matter what the rest of the ship looks like. Tremmon, work with Timmons and O'Malley to provide any support they need from the outside with your

Skaters and drones. Dorian, you know your mother's plans for the farm pods, livestock, all that right?"

"Yes sir, we have worked through all the scenarios, I can get them started until she is available again."

"Good man, you start working on those. Your mother will keep it going in the medical ward. I'm sure we will need to have that section open and fully functional first. There will be injured as we work through damage control. My wife is already down there with her. My core group meet back here in two hours. Report to me immediately if anything goes sideways. I am headed down to the medical ward now to check on things there."

Each person I had given orders to nodded back to me or replied with some version of yes sir and went to their stations or headed to the lifts. I started for the lifts also but the General stepped in my way.

"Commander, we have another situation to deal with down in your lab."

"What kind of situation?" I instantly thought of Maggie again. She had been down there somewhere, and something had happened to her. Major Bonette too. I hadn't seen her since the jump. My mind wandered over to seeing Arnold down there before everything started going haywire.

"On the surface it appears Major Bonette attempted to bring the ship down. To stop us from transiting to this system. I don't know why but your daughter was down there too."

"Why would my daughter have been down there?"

"I don't know for sure, but I felt something was wrong, so I headed down there looking for them both. There was vomit in the lift from one of them. When I got down to the lab level, the Major was screaming at your daughter. Telling her she had to stay awake and watch as the end came. Something to that effect. Bonette was holding a device in her hand, something like a remote trigger."

I didn't understand. Why would Major Bonette have a trigger device, what would she be triggering?

"Let's go have a look." I said to the General. He nodded and we stepped into the waiting lift.

When the doors opened and revealed my lab I was stunned. It was a mess. Things were floating all over the room. What had been knocked loose from the struggle that went on in here had floated away and bounced off this or that. Nothing moved quickly but lazily drifted this way or that. General Carter stepped out of the lift ahead of me and walked over to a lab table that had been smeared with blood across its surface. He picked something up and brought it to me as I stepped out of the lift myself. I reached out and grasped it in my hand to take a closer look.

"That is a trigger mechanism but for what I have no clue. Something close by. This is not a very powerful transmitter." I glanced around the room and looked at the room the soul of my ship resided in. There was blood smeared down the door leading inside, and magnetic boots secured to the floor at its base. From those boots, legs extended leading to behind a cart that had rolled free and stopped in my way. I walked over and stepped to the side around the obstacle. It was Major Bonette. Clearly dead. Blood in a floating glob around her, clinging on and not wanting to release into the surrounding area. Most of it had soaked into her uniform and a lab coat that had been draped over her.

"I wasn't sure how to contain the blood right off the bat. I was more concerned about your daughter than the mess to be honest."

"I appreciate that, what happened here?"

Pointing down at what used to be the Major, Carter responded, "Well that I know. I shot her. The rest of this," he said while turning slowly with an arm outstretched taking in the entire scene, "I have no idea. Like I said, when the lift doors opened, she was screaming at your daughter who was covered in blood and clearly incapacitated. Screaming about her destiny and the demise of the human race or some such nonsense so I shot her. She was clearly insane. I don't know what that trigger would have done but I'm sure it would have been bad for the rest of us."

I thought about it for a moment and then realized I had a video feed. I spun and pointed at the camera, "We can just look at the video feed." I pulled my tablet out and opened up the camera. Backing up to fifteen minutes before our transit I went to hit play but my comm link buzzed.

"Commander!" Dorian came across excited. "You have to see this. I am sending a video feed to your tablet right now."

"Dorian, I'm in the mid-," I cut myself off as the screen changed to a feed from outside the ship. A huge blue and green ball hovered there taking up most of the view.

"We made it sir! The skaters were so focused on damage reporting they didn't even notice it until now. We didn't see it in our scan because we were facing the sun. That is the second planet. The other dot we saw was a moon we assumed was Carterous because of its colors. We didn't even scan behind us to look for another planet because one shouldn't have been there."

I was stunned to silence. I had done it. We were here. This was my world. My daughter's world. Our species' fresh start. Another chance at a life worth living. A chance to become legend. A voice whispered inside my head urging me to move forward, to conquer this world for her. This would all be for her. For my daughter, for both my daughters. This would be our world. We would be legends.

Dorian came across again, "Sir, we are close enough I can see the surface. I can't see it clearly but there are buildings down there. Buildings. Something lives down there. Something smart enough to build structures. You found alien life. Intelligent alien life."

I looked up at the General. He peered back at me over the tablet I held up close to my face. I opened my mouth, but no sound came out. All I could do was turn the tablet to him that now showed the image Dorian was looking at. A rough grainy image of buildings. Small buildings with wood or some kind of plant-based roofs but buildings.

General Carter looked back up at me, his mouth agape. His only utterance, "Well shit."

Printed in Great Britain
by Amazon

22860801R00202